Praise for Cecilia Grant and
A Lady Awakened

"Elegantly written, emotionally powerful . . . with a compelling combination of exquisitely nuanced characters and lusciously sensual romance. Sweet, poignant, and completely satisfying, *A Lady Awakened* is a romance to treasure."

—*Booklist* (starred review)

"Grant details Regency country life beautifully, with a firm and respectful hand, and the subtle yet engrossing courtship is enchanting and gratifying as it transforms these two strong-minded and very unlikely lovers."

—*Publishers Weekly*

"This intriguing debut blends erotic themes into a plotline that has been used before, but never in this way. A desperate heroine, a wickedly sexy hero, an unexpected passion and strong storytelling along with compelling characterization mark Grant as one to watch."

—*RT Book Reviews*

"From the characters to the language to the love scenes to the plot, so much came together unexpectedly and beautifully. I loved this novel."

—Janine, Dear Author

"I'm in love with this author's voice. It is hard to explain why I love her style of writing so much, but as I read I didn't want to miss a single word."

—*USA Today*

"A marvelous gem of a book . . . I loved it!"

—*New York Times* bestselling author Mary Balogh

"If you only read one de
Incredibly sexy, surprisi
ened!"

—*New York Times* b

By Cecilia Grant

A Lady Awakened
A Gentleman Undone

A Gentleman Undone

CECILIA GRANT

BANTAM BOOKS
NEW YORK

A Gentleman Undone is a work of fiction. Names, characters, places, and incidents are the products of the author's imagination or are used fictitiously. Any resemblance to actual events, locales, or persons, living or dead, is entirely coincidental.

A Bantam Books Mass Market Original

Copyright © 2012 by Cecilia Grant
Excerpt from *A Woman Entangled* by Cecilia Grant copyright © 2012 by Cecilia Grant.

Published in the United States by Bantam Books, an imprint of The Random House Publishing Group, a division of Random House, Inc., New York.

BANTAM BOOKS and the rooster colophon are registered trademarks of Random House, Inc.

This book contains an excerpt from the forthcoming book *A Woman Entangled* by Cecilia Grant. This excerpt has been set for this edition only and may not reflect the final content of the forthcoming edition.

ISBN 978-0-553-59384-6
eBook ISBN 978-0-345-53447-7

Cover design: Lynn Andreozzi
Cover photograph: Marie Killen

Printed in the United States of America

www.bantamdell.com

9 8 7 6 5 4 3 2 1

Bantam Books mass market edition: June 2012

With thanks to Laura:
repository of medical knowledge,
tireless supporter,
all-weather friend

A Gentleman Undone

Prologue

JUNE 1815

"WHAT THE devil were you thinking, to move him?" The surgeon stank of blood. In the meager candlelight allotted to this section of the makeshift hospital, he was all crags and shadows, and slick to the elbows with the life of other men.

"None of the litter-bearers would stop for him. I waited hours." His voice bled raw at the edges, rasped to almost nothing by a day of shouting over gunfire, shouting over cannons, shouting over the thunder of two nations' cavalry.

Just as well he couldn't speak up. This was a church, or had been before its conscription into such gruesome service. Presumably it would be a church again, once all these men could be transported on to Brussels. Bruges. One of the proper hospitals, with proper beds instead of narrow benches and a cold stone floor. At all events a man ought to show respect.

"You know they have their orders." The doctor crouched by the bench on which Talbot lay, prodding at his lifeless limbs. Or not lifeless, strictly, because he was not dead. His chest heaved in a weird rhythm that seemed to bear little relation to breath. "They must take officers first, and then they look for the men we have the best hope of repairing. Lord knows we've got enough of those to keep us busy. We don't need to go foraging for desperate cases."

Surely a doctor didn't do any good to a patient by speaking that way in his hearing. Will opened his mouth to say something to that effect, and closed it again. The man's demeanor must be the least of his concerns. The essential matter, it seemed, was the state of Talbot's arms and legs. Broken as he was, he'd still been able to move fingers and toes when he lay on the field. So to transport him had perhaps been a mistake after all.

No, not perhaps. Of a certainty, but a certainty barely glimpsed through the haze of three days' exhaustion. Like some monstrous shape at some great distance, lurching to its feet to begin its shambling, implacable approach.

Time enough to deal with that later. "Well, he's here now." Command came without conscious thought, after enough practice. Brush aside what was inessential, clear a path, and set the man on it. "There's no foraging involved. All I ask is that you take a look and see what can be done for him, same as you've been doing all night."

"Did you not understand me?" The surgeon sat back on his heels, his face lost in shadow. "He's had an injury to the spine. He's got no movement or even feeling in his legs. There's nothing we can do for him."

He swallowed. It felt like downing a handful of grapeshot. "How can you know that? You've barely looked at him. The light in here is too poor for you to properly see. What if it's simply pain and prostration that's left him unable to move?" Even through the shroud of fatigue he could hear the senseless, flailing nature of these arguments. Abruptly he clamped his jaws together, and took a step back.

Something impeded his progress—someone, rather—some infantryman who'd not had the benefit of a lieutenant to find him a place on one of the pews. He lay crumpled on the stones, his wide, unbelieving eyes connecting with Will's for a second or two before his gaze veered off to the darkness overhead.

He wasn't making a sound, this one. But others were. Sounds such as one heard in the aftermath of battle, made worse by their concentration in a small space, by the echoing effect of the stone walls, by the awful irony of the setting.

Will breathed in slowly, and breathed out again. Two days ago he'd knelt in the crossroads at Quatre Bras, scrambling to reload his musket—powder, ball, paper, *quickly*—as the cuirassiers in their formidable gleaming breastplates charged in, and he'd thought, *Now I know what Hell will be like.* Some thirty hours later he'd revised the thought: Hell was a sleepless night in frigid rain with one battle behind you and another ahead, sodden uniform squishing comically as you lifted a hand and set it on the shoulder of some frightened young man you couldn't find the words to console.

Then Hell had been battle again, the noise and the stench and the comrades struck down, and Hell had been the search for survivors, and Hell had been the long wait with Talbot, the bone-weariness, the dwindling hope of aid, the desperation that had finally compelled him to pick up the man and carry him here. With his faculties intact he would not have made that mistake.

Nor would he have made the mistake of believing he'd already seen Hell. Hell, clearly, was the hopeless section of the church-turned-hospital, broken soldiers discarded like so much human rubbish on the stones, crying to

God or the doctor or their mothers for mercy that would not come.

No. A man could drown in such thoughts, and he had better things to do this minute than drown. "Please." The surgeon was rising to his feet; this was his last chance to find the approach that would compel him to *do something* for the man he'd carried into this hell. "He's one of mine. I'm responsible for him. He has a wife and child."

"For God's sake, Lieutenant, look about you. Every one of these men will be mourned by someone. Every one of them will weigh on the conscience of some lieutenant, or sergeant, or colonel who can point to something he might have done different." A hand came through the darkness to graze against his sleeve: that was meant to be comfort. "In truth, even the litter-bearers should have had a hard time moving him safely. The outcome might very well have been the same." That, too, was intended as comfort. Dimly he perceived the fact. "You did what you could. Now I suggest you get some sleep."

That was that, then. Talbot would be left to die. The litter-bearers might have brought him to the same end, but Will had done it, decisively, before they had a chance to try. "Wait." Now it was his hand, lunging out to arrest the doctor as he turned away. He forced his paltry shredded voice lower yet. "Can you at least give him something? Opium? He suffers terribly."

But God, he knew the answer even as he rasped out those words. Every damned man still breathing here suffered terribly, and opium must be saved for the surgeries. "I'm sorry," said the doctor, and Will could only let his hand fall, and watch the man's form recede.

On his left periphery, Talbot's chest was still going like an amplification of his labored heartbeat. When would it stop? He ought to have asked. He raised a hand to his own face, dragging it from his hairline down over his eyes, his too-long-unshaven cheeks, his slack mouth, his chin. He turned, and knelt where the doctor had been.

"I'm going to take you out of here." The man's eyes were closed, but his mouth tightened and he managed a sort of nod. "The wounded are too many and they can't spare a surgeon or even opium. There's no purpose in your staying." *There's no hope.* What good would he do the man by saying that aloud? "Another of the hospitals might be better appointed, and we might find you some gin, at the least."

Gin. Not likely. Unless he proposed to start pillaging corpses in search of a flask. Of course that might come to sound reasonable, between now and when Talbot's last breath left him.

Will gathered his dreadful limp form from the pew and nearly staggered, not under the weight of the man but under the weight of the man's misguided trust. He picked his way past dead and living bodies to the door, shadowed every step by a growing presentiment: there might after all be worse visions of Hell awaiting than anything he'd yet seen.

Chapter One

MARCH 1816

THREE OF the courtesans were beautiful. His eye lingered, naturally, on the fourth. Old habit would persist in spite of anything life could devise.

Will leaned on one elbow and rested his cheek on his palm, a careless posture that suggested supreme confidence in his play while also allowing him to peer round the fellow opposite and get a better view of the ladies. Not to any purpose, of course. He'd come into this establishment on a solemn errand, and courtesans had no part in his plan.

Still, a man could look. A bit of craning here, a timely turn by one of the ladies there, and he could assemble a fair piecemeal picture of the four. So he'd been doing all evening as they'd sat down in different combinations at their card table, some fifteen feet removed from the great tables where the gentlemen played. And while every one of them—from dark temptress to flame-haired sylph to crystalline-delicate blonde—gratified his eye, only one thus far had managed to trifle with his concentration.

He watched her now, her eyelids lowered and her fingers precise as she fanned out her freshly dealt hand. Not beautiful, no. Pretty, perhaps. Or rather handsome: a young man could have worn that aquiline nose to advantage, and that fiercely etched brow.

She studied her cards without moving any of them—though the game was whist and all three of her companions were rearranging their cards by suit—and glanced across at her partner. Gray-blue eyes, expressive of nothing. She could hold all trumps and you'd never know.

"No sport to be had there, Blackshear." The words rode in on a wash of tobacco smoke from his right, barely audible under the clamor of a dozen surrounding conversations. "Those ones are all spoken for." Lord Cathcart switched his pipe from one side of his mouth to the other while inspecting his hand. A queen and a ten winked into view and out. Luck did like to throw itself away on the wealthy.

"There'd be no sport even if they were at liberty. A youngest son with no fortune doesn't get far with their kind." Will replied at the same low pitch and lifted a corner of his own card, a seven of clubs to go with seven of spades.

"Oh, I don't know." The viscount's fine-boned profile angled itself two or three degrees his way. "A youngest son who's just sold his commission might set his sights beyond the occasional adventurous widow."

"Widows suit me. No taint of commerce; no worries over whether you've seduced a lady into something she'll regret." The words felt flabby and false on his tongue, a stale utterance left over from the life that used to be his. He nodded toward the courtesans' table. "In any case your birds of paradise are a bit too rich for my blood."

"Ha. I'll wager your blood has its own ideas. Particularly concerning the sharp-faced wench with the Grecian knot. Stick," he added to the table at large as his turn came.

"Split," said Will, and turned up his sevens. His pulse leapt into a hasty rhythm that had nothing to do with any sharp-faced wench. He pushed a second bid forward, and gave all his attention to the two new cards.

An eight brought one hand to fifteen. Good chance of going bust on a third card and not much chance of besting the banker if he stuck. The second hand was better: an ace gave him the option to stick at eighteen, and also tempted him with the possibility of a five-card trick, if he counted the card for one instead of eleven and if the next three cards fell out in his favor.

Were the odds decent? Twenty-one less eight left thirteen. How many combinations of three cards came to thirteen or less? With one hundred and four cards in play . . . eight aces, eight twos, et cetera, and eleven other men at the table who must already have some of those cards in their possession . . . hang it, he ought to have paid better attention in mathematics classes. Fine return he'd brought his father on a Cambridge education, God rest the man's soul.

"I'll buy another on both hands." Twenty more pounds in. Best to cultivate the appearance of recklessness early in the evening, when wagers were small. Prudence could wait until several hours hence, when most of these men would be drunk—make that drunker—and inclined to put up sums they'd regret the next morning.

The new cards dropped in and he lifted their corners. Five and three. Twenty and twenty-one. Or twenty and eleven, with two cards and ten pips between him and the double payoff of the five-card trick.

He flicked idly with a gloved fingertip at the corner of one card. Was he really considering it? Buying another card when he might stick on a total of twenty-one? His first night in the place, not two hours yet at the table, and already he was goading Fortune to do its worst.

Well, there'd be no novelty in that, would there? He had a fair acquaintance with the things Fortune could do. A loss of thirty pounds would barely merit mention.

"One more here." He pushed another note out in front of his second hand.

A knave of hearts grinned up at him when he lifted the new card, and quiet relief poured through him, loosening places that had wound themselves tight. No five-card trick, but neither would he be dunned for his recklessness. Unless the banker beat him with a twenty-one of his own, he'd have at least one winning hand. Maybe two.

"Stick," he said, and leaned his cheek on his palm again as the play passed to his left. The ladies played two straight tricks of clubs while he watched, the sharp-faced one producing her cards with smooth efficiency from their disparate places in her hand.

Cathcart could needle him all he liked. She gave a man's mind places to go, did such a girl. Let beautiful women air their attractions like laundry on a line, flapping for all the world to see. The woman who kept something back—who wore her graces like silk underthings against the skin, and dared a man to find them out—would always be the one to set his imagination racing.

Even if he couldn't afford to let any other part of him race along. He heaved a quick sigh. "What's a Grecian knot?" he said, sinking his voice again. "Do you mean the way she's got her hair?"

"Hopeless," the viscount hissed round the stem of his pipe. "Must not be a particular lot, those widows you favor. Mind you, I don't suppose your hawkish Aphrodite is any too discriminating herself, judging by the company she keeps." With a jerk of his chin he indicated a fellow down the table, a square-jawed, blandly handsome type who'd assured himself the next deal by reaching twenty-one on his first two cards.

Curiosity buzzed wasplike about Will's temples. He brushed it away. He hadn't come here to gossip. The lady's choice of protector was her own concern. "Hawkish, truly?" He leaned back and stretched his arms out before him. "Try to be civil."

Though admittedly this wasn't much of a place for that. Bottles at the table. More men than Cathcart smoking, despite the presence of ladies, or at least women, in the room. Granted, a true gaming hell was probably worse. Gillray, the artilleryman, had claimed you could actually smell the desperation by four or five o'clock of the morning. Rolling off the pigeons in waves, he'd said, a stinking sweat more acrid than the sweat of healthy exertion. And why not? Fear had a scent, reportedly—you'd think battle would be the place to find that out, but amid the perpetual cacophony of scents, no one had ever risen up and proclaimed itself as fear—so why not desperation as well?

Enough pondering in that direction. He rotated his wrists, flexing the tendons, as a corpulent fellow went bust and the next began his turn. At the ladies' table, the strong-featured girl took her third straight trick and calmly marked the point on a paper at her right hand.

Hawkish. Really. He folded his arms behind his head. And yet there was something undeniably birdlike about her nose, her blank eyes, her wren-colored hair. Cold little creatures, birds, for all their soft feathers and pretty songs. Eat your brains for breakfast as soon as look at you. The odd bits of knowledge one picked up in war.

The banker stuck on a total of nineteen, and Will was fifty pounds richer. One more small step up the mountain. He raked in his winnings and pushed his cards toward the hawkish girl's square-jawed protector.

Near his own age, the man looked. Five and twenty or thereabout, and bearing himself with fresh consequence now he had the deal. Making some minor adjustment to his cravat before tending to the cards. Tilting his head with an air of practiced condescension to grant an audience to his right-hand neighbor, who was, it happened, speaking on the subject of the girl herself. "I declare, Roanoke," the neighbor said in an audible undertone, "I should never have bet on you keeping her this long. Not half so comely as the one you were squiring about last summer. Pretty winsome thing, she was."

A small compression of Square-jaw's mouth was the only sign he took offense at the questioning of his choice. "That one gifted me with a bastard child." Green-jeweled cuff-studs glinted in the candlelight as he reached out to gather in the cards. "This one can't."

"Or so she tells you, I'm sure," was the first gentleman's rejoinder, his undertone abandoned to more generally air his wit.

"She can't." With the patience of a crown prince accustomed to dull-witted minions he made this correction. "Something's gone wrong with her insides. No monthly courses."

Charming. And quite a bit more information than any man at the table could desire to know, surely. Will threw a look to the viscount, who only lifted a shoulder in reply. Evidently this sort of discussion was usual.

And it quickly got worse. "I shouldn't mind one like that myself." A coarse-featured bounder in a bottle-green coat offered this opinion. "Available all days of the month, isn't she? Can't ever claim indisposition and turn you away. Where did you come by her?"

"Plucked her out of Mrs. Parrish's establishment." Roanoke took his time squaring the edges of all the used cards before putting the stack faceup at the bottom of the deck. "And you may believe they trained her up proper. If there's a thing she won't do in bed, I have yet to discover it."

Mrs. Parrish's. Even a man who'd never set foot in such a place knew a thing or two of its character. One heard certain reports. Accounts, for example, of a contraption that positioned a man to be serviced by one woman while another administered a holly-branch whipping. Rumors of women who'd submit to a whipping themselves, or to any foul debauchery a man could conceive. Through what perverse acts had Square-jaw made his mistress's acquaintance?

Devil take it. This was none of his concern, and to speculate so on a lady's private business ill became him. Indeed it ill became the men at the table who were now pelting Roanoke with crude questions—Would she do this? Did she allow him that?—while the lout deigned to answer only in monosyllables, vague in proportion to the heightened interest, as he dealt out the cards.

Temper sent its warning prickle down Will's spine. She must be hearing this. She must see first one head and then another swiveling to reappraise her. He could mark no change in her countenance, her posture, or the speed at which she played her cards, but with what effort did she keep that composure while hearing herself reduced to an object for the common gratification of a lot of jackals?

"Has she got a name?" That was his own voice, rising above the others. What the devil was he doing? Did he want to invite the suspicion of the entire company? A slight straightening in Cathcart's posture spoke of sharpened interest, though the viscount didn't turn.

Roanoke did. His patrician brows crept a fraction of an inch closer together, then relaxed. "Lydia is her name," he said, and spun out the next card.

Leave it alone, Blackshear. But temper asserted itself again, the cautionary prickle swelling to a ham-fisted *glissando* played on his vertebrae. "I mean a name by which it would be proper to address her." Damnation. He would never learn, would he, what was and wasn't his responsibility?

"Have you something particular to say to her?" The man looked at him with full attention, as did most of the men at the table now. A charge like incipient lightning thickened the room's air. Choose the right words, and he'd be addressing Prince Square-jaw at twenty paces.

Wouldn't *that* be a suitably ridiculous end. Called out over excessive propriety. Killed on account of a woman he hadn't even got to enjoy.

Ongoing chatter from the room's other tables shrank to something distant and obscure as the prospect took shape before him. A few insults, none too subtle, were all that was wanted. Easily enough he could probably provoke the fellow into aiming for his head while he sent his own shot ten feet wide.

How badly would such a caper besmirch the family name? Andrew wouldn't like it, of course. But Andrew's respectability could surely transcend any number of family scandals. Kitty and Martha were both already married, quite well. He couldn't blight their futures in that regard.

Nick, though. His second-eldest brother harbored political ambitions and depended on a good name even now to keep up his practice. He'd do Nick no favors with reckless nonsense.

Besides, he had a deal of money yet to win. "I've nothing whatsoever to say." He made his consonants crisp, and held Roanoke's eyes. No need to back down altogether. "I'm only unused to hearing a lady spoken of in this way, and called openly by her Christian name. But I've been out of society for some time. Perhaps the mores have changed."

"Were you in the Peninsula, do you mean?" A bright-eyed fellow who barely looked old enough to be out past bedtime piped up with this. "Or perhaps in the final battle at Waterloo?"

One encountered this sort with disconcerting frequency. Men who'd swallowed the bitter pill of staying home—heirs who couldn't be risked, unfortunates who couldn't scrape together the blunt to buy a commission—and now wanted to hear every detail of what they'd missed.

"Lieutenant with the Thirtieth Foot." Will nodded once. "In the actions at Quatre Bras and Waterloo." If the nickninny wanted to know more than that he'd have to drag it out of him with a grappling hook.

Fortunately a gentleman three seats down had some opinion to air about Wellington, which someone else countered with an insight into Blucher's actions, and from there the usual derision was heaped upon the Prince of Orange and the usual agreement ensued as to what a bright day in England's history had been June eighteenth of the previous year. The table's mood shifted; the tension between himself and Roanoke guttered like a spent candle and was gone.

Will sat back, drawing in quiet, even breaths. He could listen to such discussions, at least. Some soldiers couldn't. One heard of men who grew light-headed and must leave a room when the subject was broached. Or who flew into a rage at hearing the perdition of battle recast as some grand glorious sport, like a thousand simultaneous boxing matches improved with the addition of strategy, and flashy uniforms, and weapons that made a good loud noise.

"Slaughter," Cathcart murmured under a mouthful of smoke as he took out his pipe.

And there was that. Those men who didn't care to romanticize the event must remark upon how "near run" the whole business had been, with the best soldiers in far-off Spain or Portugal and only hapless youngsters and second-rate officers to fumble their way across the Hougoumont fields.

He'd heard it before. From a friend, it still stung. "A tremendous loss of life indeed." He steadied his voice, made it low and careless. "Slaughter on both sides, I can assure you."

The viscount shook his head. "Her name. Your barren nymph is Miss Slaughter." A card dropped before him and he lifted a corner to look. "Not the most original gambit, defending a Cyprian's honor, but usually effective for all of that."

Ah. The mistress. Yes, that made more sense. Seven years he'd known Cathcart and the man had always taken life as a string of great larks; why would he begin pronouncing opinions on military strategy now? "I tell you there's no gambit." The words tumbled out with a vehemence born of relief: he felt enough of a stranger already to old friends without introducing such rifts, and he would a hundred times rather argue over a lady than a battle. "Truly, am I the only man in this room with sisters? With any grasp of simple decency? No woman deserves to hear those things said of her." He couldn't help stealing another glance, but if Miss Slaughter had heard any part of his ill-advised gallantry, she showed no sign. Deftly she marked another point on her paper and sat back, her shoulders square, her head erect, her gaze, stark and pitiless as a falcon's, never once turning his way.

Neither did Fortune find him worthy of notice, this time. He enriched Mr. Roanoke by twenty pounds in one hand and thirty in the next, erasing over a third of the evening's gain. Let that teach him to get caught up in petty intrigues. He pushed away from the table in disgust.

* * *

*T*HIS HAD been someone's house, before it became a club of most lax membership. Walls had been knocked out here and there to create the necessary large salons and supper room, but some traces of the residential scale remained. A drawing room at the back of the second story, for example, currently occupied by ladies who did not care for cards. Will turned away from the brightness and chatter and, on the street side of the same floor, found a modest library, intact even to books. No candles lit, or fire in the grate, but that only increased the likelihood he'd have the room to himself.

A bookshelf jutted out at right angles to the single bay window, and on the shadow side loomed a shape that proved, on approach, to be an armchair. Perfect. He sank into it and closed his eyes. Through the open door he could hear the house's sounds, all remote and indistinct. Conversation. Laughter. A faint strain of music—violin?—from the ballroom one story below. No doubt there would be dancing later. Just one of those artful amenities that proclaimed this house to be no seedy Smith and Pope's, but a place of gentlemanly sport. Where a gentleman could waltz with courtesans, and drink himself into a stupor, and ruin himself to the benefit of his fellows instead of some impersonal proprietor.

And who are you to condemn them for it? He slouched deeper into the chair, folding his arms. It seemed sometimes he'd lost all ability to . . . enjoy himself, carelessly. As a man ought to do, indeed as he had used to do. Nearly eight months he'd been back in England, turning aside invitations and ducking from acquaintances, schoolfellows, with whom he couldn't seem to remember how to converse. Only thick-skinned, cheerful Cathcart had persisted, and the viscount had finally prevailed not through the power of friendship but because he'd dangled the lure of a gaming club just when Will discovered a need for several thousand pounds.

Some hard edge was imposing itself against his forearm. Some square shape in his breast pocket that he hadn't any recollection of—

Oh, Christ. The snuffbox. This was the coat he'd worn when he'd first called on Mrs. Talbot.

He felt inside his pocket and drew out the box, then stood and reached round the bookshelf until moonlight through the window bathed his open palm.

Such a pretty thing for a man of modest means to have owned. Gold clasp, gold hinges, the lid all enameled with a scene of horse and hounds. Probably it was worth a bit of money. That was why it had stayed in his pocket, once he'd seen the Talbot relations pawing over the other small items he'd returned. When Mrs. Talbot was able to be independent of those people he would put it into her hands that she might keep it for the child. She wouldn't want for money, so there'd be no temptation to sell it.

His fist closed over the box, and opened again. He tilted his hand and the enamel gleamed as the moonlight caught it just so.

Altogether too much thinking he'd done tonight. He'd be useless at cards if he couldn't quiet the rest of his brain. He closed his hand on the box again, and brought it back.

He was just stowing it in a pocket when footsteps sounded in the corridor. For no good reason he withdrew to the armchair with its shadows, whisking his legs back to keep his Hessians away from the spill of moonlight. Unaccountable reflexes a man brought back from war. It wasn't as though the French had made a practice of sneaking up on one soldier at a time. Nor, of course, was it likely that the footsteps, if indeed they were bound for this room, could represent any threat.

Two sets of footsteps there were, one lighter than the other, and unmistakably bound his way. A man and woman. Yes, he ought to have anticipated this. Often enough he'd made like use of a darkened room at some gathering in his carefree days.

Something stopped him immediately rising. The awkwardness, perhaps, of having to explain just why he'd been in here, alone, in the dark. The stubborn assertion that he'd been here first, and why should he have to give way to their sordid purpose? At all events he was still seated, all the way in shadow, when two shapes filled the doorway and came in. The taller shape swung the door gently to behind them, and as the swath of illumination from the hall grew narrower, a green-jeweled cuff-stud glinted faintly.

Roanoke and his mistress. Or perhaps Roanoke and some other woman—indeed that was the likelier case, given Prince Square-jaw could entertain his mistress at home, at his leisure, without need for skulking about. The door clicked shut and Will abandoned the idea of a prompt exit. They could get on with their business and he'd slip out while their attention was engaged. Perhaps he'd make some attempt to ascertain the lady's identity— for what purpose, though? If the man betrayed Miss Slaughter, that was nothing to do with him. Did he propose to finagle a seat next to her at supper, and drop vague dire hints of what he'd seen?

The question was moot. The pair made straight for the bay window and he knew her by her posture alone. Erect and somehow remote, as though holding herself apart from the very air through which she moved. They passed into the bay—he could almost have put out a hand and touched her skirts as she went by; thank goodness their eyes were not so well adjusted to the dark as his—and the draperies creaked along their rod; the thin gruel of moonlight grew thinner. Then, silence, save for a few vague rustles. Whatever their next order of business, it apparently required no preamble of conversation.

Doubtless there were men who would enjoy sitting here, clandestine witness to such goings-on. A pity one of them couldn't take his place. All he'd wanted was a quarter-hour of darkness and silence; now he must tax his weary brain by calculating how best to retreat undetected from this room which he, by any measure, had the better right to occupy.

He'd make his try in thirty seconds. Any sooner, and they might not be sufficiently oblivious. Much later, and he'd be more visible to their dark-acclimated eyes.

An indistinct utterance added itself to the rustles. His hands settled carefully on the chair's arms and gripped there. Twenty seconds. No more.

Confound these rutting fools, both of them. Confound her especially, for letting Prince Square-jaw make this use of her not forty minutes after he'd bandied her name about so despicably. Did she have no care at all for her dignity? Then henceforth neither would he. No more misguided gallantry for Cathcart to twit him with.

Nineteen, twenty. They sounded absorbed enough. Slowly he eased up from the chair, angling round the bookshelf for a furtive glance to assure himself they wouldn't notice him.

He stopped, half-risen.

He'd been prepared for something sordid, a brute coupling between an importunate boor and a harlot who'd learned her trade at Mrs. Parrish's. And of course it *was* sordid by its very nature, this retreat to the library, and Square-jaw himself was everything sordid, with his mouth at the juncture of her neck and shoulder and his hands groping here and there.

She, though. She was . . . Confound him if he could

even begin to find the right word. He only knew *sordid* wasn't anywhere close.

She stood with her back to the drapery, eyes closed, chin lifted, whole person swaying with pleasure. While he watched she sent her arms—ungloved, he could now see—up the wall behind her where they twisted overhead, wrists crossing with serpentine grace. Like one of those dancers in a story who bewitched men into cutting off other men's heads. Her naked fingers closed over a fold of the velvet drapery and he knew how that velvet would feel to her, thick and lush-grained, a cat's purr made tactile. Knew, too, how it would feel to be the velvet, trapped unprotesting in her hand. He found a grip on the bookshelf and held on tight.

Down her arm he dragged his attention, down the sinuous curve until his eyes rested again on her uptilted face. Had he thought her less than beautiful? In moonlight, even in such scant moonlight, he could see the truth. Her bold features carved up the shadows and threw them helter-skelter, light and darkness dancing giddily over her nose and cheeks and chin. Her skin was pale as the moon itself, pale and tantalizing as an opal at the bottom of a clear still lake. Pale throat. Pale shoulder. Pale bosom, magnificently formed and half spilling out from the disarranged bodice. But he would not let his gaze linger there. Indeed he ought to be removing himself altogether, as he'd meant to do.

One last look at her face. Her head tipped a few degrees left and then a few degrees right as though to stretch the muscles of her neck. Her chin came down, rearranging the composition of shadows and light. And her eyes opened and looked directly into his.

She said nothing. She didn't jump away from her lover, or yank up the bodice he'd tugged down, or cross her arms modestly before her. Only her eyes, widened and showing an excess of white, betrayed her consciousness of exposure. And that, for only a second or two, though the interval was sufficient to make him feel like a thoroughgoing cad.

The bookshelf's edge bit hard into his hand. He couldn't seem to look away, let alone make an apologetic bow and hasten from the room. He stood, frozen, as she regained her composure and her face hardened into the unmistakable lines of defiance: *Judge me if you dare.* Then that expression too subsided and only her falcon-like blankness remained. She looked through him, and past him, and altogether away.

He'd ceased to merit her notice. Whether he watched, or not, was a matter of supremest indifference to her. Her hands came down from their place on the curtain—even now, with a dancer's lissome grace—and settled on the oblivious biceps of Mr. Roanoke, who had continued at her shoulder and neck through the brief drama but was now commencing to haul up her skirts.

And finally Will let go his grip on the bookshelf. He didn't want to see what followed. He'd probably see it in his dreams, and that would be torment enough.

Some impulse of obstinacy made him bow. She didn't look his way, and neither did she or Prince Square-jaw glance up as he stole light-footed to the door, opened it just enough to accommodate his long-overdue exit, and soundlessly closed it behind him.

THEY DID not appear at supper. Will soldiered through three courses that did nothing to appease the foolhardy hunger scraping at his insides.

Nothing to the purpose. She wasn't for him. She pleased his eye and engaged his imagination, yes, but that hardly made her unique among women. When the time came to share himself with a lady again, he would look for a few qualities more. He'd yet to even hear

Miss Slaughter speak; for all he knew she might open her mouth and prove an empty-headed shrew.

Indeed he rather hoped she would. She'd be less of a distraction then.

Whatever had kept them so occupied as to forgo supper, they'd apparently had their fill of it by the time card play resumed. Roanoke took his seat at the vingt-et-un table and this time his mistress sat on his knee. Gone was the attentive poise with which she'd conducted herself at whist. She leaned back and rested her head on the man's shoulder, watching the play idly from under half-lowered lashes, her entire aspect suggesting a lioness who'd just gorged herself on a kill and needn't think of eating, or think of anything at all, for at least a week.

Will fixed his eyes elsewhere. He had a purpose here, a mission. He had a plan that required three thousand pounds and God knows the odds were enough against him with his wits entirely engaged.

Three o'clock came, and then four—he knew this from Cathcart's jeweled pocket watch set down between them, the room being provided with no clocks—and he was nearly two hundred pounds to the good. Men were betting with sluggish brains; some men falling asleep outright and having to be prodded awake by a neighbor when their turns came. A fellow who kept his head might do quite well here, over time.

The viscount poked him with an elbow and, when he glanced up, nodded in the direction from which he'd rigorously kept his gaze. Roanoke's head lolled on his left shoulder. His chest rose and fell with slumberous breaths. Still against his right shoulder was Miss Slaughter, who'd helped herself to his cards and was considering them with languid attention. Her hands, he could not help noticing, were still bare. Perhaps her gloves lay even now on that library floor. His skin prickled unhelpfully at the thought.

"Does she play?" No other lady had sat down to the table all evening.

"I've never seen it." Cathcart had been coming here a good deal longer and would know. "But she looks as though she has it in mind, doesn't she?"

And indeed, when the play passed to Roanoke she made no attempt to wake him. Without the smallest sign of unease she took fifty pounds from his stake and added it to his bet, eyeing the banker expectantly.

The card sailed in and she lifted its corner. "Stick," she said. And Will's whole body vibrated to the tone of her voice.

Even on an austere syllable with more than its share of clicking consonants, she put in texture, and rounded the corners somehow. A man could savor that sampling, a sweet small dose like a cordial in a dainty glass. A man could very well get drunk on a larger amount, and bathe in an abundance. She'd reserved a place already in his dreams; now he knew she would speak, unceasingly, while she was there.

She would not, however, play vingt-et-un. Sadly she proved to be no proficient. She chewed at her lower lip while studying her cards, and wagered erratically, and went bust in three of the five hands she played before fortune finally took pity on her with an ace and a ten, and the deal. Meticulously she gathered in the cards, staggering them together to break apart the turned-up hands even before shuffling, as though by thorough discharge of this new duty she could somehow compensate for her lack of tactical skill. She shuffled, had her neighbor cut the deck, and dealt.

And Will began to lose. He drew on a hand of twelve, and a king put him over. He stuck at nineteen, and she proved to have twenty. Even when he worked his pulse-pounding way to twenty-one, eight-seven-two-four, she turned up an ace and two fives to tie—to win, rather, the banker always having that advantage. Five straight times she dealt, beating him every time, until a grizzled-looking fellow hit twenty-one in two cards and mercifully took over the deal.

Ruin tasted like this. Like a mouthful of ashes, or the sweepings from a carpenter's floor. In less than half an hour his winnings had shrunk from two hundred pounds to twenty. "Bad luck, Blackshear," muttered the viscount, who had lost a mere fifty. Will didn't bother to reply.

Miss Slaughter was looking at him. Without any particular expression, to be sure, but her eyes rested steady on his. She picked up Roanoke's winnings and averted her attention to count out some bills before looking up again. Without counting along he knew—in his bones he knew—that she'd peeled off one hundred eighty pounds, precisely.

She dropped the large remainder in with the rest of Roanoke's stake. Still watching him, she folded the amount of his losses, and folded it again, and tucked it calmly into the bodice of her gown. Then she turned to the more compelling business of examining her new hand.

Chapter Two

$\mathscr{E}$DWARD WAS disposed to talk. Curse him to Hades. Why couldn't he roll over and drop off to sleep, as men were supposed to do? But of course he'd slept abundantly at the card table. She might have skimmed double from his winnings, and he would probably never have noticed.

"What do you think of a house party at Chiswell?" He lay on his back, one hand lifted above him that he might study his fingernails in the candlelight.

"In March?" The bed smelled of carnal abandon. Every inhalation brought a forceful reminder of her senseless appetites, her want of restraint. Five minutes ago she'd been ravenous for him, half out of her mind with need. Now she felt glutted and vaguely regretful, as though she'd shoveled down a pound or two of sugary blancmange. She would remember this disagreeable sensation, and next time she would know better.

No, she wouldn't. She'd had six months to know better, and she hadn't managed it yet.

"Next month, I thought. At the Easter holiday. Parliament will be out, and people in need of some amusement. Suitable weather, too, in April, or at least I should hope it will be. Deuced cold winter it's been. Long winter too. Damnably long. And cold."

If only he would not speak! When she looked at him, at his clear hazel eyes and the elegant geometry of his cheeks and chin, she could easily imagine him to be a man of information. Thoughtful, inquisitive, a sparkling conversationalist, his brain always churning away beneath that modish Caesar haircut.

When he spoke, he was like the leftover dregs of her blancmange orgy, a shameful, ravaged souvenir that she wished to her soul some servant would come and clear away.

"I'm sure your party will be everything delightful." Lydia covered a yawn. Perhaps she could make him yawn too, and hasten his progress toward sleep.

"I expect it will." The first set of nails apparently having passed muster, he was now examining those on his other hand. "Only I suppose I shall have to be ready with some indoor amusements if this weather keeps on."

"Indeed. Shall I put out the candle?"

"No need. I'll do it presently." He would not take a hint. She had no hope of sleep until he was gone from her bed, hours and minutes hence. No hope of rest, even, until he closed his eyes and went unconscious. "What provisions do you think I ought to make for the ladies?" He lowered his hand and turned his face toward her. "As to amusements, I mean? What things are fashionable now?"

How the devil would I know? My last house party was a lifetime ago. She swallowed and the words went down. "I think a play is always popular. Archery, if the weather turns fair. Perhaps some of those games with blindfolds and kissing and so forth." How novel, how thrilling such games had seemed to her once. She'd first let Arthur touch her in the darkness of his father's orangery, every breath heady with the scents of citrus and damp potted earth, every delicate negotiation of hands and lips and clothing conducted in silence, that they might not betray their location in a game of hide-and-seek.

She could probably fix the beginning of her fall to that exact occasion, if she cared to squander one minute contemplating the trajectory of her fall, and if she cared to spare a single thought for Arthur.

"Of course it must depend on the company. Kissing games might seem quaint to the ladies who were at Beecham's tonight, for example. But perhaps you mean to invite more respectable ladies?"

"Gad, no." He laughed as though she'd said something very rich. "I'm six and twenty, Lydia. I needn't think of respectable ladies for years yet."

Five years, perhaps. But he'd tire of her before that time came. And if she had not put aside money enough to secure her future, she must cast about for a new protector. Or perhaps go back to the brothel.

She could bear that, if she had to. Hadn't she borne it for eighteen months, before Edward took a whim to keep her? Indeed she'd first gone there with a will, with a plan to extinguish herself from the inside out.

She had other plans now. "I played your hand for a bit tonight while you napped." Better he should hear it from her than from someone else.

"Did you? Clever girl. Have any luck?"

Luck. Good Lord. Who could be so complacent as to leave these things to luck? "I think so. I think I may have won you some money." Four hundred eighty pounds, all told. Three hundred of it in one of his coat-pockets even now.

"Well done." He threaded his fingers together and stretched his arms straight up. "The other fellows may say what they like. I know your merits."

So do they, now. You saw to that. With all the insolence she swallowed, it was a wonder her corsets still laced. Retort after rejoinder after sharp-edged remark: *Why do you address me? What can I possibly have to say to a man who would split a pair of fives? Be quiet. Go to sleep. Go away. Come back when you have another erection.*

Sleep finally did overcome him, and after four minutes of listening to his even breaths, Lydia slid from the bed. Silently—silent as that coxcomb of a lurker in the library—she took her dressing gown from a nearby chair, pulled it on, and padded across the carpet to the candle Edward had not, after all, put out. Sheltering the flame with her free hand, she took it to the dressing room and closed the door behind her.

By the window were a chair and table. On the back of the chair was a shawl that had seen her through many such long chilly nights. And in a drawer, alongside the hundred eighty pounds she'd deftly extracted from her corset, sat four decks of playing cards, sans jokers. She took out two decks and sat down with her candle.

He might be trouble, that coxcomb. She probably oughtn't to have baited him. He played with the air of a man who didn't lose lightly and he might, after all, prove smarter than he looked. Though men so seldom did.

One by one the cards flashed by, numbers combining and recombining in all their immaculate beauty. King. Three. Five. Seven. Ace, most beautiful of all. In stacks of rank she sorted them, low to high, left to right.

Hang him, anyway. Hang him and his Waterloo heroics. A man found himself in the right campaign and his life thereafter was one long parade all embellished with fireworks and illuminations, regardless how he actually performed on the day. A man found himself in the wrong one and he perished of the ague, with no one but a desolate sister to remember that he ever lived at all.

She pulled her shawl closer against the chill. Somewhere beyond the ever-present fog, the stars were fading and the first pale traces of morning were streaking the sky. Jane would rise soon and light the fires. There would be coffee, too, to warm her and keep her brain awake.

Now then. Twelve players at the table, two decks in play, cards newly shuffled. Two cards to every player, face down. Player number five would turn up an immediate twenty-one, good for him but bad for the composition of the remaining deck. First player would buy two more cards, which meant he must hold at least three low ones. Second player would go bust. Six, six, and queen, let us say. Giving the deck a high-cards-to-low-cards ratio of approximately twenty-three to twenty-one, or one and ninety-five thousandths.

Methodically Lydia laid out the cards, tabulating as she went. Edward wouldn't wake for hours yet. She'd have time to count her way through both decks, and then to play a few hands, watching for those places where she could take advantage of her tally to wager boldly.

And night by night, through means fair or otherwise, with the help of Lieutenant Coxcomb and other men who made the mistake of estimating her lightly, she would tuck bills into her corset, and hide them away at home, and draw ever closer to the day she could buy her independence.

THE DISRESPECTABLE life was not without its consolations. A high style of living, of course. The central duty itself, where one had a skilled and agreeable partner. Entrée into places, exotic and fascinating places, that no respectable lady would ever see. And acquaintance with people who wouldn't half turn up in any sedate Lancashire supper party.

"I only mean to say I don't think you should allow him to speak of you that way." Maria crisply turned a page in her *Ackermann's Repository*. "Tell him he has a choice: to enjoy your favors, or to enjoy discussing them in public. He cannot do both."

Well might Maria issue that ultimatum to a gentleman, and expect to be heeded. Such a confection of femininity—willowy figure, ivory skin, eyes the color of a midday summer sky—was surely wasted in this world. She ought to be perched on the summit of a glass hill somewhere, smiling sadly at the princes who lost their footing halfway up, or perhaps combing her spun-gold hair on some ocean-lashed rock. Not sitting in a Bond Street dressmaker's shop, deciding how best to spend the money with which she was kept.

They weren't at all what a sheltered country girl imagined, the mistresses of London men. She'd expected, when brought into Edward's social circle, to encounter better-dressed versions of the women she'd known at Mrs. Parrish's—coarse, uneducated, with a bovine resignation to the shabby hand life had dealt them.

Instead she'd found Maria and dark rakish Eliza, both of better birth than she, both with a genteel education, and both generous enough to overlook her brothel background and address her as an equal.

Lydia shrugged, flipping a page in her own fashionbook. "I'd wager all the gentlemen speak so, when we're not about. I don't see what would be gained by asking him to pretend otherwise."

"*Civility* would be gained." Maria turned two pages, reviewing and dismissing their offerings with poised efficiency. "We're not livestock, to have our merits cried up at auction."

"Oh, I don't know." On the other side of the table Eliza abandoned her *Ackermann's* to lean forward, arms folded on the tabletop. "Who is to say but Lydia won't get a better position out of such advertising? That Waterloo fellow was certainly taking note. He lost no time in finding out your name."

"That Waterloo fellow would have done well to mind his own business." A fine indifferent tone of voice, betraying no sentiment beyond mild irritation at the memory. "And it's not as though he sought my name from some indelicate motive. He only wanted to make a grand show of what he supposed to be his superior manners."

"I shouldn't be sorry if he sought my name from any motive. Did you mark those shoulders?" Eliza appealed to both ladies opposite. "Broad as a full-grown oak. Broad as a draft horse. I shouldn't mind a closer acquaintance with those."

"His speaking up so did him credit, I thought." Maria turned a reproving frown Lydia's way. "And I'll grant him to have a pleasing appearance. Strong about the mouth; that is in his favor. Fine dark eyes as well."

"Smoldering eyes, I should say. Eyes like a pair of live coals."

Oh, for Heaven's sake. "Live coals glow orange. The gentleman's eyes are brown." But even as she corrected Eliza, she knew what the lady meant. Dim as the library had been, she'd seen the heat in his gaze. She'd opened her eyes to find herself watched by eyes that looked as if they might bore twin holes straight through her. And for an instant she'd felt naked, more naked than she'd ever felt with any paying man.

Only for an instant, though. And he'd paid for that after all. He might have bought her favors for much less, if she were of a mind to sell.

She sighed, and shoved her book to the middle of the table. "Someone else choose for me. I can't see that any of these gowns will become me better than any other." If Edward had asked, she should have told him not to waste his money on gowns, none of which would make her beautiful and none of which played any part in his essential congress with her.

Well, except for those instances of congress that occurred away from any bed. In Beecham's library, for example.

She lowered her eyes and traced the seam of one glove with the opposite forefinger as the other two ladies paged through their fashion-books, debating which styles would suit her best. She might have told them of the library incident. Eliza, at the least, would have had a good laugh, and the gentleman in question should have had to contend with more than one knowing smirk, any place he crossed paths with them.

But there was too great a risk the story would eventually reach Edward. And he might find grounds for blame in the fact that she hadn't told him herself, the very instant she opened her eyes and saw the lurker. His logic in such matters was not always sound. Better to keep her own counsel.

"This one." Maria set an open book before her. "In an indigo, I should think, with royal blue trimmings, and you must wear your sapphires with it. And this one." Unceremoniously she possessed herself of Eliza's volume and spread it out atop the first. "The overdress in dark purple; the underdress in darker purple. The darkest you can find, like a black plum. If they can make the underdress of a knit silk, to cling to the form, that will be to your advantage."

"Indeed, anything that draws the eye away from my face is to my advantage, I expect." But she felt a strange stupid fluttering of her heart, examining the plates. The first gown had a sort of Grecian draping, with split sleeves and a corded sash that crossed between the breasts and circled round the high waist. The second was comprised of an underdress, simple and narrow in shape, and a diaphanous overdress that fastened down the middle of the bust and fell open underneath, rather like a most insubstantial pelisse. No blushing young miss would wear such things. They were gowns for a worldly, formidable woman.

"Really, Lydia, you're very tedious when you speak so." Maria's lecture embroidered itself gently at the edges of her thoughts, leaving most of her attention for study of the pictures. "Ladies of no particular beauty have elevated themselves to great consequence and earned the name of *temptress*. You might do just as well if you left off reminding everyone of how plain you are. Let the gentlemen decide for themselves."

"Very well, I'll order them both. Knit silk and all." Doubtless they'd cost more than her usual gowns. Perhaps she'd better skim a bit less of Edward's winnings, the next time she played his hand.

$\mathscr{A}$ND so she did. Three nights later they were back at Beecham's, and her protector fell asleep one hand into a fresh shuffle. She'd felt him drifting, and taken note of all the turned-up cards as the first hand ended, and now she played with a good idea of what remained in the deck. She recalibrated her tally, delicately with each twist or bust, dramatically as each hand finished and all the cards went faceup.

And she won. Quietly, unassumingly, with bets not quite large enough to catch anyone's notice, she fattened Edward's stake to an amount that could pay for half a dozen new gowns of the finest Chinese silk and Indian muslin. On the last hand, with too many ten-cards remaining in the deck, she stuck on fifteen and sat back to watch man after man, including the banker, go bust.

Not Lieutenant Coxcomb, though. He glanced at her, from his place halfway down the table, as they both raked in their winnings. Perhaps hoping to see her put money down her bodice again. Well, he could hope all he liked. She shoveled what bills she could into Edward's various coat-pockets—he must count on the honesty of his companions at the table for the rest—and rose to walk unhurriedly from the room, a modest fifty pounds folded in one hand.

*T*HE THIRD-FLOOR hallway had a window overlooking the street; a good place for quiet thought and general retreat from all the activity of the floors below. The hour must be near three. A half-moon hung up above, its edges softened by the fog.

Fifty pounds. Between her corset and chemise she tucked the folded bills. Fifty plus one hundred eighty made two hundred thirty in the span of just five days. She ought to have summoned up the nerve to start playing weeks ago, when Edward had first brought her here. It would serve her timidity right if he tired of the club, and chose to do his gaming at some place that didn't admit ladies, before she'd won all she needed.

Nothing to be gained by thinking of that. Still less to be gained by reckoning the probability that he would in fact tire of her before he tired of Beecham's. That was all airy speculation, no place to get a good reckoning grip, and so it did not bear thinking of.

She reached out a forefinger to trace the narrow strip of lead that separated one diamond-shaped glass pane from another. Divide each diamond with a meridian and an equator, and you could reassemble the pieces into rectangles to arrive at the window's dimension. This one, with six courses of four diamonds and five courses of three, had an area forty-eight times as great as the area of a single pane.

Henry had used to quiz her on these matters, in the years before he'd finally persuaded Father to engage a tutor. To this day she couldn't stand before such a window without feeling her brother's presence behind her right shoulder, his giddy expectant pride as she ran through the calculations even faster than he could do.

Her hand trailed off the window and fell to her side. No doubt he'd disapprove of the uses to which she put her brain now. Never mind. He ought to have stayed home, if he meant to have influence with her. If he'd never gone away to war, perhaps he would have perceived how matters tended between her and Arthur, and perhaps he would have intervened before she could make such a disastrous mistake. Then Mother and Father would have had no reason to be traveling, that day. Everything might have been different.

Lydia swiped under both eyes with the heel of one hand. Speak of profitless speculation. She pivoted, forcefully, and started for the stairs.

She'd gone four paces when a dark shape detached itself from the shadows along the wall and stepped out into the moonlit middle of the hall. "A word, Miss Slaughter," the dark shape said.

She shrank a step backward, her heart galloping with alarm. How the devil had he got up here without her hearing? And how long had he lurked, observing her in secret and planning to take her by surprise? She went still, the better to will her heart into steadiness and to deny him any further triumph than the one he must already be enjoying. She would not speak, or even rest her eyes on him. Her remaining there, and a slight upward tilt of her chin, were all the encouragement she would grant to him and his word.

And apparently they were all the encouragement he needed. "I want my hundred eighty pounds back," he said.

Poor fool of a lieutenant, too accustomed to being

obeyed. "I don't doubt you do," she said, and pushed past him.

Or not past him: suddenly he was there, no arm held up to touch or restrain her but his body nevertheless blocking her way. Black coat. Buff tights. Broad as a full-grown oak, indeed. She would not look at his face. But neither would she draw back, this time.

Nor did he. "Forgive my not having been explicit." He spoke softly, now the distance between them was so small. "You cheated me out of one hundred eighty pounds, four nights since. I am instructing you to return it."

One brief bolt of panic shot through her, but cool outrage promptly filled up the place where it had been. "Cheated. Really." She addressed his cravat, whose arrangement, one must note, suggested no appreciation for geometry. "Can you prove this charge?"

"Do you deny it?" His breath grazed her forehead. No doubt he thought to intimidate her with his size and his nearness and his bold accusations.

Let him try. "Just as I thought. You've no proof. If you will excuse me." Crisply she cut to the left, but swift as a shadow he twisted round in front of her again. Very well. Now she'd absorbed the initial alarm, he didn't frighten her a bit. She backed up against the wall and folded her arms to wait.

He followed. Not so near her this time. He took up a position two feet away or so with his shoulder to the wall and his body turned to face her. "I watched you play tonight. I saw you stick on fifteen at the end. That strongly implies some knowledge of the banker's hand, or knowledge of what remains in the deck." Finally she looked at his face. There were those eyes, warm and intent in the hallway's moonlight. "I am persuaded your early losses of the other night were all deliberate. Your uncertainty, your ineptitude, your lip-biting all part of an act intended to put the men—and me in particular—off our guard. Nobody suspected you of any skill; thus nobody watched you for trickery when you dealt the cards."

"A pity, that." She was equal to this. "Perhaps you could have told me by what methods I cheated. As it is, I'm inclined to blame your losses on your own poor play."

His gaze went to her mouth as she spoke, and he cocked his head like an inquisitive dog. "Where were you born?" he said when she'd finished.

"I beg your pardon."

"That's no Cheapside tongue, nor any London accent I know of. Where did you grow up?"

"I fear my station has led you into some mistake, sir." Her words came out cool enough to frost the air between them.

"Has it." He made the reply absently, his attention still engaged by the study of her mouth. Like as not he'd proceeded from puzzling over her accent to imagining lewd uses he might make of her lips and tongue.

"Regarding the liberties you may take in addressing me. Asking familiar questions and making free with my name when I never gave it to you."

"Yes. Forgive that. My own name's Blackshear."

"I didn't ask. I don't care to know. And I must say, Lieutenant Blackshear—"

"It's plain Mr. Blackshear. I sold my commission." He dropped his attention briefly to the carpet, and when he brought it back he was all business, the diversions of her voice and mouth forgotten. "Why should you want to gull me out of a night's winnings?"

"This line of inquiry grows tiresome." She sent the opinion straight out before her, words marching in single file toward the opposite wall. "If you cannot offer any evidence of my purported cheating then I suggest you abandon the subject."

Silence fell between them. He moved a step away from the wall, setting one hand on the wallpaper and considering his outspread fingers. Men and their hands. Like Edward and his constant preoccupation with the state of his nails. One wouldn't think they could find so much to engross them in—

"Is it to do with the library?"

Again, the lightning-flash interval of nakedness. "I have no idea what you—"

"Spare us, Miss Slaughter. Me and yourself both." A rougher edge came into his voice, even as he kept his gaze fast on the wallpaper. He would have sounded like this when speaking to his fellows in the army. "Is that the reason for your animosity? Did it not occur to you that I might have been in the room first, minding my own business, with no desire whatsoever to be witness to any erotic spectacle?"

Did he think to shame her now? Well, he'd picked the wrong harlot for that. "Please, Mr. Blackshear." She pivoted, shoulder to the wall, to face him. "I am entirely capable of staging an erotic spectacle if I so wished. What you saw was nothing near."

That would be a fine remark upon which to exit. But she stayed. His eyes, perhaps, were to blame for that. They'd cut from his hand to her face with such an expression as . . . what had Eliza said, exactly, concerning coals? One could easily imagine a tiny man behind those eyes, with a tiny bellows, fanning the coals into full conflagration.

"I shall take your word for that." His eyes dimmed down to a steady glow. He eased his shoulder back to the wall, trailing his hand down the wallpaper, less than two feet in breadth, that lay between his arm and hers. She did notice that; the distance between them and the way his hand trailed. Once a lady had learned the better uses of men, she could not help noticing these things. "I only ask you to consider that *I* in fact may have been the affronted party in this affair," he meanwhile went on. "Dismayed by the intrusion and only wishing to get out as directly, and with as little awkwardness, as I could."

"You didn't appear, as I recall it, to be in any hurry."

"No. You're quite right." His cheek, now she looked, had a shadow below the close-trimmed side-whiskers, a texture that made her palm tingle. Three o'clock in the morning and his last shave must be a day behind him. "I did mean to hurry but I was . . . distracted from my intent. Perhaps I owe you an apology for that."

"I should think you do." Had he leaned closer? He had. That would be why her voice was creeping into this lower, warmer, not to say intimate, range.

"Very well." His eyes glimmered with sudden mischief. "I apologize if I violated whatever version of modesty permits a lady to entertain her gentleman protector in a public place. Now will you give me back my money?"

"Good God." Her voice sailed back up to its regular octave. "Who taught you how to make an apology?"

"A strict governess, whom I disregarded as often as I could. Who taught you to curse like a gentleman?"

"That's not your concern. And what soldier worth the name counts *Good God* as cursing?"

"I told you I sold out. I follow gentlemen's rules now, and gentlemen don't say *Good God* in front of ladies." His mouth spread abruptly into a lopsided grin, revealing imperfect teeth: the two front ones had a slight space between. He was teasing her, fully acknowledging that she in fact had been the one to utter the phrase, and perhaps acknowledging as well the absurdity of observing any gentlemen-and-ladies rules with such a woman as herself.

Perverse, ill-judging man. What business had he to tease her, to smile with such undisguised good nature, as though he expected good nature in return? A soldier ought to be better at distinguishing friend from adversary.

"Give me the money, Miss Slaughter." His voice went lower, honeyed and coaxing. Merriment still creased the corners of his eyes. "You've set me down admirably, and made a fool of me at the table as well. Let that be your revenge for my having seen you in *flagrante*. The money itself can be of no consequence to you."

Well, that resolved the question of whether or not he was brighter than he looked. "Please tell me what sort of life you imagine me to have, in which money is of no consequence."

"The life of a kept woman." Promptly he matched her arid tone, all traces of honey thrown off. "Someone pays all your expenses, from your fancy gowns and bonnets to the roof over your head. Perhaps money is of some consequence to you, but I assure you it is of greater consequence to me, who must pay my own way in everything."

So that was how he really thought of her. Not friend or even foe but a mere trivial creature with no weightier concern than her next fancy gown. A vision surged up of the two pattern-book plates, frivolous and accusing. Her fingers curled into tight fists. "You are a gentleman, though. A man. You have every advantage."

"No advantage that will pay my bill for candles, or keep my boots in repair."

"Indeed you do. You can find a situation. Nothing, perhaps, commensurate with the expectations and delicate tastes to which you may have been brought up, but there are a hundred respectable ways for a man to support himself, in London." Another thought occurred. "And surely you have money from the sale of your commission. They fetch a handsome sum now the war's over, I'll warrant."

"To be sure." Impatience laced his words. "But part of that profit is bound up elsewhere, and I need every penny of what remains."

"Then I sincerely hope you're not using it to gamble."

"Miss Slaughter." The tiny man had his bellows going again: surely such a stare would turn her bones to jelly. "I would have let this drop by now if the money were only for me. But other parties depend on what I can do with that hundred eighty pounds. It is a matter of utmost importance that you return it."

Her intransigence faltered, briefly, at the urgent warmth in his speech. He wasn't lying. He needed the money for some vital purpose.

Well, so did she. "Without you prove I cheated you, your other parties and your utmost importance are beside the point." She would set him the example of what tone of voice to use, in such a discussion. "I think we profit nothing by taking this any further." With a nod, she pushed off the wall and started for the stairs.

"Please, Miss Slaughter." His voice, low and unguarded, halted her steps like an arrow to her breast. "I won't threaten you. I won't cajole. I cannot, as you say, prove you took my money by fraud. I can only lay out my need before you, and make my appeal to what charity lies in your heart."

She half-turned. Not far enough to face him. "My heart." Poor fool's time would be better spent pitching pennies down a bottomless well. "Mr. Blackshear, you're three years too late." She pushed on toward the stairs, and this time he made no move to stop her.

Chapter Three

$\mathscr{A}$GAIN, THE dark library with that moonlit bay window. His grip mangling the chair's padded arms. He ought not to look this time. She'd be angry—she hadn't liked him broaching the incident in their hallway conversation upstairs—and doubtless find a way to part him from more of his money. Fool that he was.

But he could no more stop himself than he could push back a tide. Slowly, inexorably, he came up out of the chair, angling for one illicit glimpse. Another inch—another—and he saw round the bookshelf into the bay.

He could almost believe she was made of moonlight itself. Moonlight undulating, the way it did on an ocean when you'd sailed away and left shore behind. Arms twisted up above her head. Face tilted. If only confounded Roanoke weren't there to spoil the view . . . and then, as though she'd read his thoughts, one pale arm sank away from the drapes. She set her palm to the middle of the man's chest and pushed.

Roanoke stumbled backward and—most obliging of him—wavered and dissolved altogether. She opened her eyes.

Will's heart lurched up out of his chest to thunder directly between his ears. Would that instant of awful vulnerability repeat itself in her face?—but no. She registered his presence, and her generous mouth quirked, just slightly, at the corners. He hadn't caught her off guard this time. His heart rebounded to its proper place.

She didn't reach for her pushed-off sleeve. Steadily, without shame, she returned his gaze. Her arm lifted, and snaked back up the velvet. The other one drifted down and stretched toward him. She turned her palm up, crooking her forefinger.

Yes. He let go the bookshelf and stepped out into full view. And she did avail herself of the full view: her eyes raked down his form and went wide when they got below the waist.

Don't flatter yourself. She worked in a pleasure-house. She'll have seen all sizes. Whose intrusive voice was that? Ah. His own. That was certainly odd.

No matter. Things were looking promising. He could straighten out the odd bits later. He stood still a moment, to let her finish her perusal, and when her eyes came again to his face, he went to her. Shadow to moonlight, and they would play exquisitely as shadow and moonlight always did.

A sound . . . a bird? In this house in the middle of the night? No, that would be . . . he'd left a window open before he . . . for morning breezes and so he wouldn't sleep too . . . No. No. To complete any of those thoughts would bring some dire result; he couldn't quite lay his hands on it, but no, even that, to identify the dire result, might bring it about.

Urgency flared up in him as he took her face in his palms. A delicate rose-petal scent wafted from her, just as it had done whenever he got near enough in that dark hallway. Now he'd find out whether she tasted of roses too. He bent his head quickly, and brought his mouth to hers.

But she was gone. His hands sat suspended in the air where her face had been. Despair clenched his innards in its fist—he'd been so close—and suddenly he felt a touch on his coat sleeve.

She'd got behind him somehow. Slipped away like quicksilver, but no matter, because here she was turning him, backing him up against the velvet where she'd been, and then . . . and then . . . she stared at him with her falcon ferocity, and sank to her knees.

Yes. Oh, God, yes. "Hurry." His unaccountably clumsy fingers stumbled over his buttons. "It's a dream, you see, and we have to finish before I . . ." But no, that had been a mistake, to say so out loud. Already the velvet was feeling like linen at his back, and the midnight darkness was beginning to lift. "Hurry, please." Though *please*, he already knew, had no effect on her. "If you could at least get—" No, she was wavering just as Roanoke had done, even as he moved frantically from one button to the next. She leaned toward him, slowly, her lips parting, but he could hear traffic from the street below. Horses. Someone shouting. Confound his open window.

He finally got himself free of his breeches and felt a single faint, dissolving touch from her lips . . . and it wasn't enough. He came awake, hard and ravenous and alone in his bed.

Will swept a hand across the mattress's empty expanse. One of these mornings, surely, he'd wake to find a woman there. One morning he'd wake to a better comfort than his own right hand.

He touched himself nevertheless, eyes closing as his fingertips roamed over the sensitive skin. What he needed, once the time came, was a lusty, carefree sort of partner, with blitheness enough for the both of them. A lady who knew how to take things lightly, and who risked nothing by being with him.

What he didn't need was someone else's mistress, and a ruthless one at that. Bragging of her heartlessness. Taunting him with mention of erotic spectacles. Helping herself to his money at will.

His breath came quicker as he wrapped his whole hand. How unearthly she'd looked, kneeling before him. Her posture submissive, but her eyes the eyes of a creature who would eat you alive and spit out your bones. He'd shaped her that way, of course—it was his dream—and what did that say of him? More evidence he'd come home to England unsound.

No matter. His hand was sending quick spirals of pleasure from his loins to the top of his skull and he need not think at all now, unless it was to imagine her ruthlessness put to most gratifying use. And then to imagine the ruthlessness with which he would answer, laying her out right there on the library floor and showing her that what she'd heretofore believed to be pleasure was but a pallid facsimile.

Yes, she would say in that liqueur of a voice. He could hear it. She'd render his name like some complex, bittersweet confection and she'd give up the most sumptuous, maddening moans ever heard by mortal ears as he drove her from one climax to the next.

He gasped, and arched up off the mattress, and spent himself in the sheets. Breath burned in his throat, his mouth, leaving behind a faint flavor of shame as he sank back down to his solitary bed. Lord. Without question he was wrong in the head. He might never be fit for a proper woman again. To say nothing of a proper lady. What did he mean, dreaming so of a demimondaine who'd made her contempt for him clear?

Too long a stretch of abstinence did this. His black moods had been so frequent, in those first months home, and so potent that to share any bit of himself with a woman had seemed unthinkable. Even now, with those moods relaxing their grip, he felt . . . well, he had lingering debts, hadn't he? Accounts to square; solemn trusts to keep; atonement, of a sort, to perform, before he could turn his thoughts to the pursuit of pleasure.

He threw off the covers and swung himself out of bed into the shock of cool air on his sweat-damp body. Yes, he knew he'd left that window open for a reason. No lying abed this morning; his sister was due here in a bit above an hour and then he'd be off on his latest trial of penitence. Now what had he done with his best waistcoat?

*L*YDIA PINCHED at her reticule and wound its strings more securely round her wrist. No cutpurse had accosted her on the long walk from Clarendon Square to Threadneedle Street, and certainly none was likely to do so now that she actually stood within the imposing walls of the bank. Still she held tight, rubbing silk back and forth over the bills on which she would begin to build her future.

One hundred in her purse. One hundred thirty waiting in the drawer at home. Only seventeen hundred seventy more to go.

Two thousand pounds, invested in the five percents, would bring her one hundred pounds per annum. One hundred pounds was income enough to buy a single lady a respectable life. Not a luxurious one—the house would be small, the candles would be tallow, and she must probably learn to like her tea without sugar—but everything would be in good repair, and she'd be able to spare perhaps ten pounds a year for a maidservant.

She glanced over to the bench where Jane sat, waiting patiently for her mistress to progress to the front of the line. She was a good girl, the maid was—industrious and uncomplaining—and she deserved better than to be dragged across town on obscure errands.

But a respectable lady wouldn't go abroad, and certainly wouldn't go into a place of business, without a companion. And since Lydia was counterfeiting to be a respectable lady today, Jane must counterfeit to be the companion.

A clerk in a frock coat finished his dealings with a bespectacled man and finally it was her turn. Jane came obediently to join her, favoring one foot as she walked. Likely she'd raised a blister on the two miles from Somers Town. They'd be in for a difficult trek home.

Time enough to think of that later. She sat, arranging the skirts of her plainest, most respectable dark blue gown. Jane sat some seconds after—she'd paid careful attention when Lydia explained the rules by which a lady's companion behaved—and then the clerk sat, too, folding his hands atop his desk. He smiled, a sheen of amused indulgence already polluting his countenance from the crown of his wig to the tip of his insufficient chin.

She cleared her throat and sat as straight as possible. "I'd like to purchase a certificate of annuity." Had she said that correctly? "To invest in one of the annuity funds. The Navy annuity, to be specific."

"We're all eager to support the Navy, aren't we?" The indulgence leaked into his voice, too, as he bowed his head in acknowledgment of her patriotic fervor. "But that's just one of the annuities we offer, and one of the newest at that. Perhaps you've heard of the consolidated annuities? They've been a reliable investment since the last century. A good choice, I've found, for ladies who like a guaranteed income."

Good Lord. He thought her a cork-brain. "As I understand it, an annuity by its very nature guarantees an income. And the Consols are paying only three percent now. The Navy pays five." She turned an imperious glare on Jane. "Isn't that what you read to me out of the paper, Miss Collier? Five percent?"

Jane took the cue beautifully, nodding her bowed head while directing one apologetic glance toward the clerk.

"So I thought. I am decided on the Navy funds."

The clerk tilted his head back, as though to estimate her from a broader angle. "Have you a man of business?"

Do you suppose I'd drag myself into this bank all alone if I had? "My means are not so great as to require one." No looking down. No looking away. And for God's sake no wavering in her voice. "At present I wish to invest only one hundred pounds."

She saw the little jump in his eyebrows before he leaned forward to possess himself of a dry pen, which he then tapped several times against his lower lip, with a meditative air. "That's a small amount indeed for investing. Even the Navy annuity would net you only five pounds additional at the end of a year."

"Your calculations agree with mine." *Really, do you get many customers who can't work out five percent of one hundred?* "It's five pounds more than I'd have if I didn't invest."

His pen kept tapping. An odd look came into his eyes and his brow knit slightly, as though she and her hundred pounds were not only absurd but vaguely troubling to him.

Impudent coxcomb. She inched forward in her chair. "The hundred pounds are a beginning. I hope in time to be able to add to them."

"Have you done business with us before?" His gaze darted from her eyes to her mouth to her tasteful gold necklace and the crease in his brow etched itself deeper. He scratched his nose with the end of his pen.

"No, I've never yet had the pleasure of—" The words broke off. She hitched a breath. It felt like a lungful of brackish water.

Something in his gesture, or some angling of his head, had unlocked a certain cupboard in her memory, and now the contents of that cupboard came thundering out.

She hadn't done business with the bank before. But she had done business with him.

She dropped her eyes to her own hands, twisting her reticule strings tight enough to stop her blood. She'd looked at faces as little as possible in the brothel, and she'd willed herself to forget what faces she saw. Not, however, with complete success.

She cleared her throat, as though that had been the impediment to her speaking. "I haven't had any dealings with your bank, no." She forced her chin up.

His odd expression made sense now: he was trying to work out where he'd seen her before. And she saw the exact instant when he knew. His brows dashed together and his nostrils flared. His mouth curved slowly, all smirking prurience, and he set his eyes roving with thorough liberty over her person.

Then over Jane's.

Lydia shot to her feet. She might have stayed and borne the insult, if it had been hers alone to bear. Lord knows she had practice with that.

But Jane was guilty of nothing more sordid than taking a position as housemaid to a gentleman's mistress. She'd likely never even heard of Mrs. Parrish's, and she didn't need to be told of it now.

"I've no more time to waste on your pointless questions." She edged in front of her maid to shield her from the man's foul view. "I see you consider a lady's hundred pounds too insignificant to merit your attention. I shall seek some other home for my investment. Come along, Miss Collier."

The clerk didn't even rise. He only looked at her, and looked round her to Jane, with an expression that roiled all her insides. She turned away and left the bank as quickly as she could, or rather as quickly as her bewildered maid could follow with her one foot sore. Curse her selfishness. Two miles she'd dragged the girl and now two miles she must drag her back, all to no purpose. The hundred pounds wouldn't earn her even five more.

$\mathscr{M}$ARTHA DROVE up in a red-wheeled curricle, of all things, her straight, stern person at odds with the flashy equipage, her subdued dress quite put in the shade by the stylish green-velvet livery of the groom perched behind. "You may believe it was not my idea," she said after Will climbed up beside her and took the ribbons, "but Mr. Mirkwood insisted. He said it was the only proper conveyance for a social call."

"Did he drive this same rig while he was courting you?" The horses felt marvelous from this end of the reins; springy and responsive. And they were, of course, a perfectly matched pair, glossy black and just of a height.

"He didn't court me, precisely. He couldn't have done." Martha stared straight ahead. "We formed an acquaintance during my early widowhood, and his conduct as a landowner earned my esteem. Then when Mr. Russell's estate passed away from me, Mr. Mirkwood was so good as to offer for my hand." Her cheeks had gone progressively pink as she spoke, ending in a full-fledged blush.

Things changed while a man was away. Life moved on without him, sometimes in unaccountable directions, and the people to whom he returned were not quite the same ones he'd left. His unsentimental little sister had developed a taste for matrimony in his absence, and married not once but twice. The first husband must remain a bit of a cipher, having perished before the marriage was a year old. The second was only too much in evidence: a great lusty extravagant fellow who'd lost no time in getting a child on her and who inspired her to blush with disconcerting frequency.

"How does little Augusta get on?" He pulled lightly on the reins to let a walking-party cross in front of them. The team needed no more than a suggestion.

"Quite well. She's robust." That, of course, was something no Blackshear parent would ever take for granted, with as many of his siblings miscarried or lost in infancy as there were grown up. "Crawling all about, lately. Pulling herself up on furniture to stand. The usual accomplishments, I expect, of a baby ten months old. I don't delude myself they're of much interest to anyone besides the mother and father."

"I assure you those things are of interest to uncles as well." God. How exactly had this come about? Wasn't it only yesterday they'd sat side by side in the schoolroom, seven and ten years old, she upright and attentive, he with every muscle poised against the moment Miss York would dismiss them and he could go tearing outside? "Does she say any words yet?"

"Mr. Mirkwood thinks so. I have yet to be convinced. But you may come by and see for yourself any time you like." She turned her dark gaze on him. "I wish you would." Ah, here came the concern. The attempt to draw him deeper into the circle of family, where he might properly heal from whatever ailment was preventing him matching up exactly with the brother of her recollections. "Perhaps I could give a dinner party, and invite this lady upon whom we're going to call."

"Have you learned nothing from Kitty of how a married sister ought to behave? You must invite young ladies of your own choosing, and foist them upon me with adamance directly proportional to my lack of interest." He took one hand from the reins to pinch the brim of her bonnet. "However we should leave Mrs. Talbot off your list in any case. She's no prospective sister; only the widow of a fellow I knew in the Thirtieth. I promised him I would look in on her sometimes, if things turned out . . . as in fact they did. I hope you haven't grown too grand to step foot in Camden Town."

He kept his eyes on the road, watching for a chance to cut left and round the slow-moving dray ahead of them, but he could feel her steady attention. Felt the way she parsed his explanation, gently swirling and resettling his words as though they were tea leaves at the bottom of a diviner's cup. "Have you looked in on her very often?"

Will shook his head. "I called some months ago to return a few of Talbot's possessions. Letters and so forth. For a purely social visit I thought it best to bring a female relation."

"Yes, that's proper."

"Proper and pragmatic. I should soon run out of conversation to make on my own, but she has a child—a little fellow two years old or so—and I expect the two of you can fill fifteen minutes in comparing what you know of babies."

"Camden Town." She brushed at her skirts, soft swish of kid over wool, as though the knowledge of their humble destination required her appearance be more impeccable even than she'd originally intended. "That's a long way to travel from St. James's for a fifteen-minute call."

"No distance seems long to a man when he has a fine curricle to drive." He flicked the reins and chirruped to the horses as a space opened up left of the dray. "See if your husband doesn't second me on that." He could feel her quiet disappointment at this resort to flippancy. He wasn't beyond a slight sense of gnawing grief himself, at the want of openness between them. But what could he ever say to make her understand the nature of his obligation? He only wound the reins round his left hand, and gave his attention to steering the horses into the clear.

$\mathscr{A}$ND FIFTEEN minutes, thank goodness, went fairly quickly. Not that there was anything to object to in Mrs. Talbot. Indeed he could easily see how a soldier might sustain himself with thoughts of coming home to her; to her gentle grace, her warm, unaffected manners, the sweetness in her clear blue eyes.

She brought out the child, whom Martha duly admired. "He features his father, I think?" his sister said after patting the boy's mop of unshorn auburn curls.

"He's quite the image of Mr. Talbot. I hope he will continue to be so. My husband never had so much as a miniature portrait made, so Jamey is all I have in the way of a likeness." Mrs. Talbot watched the child as she spoke, and then raised her eyes to Martha with a smile so abrupt she must have pasted it on to cover melancholy feelings.

Will looked away. At his hands. No. At the sofa cushion, a blue brocade faded and worn thin enough almost to show the stuffing in places.

"He may not have left a picture, but he did leave a good sum of money for when the boy comes of age. Not many children are so fortunate." This was the other Mrs. Talbot, wife of Talbot's brother and mother of several children who had not been so fortunate as to lose their father and gain the prospect of an early independence. "It's a pity he didn't arrange it so Mrs. Talbot could get at some of the money to help with the rent and other expenses. I'm sure nobody with any pride likes living on charity."

"Indeed I should have asked him to do that, if I'd known of the investment." The widow Talbot was blushing, her gaze averted to the floor. "But we weren't in the habit of discussing such matters." Her stick-straight posture alone spoke volumes. She had probably not relaxed for two seconds since coming into this house, where she must be reminded at every turn of the burden she and Jamey made.

He looked again at the worn cushion, and dragged a fingertip over one flower in the damask pattern. Lord, how he hated the feeling of helplessness. She needed to be taken out of here, delivered into a home of her own, and he didn't have the power to do it and couldn't say when he would.

The remainder of the call centered round the topic of small children and their ways, with particular emphasis on when teeth might be expected, and at last the fifteen minutes were through and it was time for him and Martha to take their leave.

"How did her husband die?" said his sister as he stepped up into the curricle. To keep his footing suddenly required a conscious effort.

"At Waterloo. I don't . . . ah . . ." He sat, gathering up the reins, and angled his head to face her indirectly. "I can't imagine you want to hear the exact nature of his wounds."

"Wounds." She considered the word. "Not an immediate death?"

"Not immediate, no." No need to trouble her with more information than that. Better she should be kept in ignorance of just how long a man could linger, a wretched bit of refuse that neither Life nor Death felt much moved to claim. "Though I've told Mrs. Talbot otherwise." He flicked the reins and the horses started off, their heads bobbing in steady rhythm.

You did what you could, the surgeon had said. *The outcome might very well have been the same.* He'd repeated the words to himself so many times. Why could he never hear absolution in them?

"That's very good of you." Like sewing pins poked into him, his sister's words of praise. "She was grateful for the call, I could see. I expect it's rather a dismal existence, in such close quarters with that disagreeable sister-in-law." Sidelong he could see her turn her frown on him. "How is it she must rely on family charity? Shouldn't a war widow have some sort of pension?"

"Talbot wasn't an officer." He settled his feet, one forward and one back, and eased his clutch on the reins. "The army tries to keep married men out of the enlisted ranks, and it doesn't provide anything to the widows of such men."

"Then he knew the risk he took, I suppose. Only it's unfortunate that a widow should suffer for choices her husband made."

He suffered too, Martha. Believe me, he suffered beyond anything you can imagine. And thank God you can't. He'd been fighting a black mood since halfway through the call at Mrs. Talbot's, and of a sudden he was tired of fighting. Let them come, the sorrow and anger and bleakness and oh, the tireless self-recrimination that swirled up from the pit of his stomach like plumes of coal dust. He was nothing if not accustomed to their company.

"Unfortunate, to be sure," he said in as light a voice as he could manage. "It's a pity nobody's undertaken to establish some policies for the welfare of widows."

Here was just the sort of topic to consume his sister all the way back to St. James's, with little need for him to contribute anything beyond the occasional grunted assent. Indeed by the time they were approaching High Holborn she'd proceeded from the plight of the military widow to the fundamental unfairness of the commission system to God knows what else. He'd lost the thread, somewhere along the way.

But a change in her voice hauled his attention back. "Look at those poor women." She reached across him to point to the near side of the road. "I think one of them is hurt."

Will looked. If the women had been facing away, he would not have recognized her. Nothing in her posture or her person was familiar. She wore a plain, high-necked dark blue gown, and she walked slowly, one arm about the waist of a girl who was leaning on her and taking every other step on the ball of her foot. Her face was bent near to the girl, and she was saying something. Words of encouragement, no doubt, or whatever words could just move them one step nearer to wherever they had to go.

He breathed in, deeply. He could feel the fragile burden of that girl's arm as though it lay across his own shoulders. He knew everything about how another person's weight took your balance off center. A person carried on your back required you to cant your posture forward. A person carried in your arms meant you must sink your center of gravity down into the pelvis. A person at your side would no doubt leave you with an aching spine and shoulders.

He exhaled. "I know that lady." Was this an acquaintance he wanted to acknowledge before family? Too late; he'd just done so. "The taller one. At least I've met her." Already he was steering the team to the side of the road. He was helpless to do otherwise.

She doesn't like you, said a coal-dust-tainted voice in his brain. *She won't welcome your aid. And don't go thinking this is a chance to get right what you got wrong with Talbot.* That voice could go to the devil. She was in need, and nothing else mattered.

His heart pounded with unexpected resiliency as he leaned over the side of the curricle, and called her name.

Chapter Four

"M<small>ISS</small> S<small>LAUGHTER</small>!"

Lydia looked up. Stopped at this side of the moving traffic was Mr. Blackshear, in a lacquered curricle, with a young lady at his side.

Heat raced into her cheeks. She should certainly never have spoken so freely with him, in their last meeting, if she'd known there was a young lady in the case. An exceedingly pretty young lady at that, dark-eyed and slight-figured, in a fawn-colored gown with a matching pelisse.

He swept off his hat, the reins clasped tight in his other hand. "May I present my sister, Mrs. Mirkwood?" he said, and suddenly the resemblance was obvious. Lighter-colored hair, to be sure, peeking out from under the bonnet, and no hint of mischief about the mouth, but those eyes had unquestionably come from the same stock. "Martha, this is Miss Slaughter." He nodded toward Jane. "Has your friend hurt herself? Can we be of some assistance?"

As though she weren't ashamed enough already of what she'd imposed upon the girl. "No real injury. Only

I'm afraid I've made Miss Collier walk a long way today, and she's raised a blister on her heel."

The sister leaned forward. "Where are you bound?"

"To Clarendon Square, in Somers Town." A spark of hope kindled, irrationally. The curricle wouldn't hold another person.

"Why, we've just come from that way. We've been calling on an acquaintance in Camden Town." She said something to her brother, who answered at the same unintelligible volume. Then he put the reins in her hands and jumped down.

"Would you be so good as to let Mrs. Mirkwood drive you there?" He spoke with a self-conscious formality, miles removed from the man who'd trailed his hand down the wallpaper and accused her of cheating at cards. "I've rather been craving a walk, and that would make room for you both, if you don't mind a bit of crowding." He waited, still and poised but for the fingers fidgeting on the brim of his hat.

Jane's arm tensed across her shoulders. Was she hoping for a ride, or was she shy of these strangers? "May I have a word with Miss Collier?" Lydia said, and Mr. Blackshear stepped backward with a bow.

"I think you ought to go with her." She pivoted round to shield their conversation from the others. "I don't care for crowding and I don't mind the walk, but you ought to ride. The sooner you're at home, the sooner you can sit in an armchair and put your foot in warm water."

"They're worthy people, aren't they?" Jane threw one anxious glance back toward the curricle. "I shouldn't like to go with a stranger, unless you're sure of them."

That the girl should trust *her* to render judgment on the worthiness of such obviously respectable people sent a bittersweet pang straight to Lydia's core. She did deserve better. "I'm quite sure of them. I wouldn't countenance your going unless I were." She caught the maid's hand and gave it a quick squeeze. "Do your best to be discreet in speaking to her, but I don't suppose it's any disaster if she learns a gentleman pays my bills. I'm not likely to see her again."

Jane nodded, and Lydia turned them both back about. "You're so kind to offer. I'd be greatly obliged if you would convey my maid home. I shall walk, myself."

Mr. Blackshear stepped forward at once and the green-liveried groom sprang down from his perch at the rear. Together the men boosted Jane up to the seat, from where she surveyed her surroundings with not a little satisfaction. The brother and sister made some arrangements for meeting again, and then she lifted the reins and took the vehicle smoothly out into the road, the groom back aboard and Jane turning to wave over one shoulder.

"That was very good of your sister." They stood side by side, watching the curricle pull away. Now she would say what needed to be said if the effort killed her. "Even better of you, everything considered." She could see how he turned his head to regard her though she kept her own eyes fast on the receding carriage. She drew a breath. "I thank you for not allowing any prior unpleasantness to stand in the way of your aiding a lady in need."

He looked away from her to his hat, which he still held in his hands and now rotated several times. "It pleases me to be of use," he said after a moment. Then he pivoted to face her and restored his hat, one hand at the front and one at the back angling it just so. "Somers Town, you said. Shall we set out?"

A jolt of surprise raced through her limbs, and then a jolt of self-impatience because she had not foreseen this misunderstanding. "I beg your pardon." She put a step of distance between them, and her voice put half a mile.

"I intend to walk alone. I ought to have made that clear."

"Come now, Miss Slaughter. You cannot expect me to allow that."

It was exactly the wrong thing for him to say. And it was exactly the thing she needed, the rope she could seize and climb to escape the slough of unwelcome sentiments in which she'd floundered all day. The panic at being recognized by that clerk. The vexation at failing in her errand, at failing to take proper care of her maid. The shame, in that instant when she'd believed Mrs. Mirkwood to be something other than a sister. All these she could leave behind, if she clung instead to outrage at yet another man's presumption.

She swung to face him square, and wrapped her reticule-strings another turn about her wrist. "It is not for you to allow or disallow anything where I am concerned." Without even a curtsey she spun and started walking.

She must not have taken him aback for so much as a second. All at once he was there, just as shadow-quick by daylight as in the dark, filling up the place where she'd intended to be, albeit at a respectable daytime distance. "I chose my words poorly." He inclined his head to grant her this point, but raised it with undiminished purpose gleaming in his coffee-dark eyes. "What I mean to say is I will not send you off on your own through the streets of London. I can't believe you supposed I would. I should never have agreed to spiriting off your maid, if I'd known this was your intent."

No. Don't you dare have a care for me. "I'm sorry you should have misunderstood." An inhalation brought her the faint scent of starch: he'd taken extra trouble with his cravat today. Or perhaps with his shirt, whose crisp linen rose and fell with his breaths under a copper-colored waistcoat and—

Never mind. She gave herself a quick shake, on the inside. "If you reflect for two seconds I'm sure you'll agree that to be seen walking with another man, particularly another man who has already brought himself to my protector's notice in a pointed discussion of me, can be nothing but detrimental to my interest."

Mistake. Mistake. His eyes widened and his jaw went tight and he loomed, somehow, taller and broader than he'd been an instant before. He reached across to catch her by the shoulder and then drew his hand back again, abruptly as if he'd touched hot iron. "Does he—" Up and down her face he looked, combing for clues. "Do you mean to say you have something to fear from him?"

Her insides all writhed under the ferocity of his attention. He had no right to ask, or to look at her so. He was utterly mistaken in his assumptions and this was not his business in any case. "He doesn't beat me, if that's what you imagine. But if he thought me unfaithful I could lose his protection. That's more than adequate grounds for fear, I assure you."

He studied her the way he must often have studied unreliable soldiers, his thick black brows pushing low over the bridge of his nose as he weighed the probable veracity of her words. "Very well," he said at last. "I shall follow you, six paces behind. No one will see that I'm with you."

"A block behind would be better."

He shook his head once, adamant. "A block is too far for me to be of use."

"I don't know what use you're imagining I—"

"Your purse," he said, though his eyes never left her face. "From the way you're holding it I suspect you've got more than a fan and a handkerchief in there. Any thief with half a brain is likely to draw the same conclusion. And I can run down a man with a six-pace head start, but I shouldn't like to try a whole block."

He looked capable of running down the fastest entries at Newmarket, with his muscular build and his fierce determination. More than capable of running herself down, if she attempted to bolt. She lowered her eyes to her reticule, and repositioned the strings.

"I'm sorry, Miss Slaughter." These words came in a lower pitch. "I know I sound peremptory, and I can see how that offends you. But the long and short of it is you will not dissuade me from seeing you safely home. And the longer we stand here arguing, the greater the risk of our being seen together, as you feared."

She glanced up and caught a flicker of some stark emotion in his eyes. *He needs this.* The knowledge floated in, delicate as thistledown. A disreputable lady developed a skill for divining the things men needed, and not only the fleshly things.

She walked. He moved nimbly aside and, one must presume, fell into step six paces behind. Among the many boot heels sounding about her, she couldn't be certain of his.

It wasn't so much a question of concern for *her,* then. He was one of those men who must always be concerned for someone or something, who went racing out to tilt at dragons wherever he could find them. He'd shown his colors that first night, hadn't he, when he'd broken into a conversation that was none of his concern to stand in defense of a lady he didn't even know.

Of course, not an hour later he'd stood in the library darkness, having a good long look at what was not for his eyes. More man than noble knight in that moment. She'd do well to remember.

And so she did remember, when she finally turned the corner into Clarendon Square. The sinews in her shoulders tensed. If he had untoward intentions—if he expected some sort of recompense for his chivalry—now was when he'd make the fact known. With a few long strides he'd catch up to her and show his gentlemanly solicitude to be a sham. And she'd answer his presumption with the blistering contempt such falseness deserved.

He didn't come. On the doorstep of her house she finally glanced back and saw him, halfway down the square, his attention seemingly on the grand polygon buildings in its center. One, then another of her shoulder-sinews relaxed. Then all of them.

She made a small gesture, fluttering the back of her hand at him. *Very good. You're free to go.* He answered with a rolling motion of his own hand, and a jab of one finger. *Finish. Open the door. Go inside.*

So she did. On her way upstairs she stopped at the first floor and went to the front of the house. Out the window she spied him, a distant figure in a charcoal-gray coat, starting his long journey back to wherever he lived. Eastward he went, along the square's southern edge until the polygon buildings blocked him from view. A thought slipped in just as his shape quitted her prospect: not once had he mentioned the hundred eighty pounds.

Lydia touched a knuckle to the pane of glass that had last framed him. Then she gathered her skirts and hurried up the next flight to see to Jane.

I DARESAY YOU could poach her with a bit of effort." Lord Cathcart slouched on the Beecham's ballroom wall, arms across his chest and one boot-heel up. He nodded toward the place where Miss Slaughter was working her way through the set, as though Will's attention were not entirely engrossed there already.

"You're wrong. I sense she's taken a dislike to me." He folded his own arms. "Besides I haven't the means to keep her. And if I crossed Roanoke in that way, I suspect

I'd be unwelcome here altogether." He shook his head. "Not worth the risk." Truly, it wasn't.

"Beecham's is but one club among dozens. You'd find another." Cathcart changed feet, shifting his weight and putting his opposite heel against the wall. "You might try one of the higher-stakes houses, if only for the sport of it. I expect I could get you into Watier's some night. Or we could visit one of the truly down-at-heels properties, if you've got a taste for adventure."

The prospect had its temptations. Nine days into the month of March, his third night now at Beecham's, and between wins and losses he'd gained only sixty pounds toward the three thousand he needed to hand to Fuller by the end of April. One good night at a high-stakes hell and he could have the full amount.

One bad night and he'd lose not only the sixty, but the eight hundred he'd kept from his commission.

"The clubs, I'll consider. The mistress, I won't." *Liar.* He'd considered her in lavish detail this morning, after waking from a dream in which she'd thanked him— tirelessly—for his kindness in seeing her home.

That was as far as it could go, of course. He'd learnt enough, in that brief conversation on Tottenham Court Road, to redouble his resolve against any dalliance. His gaze slid from Miss Slaughter to Mr. Roanoke, who was partnered with a different lady and just this moment bending to murmur something in her ear. Will's blood stirred, darkly.

No, no, no. He already bore the burden of one lady who wasn't his, and that one had every claim on his sympathy as well as on his sense of honor. Why the devil would he want to get involved in the fortunes of a woman who bridled at his well-meant overtures? Who'd cheated him, for God's sake, of a hundred eighty pounds he couldn't afford to lose?

"I'm for the card room," he said abruptly, and pushed

off the wall. Discipline. He'd come here to win money, not to moon about over unsuitable women. Henceforth he'd keep to the task.

And so he did, admirably, even after Roanoke wandered in and took a seat opposite, mistress on his knee. By four in the morning he had a hundred pounds more than what he'd brought, and a mind no less agile than when he'd walked in the door six hours since. The usual number of men had fallen asleep all round him, with several of the remainder drunk enough to make ill decisions when it came their turns to deal. Prospects looked promising in every direction. Naturally, then, Miss Slaughter, having taken over Roanoke's cards an hour or so past, must turn up twenty-one on the deck's last hand and secure shuffling privileges as well as the next deal.

Will slid his cards faceup across the table and let his hand loiter, lifting it just in time to effect a slight glancing collision between his fingertips and hers. For the first time that evening, she looked at him.

He wouldn't compromise her in any way. But if she was at all inclined to read him, she could not possibly mistake what was in his thoughts. *I'm watching how you handle those cards. Don't expect to make a fool of me twice.*

She gave him no reaction whatsoever. Her impassive eyes considered him the way they might consider wallpaper while her hands swept cards in from all directions. She shifted her gaze to some other man, and when she'd formed a haphazard stack, finally dropped her attention to the deck.

Whatever trickery she employed must come now. But she only straightened the cards and shuffled, in rather stolid fashion, and passed the deck to her left neighbor to cut. Then she dealt them out, an initial card on which each man might determine his bet.

His fingers and thumb took hold of the card at the

very place where she'd touched it, his prints mingling with hers. Ace of diamonds. Damnation. She *would* tempt him, wouldn't she?

Across the table she was studying her own card, a single slight crease in her brow. Maybe she was playing fair tonight. Maybe his warning look had done its job. Last week she'd watched the cards as she'd gathered them, and intermixed them with such care as suggested, in hindsight, some deliberate arrangement. This time she'd raked them in without looking.

And hell. It was an ace. A sad excuse for a man he'd be if he didn't risk a little. He pushed twenty-five pounds forward.

A second card came round to each man and he lifted the corner to find a three of spades. Soft total of fourteen. Four, if he preferred. No chance of going over on the third card; two different paths to twenty-one. Of course if he turned up a ten next, that would change the outlook. Hard fourteen was a considerably less attractive hand.

The fellow at his right side finished his turn and Miss Slaughter's eyes came once more to him. "Do you care to buy another card?" she said.

"I might twist as well, recall. Unless you've effected some change to the rules." Their first words exchanged since he'd convinced her to let him follow her home. His consciousness of that fact—of their nightlong pretense to be less acquainted than they truly were—was the only possible excuse for his failing to be struck immediately by the oddity of her question.

"Of course," she murmured, chin dipping as though chagrined by the mistake. "Buy or twist."

Now it did strike him, with full force. She knew the rules. Of this he had no doubt. She'd said what she'd said on purpose: she was telling him to buy.

For whose benefit, though? Did she mean to help him,

or to amuse herself by taking him in even when he ought to know better?

She'd brought her chin up again and watched him, all disinterested patience. Damn his sluggish instincts and her placid mask; he couldn't read her worth a farthing. If she had his ruin in mind, her eyes and mouth showed not the smallest hint of twitchy eagerness or ruthless resolve.

He set his head on an angle, peering at the underside of the ace. "Another, facedown," he said, and counted out twenty-five pounds more.

The new card dropped in and he palmed it up. Two of clubs. The back of his neck prickled as all his short hairs stood on end. Two plus three plus one made six. He was more than half the way to a five-card trick, with fifteen pips to give.

What the devil was she about? If she'd done anything irregular to arrange this, he hadn't seen it. Yet what were the chances he would draw three consecutive cards so low, without some manipulation on her part? He threw her a quick look but her face, as always, gave away nothing.

Without question he must buy one more, at least. A five or anything lower would guarantee him the trick and the double payoff. He slid his money forward.

And of course the next card was a six. Hard total of twelve: a ten or a court card would be fatal now. If pure chance governed this hand, he was due for one. If the vexing creature across the table was pulling the strings, she could dismantle him in brutal fashion, having lured him down the garden path with her twos and threes and aces.

Buy, she'd said. Pure chance was nowhere to be found in this room.

Will sat back in his chair and tapped his fingers to his lips, letting his eyes settle on her in absent fashion. If she would give him some sign . . . he still wouldn't know whether to credit her. He might imagine something kindling in her empty eyes; some cryptic message meant just for him; some scrambled communiqué that he would decode until it spelled out *Trust me*. And then could he?

Little matter. He was bound by the rules to take another card: the only decision was whether to twist or to buy. She had him for seventy-five pounds already, if she was fleecing him. The twenty-five he'd save by pulling up now wouldn't be near enough to repurchase his pride.

He sat forward. "In for a pound, in for a hundred," he said, and found two tens and a five to throw in.

Like some part of a spring-loaded machine her thumb moved, a single efficient motion tugging the top card off the deck to be caught by her fingertips and tossed down before him.

He turned it faceup. Ace of spades. His lungs filled with lovely tobacco-tainted air and only then did he realize he hadn't taken a proper deep breath since she'd first begun to deal.

"Nicely done, Blackshear." The fellow to his left was addressing him, an unexpected nudge of generosity from a gentleman whose name he hadn't bothered to learn. He grinned—oh, and didn't *that* face come easily!—and acknowledged the kindness with a nod.

Good Lord. Two hundred pounds in a single hand. His one-eighty back and twenty more besides. Double the amount he'd worked the six hours previous to amass; more than three times his total Beecham's take before he'd sat down here tonight. The cards snapped delightfully as he turned them all faceup. Miss Slaughter didn't even look at him: already she'd progressed to the next man's turn.

Play continued round the table, though the game could hold little interest for him now. To quit in the thick of success was discipline of the sweetest sort. And he should hope he knew better than to misprize her gift or to tempt fate—or hell, to tempt her—by staying to risk any of his windfall in even one more hand.

When the last man had gone bust, and the banker had counted out payment to the three players whose totals bettered her own, Will pocketed his winnings and rose. He hesitated where he was for a second, battling a desire for some tiny acknowledgment of what had passed, intelligible to him and her but opaque to everyone else.

She didn't glance up. Rather, she leaned back, all heavy-lidded languor, against the shoulder of the man on whose lap she sat, and lifted an absent hand to graze her knuckles along his jaw.

Right. Let that be a reminder of what was what. He caught up his gloves and left, jamming his fingers impatiently into their respective sheaths as he went.

She doesn't like you. She doesn't want you. She's neither generous nor kind. Good, bracing phrases, worth repeating to himself all the way home.

But every repetition prompted the question: what, then, had possessed her to restore his hundred eighty pounds?

Chapter Five

$\mathcal{T}$HE WOMAN in the glass wore a faint, enigmatic smile as she smoothed her hands down her indigo front, over the blue silk cords that crossed one another in the center of her bosom and wrapped round beneath it, fettering the gown's fullness in that crucial region. Where most of her gowns merely hinted at curves, this one owned them outright, without apology or coy reserve. This was the shape that belonged to her.

"That gown becomes you very well. Just as I knew it would." Maria, having already approved the fit of her figured white muslin, made a picture of perfect self-satisfaction as she looked on from one of the modiste's chairs. "The style shows off the merits of your form without being quite so daring as the purple gown."

"I prefer the purple." Eliza, at the next mirror, craned over her own shoulder to admire the back of her gown, a gold-threaded creation with a wide band of scarlet at the hem. "This one leaves everything besides your bosom to the imagination. The purple one will cling when you move."

That it would. The knit silk underlayer had been cut very close to her own dimensions and would scarcely allow for one petticoat underneath. The overdress had a more traditional shape, but was of such thin sheer mull as to leave the underdress, and its close fit, entirely visible to anyone who looked.

"They're both very grand." Maria left her chair to come and make some adjustment to the split sleeve, smoothing the indigo layer away to show more of the royal blue silk underneath. "But I think this is the one you must wear to Mr. Moss's musical evening."

That brought a groan from Eliza. "He's not truly expecting us to attend, is he? It seems to me a fallen woman could be spared such dreariness. It's really too bad I should be subjected to insipid harp-pluckers and persons warbling in some language no more than half the room understands, same as any respectable miss."

"Courtesans *are* respectable. Will you never grasp that?" Maria frowned into the mirror as she fussed with the layers of the second sleeve. "Even a Philistine with no taste for music should appreciate the social occasion. Heaven knows it will make a welcome change from the gaming club."

Lydia ran her palms once more down her silk front. She ought to change out of this gown, and have it wrapped. "Mr. Roanoke speaks of giving a country house party next month. Has he mentioned it to either of your gentlemen?"

"A house party." Eliza swiveled to meet this news. "Now there's an idea with promise. Do you suppose he'll invite Captain Waterloo? House parties are always better with unattached masculine guests."

Unattached masculine guests, indeed. Captain Waterloo, indeed. "He's not a captain, you know. He was a lieutenant but he's sold his commission, so I don't suppose he's anything now." The words rang gracelessly in her own ear. Fine way to answer his charity to Jane.

But she'd made her answer at the table, hadn't she, three nights since. No need to go turning generosity into a habit. "He's a gentleman, merely," she added after a moment, because decency demanded that much. "Plain Mr. Blackshear, if you want his name. I heard someone say so." She beckoned to one of the assistants and moved away toward the dressing closet at the back of the shop.

"Blackshear." Eliza bit into the word the way she might bite into a juicy piece of orange. "I like that."

Well, maybe Eliza would like to amuse herself with him when they all went to Chiswell. Why should she not? Likely it would do him some good. If he could set aside his hopes of rescuing, he might have a very fine time. So might Eliza.

She held her arms up as indigo silk rustled away, its cool touch at her shoulders, at her neck, at her face, over the crown of her head. The dressing-closet had a mirror too, a smaller, dimmer one. Very little enigma to the woman reflected here. In chemise and stays she looked like nothing so much as the sum of her disappointments. Abandoned. Orphaned. Left barren. Tired and forlorn, and long past rescue.

Lydia turned her back on the reflection even before her old gown came over her head. What rot. Rescue. That had never been possible. And even if it were, she would not welcome it. She would laugh in the face of any man who tried.

Out in the shop there was a burst of merriment from the ladies, perhaps still on the topic of Captain Waterloo. But for herself, she was finished with that subject.

Claret-colored satin shut out the world as her gown slipped on. He'd shown her kindness. She'd repaid him with what she valued most. Now their accounts balanced, and she could devote her attention to more important things.

* * *

$\mathcal{J}$ACK FULLER wore his scars on the outside. He'd been a laughing, sandy-haired devil of a man when they'd met in the Thirtieth, two years since. Logic suggested that his hair must still be sandy, though only patches remained, and those severely shorn, perhaps to minimize contrast with the places where hair would never grow again. He was, by general reckoning, lucky to be alive. What might be his own reckoning on the subject, Will had never yet discerned.

"It will be three-masted and ship-rigged like this one, but bigger. Three hundred fifty tons to this one's mere three hundred." He made his way to the port railing, his stout walking stick bearing a bit of his weight on each step. Besides the burns he'd come home with a limp. No one had bothered to amputate, on a man not expected to survive, and his wounded leg had healed up uneven.

Will followed. Past the port side was the massive dock lined with warehouses where cargo from the ship's last journey had been unloaded, some days since. "It's a good time to be in timber, I expect."

"Better than you know." Fuller swiveled and pointed with his stick. "Do you see on the south bank, where they're building? New docks, dedicated to the timber trade. We'll have a warehouse there in time, I hope, just suited to our cargo."

The ship rocked tranquilly in the river currents. The yards and all the rigging had been brought down from the masts and lay about the deck in what looked, to a land-dweller, like riotous disarray. The scent of oakum edged his every breath, stirring memories of the trip across the Channel and the trip back home. A mere step across a gutter, by the side of what this ship did.

"And then of course the American market's opened now, as it wasn't just a few years since." He brought the walking stick back and stowed it under one elbow. "Wide open to the independent trader. No East India to grab it all up for themselves as they've done with tea."

"You do remarkably well, considering you never planned to run the family business."

Fuller laughed, a single bark that stretched his mouth painfully and made no impression in the ruined skin about his eyes. "I do remarkably well considering I ought to be mouldering in a mass grave at Hougoumont, you mean, and my brother still calculating how many emigrants must pay passage to Newfoundland and how many barrel staves and great oak masts must come back to make a profitable voyage." He pivoted to look out at the north bank again. "He was the one with a gift for this, and our father before him. I think it's only a perverse family pride that stops me from letting it all go to the devil."

Score a point for perverse family pride, then, and another point for the practical-minded resilience of the merchant class. They were an admirably resourceful and industrious lot. Any blue blood who'd come home in Fuller's condition would probably not have had the mettle to refashion his life on these new terms. Without question a gentleman investor would do well to put his money in such hands.

The question was whether the merchant ought to put his faith in the investor. Three thousand pounds, he'd promised the man. At present he had eleven-hundred-sixty, and that was counting money that must go to rent and living expenses.

Will stooped to pluck up a bit of the pitch-and-oakum caulking that had come loose between two planks. They had to replace the stuff constantly, Fuller had said, while the ship was at sea as well as in port. Someone or other must always be mending a sail, fashioning a new spar, wetting down the deck with salt water. No time for idle meditation on a sea voyage. "Do you ever think of going along?" He twisted the fibers between his fingers. "Getting a glimpse of the New World for yourself?"

Fuller shook his head. "Too much risk. Storms, sickness, rations that can spoil or run out. I've looked death in the eye once already. I don't expect it to blink a second time. You, though?" He threw a glance over his shoulder. "Think you'd fancy an Atlantic crossing?"

"Not the storms and spoilt rations, certainly." Pitch was rubbing off on his gloves. Stupid of him. He couldn't be throwing away money on a new pair. "But I admit there's an appeal in the notion of leaving all one's encumbrances behind to make a new start."

"I haven't that option. This face follows wherever I go." He dipped his head to gaze down into the waves. "And encumbrances don't sound half so encumbering when they're put beyond your reach. A leg shackle, for instance. If I'd known I was going to come back as damaged goods, I should have married the first girl who'd have me. She'd be stuck with me now, scars and all."

"I suspect most men come back damaged, one way or another." Tentatively the words hung in the air, as though looking over their shoulders to see whether any more would follow. "If not in a way that prevents marriage, then perhaps in a way that makes an unjust encumbrance on one's wife. I know I shouldn't have liked any sister of mine to marry a man who would burden her with nightmares, or with forgetting his whereabouts and imagining himself back on the battlefield whenever he hears a loud noise."

"I've heard of such afflictions." Fuller nodded but didn't turn, inviting just as much confidence as Will cared to impart.

"Nothing so capricious plagues me." He twisted to drop the bit of caulking over the side, and lost sight of it at once among all the other rubbish littering the Thames's surface. "It's only that my disposition has changed. I think marriage requires a certain . . . hopefulness of outlook, and I can't seem to . . . be hopeful, quite as I used to do."

The flotsam danced over the waves below. He stood still with his back to the railing, only his shoulders twisted, away from where Fuller stood at his left, to look down into the water. Words danced there too, words he'd once been so arrogant as to say aloud.

I'll get you to the hospital. And then I'll get you home to your family. I swear on my soul I will not let you die.

Other words, words he would never say aloud to anyone:

The outcome might have been the same if I'd waited for the litter-bearers. He might have been lost in any case. But I'll never know.

And *He trusted me. He looked to me as a leader and he believed a promise I should never have made.*

And then the pitch-dark bit of flotsam, too dark for words. Incomplete fragments of memory stored in his senses: the clammy chill of that early-morning hour. His hands. The pulse in Talbot's throat, ticking patiently against his thumb. The sounds.

What else were you to do? Leave him to suffer for God knows how many hours more among corpses on the field, or in that hellish church?

Will drew a sharp cold breath. This was a mood. That meant it would pass. He'd come safe to the other end of every mood before, and so would he do with this one.

"I'd be surprised if that weren't common. A want of hopefulness." The sound of Fuller's voice told him he'd raised his head and was now addressing the horizon. "Still, I think a woman could be the cure. A warm sort of woman. Patient. With a hopeful nature that can brace you up when your own is lacking; remind you of what's good and worthwhile in yourself as well as in the world.

Nothing better for attaching a man to life unless it's children, and if you're lucky those will follow."

Sorrow prickled up and down Will's throat, leaving a metallic tang in its wake. Never mind his own unfitness for such a woman, for children. Fuller himself could have little hope of ever gaining the comfort he described, and described in such terms as suggested no small degree of longing. What a perverse place the world was, all in all.

"I don't doubt you're right." He brought his shoulders back round so he was facing out over the deck again. "Only I find I haven't much patience for the events at which one encounters such women. Routs. Musical evenings. Card parties for polite small stakes."

"Musical evenings?" Fuller cocked his head, like a hound catching an unexpected scent and contriving to isolate it from among the general bouquet.

"An idle pursuit of the well-born." He rubbed at the pitch on his fingertip and thumb. "Some lady who wouldn't dream of performing in public stands up and sings, or perhaps plays the pianoforte, and everyone claims to enjoy it whether they do or no."

"Singular. But I confess I had this sort of thing in mind, when I invited you to buy in." He waved a hand vaguely. "You have the air of a gentleman about you, with your bearing and your knowledge of musical evenings. I fully intend to trot you out before the Americans, when they pay their visit here. You'll make my business look a sight grander than if it's just me."

Will laughed and nodded, even as uneasiness stirred in the pit of his stomach like silt kicked up from the bottom of a stream. *I must tell you I'm not at all sure of having the money by April's end. I cannot in good conscience advise you to make any plans that depend on me.*

No. He would get the money. Somehow. March wasn't

even half over yet. He must not be as lacking in hope as he'd thought, because he was not ready to give up.

"Musical evenings," he muttered instead. "I suppose I'd better make myself an expert, then. Indeed I think I may have been invited to one this very week."

*S*ELF-PITY WAS a vice for the feeble of spirit. Not for her. If she had, at one time, known the pleasure of singing before an audience of cordial neighbors, well, it would behoove her to recall she had never been but the third or fourth young lady entreated to perform for the company, after the more talented took their turns.

Lydia stripped off her second glove and dropped it across her lap. Decidedly Mr. Moss had too much money. She'd peered into three doorways along this hall, and each time found at least half a dozen lit candles and a fire in the hearth.

And in this room, finally, she'd found a game table.

She split the deck and shuffled, cards accommodating one another with a dulcet ripple reminiscent of music-room applause. There was all the accolade she required. She could feel, but not hear, the place where eight cards went by undisturbed, admitting not a single card from her other hand into their number. Let any drawing-room nightingale try *that*.

Eight cards, nine cards, ten, and eleven had passed through a shuffle intact when a black-coated shape loomed into the open door on her left periphery. At the back of her neck, a muscle ticked once. Mr. Blackshear. She knew without turning. She'd glimpsed him in the last row of the music room, when she'd made her way out at the interval, and apparently she'd taken better note than she'd realized of what coat he wore.

What waistcoat as well. He'd put on that same copper-colored one she'd first encountered out on Tottenham

Court Road, when he and his sister had been coming from a call in Camden Town. Even from the corner of her eye she could see its threads burnished by Mr. Moss's exorbitant firelight.

Who in Camden Town had merited such finery? She hadn't stopped to wonder until now.

Not her concern. He could pay calls wherever he liked. She'd given back his money and thus ended the intersection of his fortunes with hers. She dealt two cards without looking up. "Have you come to spy on me, Mr. Blackshear?" In case he supposed he was taking her by surprise again.

"Not at all. Forgive the intrusion." The threads in his waistcoat winked as he made a slight bow. "I noticed you'd left the gathering."

"I was under the impression we had an interval."

"Yes, of course. I mean you left the company, where they were gathered in the room with the refreshments. Nothing is amiss, I hope?"

"Nothing whatsoever." She turned up the first card—ace of clubs—and the second—king of clubs. "And I must say I liked you better when you marched up and accused me of cheating. I haven't any use for chivalry or nice manners."

"Some plain speaking, then." How quickly he shucked the cloak of gallantry. That was interesting. "I came looking for you because there's something I want to discuss. I expect you can guess it."

Oh, she could guess it, surely enough. Unless he was a royal nodcock he would naturally have questions about last Saturday night at Beecham's. She'd known that before dealing the ace of diamonds, and she'd dealt it just the same.

Well, he could have all the questions he liked. He would see in what style she chose to answer. "Indeed." She lifted her chin finally and faced him, angling her body his way, laying one forearm on the table and the other along the back of her chair. "I surmise you've sought me out to compliment me on my new gown."

"You surmise incorrectly. I've come for something else." He paused, though, his gaze flicking down over the yards of indigo silk and back up. "But I'll grant you the compliment, willingly. I suspect there's not a man alive who wouldn't appreciate that gown."

"Possibly. Though I might advise you to reserve your panegyrics until you've seen my other new gown." She palmed up her king and her ace with a smart flourish.

"Are you . . . flirting with me, Miss Slaughter?" His eyes narrowed briefly, like a sailor trying to make out the colors of a ship on the horizon. Then his mouth curved and sent smile-echoes through his whole body, loosening his posture as he folded his arms and leaned his shoulder into the doorjamb. "You must want very badly to divert my attention from the topic I came to pursue."

Now *here* was a man she had use for, spirited and ready to spar. "Nonsense." King and ace went back into the deck at precise intervals. "If my purpose were to distract you, I should have commenced my erotic spectacle."

Oh, he did like that. His eyes narrowed again, or rather, the lids dropped halfway and his lopsided smile took a turn for the wicked. "It's a solo act, then. I'm intrigued."

"Perhaps." Ha. Did he think she was so easy to shock? "Or perhaps it's an act that requires the participation of some willing audience member." She owed this man nothing. She didn't have to mind her words with him, the way she did with Edward. She could say any reckless thing she liked.

"Now that, I'll grant, might have succeeded in diverting me. Mere flirtation will not." He held that same relaxed posture, weight against the wall, but he was undeterred in his purpose. "I'd like you to explain to me what took place at the table, when we were last both at Beecham's."

She divided the deck and shuffled. "You had an admirable run of luck, as I recall."

"Rubbish. You fed me those cards." She didn't look up but she could feel his cool patience. He had no intention of leaving this room without an answer. "I'm nothing but grateful." Ah, that lower pitch. The same one with which he'd finally convinced her to let him see her home. "Only I can't guess for the life of me how you did it. Or why."

She did something with her brow, something to make her look more than ever absorbed in the cards, and bent her head for good measure. "Nobody but you has ever accused me of cheating."

"I expect that's because you're so good at it." Flattery. And probably true. "You must know I won't tell anyone. It wouldn't be in my interest, would it?"

Maybe. Maybe not. But that was nothing to the purpose. Regardless of whether it was in his interest, he would not tell. Certain things a lady could discern about a man after a few meetings, and this was something she'd discerned about him.

She ought to send him away, of course. Closeting herself with another man, particularly with Edward on the premises, would be imprudent.

But Edward was in his cups, and would probably sleep through the second half of the concert and never notice whether she came back or not. Besides, she was in his very good graces this evening in consequence of the new gown, which had come off once already when he'd arrived to collect her, and would doubtless come off again when he took her home.

And it wasn't as though Mr. Blackshear sought her

out for any improper purpose. He'd come to ask her about cards.

No one ever asked her about cards.

"Close the door." She turned the deck and struck its edge on the table. "Come take a seat."

Six strides brought him to the chair at the game table's other side. For a man who must have drilled at marching in formation, he had a remarkable ease to his walk, all nonchalant, unself-conscious grace. She hadn't had the chance to notice, when he'd been walking six paces behind.

He sat. She leaned a bit forward to set the deck before him and caught an unexpected scent. Bay rum. That hadn't been there in the upstairs hall at Beecham's, when he'd stood so near her. Whatever occasion had warranted the fine coat and waistcoat apparently demanded new soap as well.

Not her concern. "Deal out ten hands." She straightened, the bay rum receding like the last wisps of an agreeable dream. "No fewer than three cards in each hand, no more than five."

He dealt, smoothly and unspeaking. He didn't ask why. That was to his credit.

"Good," she said when he'd finished. "Please turn them faceup, with every card showing." In her wrists, in her throat, in the middle of her chest, her pulse thrummed, fretful with anticipation, even while her thoughts went calm and all the room's sights and sounds lurched into perfect clarity.

A sweet mellow percussion, his fingers striking the tabletop, sliding over the backs of the cards, then the muted slap of cards going faceup, soughing over one another as he edged them apart to show her each king and ten and seven and three. He sat back and when she raised her eyes he was watching her expectantly, brows edged a wary fraction of an inch together.

She clasped her hands on the table. Straightened and curled her bare fingers. Gave her mouth permission to issue a Sphinxlike smile. "Now then. Speak, please."

"Speak?" He'd caught her smile; it hovered at the corners of his own mouth. "On what subject?"

"Any subject you like. Your aim is to distract me." Eyes still on his face, she sent her hands out after the cards.

"Distract you." His brows jumped and then bent at devilish angles. "I'm afraid I neglected to rehearse my erotic spectacle."

Good. This was exactly the right sort of thing. "I shouldn't have permitted it anyway. Your distraction must be effected through speech. However I will allow any subject. Until I've gathered up the last card, you have license to speak with just as much familiarity as you like." The cards fairly sang as she swept them in, feeding each one deftly into a growing small pack.

"That sounds very like a dare, Miss Slaughter." He sank into an outright slouch, one wrist resting on the table's edge. Really, he ought to give up that chivalry business altogether. He was infinitely more interesting this way. "You're wearing stockings, I suppose?" And here was the voice he would use for seduction, its soft rasp a kind of promissory note for the touch of his weather-beaten soldier's hands.

But she would not permit the use of hands, and the only kind of seduction worth recognizing was the kind that came with an offer of carte blanche. "Of course I'm wearing stockings." No change whatsoever in the timbre of her own voice.

"What color are the garters?" His eyes were steady on hers.

"Blue, tonight." So were hers steady on him.

"Blue." He repeated the word as though to take possession of it. He might possess a lady piece by piece in this way, if she weren't strong-willed and otherwise occupied.

"Blue, indeed. That's one point settled. Is that your idea of distraction?" She ought, of course, to feel his hot attention creeping up like fingertips to the place where her garter was knotted on her thigh. Perhaps she would, later. For the moment his words only redoubled the lucidity with which the needful facts came to her. Here would be a queen of clubs, and her left thumb knew precisely the spot at which it must slide into the deck.

"Give me time." His voice sank a few notches down the scale. "Dark blue like the body of your gown, or medium blue like the trimmings?"

"Royal blue, it's called. Not medium. And I told you your time is limited." She gave her head a slight toss, just to show how little she was affected. "If you mean to make an inventory of my underclothes, you'd better pick up your pace."

"Hasty men miss so much. There's a pleasure in lingering over these things."

Lingering, indeed. And over garters, of all things. "What a vexing sort of lover you must be." Three more cards to go. "All that meandering about would drive a lady to distraction."

"That, as I recall it, was my mission. Did I succeed to any degree?"

"See for yourself." She clapped the cards once against the table, edgewise, to make them all even, and set the pack down before him.

He picked it up. Ace of clubs sat on top. With his long agile fingers he peeled off that card, and peeled off the next, and the next and the next.

Assuredly she was vain. How could she not be, watching all his features soften with wonder as he turned over card after perfectly sequenced card? Aces, twos, threes, fours, and he shot her one glance. Fives, a six, sevens, and one eight had got in with the sevens, not due to any distraction but simply because her fingers sometimes misjudged the count. By the time he set down the king of spades he was sitting up straight, his whole face alight with such a look as Paris of Troy must have worn when those three goddesses showed up to demand he judge one of them most beautiful.

No man had ever looked at her that way. No man would likely ever do so again. But he made her insides feel like clockwork for a moment, ingenious subtle clockwork instead of fallible flesh, and it occurred to her she might stay in that moment forever, given the choice. She might bask wordless in such a transformative gaze for as many moments as remained to her life.

No. Not transformative. This was who she was, quick and gleaming and intricate. She'd known that already. Now someone else knew.

Chapter Six

"How the devil did you do this?" Will sat motionless, all energy diverted to receiving her reply. She faced him like a Grecian goddess, sure, potent, ravishing, and for all that the goddess-style gown still draped her, advertising the bounty of her figure and deepening the blue of her eyes, he couldn't shake the feeling that she'd just undressed for him.

"Through a certain facility with numbers and an excellent memory for what I've seen." On the tabletop, she folded one hand in the other. "Practiced fingers as well, of course."

Undressed? Devil take her. She was parading about the room naked now. He touched a finger to the king of spades, topmost on the pile. "You looked at these cards when I turned them up, and remembered the contents of all ten hands without looking again?"

"I had a picture in my mind." Quiet pride lit her features and simmered at the bottom of her voice. "I remember things that way. If you recited a list of thirty-eight cards, I doubt I could repeat them all back. But if I see them laid out I can make a sort of map."

"Thirty-eight. Did you count them?"

"Not deliberately. But the hands had three, three, five, four, three, four, five, four, four, and three cards."

"Good God." He didn't even try to check her addition. "So your memory tells you where each card is, and a numberish brain gives you the proper stacking order. But how do you then put them in that order? You didn't look away from my face even once."

"Practice." She turned her hands palm up and flexed them. "I've taught my fingers to know the feel of six cards, of nineteen cards, of thirty-eight cards. I daresay you might have seen me feeling for the right place if you'd watched. But when I told you to distract me, I wagered you'd pick a topic distracting to you as well." That smile crept back, knowing and seductive, the same one that sent his wits out the window and impelled him to talk about garters. "I don't usually have to place them so precisely, you see. Usually what I want is just to alternate high cards with low. Or, in the case you witnessed the other night, to set up a run of all low cards. That's easier, as you may imagine."

Hell and damnation. She plied six kinds of witchcraft and discussed it the way she might chat about a sampler she'd sewn. He wrested his gaze from her, to study the cards. "But surely your whole arrangement must come undone when you shuffle."

"If you shuffle cleverly, you can keep a sequence of cards from mixing with the other side. All it requires is nimble thumbs and plenty of practice."

"Very well, but someone else cuts the cards. I distinctly remember the man to your left doing so on the evening we're discussing. You had no way of controlling how he arranged the deck."

"That's the easiest bit of all." She leaned forward to catch up the thirty-eight cards and add them back to the fourteen that had sat this exercise out. "Cut the deck, if you please." The pack came down smartly before him.

He closed his fingers on a good half the deck and lifted it away.

"Stop." He did. "Do you see where you've divided it?" If he put out every candle in the room he could see whatever he liked, by her prideful radiance alone.

"A bit more than halfway down."

"Sixty percent, approximately." She nodded toward his hand. "Everybody divides it there. Simple as that. Put the cards you want sixty percent of the way down, and the person who cuts the deck will set them at the top for you."

Confound her. A thousand times. Confound her boldness and her incandescence and the crafty skills that made him feel giddy and lighthearted as a boy watching a juggler at the fair, when he had abundant reasons to never feel lighthearted again. "Still, though." Giddy he might be, but he hadn't lost the capacity for rational thought. "You had to deal cards to men before me, and you couldn't have known exactly how many each would take. You must have had a good long run of low cards to insure I got them, and then how did you avoid gifting the men on either side of me as well as myself?"

"They weren't all low." She held out her hand, palm up.

He surrendered the deck, his fingertips tingling as they met the tender flesh at the heel of her hand.

"I did include a few court cards, for that purpose." She squared the deck's edge on the table. "Only I took care to not give you one. If your thumbs are accomplished and well rehearsed, you can draw back the top card enough to get a quick look at its underside. And then if you don't like it, you catch the second card, where you've exposed it by drawing the top one aside, and deal that instead, right out from under the first." She suited action to words, he must assume, though for the life of him he couldn't detect anything out of the ordinary. "See? King of hearts." With a forefinger she mimed turning his card over. "King of spades was topmost."

The king of hearts, a rather vacuous-looking fellow in this particular deck, stared up at him when he flipped the card. A second later the king of spades fell faceup beside it. As though she could really have believed he'd require any proof.

He sat back. "You've staggered me, Miss Slaughter." Probably he was wearing an expression not altogether unlike that red king's. "Where on earth did you acquire such skills?"

A change came to her face, though as usual he couldn't scry its meaning. "We used to play cards to pass the time, in the establishment where I was formerly employed." Her gaze slid to somewhere over his right shoulder. "I learned those shuffling and dealing tricks from a woman there, and once I'd mastered those, it occurred to me I could make an advantage of my memory and my fluency with numbers. One wants occupation for the mind, in such a . . ." She curbed the thought the way she might curb a headstrong horse, and brought her eyes back to his. "I do well at vingt-et-un, though, even when I'm not dealing, because I always keep a tally of what remains in the deck. And that's not cheating. Just being attentive."

"An important distinction to you, I'm sure."

She grinned, all delinquent swagger once more, and then the grin subsided. "I could teach you."

"I beg your pardon?"

A keen, calculating light had come into her eyes. She sat up straight again, and even leaned a bit forward. "Not how to remember cards exactly as I do. I don't believe that can be taught. But I could help you practice some ways of shuffling and dealing such as I've shown you tonight, and I could teach you how to keep a reckoning when you play vingt-et-un."

"I presume you'd want something from me in return." Though for the life of him he couldn't guess what it would be.

"I have some money I'd like to invest in an annuity." No, he certainly would never have guessed *that*. "I need some gentleman, some solicitor or clerk, to act as my man of business." She set her hands atop the table, one over the other, and studied them. "It occurs to me you must have developed a broad acquaintance in the army. Perhaps you know such a man, and perhaps you might . . . prevail upon him, for reasons of friendship, to do this service for . . . such a woman as myself." By the time she'd finished speaking her cheeks were pink. She didn't look up.

Where did this discomfited manner come from? Before today he'd never seen the least sign she felt any shame over what she was. Even when he'd faced her round the groping, rutting body of the man who paid her bills she'd stared back unabashed. What could account for—

Something broke through his preoccupation, like pebbles dropped into a pond. Into the room's quiet, above the pop and murmur of the fire, fell notes from a distant harpsichord.

"Good God." He sprang to his feet. "The concert. I forgot completely. You've got to go back."

She blinked up at him, and furrowed her brow.

"Surely Mr. Roanoke will notice your absence. If he notices mine as well it could do harm to your prospects." What the devil had he been thinking? Shrugging off any care for her welfare the instant she offered him a chance to play at rakishness. Gaping like a foolish boy at card tricks when he ought to have been a mindful grown man, and sent her back to the company.

Her brow went smooth. Her whole face went placid, masklike. "I assure you he's not in a noticing frame of mind tonight. And I confess I dissembled somewhat, that day on the street, when I spoke of the hazard of being seen with you. Whatever he might think of you, he's entirely sure of me. I'd have nothing to fear."

It was like facing her across the table at Beecham's all over again: he had no way to tell whether she was lying.

That didn't matter. He knew what was proper to do. "Nevertheless, I'll take my leave now." He stepped behind his chair and pushed it neatly in. "I'm going home. One person returning late to the concert will give people less fodder for speculation than two."

"Do we have an arrangement, though? I'll teach you to better your play and you'll help me find a man of business?" On the tabletop, her clasped hands tightened. "We might start the next night we're both at Beecham's. We could meet at midnight, in one of the rooms on that top floor. No one ever goes there."

Just what I need. To be alone with you at midnight in a room where no one ever goes. Refusal, sensible, grown-man refusal, poised itself on the tip of his tongue.

But an inconvenient recollection came: the smell of oakum and the gentle rolling of the deck beneath his feet. Everything depended on his winning money at a better pace than he'd so far done.

"Midnight, then." He let go the chair-back where he'd been gripping it. "Vingt-et-un only, and only honest play. I haven't the temperament for the other business." That was judicious. He had sound, solemn reasons for agreeing to be tutored. And still he rose from his farewell bow with a creeping sense that he was embarking on something monumentally unwise.

* * *

*S*HE HASTENED up the aisle in the lull between two songs and slipped into the place beside Edward, who didn't wake. Mr. Blackshear had been wrong to worry. Not to mention presumptuous.

He stirred in his sleep, her protector did, and the length of his thigh pressed against the length of hers. She pressed back until she felt the clear outline of her garter, her blue garter, and the top of the stocking it tied. That garter and stocking had lain crumpled on the floor with her gown earlier this evening, spoils of a swift, purposeful conquest. Edward was not a man to *linger,* over garters or anything else.

Her hands curled into fists in her lap, snagging a bit of silk skirt on the way. He knew what she liked. He gave it to her. There was the beginning and the end.

You've staggered me, Miss Slaughter.

Never mind. She had other ways of staggering, and more suitable men to stagger. She crept her chin round to get a view of Edward's profile. A jaw like granite. Cheeks that might have undergone a carpenter's plane. Lips that smiled with consummate symmetry to reveal a mouthful of teeth that would do a horse proud. She'd never bedded a handsomer man—at least so far as she remembered—and this one prided himself on satisfying her. That was more than many women might ever enjoy.

She slid her hand over and let it rest on his thigh. She would lay waste to him tonight. To herself as well. She would hurl herself against him like a wave breaking over a rock. She would claw her way to oblivion as many times as she must, until no fragment of human feeling remained.

Her fingers inched along until they met his breeches-buttons. His eyes half-opened, groggily, and when he'd blinked about enough to sort out the circumstances, his mouth spread into a smile that promised her everything, everything, she could ever expect from a man.

Chapter Seven

*N*o FLIRTING this time. He would devote all his attention to the substance of what she taught, that he might keep their time away from the company short, and keep them both out of trouble.

Any number of such admonitions Will had for himself, two nights later at Beecham's as he waited for the appointed hour. He'd been too free with her at Mr. Moss's house. If he could not keep his own dignity in mind, he must remember to think of her interest. Safeguard her place with Square-jaw and all of that. It was the honorable thing to do.

Four times over the course of the evening he slipped away from cards or supper to work at provisioning a room upstairs, and when midnight rolled round it was ready. From a hodgepodge of furniture piled in a room at the end of the hall he'd picked out a game table, two chairs, and a candle-branch, now alight with three candles pilfered from the supper room. Also a carpet, in the interest of keeping noise down. A far cry from the Mayfair drawing room where they'd last sat down together, to be sure, but it would serve its purpose.

He was standing in the doorway, arms folded, facing

the stairs, when a creak on one of the treads announced her approach. A single spark of anticipation hurried up his spine: he would not let it catch fire.

Stair by stair she ascended into view, her back to him, all pale gown and pale arms in the stairwell's dim, a specter on a mission. She reached the last step and rounded the railing to face him. Face the moonlight, too, filtering in from the window at the hall's street-side end to bathe her features.

Blank eyes. Sharp brow. Hair the color of weak coffee, and a frankly prodigious nose. *Solve me,* that face said to him, the way it always did. *Unwrap me. Find me out.* More sparks went up his spine. This rendezvous might have been a terrible idea, altogether.

She paused some ten feet away, taking in his own person and posture. Some shift occurred in her countenance as her eyes came back to his. "You've done this before. Coaxed a lady to leave a gathering and meet you in some secluded room. I can see it in your stance."

You're not going to make this easy, are you? "As I recall, the coaxing was all on your side." He unfolded his arms and stepped away from the door-frame that she might precede him into the room and that he might not betray anything by stance. Another remark shaped itself, as to pots and kettles, glass houses and stones, the library downstairs; prudence smothered it.

"Perfectly true." She moved past him into the room. "Only it occurs to me you're not nearly so much a gentleman as you strive to appear."

"On this occasion, I am." Now she'd brought the conversation into indelicate territory, he could at least make use of the candor. "Forgive my bluntness, now. This will be the third time we've met somewhere away from the company—fourth, if you count my walking behind you on the street—and it's my duty to assure you nothing improper will occur." *More improper than closeting my-*

self with another man's mistress, that is. "I won't attempt any liberties. You have my word."

She stood at the white stone chimney-piece, the candlelight flickering over her birdlike gaze and her slight, slight smile. "Very good. Close the door and sit down."

He did. She didn't join him.

"We'll begin with a bit of theory." She clasped her hands behind her and began to pace, quite like a lecturing schoolteacher. "Tell me why no gambler with a brain would ever play at roulette, for example, when he could be playing vingt-et-un."

"I suppose because the outcome in roulette is dependent entirely on luck. Is that your other new gown?" No. Emphatically the wrong sort of thing to say. Only her smile had sunk into his skin somehow, and her gown had caught his attention as she walked, and then the question had sailed forth of its own accord.

"This? I should hope not. Didn't I say it was a gown suited to a gentleman's taste? I know better than to believe any gentleman would be stirred by plain white muslin." Her pacing had brought her nearly to the door; now she spun and started back. "And as to your answer, let that be our last reference in these sessions to *luck*. A wise gambler recognizes only odds."

"Odds, of course." Hanged if he didn't feel a bit like he was squirming under the gimlet gaze of his old governess once more.

"To be specific, in most games the odds start fresh every time. Every roll of the dice, every spin of a roulette wheel, the odds of each possible outcome are the same as they were on the last turn." Those hands clasped behind her made her shoulders draw back, elevating her bosom and pulling her bodice snug. He sent his gaze past her to the wall. "In vingt-et-un, however, the odds keep changing until the deck is shuffled again. The player who keeps a reckoning can wager accordingly."

"Naturally. High wagers when he's likely to get a good card; low when he's not."

"Naturally. You have some grasp of odds, then? As opposed to luck?" Her head tilted to a considering angle as she halted behind the opposite chair, and her voice betrayed an ungratifying degree of doubt.

"Enough understanding to gamble, I should think."

"Very well. We'll play a game. Not vingt-et-un, just yet." She palmed up the pack of cards he'd set out. "Do you care to wager?"

"Risk more money with you? Not likely." He sat back in his chair, arms folded. "I'll consider other stakes." Yes, that *sounded* provocative, but he'd already assured her of his honorable intentions. She knew she had nothing to fear.

And fear, indeed, was nowhere to be found in her eyes when they snapped round to where he sat. She'd been sorting through the cards; now her hands went still. Her gaze lingered for a few speculative seconds on his face. Then down it roamed, clinging and unhasty as half-melted ice cream sliding from a tipped-up plate. Cravat. Shoulders. Hands, resting before him on the table. The table itself, under which the rest of him lurked. Then back to the cards, and her brisk sorting recommenced.

"Good Lord, Miss Slaughter." Her audacity woke half a dozen impulses in him, not least an ill-advised impulse to laughter. "Did you just mentally unclothe me and find me wanting?"

Her mouth tightened into a private smile, for the benefit of herself and the cards. "How could I have made any such judgment?" She twitched a card out from the pack and set it on the table. Three of hearts. "It's an imperfect art, mental unclothing. One relies to a woeful degree on one's own imagination. At least as far as all the interesting particulars are concerned."

"I'll spare you the effort. It's big." Splendid. Not five

minutes in her presence and he'd come to this. "And before you make a reply, let me assure you that you'll have to take me at my word. I've no intention of furnishing evidence, as part of a wager or otherwise."

Her smile went wide, as abruptly as if he'd reached out and tickled her. "Of course I wouldn't doubt you. All men are so favored, aren't they? Certainly every man a harlot beds is the biggest she's ever seen." Two of diamonds took its place beside the three of hearts. "However, the truth is I won't make that kind of wager either. I was provoking you merely, because of your decorous manners. I'll try to refrain in future."

"Yes. Please do try."

Smiling all the wider, she set down the ace of spades with the other two cards and finally took the opposite seat, pushing the remainder of the deck to rest by the candle-branch. "What wager, then, Blackshear?" In an entirely businesslike manner she started peeling off her right-hand glove.

Several of his internal organs changed places at the sound of his name without the honorific. He glanced away from where she was gradually baring the alabaster-smooth skin of her arm. "A question." Yes, that would be the way to put her off balance. "If I win, I'll ask you a question and you must answer. If you win, you can ask one of me."

She drew the glove off and dropped it in her lap. "I might lie, you know."

"I know that very well."

She tugged at the second glove. "And you don't even know what game I'm proposing."

"More than that; I know you have no qualms about cheating." He shrugged. "Let's play."

"It's not even much of a game for wagering. But so you'll see." The glove slipped off and fell with a whispered slap of leather against the other in her lap. Her bare hands stole forward to sweep the ace and the two and the three off her side of the table, out of his sight. She did something with the cards, a tiny frown at one corner of her mouth. Then back they came, facedown, set before him in a row. "Tell me which is the ace, and you may ask your question."

"None of them. You switched it out while I couldn't see."

Again, that smile so sudden it seemed as though pleasure had caught her unawares. "No. But I like your thinking so I'll give you another chance. Guess again."

"I hope you know I'd never make this wager with money, any more than I'd play roulette." Nevertheless he tapped his first and second fingers on the middle card.

Her hand came forward but instead of turning over his card she flipped the one on its left. Two of diamonds. "Now, Mr. Blackshear." Her eyes reflected the candle-light with a peculiar intensity. "If I offered you the chance to change your pick, would you do it?"

"Will," said his lips and his teeth and his tongue without sanction from his brain.

The space between her brows pleated, hard.

"I'm giving you my Christian name." He cleared his throat. "And permission, of course, to use it." His face felt suddenly warm. "And I don't care to switch, thank you. I'll stay with the middle card."

"Then you don't understand odds as well as you think." His name apparently made no impression at all.

"What precisely do you think I misunderstand?" Really, she needn't be so pert. "Two cards remain. Each has one chance in two of being the ace. All else being equal, I prefer to trust my original impulse."

"Oh, good Lord. Please don't tell me you give any weight to *impulse* in gambling." You'd think he'd just said he based all his play on numbers given to him by Gypsy fortune-tellers. She leaned forward, forearms on the table, whole person suffused with officious purpose. "Your calculation of the odds is incorrect. Your original choice has one chance in three; the other card has two in three. You're a fool if you don't switch."

Had she gone mad? "There are two cards. One is the ace. How on earth do you calculate the odds as anything other than even?"

"Because there were three cards to begin with. Your chance was one in three. That doesn't change just because we have a look at one of the other cards." Her upper body inclined lower, closer to the tabletop. "Think, Blackshear." He could see the agitated rise and fall of her bosom. Her features were fierce with concentration, willing him to understand. "You said you would never risk money in this wager. Surely that's because you didn't like the odds."

"Not to begin with, no."

"In other words, with odds of one in three, you knew your pick was likely to be *wrong*." Her attention had heat and weight; he could feel it like a pair of warm hands pressed to his face and dragged down his front. "Odds tell you the ace was more likely to be one of the two cards you *didn't* pick. Will you dispute that?"

Well, no. He couldn't, really. Her tirade was beginning to assume a faint aura of logic.

"Then forget everything else and remember only that: your first pick is probably wrong. So why in God's name wouldn't you switch from it, given the chance?" She wore that alluring flush of a woman both mastered and powered by passion, and he would bet all of his eleven hundred sixty pounds that no mere lover had ever inspired such ardor as she felt for her numbers and her odds.

And to her question, he could make no good answer. Or no, maybe he could. He set his elbow on the table, chin in his palm, and with his free hand, turned up the middle card.

Ace of spades. He looked from the card to her, allowing himself the smallest arch of one eyebrow.

Oh, but he'd stepped in the hornet's nest now. She stared at him, throat working silently, mouth a straight shut line, bosom keeping its dainty rhythm.

Without question he'd come home as warped as Jack Fuller's leg. What else could account for the lightness in his heart as he awaited the next fusillade of abuse from a woman who was anything but warm and patient? She had none of those qualities that could remind a man of what was worthwhile in himself or the world. She could never provide the children that would attach him to life.

But devil take children. Devil take the world. Devil take himself and whatever worthwhile remained in him. Those things must bide their time out in the hallway, on the other side of the shut door. For these few minutes she and her fiery attention were all the world, all the life he required.

$\mathcal{G}$OOD GOD. He was hopeless. Either he truly didn't grasp the concept, or he placed a higher value on his contrary games than on the solemn truths she'd labored so to impart.

Lydia flattened her hands on the table, fingers spread for maximum stability, and took a deep calming breath. "Yes, one out of three times your choice will prove correct." The calming breath had predictably brought his gaze to her bosom, where it now lingered. "That's exactly what one-in-three odds means. Over time you'd do better to switch. And please have the courtesy to look at my face when I'm speaking. You may review my bosom during the silences, if a bosom is indeed such a novelty to you as to require scrutiny."

His eyes came back to hers and his mouth spread into a smile of pure crooked delight. "Please tell me you speak this way to Prince Square-jaw."

"To whom?" But there could be no doubt of who he meant.

"Your flash man with his big square chin. Tell me you dictate when he may and may not look at each part of you. It makes a most agreeable picture for me."

She'd encouraged him too much, with her flirting. She must reel him back to business now. "His name, let me remind you, is Mr. Roanoke. My transactions with him are not your concern. I'd be obliged if you would return your attention to the lesson at hand."

"The lesson, yes." He frowned down at the cards as though seeing them for the first time. "I believe I've won the game, Miss Slaughter. Are you ready to answer a question?"

"Yes. Ask."

A smile flared over his features but when he raised his chin to address her he'd scrubbed away all traces of playful triumph. He eyed her without tilting his head, or pursing his lips, or bringing a considering hand to his chin. He knew exactly what he wanted to ask. Perhaps he'd known for some time.

"What happened three years since?" In a perfectly conversational tone of voice he launched the words.

Her hands, still spread atop the table, slid back until she could hook her thumbs under the edge and take a grip. He remembered. *You're three years too late to do business with my heart,* she'd said, or some such flippant remark, and he'd plucked it out of air and put it in a pocket and kept it ever since.

He watched her, waiting. He knew he couldn't read her. He must take what answer she gave.

Lydia dropped her gaze from his. One of her fingers found a scar of some sort on the tabletop. A dark indentation, perhaps where some lout had dropped a cigar and, too drunk to notice the loss, had let it lie until it burned this shallow channel just wide enough and long enough to fit the end joint of her last finger. "A number of things went wrong that year, culminating in the loss of my parents."

"Both at once?"

That was a second question. She'd only agreed to one. But she could answer this, and still keep a great deal back.

She nodded. "They were traveling. There was an accident." Even these incomplete truths felt like handfuls of flesh scooped from her by some creature with claws.

"I'm sorry." She didn't want his sympathy. "I've lost both parents as well. Not at once, but it's a fearsome blow no matter how it comes. I know."

Do you, really? Did you lose them with their hearts broken from the shame you'd brought on the family? Did you lose them after you'd thrown away everything else? If he dared to speak further on the subject she might say something injudicious.

But he didn't. He took up the three cards and shuffled them one behind the other. "Now I presume you'll want to repeat this exercise two or three dozen times to prove your contention as to odds?"

"Yes." She lifted her attention away from that scarred place on the table, and let her hands relax their grip. "Yes, that's exactly what I wish to do."

*T*HE TRIAL of repetition proved her correct. Of course. Thirty-six times they repeated the exercise, and in twenty-two instances Will picked the wrong card. Really, it was as simple as that. The card she showed him would never be the ace; the ace must be either the card he'd picked or the remaining card he hadn't. Ergo, it all came down to whether he'd picked correctly to begin with, and with odds of one in three, most often he did not.

"Do you begin to see?" Something had changed in her, over the past half hour or however long they'd been in here. Alongside that prideful, purposeful intensity was something new. Some almost-vulnerable desire—he knew better than to call it *need*—to share what was meaningful to her, and to see it grasped and properly prized by someone else.

Had he effected that change? With his question, had he pried open a weak joint in her armor through which he might reach her now?

Time enough to dwell on that later. "You've convinced me." He closed up the pocket-book where he'd kept count of his right and wrong guesses, and stowed it back in his pocket. "Or rather, the results have convinced me. I grasp the essential principle now, for all that my intuitive sense of logic first revolted against it."

"Intuition is no more to be relied upon than impulse." She swept up the three cards and fed them back into the deck one by one. "If you will give up consulting such things, and trust strictly to what you know of odds and chance, you'll have an advantage over most of the men against whom you play. I hope tonight's lesson may have begun to persuade you of that."

"Are we finished, then?" His voice rang hollow with forced lightness. Until this instant he hadn't realized just how ill-prepared he was to forsake this circumscribed world in which one's worth depended on nothing but the ability to master odds.

That his voice had betrayed him was evident from her response. Her lips pushed together in a slight symptom of effort while her eyes flicked back and forth across his face. As though his sentiments were actually written out there in paragraphs. "I think we ought to be," she said at last. She put down the deck on his side of the table. "I recommend we return to the company five minutes apart, and return to different rooms. I'll go after you, and appear in the ballroom. You may choose any other room you like."

"Very good." He pocketed the cards and rose. "Shall I count on another such midnight session the next time we're both here?"

She nodded, studying the way her fingers laced with each other on the table's smooth top. She didn't speak.

Will pushed his chair in. She didn't glance up. Her brow sank with severity as she worked her fingers harder together. Reviewing and regretting, perhaps, every familiarity she'd allowed tonight. Patching that weak place in her armor. Totting up the inches of distance she'd ceded, that she might take that much back again.

Nothing he could do but leave her to it. He bowed and made his way across the carpet.

"Mr. Blackshear," she said just as his hand fell on the knob. "Will."

He turned. She'd made a tight double fist of her hands and stared at it as though some oracular wisdom were clutched on a slip of paper inside. Her cheeks, if he did not mistake, had gone faintly pink.

"I believe you've heard my given name. I don't know whether you will remember."

"Lydia." It tumbled off his tongue like a commonplace, like the answer to a most mundane riddle, because that was the way to put her at ease.

She nodded, looking already as though she would retract the overture if she could.

So he left without giving her the chance. And all the way to the supper-room he rolled her name round his mouth like rare wine, and if his foot touched one single stair on the way down, that was more than he could tell.

Chapter Eight

Prince Square-jaw. Really.

With the first two fingers of her left hand Lydia tipped Edward's chin up and back. With her right hand she applied the straight razor. The tiny rough beginnings of a beard ticked against the blade and gave way, up the column of his throat, up the underside of his jaw, to the clean right angle of his chin. She swished the razor in her water bowl and wiped it deftly on a towel, one side and then the other.

He'd closed his eyes while she was brushing on the soap and still sat that way, head tilted, outspread hands resting on his trouser-thighs, as calm and relaxed and accustomed to this as . . . well, as a prince. Perhaps a square-jawed one. She applied the blade again, clearing another path of smooth skin among the lathered stubble.

In the mirror she saw her own shape behind him, prim and workmanlike, the prince's diligent valet. Often she did this naked, or in some interesting state of dress. Today she wore her plainest high-necked nightgown, and a flannel dressing-gown belted tight. She had a lesson to prepare, and no time to squander on a dissipated romp.

"By the by," he said as the blade came off his chin and arced through sunlight to the water bowl. "I'm afraid I must ask you to give up the diversion of taking over my cards sometimes at Beecham's."

"I beg your pardon?" Her hand froze where it was, just above the bowl.

"Only the proprietors have a certain image they'd like to keep up." He didn't open his eyes. "To have a lady playing with the gentlemen is a bit too reminiscent of one of the lower hells, or so it was put to me. I'm sorry, love. I know that was one of your pet amusements."

Don't call me love. She plunged the blade into the water. Really, what he called her was the least of her concerns.

She'd known her time at the table might end. She ought to have been better prepared. "I hadn't realized I offended anyone." Four hundred and ten pounds sat in the drawer of that table by the window, and four hundred and ten pounds were not nearly enough.

"Nor I, else I should have said something before. But now we're both the wiser."

Indeed. The razor beat a bitter chime against the china bowl, striking resolve into her marrow. If one path was blocked to her, she'd just have to find another. She touched the blade to the towel again, and spoke lightly. "There are gaming hells where ladies play?"

"I shouldn't call them *ladies.*" His half-smooth, half-stubbled throat rippled with a chuckle. "Desperate creatures, and the proprietors know it. Think nothing of raking in a woman's last farthing and allowing her to play on for graver stakes."

"Those sound like dreadful places, altogether." One more stroke up the length of his throat. "Do you mean you must play against the house itself? Not against each other, as at Beecham's?"

"To be sure. The fellow who deals the cards, or spins

the wheel, is in the establishment's employ. No chance of him forgiving a loss."

No chance of getting a turn with the deck, either, and ordering the cards to her liking. She swished the blade in water and watched in the mirror as it cleared a swath of his jaw. "I don't know why anyone would wish to play under those conditions. To never be the banker puts you at a disadvantage in games like vingt-et-un, for example, where ties are awarded to the banker."

"Oh, but the rules differ." Ah. Now they came to it. "I think there are houses where a tie simply counts for a tie, no money passing either way. And some houses place constraints on the banker's play."

"Constraints?" Mildly she repeated the word, while her attention sharpened to an edge that might put the razor to shame.

"There are houses where the players may stick at fifteen but the banker must keep drawing cards until he reaches seventeen. And then he *must* stick once he's reached it. And often you see the first card dealt faceup."

She'd held the blade away from his face while he spoke, and a sudden jagged glitter of light told her her hand was shaking. She doused it, razor and all, in the basin, shaping that chaotic agitation into a few fierce flicks of the wrist. "The banker's first card shows?" she said, because she must say something.

"The player's first card as well. So I don't suppose there's really any advantage."

Fool of a man, there was *every* advantage. The visible cards alone! Late in the deck they would make a tremendous difference in her knowledge of what cards remained. Even early in a shuffle, the banker's first card could tell her things. If he showed an ace, she would know his prospects were good, and she could wager accordingly. Add to this the unutterably elegant constraint of the banker's continuing to draw until he reached seventeen . . .

Something overhead caught her eye: a dozen spots of sunlight dancing to the rhythm of her razor in the washbasin. She let her hand go still and watched the spots slow and subside, each sliding into its proper place like a number in a solved equation. She might devise some calculations. The variables were too many for her to know exactly how to play every hand, but with pencil and paper and hours of rigorous, satisfying work she might—

"Lydia." The word barged into her sweet symphony of thought like a screech from one of the reed instruments. Singular. She'd never supposed there might be a right way and a wrong way to pronounce her name. "Have you gone into a trance, there?" He'd opened his eyes, finally, to investigate the lapse in her ministrations.

"Forgive me. I was distracted by the light." She wiped the razor dry and glanced at the mirror to find he'd closed his eyes again.

Some men there were who knew how to look at a lady, and make her feel she'd been seen. Or perhaps there was no question of knowing how. Some men just looked at ladies that way.

Nothing to the purpose. Here was the man to whom she'd attached herself, and here was the task immediately before her. She angled the blade, set it to his cheek and drew it back, the soap mounding up as she went. But some men, one couldn't help observing, would have kept their eyes open. *Tell me what absorbs you so*, such a man might say. *I wonder at your thoughts*. He might even guess: *It's to do with cards, isn't it?*

She brought the razor away and tipped it above the washbasin, its dollop of lather and bristles sliding off to land with a faint *plash* among the rest of the sudsy flotsam. Some men had no valet or even mistress, and must see to their own shaving. Standing shirtless before a mirror, perhaps, the towel draped carelessly over one well-articulated shoulder.

Not that anything was amiss with Edward's shoulders. Indeed his whole form could bear comparison with any man's. Still, when she'd shaved her last stroke, wiped the remnants of soap from his face, and then glanced in the mirror to find him eyeing her with the first stirrings of unmistakable intent, she pivoted away to catch up his waistcoat.

"Perfectly timed." She gave the waistcoat a brisk shake. "I do believe that's your phaeton I hear outside." Perfectly timed, indeed. The shave was usually followed by several minutes of more particular attentions, if not a full-scale return to the bed.

He glanced over his shoulder at the window, though of course he could not see to the street below. One corner of his mouth pulled down with indecision. His palm, flat atop his right thigh, smoothed the nankeen of his trousers. Clearly he was struggling with some personal calculus involving the questions of how quickly she could work, how long he could decently keep his driver waiting, and whether or not his appetite had been roused to such a pitch as to render the first two questions moot.

She moved her thumb infinitesimally over the fine stitching at the waistcoat's armhole, her only outward manifestation of unease. What would she do if he should bid her come and kneel? She'd never refused him before.

No. I don't want to. The novel words loitered just back of her teeth. She could taste them. She could feel the way they would resonate from the roof of her mouth to the bridge of her nose. She could picture Edward's astonishment, but her brain balked at picturing what might come next, in answer to such open defiance.

Never mind. A clever woman needn't resort to defiance. "What a fine waistcoat this is." She moved a step nearer. "Did you choose it on purpose because you knew you'd be going to luncheon at your mother's house?" She would mention his mother just as many times as were necessary to wilt his ardor.

"Hang it, Lydia." He got grudgingly to his feet. "Why did you have to squander so much time in staring at the ceiling and talking of cards? I had no idea the hour had grown so late. Next time you must keep to the task."

"Indeed I shall," she said as she helped him into his waistcoat, and "The fault is mine," and "Your mother is fortunate to have so dutiful a son." Near a dozen such trifling pleasantries she'd uttered by the time the front door closed behind him.

She stood for a moment with her back pressed to the door, her palms flat against it at thigh-height on either side. Her muscles all tensed, unaccountably, gathering themselves as though Edward might turn about and pound on the door to demand his indulgence after all—of course he wouldn't—and as though she might dig in her heels and oppose his efforts with all her weight and strength.

She wouldn't. She couldn't. But she stood nevertheless, poised above her own revulsion like a tightrope-walker above a moat boiling with sharp-toothed eels, until she heard the clop of horses pulling his phaeton into the street. Then she mashed the strange sentiments small, put them away, and went to begin her work.

I vow I can't tell one from another. You?" Nick spoke in an undertone, though there was little chance of his being overheard.

"The tiny red-faced one that can't so much as lift its head is Andrew's latest. Master Frederick. Kitty's got him now." Will nodded toward the corner of the room where babies were being passed about.

"Well for Heaven's sake I hope I know *that* much." Indeed they'd all been invited expressly for the purpose of viewing that most recent addition to the family, though by some obscure process the event had mushroomed into a full-on celebration of Blackshear fertility. Already there were ten children in the next generation, and all ten were present in his eldest brother's drawing room, some doing their best to sit straight and be worthy of the honor; some conducting themselves with blissful infant ignorance of manners. "Keeping track of the very smallest is no trick. It's when they get a bit older that they all start to blend together." Nick gestured at the sofa nearest the bow window where they stood. "I believe one of the two climbing on Mirkwood may be my godson, but I'm hanged if I can tell you which one."

"Don't look to me for help. I would have sworn those were both girls." He oughtn't to say so—doubtless he'd offend some parent if he was heard—but his brother's poorly stifled snort of laughter was a tonic he couldn't resist. It seemed years since he'd laughed so easily, so carelessly with Nick. With any of his siblings, for that matter.

Across the room his elder sister glanced up from the baby she'd been admiring, and smiled. Kitty was Miss Slaughter's precise opposite, wasn't she? All he needed was half a second to see her fierce joy and relief at the sight of her two younger brothers giving way to some secret hilarity, as they'd been wont to do in simpler years.

He cut his own gaze away from the emotion in hers, fixing vaguely on the sofa where Martha's Mr. Mirkwood was in conversation with Kitty's Mr. Bridgeman. Surely he would soon come to feel as though he belonged among these people once more. They were his kin, after all, his blood, the only souls in the world who shared his memories of a delicate mother and a sober-minded father who'd both left the breathing world too soon.

And yet he'd found himself making excuses to avoid them, these months since coming home. He'd had more to do with Nick than any of the others, but that had been largely on account of business. Even now, though he might have gone on joking about the little nieces and nephews, a particular obligation was tugging at him. He brushed a bit of lint off one cuff. "Do you remember that Grigsby fellow you introduced me to? The one who set up the trust?"

"Saw him just yesterday by Lincoln's Inn." Nick swung about to fix him with the full force of his curiosity. "What, are you wanting his services again? Found another orphan in need of an anonymous benefactor?"

Will shook his head. "Rather I'm hoping to do a service for a lady this time."

"Not the boy's mother, I hope. According to what Grigsby tells me, you've already done more for that family than anyone could reasonably expect."

Grigsby needed to learn a bit of discretion, clearly. And he was in no position to render judgments as to the degree of Will's obligation. "No, it's another acquaintance and the money is all her own. She's put a bit by and she'd like to invest it, but she hasn't the means to retain a man of business. I offered to see whether I couldn't find someone to help." He laced his hands behind his back and stretched his shoulders, a gesture that would, with luck, suggest an attitude of casual indifference.

"What is she, someone's spinster aunt?" His brother's eyes held more bafflement than suspicion; that was to the good. "What sort of company are you keeping these days?"

He nodded vaguely, with uncomfortable thoughts of

perjury. "She's a connection of someone at the club I frequent." That was entirely true.

This prodded Nick's curiosity in another direction, and he was now obliged to tell a bit about Beecham's, in terms that left vague the character of the place. Nick had never set foot in a gaming establishment of any sort, and heard the club's name without a glimmer of recognition.

From the corner of his eye, however, Will saw Mr. Mirkwood straighten and throw one quick glance their way before taking a sudden animated interest in some story Kitty's Bridgeman was telling.

World's worst dissembler, his little sister's husband. He'd been a bit of a good-for-nothing before marriage, if Andrew was to be believed, and obviously the name of Beecham's wasn't new to him.

And indeed, no sooner had Nick gone off in search of some refreshment than the fellow hoisted himself up from the sofa, one child in the crook of his arm, and made his painstakingly casual way round to the bow window. "Hold this for a moment, will you?" he said, brandishing the child with both hands.

A dirty trick, that. Will couldn't very well excuse himself and dash away if he was holding the man's child. "Does my sister know you refer to your daughter as *this*?" His hands fumbled for a second—even a sturdy baby seemed an impossibly fragile thing—but then Mirkwood let go and her weight was all his, her arms flung out to either side and her legs pedaling in the air as though she thought she might lift off like a bird.

Panic simmered up his spine. If he should drop her . . . those tiny vulnerable bones . . . He hauled her in against him, his elbows bent awkwardly out, his hands clutching her under her arms, his heart thudding so hard she must feel it. Confound people and their young. Clearly this wasn't the right way to hold her, but—

"Not on the shoulder. You see what she's done to

mine." Mirkwood had pulled out a handkerchief and was dabbing at a damp patch on his expertly tailored coat. "You might sit her at your waist and support her with one arm round her back. That way she can look about. See who's holding her. You have the sort of face babies like."

"Indeed. What sort of face is that?" Carefully he rearranged her. She'd been a mere insensate bundle of three months when he'd last held her, on his one visit to Martha's grand Brook Street residence. She'd grown a good deal less floppy since then.

"Dark hair, dark eyes. Brows. She's very fond of looking at Mrs. Bridgeman, too." He folded his handkerchief to produce a clean spot, and wiped her chin. She was drooling like some rabid thing and she was, as her father had promised, studying Will's face with rapt attention.

Lord, but she was absurd in her innocence. No idea in the world of the mistakes a person could grow up to make; the wreckage he might leave behind. To her he was nothing more than what her eyes could see: black hair, black brows, brown eyes, and a mouth threatening all in spite of itself to smile. "She'll feature you, won't she?" With his free hand he lifted one wavy lock of her pale hair, paler and wavier than anything his own bloodline had yet produced.

"I think so. Mostly." Fool was scrubbing at his shoulder again, as though Will would not know a pretext when he saw one. "Everything but the eyes."

"You've got proper Blackshear eyes, haven't you?" He wouldn't croon, as some people did when addressing a baby, but he did pitch his voice to let her know that his words were meant just for her. Her downy infant brows pushed together in response, giving her the air of a scientist confronting some puzzling outcome.

Did he look at all familiar to her? She wouldn't remember him from that earlier visit, but might his eyes remind her of her mother's eyes? He sent her a smile and abruptly she returned it, in such open-mouthed, toothless glory that he nearly had to avert his gaze.

"I knew you were her sort." Bastard was playing him like a fiddle, for all his clumsy subterfuge. He folded up his handkerchief, finally, and stowed it back in a pocket. "Listen, Blackshear." Now they would come to it. "The fact is nobody here much likes me."

"I should hope Mrs. Mirkwood does."

"To be sure." He nodded once, his mouth straightening into what must pass for a serious expression, with him. "But between persuading her into remarriage so early in her widowhood, and . . . well, and some general concerns in regard to my character, I suppose, I've never quite found my footing with your brothers and your elder sister. Altogether I'm in need of an ally in this family."

Will waited, a wary humming in his blood.

"So if I could put myself in the way of doing you a service, I should consider it a favor to myself, really."

Oh, God. Charity. Of all insupportable things, charity under the guise of fraternal fellowship. He angled his head to face the baby again and touched her small fingers, which curled immediately round one of his.

"I have a great deal of money and no dependent relations. Pardon me for saying so." From the corner of his eye Will could see him glance down at the carpet as though considering whether to proceed. "For all I know you might frequent Beecham's for the company. But most men don't. And damn it all, I don't see any sense in letting some members of a family want for capital, and perhaps pursue it through imprudent and degrading means, when others have more than they need." His well-intentioned words fell like hot cinders, and clearly he knew it, and the fact that he knew it somehow made it that much worse.

"That's quite generous of you." He sounded like a schoolboy slogging through an ill-rehearsed recitation. "If I ever find myself in such a position of need, I shall remember that offer." Every word of this was delivered to the baby, who listened with an increasingly sober face.

Probably he was being perverse. But it wasn't Mirkwood who'd promised a dying man to look after his wife. The promise, the penance, the debt was Will's to shoulder, and what would he be worth if he allowed some other man to relieve him of that burden? "She's a charming child, your Augusta." He caught her under the arms and lifted her briskly toward her father. "You must be quite proud."

"Prouder than I've ever been of almost anything." Bless the man, he knew when to quit. "Martha has been wishing you'd come to visit. Nothing formal." He busied himself with arranging the baby in the crook of his elbow, attention half averted as though he knew that this, too, might be an uncomfortable topic.

"So she said. I must see whether I can't find a day soon. Now if you'll excuse me, I've been waiting for a chance to address my other sister and I see she's between conversations." And away he hastened, lest enough time spent under the influence of kind intentions, and a winsome child, might after all shred his resolve and persuade him to succumb to charity.

*I*N A full deck, how many cards have a value of ten?" Miss Slaughter's sharp features warmed as she leaned near the candles, removing her left glove. She'd arranged her hair to include a few curls tonight, about the cheek and temple, and they swayed distractingly when she moved.

"Sixteen." He dragged his mind back to business. "Tens and court cards; four of each. And that leaves thirty-six cards of other denominations, in case you intended to ask."

"Good. You're on the right path." She bunched the glove down to her wrist and started working her fingers free. "Tell me the ratio of non-tens to tens."

A simple problem of division oughtn't to be beyond him. Sixteen into thirty-six went . . . "Two times, with four remaining. Two and a quarter. There are two and a quarter times as many non-tens as tens. That's not the new gown, is it? I'm almost sure I've seen you in it before." It was a dreary reddish thing that didn't near emphasize her curves.

"I assure you, Mr. Blackshear, when you do see that gown, you'll know it. There'll be no need to ask." She punctuated this stylishly, with a little toss of her head that set the curls dancing while she meanwhile drew her glove off and dropped it in her lap.

"I begin to doubt the existence of this gown altogether. Very soon I may begin to doubt your knowledge of vingt-et-un. Last week we spent the whole lesson looking for the ace of spades, and now you quiz me with division problems. Shall we ever actually play a hand?"

"We'll come to that in good time." That voice of hers could make anything sound like a lascivious promise. She dispensed with her second glove and picked up the cards. "I'm going to deal out the deck, slowly. You keep count of tens and non-tens." She turned over the seven of hearts, her thumb releasing it with a snap. Queen of spades followed, and three of clubs. "Count?" Her head tilted slightly toward the table, she looked up at him from under her lashes and her sternly arched brows.

"Thirty-four; fifteen."

"Ratio?"

Lord, he knew she was going to ask that. "Two with four left over. Two and a third, nearly."

"Two and four-fifteenths. Closer to a quarter than a third." She dealt a knave. Nine. Ace. Four. Paused to shoot him that look again, wordless this time.

"Thirty-one; fourteen. Meaning a ratio of . . ." Christ. This was beyond him.

"I can see you thinking. I don't want to see you thinking."

"Ha. *There's* something I don't suppose you often need to say to Square-jaw." Barely under his breath those words emerged, as if of their own accord. "Two and . . ." three left over; three into fourteen . . . "A bit more than one fifth."

"Three-fourteenths. No need to round. And please confine your attention to the cards. Prince Square-jaw is my own concern."

Three. Seven. King. Eight. Twenty-eight; thirteen. He could see how the counting bit would get easier with practice. Perhaps the division bit might as well.

She gave a sudden shake of her head, as if to relocate a curl that had fallen so forward as to encroach on her vision, and he glanced up at just the instant when her face was turned fully toward the candles.

And now she might as well have been laying down the twelve of sickles and the princess of petunias, for all he could see of the cards. Pity any woman who didn't have such a profile. Pity dainty noses, rosebud mouths, insipid brows, and delicate chins. By the side of Lydia Slaughter, a pretty girl must look like the work of a sculptor who hadn't known when to stop, but had gone on chipping and nicking away until the forceful beauty of the marble was all smothered and subdued.

"I've lost it." No point in letting her go farther. "I've lost the count."

She nodded, lips pressed together. She'd expected this. "It's twenty-six and twelve. Keeping a tally takes practice. You're doing respectably, for a first try."

"I confess I'm not grasping why I must organize them so. Tens and non-tens."

"Do you ever go into gaming hells, Mr. Blackshear?" Ten, ace, queen. Twenty-six, nine.

"I haven't. I fear ruin."

"One hears of it, to be sure." Six. Knave. Ace. Seven. "But one hears also of certain intriguing variations such establishments apply to the rules of vingt-et-un."

"Oh?" Twenty-four, seven. Three and . . . something.

"For example, I've heard that in some hells, the banker is not permitted to stick below a total of seventeen. And that he *must* stick once he reaches that total. Do you see how those facts might change the game?"

"Of course. A player would never stick on fifteen or sixteen, for example, unless he knew there was a good chance of the banker's going bust." Ah. "Unless, let us say, he knew there was a high ratio of tens to non-tens remaining in the deck. And I'm afraid I've lost the count again."

"It's nineteen and six. Three and one sixth. Not at all favorable." Abruptly she set down the cards. "I've been told I'm no longer welcome to play at the gentlemen's table here. It's unseemly, I'm informed."

"I'm sorry to hear it." He'd be sorry indeed not to watch her deal anymore, knowing he alone was privy to her witchcraft. "Are you—do you mean to try your luck in the hells?" One heard of some clubs where ladies played alongside the men.

"I don't mean to *try my luck* anywhere. Good Lord." What an ill, ill man he was, to enjoy her scolding so. "I've told you already I spare no thought for luck. I have a plan."

Of course she did. And it almost certainly meant he'd see her here less often. He sat forward and gathered the cards, to engage himself with something other than the sudden dull weight of disappointment. "Prince Square-jaw has no objection, then, to spending his evenings in such venues?" And taking his woman there, too. You'd think the man would have a bit more pride.

"Prince Square-jaw has nothing to do with it. Haven't you been paying attention, Blackshear?" She clasped her hands before her and looked him dead in the eye. "I'm going to do this with you."

Chapter Nine

He DIDN'T altogether like that. The sharp vertical line between his brows told her so.

Maybe she ought to have softened him up with more flirtation. Maybe she ought to have worn the purple gown. Nothing for it now. She leaned forward.

"Neither of us plays for amusement. Other people are depending on you, you once said, and I am depending upon myself. I need to win a certain amount of money, quickly."

"I as well." He was turning the cards over one by one, that crease still present between his brows. He glanced up. "Are you in some trouble?"

"No more than any lady is who depends on a gentleman's whims for her security. I'd like to free myself from that state, and I calculate I can do that with two thousand pounds."

"Won't Mr. Roanoke provide for you?" He addressed these words to the cards, with a frown. "I thought that was the custom, when these things had run their course. I thought you worked out a settlement right at the start."

"Generally it's done that way." She cleared her throat. "But as you may recall hearing, I was employed in a disorderly house at the time Mr. Roanoke decided to engage me. I knew nothing of settlements or negotiation."

"He did, though." A muscle tightened at the corner of his mouth. "He ought to have told you what was customary."

"He paid a generous sum to Mrs. Parrish to procure me, and for all I know he may yet settle money on me. But in the absence of a contract, I cannot count on that." She sat straighter. He was taking her off course. He'd be trying to ask more questions about her past, soon, if she wasn't careful. "I have four hundred and ten pounds at present. Obviously, I need fifteen hundred and ninety more. Now that I cannot play here, I think the hells may be my best and only chance."

His mouth twisted. He picked up the seven of spades and turned it in cartwheel fashion, his fingertips touching one corner after another. "I need a bit more than you. Three thousand, all told, and I need it by the end of next month. At present I have four hundred I've won here, and another eight hundred left from the sale of my commission, though I depend on having some of that to pay my rent and expenses while I wait for the three thousand to do its job." His eyes strayed from the card to her face. "The hells have not been anywhere in my plan."

"I know you fear to lose money." She inclined forward, just a few degrees. "But once you've learned to keep count of tens, and to wager accordingly, you'll be better off in a hell than at Beecham's because of the different rules. I promise."

A tiny spasm crossed his face. Clearly her promises weren't worth much.

Speak of something else. Lull him. "What plans do you have for your three thousand? I expect it's something more stirring than the five percents."

The seven of spades went through several more rotations. He was unaccustomed, obviously, to discussing such matters with a slight acquaintance—a woman at that—but there seemed something else at work in him too. The subject was even more delicate than it ought to be. "I have an acquaintance who imports timber," he said at last. The card cartwheeled on. "He'd like to add a second ship, and needs capital for the purpose. I'd be a part owner, with a good share of the profits."

"Good enough to provide for you and someone else as well."

"Indeed." The card turned faster. His brow sank, and he watched his fingers.

"Is it a lady?" Good God. This wasn't her business.

"I beg your pardon?" The card halted, pinched between two fingertips. He raised stricken eyes to hers.

"I don't—Only I thought . . ." Unaccustomed heat flooded her cheeks. Suddenly she couldn't meet his gaze, and must turn hers to the row of candles burning at her left. "That day I met you on the street, when you'd been to Camden Town. You wore fine clothes and I . . ." *What in God's name was she doing?* "Clothes such as one might wear to call on a lady."

"I was. I did." Terse, minimal replies, as though he couldn't trust his voice to stay steady if he spoke at length.

"Only I wondered. It doesn't matter." She was too near to the candles and the smoke hurt her eyes. Brilliant. He'd fancy her brought to tears by the knowledge of this other lady. "At all events I hope you'll consider my plan, or at the very least consider helping me to discover which clubs permit ladies and which of those utilize the rules I've mentioned. Would you happen to know the time?" Regardless the hour, they'd been in here too long.

He felt about, somewhere on his person below the table's edge, and brought out a watch. She touched a knuckle quickly to both eyes as he flicked it open. "A quarter after midnight. We can stop the lesson here. I have the hang of it; I'll just need practice now." He regarded her for a moment, watch still open in his hand, looking as though there were something he wished he could say. Then he smiled. "A great deal of practice if I'm to keep up with you in the hells."

He'd assented. Relief flowed through her in warm torrents and took out the connection between judgment and her tongue—or maybe it was the smile alone that undid her. "You ought to practice soon. Build on your skill before it can begin to slip away." She held the next words like potatoes hot from the hearth, shifting them from hand to hand and half inclined to drop them altogether. "You might call at my house. My days are my own after three o'clock or so. I spend most afternoons occupied with this sort of thing anyway."

She'd bent her head to gather back the cards, so she could only imagine the effect upon his face of this speech. "I'm sorry." His watch snapped closed, its crisp percussion muffled in his palm. "But given all the circumstances, I think that would be prodigiously unwise."

He was right. That was the worst of it. She knew better than he did how ill it might go if Edward found out another man had called. And to burden Jane with keeping such a secret would be unjust. "As you think best." She pushed the cards across the tabletop and fumbled for her gloves. Enough time spent on fitting her fingers just so, and she needn't raise her eyes again before he was gone from the room.

His chair creaked as he pushed it back over the carpet and his black-coated form rose up into her peripheral view. Perhaps he would bow. She'd be too busy with her gloves to see. She tugged the right glove up over her wrist and wiggled her fingers to work them in. Vaguely she saw him pocket the deck and move out of her field of vision. One, two, three, four steps across the carpet to the door. That was that.

"Lydia." His voice was like a long arm reaching all the way back to catch her by the chin and make her turn. He himself had not turned. "Damnation. Do I need to say it aloud?"

"I don't know. I don't know what you mean." Her pulse hammered in her throat.

He heaved a sigh that elevated his shoulders and dropped them again. His face angled a few degrees to the left, not even far enough to show his profile. He kept his hand on the doorknob. "I want—very badly—to take you to bed."

"You said you wouldn't." Parched and panicked, she sounded. Like a lady who'd woken to find her bed-curtains on fire.

"And I won't. There are more reasons against it than just Mr. Roanoke." His hand turned and took another hold on the doorknob. "We flirt for sport here, and we can continue to do so. You needn't fear I'll . . ." He trailed off and she was left to imagine all the things she needn't fear he'd do. "But don't mistake me. I want you. I've wanted you since that first night when you fleeced me."

His voice had got lower, half made up of shadow, half made up of the same rich chocolate that colored his eyes.

"And if I were in your house, with your bed but a closed door away, I fear I would forget your best interest and my own as well. And I cannot—" His voice broke off, suddenly, and he tilted his head to gaze upward, near the top of the door. "I've made mistakes enough, believe me. I don't need to add this one." A second of heavy silence. Then he inclined his head and was gone, closing the door behind him without waiting for a reply.

Just as well. Between the tempest in her brainpan and the stoppage in her throat, he should have had a very long wait.

*D*o you never mean to wear this gown?" Jane stood at the clothespress, lifting the tissue-thin purple outer layer between thumb and forefinger. "You've had it a week and a half now and I vow Mr. Roanoke hasn't seen it once."

"I'm saving it for a suitable occasion." With her pencil hand Lydia pushed a stray lock of hair back behind her ear. "And Mr. Roanoke likes the gown I have on very well."

The girl made a small sound in her throat, considering. "Is this sarcenet? The black part?"

"I don't know. Knit silk of some sort. And is it black? I had thought it a very dark purple." Her pencil was growing blunt. Twice already she'd pared it to a better point, and she'd need to take up the penknife again soon.

Three essential problems confronted the serious player of vingt-et-un. First, how to play a given hand. Second, how to wager on that hand. Third, how to manage one's stake over the long term. Because proper strategy relied on the power of odds, and the longer a time one gave odds to work, the likelier they were to *I want very badly to take you to bed.*

She screwed her eyes shut. No. Opened them. Fixed them on her paper, with its numbers and letters and braces and square-root signs, none of which had yet added up to an ideal strategy. Her deft, easy hold on the pencil had turned into a rigid gripping fist.

This was ridiculous. She was no blushing virgin. And Mr. Blackshear had flirted with her enough by now that she might have deduced he wouldn't mind a tumble. He was a man, for Heaven's sake. Men liked bedsport wherever they could get it. Why the devil should his plain statement of the fact make her insides race and wheel about like a frantic flock of swallows?

A soft throat-clearing sound brought her attention back to where her maid stood by the clothespress, her hands now folded before her. "Do you plan to wait up for him very much longer?"

She swiveled to squint at the clock on her candlelit dressing table. It was past midnight. Edward had said he'd call at ten. She put down her pencil and rose. "I have a good bit of work to do yet. But I can do it just as well in nightclothes. I suppose Mr. Roanoke must have changed his plans." This happened from time to time. Jane dressed her and did up her hair in some style suitable for an evening out, only to take it down again when Edward found some more compelling way to spend the night.

It made a poor impression for a young lady. *Proper men aren't like this,* she ought to say. *A man with true regard for you will keep his promises.* But how could she say so? Arthur's regard had been true, and still his promises had given way like rotted-out floorboards under the weight of his parents' disapproval.

Too many men shouldering their way into this small room. Edward. Arthur. Mr. Blackshear and his bold declarations. "Are you familiar with the martingale system of wagering, Jane?" She crossed to the dressing table and sat. She would force her mind back to business.

"I don't think so. I've only ever played for pennies."

Jane undid the circlet of pearls she'd pinned into her hair some hours since.

"The principle is simple: each time you lose, you double your next bet." This was better. Already she was feeling more herself. "Let us say you bet a penny, and you lose it. You follow by betting two pennies. If you win, you've gained back the penny you lost plus a penny of profit."

The girl nodded, rather dutifully, as she straightened the pearls and set them on a lacquered tray.

"Of course you might lose as well, and then you'd be down threepence. But if you bet four pennies on the next hand, and won, you'd have back all three plus one more in profit." She closed her eyes and tipped her head forward to have the hairpins drawn out. "The principle and outcome are the same no matter how many times you must double your bet: eventually you win a hand, and recover the amount of your losses plus one penny profit. However the martingale system has several obvious flaws." She opened her eyes again to address her maid's reflection. "Perhaps you perceive them?"

"Only it seems a deal of trouble for a profit of only one penny." Jane dropped a handful of hairpins into a dish and took up the hairbrush.

"The betting unit needn't be a penny. It's more likely to be ten pounds, fifty pounds, one hundred. Martingale, in theory, recovers your losses and returns one betting unit besides, no matter what the unit might be." A disloyal thought flitted through: *Mr. Blackshear wouldn't have needed this explained.*

Then a worse thought: *He might have liked to discuss it, though. Naked, with his head on a pillow.*

This was Edward's fault. Leaving her alone here to fill her idle imagination with other men. "The system's chief flaw is that it depends on an unlimited stake." She put up her arms, that Jane could undo the latticed cords of her gown. "A long run of losses is improbable but not impossible. If you went into a gaming establishment with one thousand pounds, then even if you began with a wager of only one pound, nine straight losses would be enough to do you in. You'd be down five hundred and eleven pounds, only four hundred eighty-nine pounds remaining, and no way to put up the five hundred twelve that must come next in the martingale sequence."

"I've never known such a lady for reckoning numbers as you. Stand now, if you please."

Indigo silk—or "dark blue," as some called it—shut out the world for several seconds, imposing a break in her lecture. Two full-length petticoats followed. Then there she was in the mirror, down to her corset and chemise and rattling on once more. "The more pertinent shortcoming however, in regard to my present efforts, is that martingale presumes the same odds on every wager. An astute player of vingt-et-un recognizes *varying* odds from wager to wager. You must make larger bets when the deck is favorable, and smaller bets when it isn't. The last thing you want to do is double your wager in an unfavorable situation."

"I see." Jane had learned to say this at suitable intervals, whether she saw or not. "I don't doubt you'll invent something better, then." She gathered Lydia's hair and laid it forward of her shoulders on either side before starting on the corset-strings.

"If I do I shall certainly teach you." Lydia let her head fall forward again. "You'll rob your friends of all their pennies."

She made a vaguely feral sight in the mirror, peering up from under her lashes and out between twin curtains of unbound hair. This would be a man's view of her, if he should wish to undress her with his own hands before taking her to bed.

A whiplash of impatience cracked through her and she forced her gaze away from the reflection. *Bed.* That was quaint. As though they couldn't make do with that faded carpet on the upstairs room's floor. For that matter he could just bend her over the card table and toss up her skirts, or back her up against the door on tiptoe.

No. Even tiptoe wouldn't bring her high enough. He should have to crouch in that ungainly way taller men did when they took it into their heads to couple upright. She might prevent that, though, by scaling his body as if she were climbing a tree, one leg hooked over his hip and the other wound high across his back. No niceties would be possible in that position. No lingering. They'd satisfy their curiosity with ruthless, unsentimental efficiency, and be done.

They wouldn't, though. He had reasons against it. So he'd said.

She picked up a scent bottle and turned it, the facets catching candlelight one after the next. A lady didn't have to puzzle long to deduce what his reasons would be. He was promised elsewhere, or at least paying attentions, and he would not dishonor that connection by indulging whatever appetite he'd worked up for her.

That was to his credit. A man who could master his impulses would be likely to keep his head in a gaming hell. That was the important part of all this. The rest was mere distraction.

She set the bottle down firmly. They had a bargain. She would teach him to play with a reckoning, and he would scout the hells for her and find her a man of business when the time came. That was all. "I think I must consider the difference in odds for a deck whose composition is known as opposed to a deck of unknown proportions," she said, and watched Jane's face settle into lines of patient resignation.

* * *

$\mathcal{S}$UNDAY MORNING. He ought to have stayed in bed.

Bells rang out from the dark brick tower of the Church of St. James as Will walked past. People in their sober Sunday best were streaming the opposite way and he must fight the current, threading a path through like one of those fish who braved rapids and waterfalls to find its way home.

He hadn't yet been inside that church since coming back to England. Nor had he darkened the doorstep of St. George's in Hanover Square, though Andrew or one of his sisters must always be extending the invitation. Difficult to be sure of the proper protocol, when one had cast away one's immortal soul.

He shoved his hands deep into his pockets and pulled his greatcoat closer against the chill wind. Not for him to judge, of course. Soldiers of the world would be in a sad way if taking a life meant absolute condemnation. Indeed, enough of them filled the churches on Sunday to suggest a general hopefulness of outlook on that point. His case was just different enough to prevent him joining them.

A stray end of his muffler flapped; he caught it and tucked it into his coat. Eternal damnation. Jolly subject for a long morning walk. Still, it kept him from dwelling on what he'd said to Miss Slaughter. To Lydia. He shook his head as though he might scatter the memory. What on earth had possessed him to speak so?

Yet he must have said something of the kind, sooner or later. She would surely have guessed before very much longer. He hid his sentiments poorly. This way, at least, the cards were laid out on the table between them. But he wouldn't dwell. He'd said what he'd said, and he could not take it back now.

South and east he walked, through the Sunday-quiet

streets of the City until he reached the London Bridge with its view of the Upper Pool. More than once, lately, he'd come down here to watch the boat traffic and test his recollection of what he'd learned from Fuller or read on his own. This nearest vessel at anchor was a two-masted brig, not large enough for an open-sea voyage so probably engaged in some coastal trade. Coal, perhaps, or wool. Something produced in the hinterlands of the north and brought down to supply the needs of London. Rather miraculous how it all worked, when one paused to consider.

He folded his arms atop the stone railing and leaned into a breeze that stirred the surface of the river and tasted faintly of salt. To be part of this might be a fine thing. Of course the urgent matter was to secure a profit that would make Mrs. Talbot's independence possible. To deliver her from such unfriendly confines, and to make his word worth something again.

Beyond that, though, and beyond assuring himself of an income sufficient for his own expenses, he would gain a certain satisfaction from knowing he had some small hand in all this industry. This honest commerce. People might one day live in houses built from timber his own ship had hauled across the sea.

Not the life he'd been brought up to, of course, and Andrew would probably blanch when he heard of a Blackshear brother having even so glancing a connection with trade. But an eldest son must always have more use for the gradations of rank than a youngest, to say nothing of a youngest who'd stood shoulder to shoulder with butchers' sons in square combat formation on the battlefield.

He turned to lean his back against the railing and look to his right, where the buildings of London rose. The City. St. James's. Clarendon Square, somewhere beyond what he could see. What hopes he held for the future were coming to depend in large part on his association with Miss Slaughter. He must be mindful, henceforward, of all he stood to lose by being careless with her. More than ever, he would practice circumspection. Now he'd confessed his attraction, they could surely set that matter aside and devote all their energy to the intricacies of vingt-et-un.

Chapter Ten

BUT THERE was more than one way to scuttle their bargain, and two nights later she had him on the brink of doing just that.

"How do you not see that three-eighths is greater than five-fourteenths? How do you not see?" She stood dumbfounded, hands on her hips, her vexed pacing of the past five minutes temporarily arrested that she might aim her wrath at him with optimum accuracy.

"For God's sake, Lydia, my brain doesn't work that way. Most people's don't." He sat with his elbows on the table, his hands at his temples, his weary fingers pushed through his hair.

She walked three steps away and came back. "Surely if you make a picture—"

"I can't make a picture."

"A simple one, I mean. Two rectangles, side by side, equal in height. Divide one with seven horizontal lines and the other with thirteen. Then surely you can see—"

He had to laugh. He could not forbear. "Good Lord. It really is that simple for you, isn't it? And you really have no idea of its not being like that for the rest of us."

She took one step closer, arms dropping straight at her

sides and hands curling into fists. "This isn't a *jest,* you know. This isn't meant to *amuse* you." Everything in her demeanor suggested a young girl furious at some elder who would not take her seriously. Did she have elder siblings? Any siblings at all? That wasn't where his thoughts ought to be. "I have spent hours and hours, and used up a whole pencil and countless sheets of paper, attempting to devise a system by which you can consult the degree of your advantage in order to determine the proper amount to wager. I can only think my time and effort will have been wasted if you haven't the necessary understanding to even keep track of your advantage."

"Perhaps your time and effort were wasted indeed." He let one hand fall to the table where his fingers drummed lightly, to let out by increments the irritation that simmered in him. "Let me posit, though, that the fault may not be with my common understanding, but rather with the decision to concoct a wagering system that depends upon a common brain's recognizing that three-eighths is greater than five-fourteenths."

She stared at him, baleful as a hawk come face-to-face with a rival in her hunting grounds. Her eyes skipped back and forth, considering him. "You shall have to learn everything in hundredths," she said with new and sudden resolution. "Three-eighths is thirty-eight hundredths and five-fourteenths is thirty-six hundredths."

Oh, good God. He seized the edge of the table and levered himself up. "Lydia, I *cannot do that.*"

"You can with practice." The suggestion of violence in his movement seemed only to spur her on. Briskly she came back to her place opposite, pulling out her chair. "Surely you learned division in school. Just round everything to two places beyond the period." She sat. "Likely you'll need to practice with a pencil and paper, to begin, but if you spend a little time on it each day then I should think—"

"No." He put everything he knew of calm and reason into the one syllable. "I'm sorry, but I should consider that a waste of my time." More calm and more reason, to smooth away the piqued creases in her forehead, to soften the tight line of her mouth. "The chances of my ever attaining such proficiency as would allow me to execute those calculations while keeping up with a game of vingt-et-un are simply too slight to justify the investment of hours." He released his hold on the table and straightened. He'd been sitting for some while and his legs were in no hurry to take the chair again.

She swiveled her chin to the left, as though she believed the candles more worthy of her wisdom than he. "I see." One flame swayed and buckled before her breath. "You are unwilling even to try. That, in case you wondered, reduces your chance of success from slight to nonexistent."

Three backward steps brought him to the wall, where he leaned, arms folded across his chest. He sifted words, though really, why should he take any care at all in answering her petulance? "I am trying very hard to remain civil, Miss Slaughter, and to make allowance for what must be your feelings, on hearing one of your favorite pursuits dismissed as a waste of somebody's time."

"I do not want you to make allowance for my *feelings*." *Impulse* and *luck* had nothing on *feelings* when it came to arousing her distaste. "I've never asked you to give the least consideration to my *feelings*." He could picture her holding the word with fingertips at arm's length, like a scullery maid disposing of a dead rat she'd found in the larder. "All I've asked of you is that you take this game seriously, and apply some small fraction of the effort I myself have applied toward giving you every possible advantage when the time comes to wager.

I'm very sorry you find yourself unable to do so." Everything in her aspect—the rigid posture, the averted face, the arms converging to suggest hands tightly clasped beneath the table's edge—made a silent rebuff to any sympathy or cordiality he might dare attempt.

He expelled a slow, weary breath, tilting his own eyes to the ceiling. No one to blame but himself. He had an excellent idea of how to account for her irritability.

He pushed off the wall and came round to the candle side of the table, where he crouched until his eyes were level with hers.

She peered at him through the flames. Her lips thinned, warily, but she didn't turn away.

"Tell me the truth." At this distance—two feet at most—he didn't need to weight the words with any particular inflection. Their meaning alone would be sufficient. "Are you angry at me because of what I said to you the last time we were in this room?"

"You *would* think so." Her gaze shifted: though she still faced him, she'd gone back to addressing the candles. "You can't believe the cause of my frustration could truly be what I've stated. No, because I'm a woman, it must be some slight to my *feelings* that's put me out of countenance." Again, the scullery maid and the dead rat, though this time she seemed set to swing it by the tail and pitch it over a far hedge. "Or some injury I'm nursing in response to some one of the many things you said here, three nights since."

"Lydia." He set his hand on the table's edge, four fingers atop and thumb underneath. "I know you're not naïve. I know you recall the exact thing to which I refer." He let those words stand, and waited.

She glared into the candles until he could see her eyes watering. No trembling about the lips—she wasn't weeping—rather it was as though she were punishing herself, deliberately, for some obscure failing. She blinked hard, one, two, three times. Water welled over and made its haphazard way down both cheeks. It glittered against her skin in the candlelight, stark as an accusation, and she made no move to wipe it away.

She looked past the candles to him. "I'm not angry at you for that. I should be a comical character indeed if I took offense at a man saying such things."

He watched his fingers curl and straighten on the table's edge, flesh against faded oak. That wasn't the answer he wanted. He had rather she be angry at him, Will Blackshear, for the particular words he'd said to her than that she should absolve him with the same sardonic policy that could exculpate every man in the world. He slanted his head a degree to the right and spoke, carefully. "It's not untrue, what I said that night. But with all my soul I will wish it untrue if it means the loss of what cordiality we'd attained. I spoke impulsively, without giving sufficient thought to how those words must be received by a lady who has your experience of men. I don't want you to see me as just another lout looking to make use of you."

"Why should you care at all what I think of you?" She all but squirmed in her skin at the notion, and one more fact about her came clear: *I want you* didn't discompose her nearly so much as *I like you and I want you to think well of me.*

And it was an excellent question she'd asked. Why indeed did he care so much for her good opinion? He tightened his grip on the table. "There's the bargain, of course. I need to learn what you can teach me and I cannot afford to jeopardize that with ill-timed candor." He would give her a bit more. She'd told him about the loss of her parents, after all; this would bring him even with her. "Also, this is the first truly new acquaintance I've formed since returning from the Continent. You're the first person to build her opinion based solely on the man

I am now." His stomach was threatening to turn somersaults but he would forge on, even if he must fix his gaze on the unlit candle at the end of the branch. "I have more doubt than I once did about meriting a lady's good opinion."

The room was so quiet he could hear her breathe. Lord only knew what she was thinking. She cleared her throat. "Because you were changed by war, do you mean?" A quick glance found her busying herself with one of her gloves, a finger tracing along its seam.

"It's difficult to explain to a woman—that is, to anyone who's never served." Again he looked to the end of the candle-branch. "But I suspect few men come home unaltered."

"I can see how that might be." The satin of her glove whispered as she rubbed it between finger and thumb. "My brother was a soldier. Though he didn't come home, altered or otherwise."

"I'm sorry." He plucked the cold candle out of the branch. "Was he your only sibling?" Perhaps he would have given her a home, and spared her the descent into her present station.

She nodded. "Henry was his name." In the pause, he could almost hear her deciding whether to tell him more. "Do you remember the Walcheren expedition, seven years since?" Her fingers stilled on the glove and she angled her head to face him.

"Of course." A sorry mess that had been, troops stationed in swampy ground, more men dying of sickness than by bullet or cannon. He touched the candle's wick to a flame. "Is that where you lost him?"

"To the ague." Her eyes glittered like ice before the sudden flare of the candle. "He hadn't even the honor of dying in battle."

"There's very little honor involved. You may trust my word on that." He put the candle back, finding the place by feel so he need not take his gaze from her. "Was he clever with numbers too?"

Surprise flashed over her face—she hadn't expected this question—before giving way to a very sunrise of a smile that seemed to warm and loosen every knotted-up thing inside him. "*Clever* doesn't begin to tell it, Will. Where I have a sort of dumb genius for calculation, he had depth of understanding, and an interest in abstract concepts that I don't share. By his side I always felt a bit like one of those trick horses at the fair, pounding out answers with one hoof."

"He must have been proud to have such a sister, I imagine." Seven or eight thoughts and feelings were running riot all through him. Chief among them: *this is what she looks like, sounds like, when she loves someone.*

"I suppose he was." Her smile subsided. He'd said something wrong, or perhaps she'd simply moved from remembering her brother to remembering his loss.

The compulsion to cheer her was primal, of a sudden, the same sort of drive that could keep a man staggering through a desert for days toward a rumor of water. Numbers. Cards. That was the way. "I wish I could claim either a depth of understanding *or* a dumb genius, but I think we must face the fact that I'll never be as proficient as you'd like at keeping the tally." He let go the table and came upright again. "Might there be some way you can keep that reckoning, and pass the information secretly to me?"

Her eyes widened a fraction, and he could see—he could nearly see past them to the furor of fireworks whizzing and spitting about her brain. Good Lord. He'd said absolutely the right thing this time. In fact he might have stunned her with a clever idea.

"Yes." She'd completely forgot about war and ague and trick horses at the fair. "Yes, that's exactly what we'll do. I'll manage everything. I'll tell you how much to wager, and whether to buy or stick. We'll devise a system of codes." Her brow furrowed fiercely as she sent her gaze to the table. Four seconds later she looked up. "Mr. Blackshear, do you know French?"

*L*YDIA LEFT first this time, pulling the door shut behind her with a clean, immensely satisfying click of hardware. The prospects that had looked so grim but an hour before were looking crystal-chandelier-brilliant now, and if Mr. Blackshear truly cared to earn a lady's good opinion he need only keep coming up with ideas like the one he'd voiced tonight.

For Heaven's sake, why hadn't she thought of it herself? She would manage the reckoning, and he would supply the larger stake that could weather the inevitable fluctuations in outcome. He would have to trust her, of course, and she would have to prove herself worthy of his trust. But with their interests lying on a common path, that part should see to itself.

Down the staircase she went, light on her toes and in charity with all the world, until she turned at the landing to find Maria waiting at the foot of the steps, arms folded, posture rigid with disapproval, eyes fixed on the flight that led down to the next floor.

Apprehension seized at her with cold fingers. She caught up her skirts and hurried down the remaining stairs. "What is it?" *Don't act guilty. You've done nothing wrong.*

"Mr. Roanoke came to the retiring room some half hour since, looking for you." Maria kept her gaze averted. "Eliza talked him into dancing a set with her in the ballroom. They must be on their second set now, and if he hasn't grown suspicious you're greatly in her debt."

"How did you know where to find me?" She took a

tight grip on the balustrade, because it felt as if the floor were dropping out from beneath her feet.

"Do you suppose us entirely hen-witted?" With one sharp turn of her head Maria subjected her to the full force of reproof. "Eliza noticed when you went missing two Saturdays since, and you know what sort of conjectures she likes to make. When it happened again this past Friday she looked about and made sure of which gentleman was absent at the same time. Guessing where you'd gone wasn't so difficult—there aren't many places here where two people may effectively closet themselves."

"We were only playing cards." Why did the truth sound like such a feeble trumped-up tale? "You know how fond I am of cards." But Maria didn't know. She had no reason to believe cards meant anything more to Lydia than they did to the other ladies. Only Mr. Blackshear knew that part of her.

"I don't concern myself with what you do. Mr. Roanoke has merited only the poorest claim to your loyalty. But surely you recognize the value of discretion. And the longer we stand here discussing it, the more time you give people to notice your absence."

"It was only cards." She lurched from her standstill, catching up her skirts and starting down the next flight as Maria trailed behind. She would not panic. Edward wasn't as observant as the ladies—likely he'd formed no suspicions.

But she must not risk giving him anything to suspect. With quick decision she spoke over her shoulder. "Nevertheless I shall tell the gentleman we must give up meeting. You were very good to warn me and I promise you won't be put to such trouble on my account again." She and Mr. Blackshear would have to make other arrangements. She had no idea what those could be.

She reached the ballroom to find Edward altogether

engrossed by Eliza, who was always happy to engross a man in service to a worthy cause. By the time the set broke up Lydia had concocted a tale of a passing headache and the interlude outdoors that had cured it, and this, combined with her protector's residual enjoyment of the dance and followed by the half hour in the library for which he'd originally been seeking her, proved sufficient to satisfy him on all points.

"I hope it was a first-rate game of cards," said Eliza some while later as she and Lydia stood side by side along the ballroom wall. Her gaze rested innocently on the dancers in the middle of the floor; her voice crept and twisted with merry insinuation.

"I swear on my soul it was nothing more. Did Maria tell you otherwise?" She felt for a lock of hair that had come loose in the library, and busied herself with pinning it back in place.

Sidelong she could see Eliza shaking her head. "You know she has a disdain for gossip. And I think she believes you. Indeed I suppose I may end by believing you myself." Her near shoulder rose and fell in either a shrug or a sigh. "You're not likely to lie, are you, when you know such a scandal would only garner you more of my good opinion?"

"I hope I'm sensible of your goodness in crediting me. Yours and Maria's both." Lydia pressed her lips together. She wouldn't answer the unvoiced questions. *Why Mr. Blackshear? Why in secret? When did you arrange it, and what makes it worth risking your position?* She wasn't in the habit of confiding. How to account, then, for her speaking of Henry the way she had?

"Mind you I say nothing of *his* motives. I wouldn't be surprised if this business of cards were but the first step in an elaborate campaign."

"Then he's been a deal too slow about moving to the second step, hasn't he?" Enough of this conversation.

She pushed off the wall. "I shan't be withdrawing upstairs with him anymore after tonight. So I told Maria,
and so I shall tell the gentleman himself."

And so she did, in a moment when he happened to be
at the end of the ballroom where a cluster of potted
palms offered partial screening for such a conversation.
He nodded, his face tight with concern. Clearly he was
blaming himself for the lapse in prudence, though he
would not do so aloud because it would unnecessarily
prolong what must be a brief, inconspicuous exchange.

"We're nearly ready to go into the hells as it is," she
said before he could suggest they abandon the scheme
altogether. "Only we'll at least need to consult after
you've scouted the establishments."

"I might be able to arrange a meeting place." He furrowed his brow at the nearest of the potted palms. "I
have a friend who . . ." He checked his thoughts, angling
his face back to her. "Can I write to you?" His efficiency
sent a pleasant tingle down her spine. So quickly he absorbed these new terms and took the necessary tasks
upon himself. Habit from his years as a soldier, no
doubt.

"I'll write down my direction. I'll leave the arrangements in your hands." Ordinarily she'd at least want to
know what sort of meeting place he had in mind. But
she was going to have to depend on him in the gaming
hells. She might as well practice depending on him now.

*H*IS FIRST impression, on setting foot in his first high-
stakes gaming club, was that the men who'd told him
tales of these establishments had neglected to give sufficient due to the décor. Clearly Beecham's was aiming for
this, and clearly Beecham's was falling far short of the
mark.

"Try not to gape," Cathcart murmured at his left. "They'll mark you for a pigeon straightaway."

And Will made a mental note: *gape*. When he came to a hell to gamble in earnest, he would do well to look like a man who didn't know his way around a pack of cards.

Not that the astonishment would be hard to feign. The climb up a dim, nondescript stairway, three separate doors closing behind them to mark the stages of their journey into the *sanctum sanctorum*, had prepared him to expect something drab and utilitarian, its smoke-begrimed walls perhaps garnished with a painting or two, bawdy in subject matter, indifferent in execution.

Instead the room fairly sparkled with splendor. The enormous chandelier *did* sparkle, its illumination thrown back and amplified by grand gilt-framed mirrors that were probably meant to facilitate cheating at cards, but were no less handsome for that. The ceiling had been worked in a pattern of recessed squares, white with a relatively restrained gold outline. They neatly echoed the squares of the polished parquet floor.

For a room of such ill purpose, it was remarkably pleasing to the eye. But then, it had better be, with no windows to offer a prospect on any world beyond this one.

And then again, the splendor must go largely unnoticed by the establishment's clients, intent as they were on eight feet of green baize, the racket of a wheel, the somersaulting of a pair of dice, the spring of the topmost card from a faro box.

"Well, you've seen it. Can we go now?" Nick, on his right, dusted one cuff as though some foul particles of the place had managed to land there in the ten seconds since they'd entered the room. But doubtless Nick had made up his mind to be unimpressed well in advance.

I begin to grow weary of Beecham's, he'd said to Cathcart. *What do you say to visiting a few hells?* And

Cathcart, of course, had risen to the occasion, plotting out a long night of profligacy and suggesting they drag earnest, industrious Nick from his chambers to join them. Already it felt a bit like being at university again: into how many such pranks or dubious errands had the viscount cajoled them during the two years they'd all overlapped there, and how many times had his brother declared he'd never be drawn into such nonsense again?

"Show a little spirit, Blackshear." Cathcart wheeled out front to precede them, walking backward, toward the tables. "At the very least you'll be able to describe the evils of these places in detail at one of your political salons."

"More likely it will be used against me." Nick flicked at the other cuff, in case his first such gesture had not made his disapproval clear. "Some opponent in court will question my fitness, and produce all manner of wastrels who'll attest to having seen me in a hell. In multiple hells. How many did you say we must visit?"

"As many as are wanted to sate my curiosity." Will clapped his brother on the back. "Come along. The sooner we start, the sooner we finish."

"What will it be, then, Blackshear?" The viscount nodded from one table to the next. "Hazard? Chemin de fer? Roulette? Which path to damnation do you prefer?"

"Something that will allow a small bet. I shouldn't like to ruin myself in the first stop of the evening." No women in this club, so he needn't scout the vingt-et-un table. But neither need he make his companions suspicious as to his true errand, so he'd stay a bit before proposing they move on to some other establishment.

"Roulette, then. It will afford your brother the greatest opportunity for disapprobation."

The other two fell to good-natured sparring of a style honed in their years at Caius. Will sidled after them into the crush of bodies standing round the table where the great wheel spun. A long night stretched out yet before him, and he didn't feel tired in the least.

$\mathcal{F}$IVE DAYS later, and nearly a week since he'd seen her last, he fought the urge to offer Miss Slaughter his arm as they walked down the east side of Russell Square. In public they must always be the remotest of acquaintances.

"I haven't told him how I'm raising the money." He folded his restless arms behind his back. "I've represented this whole gaming-hell affair as something of a lark; a favor I'm doing for you."

She nodded gamely. "He won't learn otherwise from me." Her chin came up and her face angled itself his way. "What does he suppose to be the nature of our connection?"

"I've left that vague. He knows we have a need for discretion, so he may have drawn the obvious conclusions. On the other hand, he must see that if we'd intended anything truly iniquitous we would simply have gone to my rooms. Whatever his suspicions, I assure you he's too well-mannered to let on."

"That should be interesting." She sent him a grin, good-natured and mischievous as if she was indeed his mistress. Or perhaps his friend.

He was fortunate in his friends. Jack Fuller had listened stone-faced to a most irregular request—*I have some business to discuss with a woman and I'm in need of a place where we may meet, out of the public eye*—and offered up the use of his parlor without so much as a raised eyebrow.

Of course, a raised eyebrow on Jack Fuller would be no easy thing to detect. "One thing for which I must prepare you." He spoke quickly as they drew near the front door, and bent a bit toward her to keep the words confidential. "He was badly burned in the fire at Hougoumont and the resulting scars have given him rather an alarming appearance. I shouldn't like you to be taken by surprise."

She nodded again, silently making whatever preparations a lady must make before meeting a fearsome-looking man. And when they entered the house, and were shown by a footman into the parlor, Will admired all over again the ability her face had to keep her secrets. She bore the introduction with perfect aplomb, no fixed quality in her smile; no wandering of her glance to the damaged leg as the man came forward from behind his desk to greet them. One would think there was nothing remarkable in Fuller's appearance, or else that Miss Slaughter met men with burn-blasted faces every day.

She was more than polite: within ten minutes he could see she liked the man, and that Fuller was thoroughly diverted by her. She explained her scheme for winning at vingt-et-un, and spoke of the thousands of hands she'd dealt in her solitary hours in an attempt to gain some knowledge of odds. Then the talk turned to timber, and the glittering prospect of a new-built ship with a capacity of three hundred and fifty tons.

"How on earth do they determine the tonnage?" She'd taken a seat on a high stool at the table where ledgers were kept; she sat with her feet on a rung and her hands gripping the sides of the seat, looking, despite the gown, like a young clerk who'd left off managing the accounts for a few minutes of affable conversation. "It sounds like a matter for Archimedes's rule of floating bodies displacing water, but I know there can be no suitable tank for the purpose."

"Prepare to be shocked and dismayed, Miss Slaughter: what we call tonnage isn't true tonnage at all." How long had it been since anyone had visited Fuller? He looked happy as a boy come home from school for the holidays. "They measure the ship's length and breadth, and make some calculations using those figures."

"Length and breadth?" She sat up straight as a spindle. "Don't they include the depth?"

"The depth of the hold is reckoned as half the breadth of the ship's widest point. There are other adjustments, to account for the curving of the hull and so forth. Guesses, though, all of it but your length and breadth."

"Then it seems the clever thing to do is build a ship with a narrow breadth and a very deep hull, and run more cargo while paying the lower port dues and pilot fees." How eagerly she entered into the mechanics of this business. Wave a few numbers in front of her and you could lead her anywhere.

Will sat back in his armchair by the fire, stretching his legs out before him. "Not so clever, though, when a low tide runs you aground while your shallow-hulled competitors sail past you." He threw her a smile that was nearly accompanied by a wink.

"Ah. I didn't think of that." Her voice softened with chagrin and her straight form wilted slightly. Apparently she expected of herself that she should grasp the intricacies of shipping, and probably everything else, just as readily as she grasped odds and calculation.

Fuller proceeded to assure her that ships frequently *were* built on just that plan for traders willing to risk the hazard Mr. Blackshear had mentioned, and the deepest of them quite often did run aground and sometimes even tipped over when the tide receded from beneath them. Will crossed one booted ankle over the other and simply listened, glancing from left to right; from the merchant at his desk to the sharper perched atop her stool.

It wasn't so difficult to imagine, in a drowsy sort of daydream fostered by the fireplace's warmth, a life in which the three of them might meet often. When she'd bought her independence, she could visit wherever she liked. Perhaps she'd like to visit here, browsing through the ledgers and playing the occasional hand of vingt-et-un with two gentlemen she might come to count as friends. It *was* possible, wasn't it? That out of such an adversarial beginning, they might safely navigate the shoals of flirtation and attraction, and end as friends?

The time came at last to conduct the business that had brought them there. He took out his list of the most promising hells, and as he gave his opinions of each she listened with such keen-eyed reliance on his judgment as made his skin seem to shrink a size. Would he ever again in his life feel comfortable in the face of someone's trust, even on such a small matter as choosing which hell to visit first?

But he did make his recommendation, and they agreed on a night, and a time when he would come to fetch her. It was all down to odds and fate now, and the efficacy of her scheme.

"Well done, Blackshear," Fuller said when she'd left for home in a hackney the man had insisted on hiring. "Where the devil did you find her?"

"At a club. On another gentleman's arm, which is where she'll remain." He turned from the street, where they'd stood watching the hackney roll away, and stepped back into the house. "I'm pleased to do her a service, but it can go no further."

"Pity. She likes you." Fuller followed him in.

"I think perhaps she does. She didn't, at first." A foot-man stood in the entry hall with his coat and hat; he shrugged into the coat. "But we seem to have attained a solid mutual regard."

"Solid mutual regard, my arse." His mouth was stretched into one of those painful-looking smiles. "There's got to be a reason she asked you instead of that other gentleman to do this with her."

Well, yes. She knew he needed the money, and she almost certainly believed Roanoke would disapprove of her playing in a hell. The former reason, he could not offer to Fuller. The latter was Lydia's own business. "I suppose there's a lack of volatility in a plain friendship, as compared to a relationship with the element of passion, that makes it better suited to the sort of business we mean to undertake." He took his hat from the footman and settled it on his head.

Fuller only nodded, and if the scarred flesh about his eyes had not robbed him of subtler expression, there would almost certainly be a wry flavor to his persistent grin.

But it was true, after all, the bit about the lack of volatility. So Will told himself as he took his leave and started the walk home. They must both bring sharp, uncluttered minds to the gaming table. They didn't need the distraction of wondering at the state of each other's sentiments.

She likes you. Very well. So did he like her. But the more important fact was that she must rely on him, in the hells, and he must do whatever was necessary to uphold her reliance. If that meant smothering all improper impulses, then smother he would, for the sake of her trust.

Chapter Eleven

"Wʜᴀᴛ ᴋɪɴᴅ of place is it?" Jane stood back of Lydia's right shoulder, her eyes skipping about to avoid settling on any part of the scandalous image the pier glass showed.

"Not an altogether respectable one, truth be told. Not like the club to which Mr. Roanoke takes me." Her hands lifted to smooth her sarcenet front, but she checked the impulse and brushed fingertips over her curls instead. "The women who usually go there aren't the nicest sort, so I must wear something like this, so as not to seem out of place."

"You will wear the overdress, though?"

"Oh yes, of course. I only wanted to be sure this underlayer fell properly first." *Properly.* That was rich. The purple silk flowed over her body like cream poured from a pitcher, delineating her nipples for the edification of anyone who cared to look.

And who could blame Jane for wondering just how undressed she planned to be? Not one petticoat came between her and the sarcenet, and the chemise she wore was hardly a chemise at all, having had its neckline lowered to meet the top of her corset and its hem raised to well north of her stocking-tops. The knots of her garters announced themselves when she moved.

The mull overdress, when she put it on, made her . . . marginally more decent. It fastened down the bosom to the high waistline before falling open. It would float out to the sides when she walked, no doubt, giving the world a view of the way the silk skirts clung.

So much the better. They could notice that, and forget to heed anything she did at the table.

"Well, then. No need for you to wait up." Her voice was striving a little too hard for cheerful unconcern. "I'll watch for Mr. Blackshear and open the door myself when he comes. We'll be leaving directly for the club."

"If Mr. Roanoke calls . . ." Jane had gone to the dressing table and now fidgeted with the comb and brush.

"He won't. He never does, on Wednesdays." She crossed to the table, that her maid must look her in the eye. "You remember, don't you, that Mr. Blackshear is a gentleman? You remember he gave up his seat in the curricle for you? He's not the sort to do anything improper."

Jane nodded, though that might have been a rote response.

"He'll go with me a few times to these clubs, we'll each win the money we need, and that will be that." She hesitated. "I want to have a respectable establishment, Jane. I'd like to pay my own bills, instead of depending on a gentleman. I need money to do that, and I know of no better way to get it than by playing cards in a high-stakes club." Her pulse was ticking hard in her throat. She'd never confided quite this much to the girl before. "All those hours you've seen me play at cards all by myself? All those papers covered with scribbled numbers?"

The maid nodded again, this time with conviction.

"This is how I mean to reap the fruits of that labor. All

those hours have led up to this night." Indeed more hours than those had led to it. Long mornings with the tutor, Mr. Sinclair. Those puzzles Henry was always setting her with diamond-paned windows, or the multiplication of one three-digit number by another while he softly counted off the seconds it took her to call out an answer. Finally, tonight, she would do the thing she'd been preparing for all her life.

Jane retired to her room and Lydia waited on a bench in the entry hall, wrapped in her cloak, until the creaking wheels and clopping hooves of some conveyance drew to a stop outside. She jumped up and pulled the door open.

Mr. Blackshear—Will—was already out of the hackney and halfway up the steps, his face lit with a smile that would have exactly mirrored her own, had she the lopsided quality and the irregularity between the front teeth. He cut a rather Byronic figure in his carelessly draped greatcoat, with his cheeks unshaven and one of those faddish handkerchiefs in place of a cravat. The very picture of a man poised to ruin himself in romantic fashion, a pigeon ripe for the plucking, which of course was the role they'd agreed he would play.

"Come in." She stepped back. "I'm ready. Just let me fetch my reticule."

In fact she'd left it on the hallway table and had only to turn away, swipe it up, and turn back. But in that interval his countenance underwent a change. She faced him again to find his smile gone, his gaze pitched to the bottom of her cloak, his attention keen as a bird dog's. "I've never seen this gown," he said, and his eyes rebounded to hers with an unvoiced question.

"Ah, yes. Well, you'd better have a look now so it won't distract you at some critical moment." Often enough she'd spoken flippantly of this gown and its powers, but her insouciance now rang false in her own ears. When she caught her cloak's edges and swung them apart, she found she must look elsewhere than at his face.

Like him, she had a role to play: courtesan trolling for a moneyed protector. He knew that. He wouldn't be shocked to find her wearing something a bit brazen. Still her nerves prickled along the cut edges of her too-short chemise, and the knots of her garters felt conspicuous as a man's ill-timed erection.

Well, he'd seen it. Now they could go. She shrugged to flip the edges of her cloak to, and—

"Wait." His voice came out half strangled and his hand shot across to stop her covering herself.

"What is it?" But she could imagine. *You can't possibly go out in that. Do you have any idea what sort of men frequent these places? At least put a petticoat on.*

"Nothing. Just . . . wait."

She let herself look at him. He didn't notice. His hand still gripped her right wrist, holding that side of the cloak away, and his gaze ran over and over her gown as though he would never see it again and must fix the sight in his memory. She heard him draw a breath through his teeth.

A sizzle ran from the nape of her neck right up over her scalp, and some base part of her brain scrambled to life. *Take him upstairs. The hells can wait. You'll never have a better chance.*

That base part could say whatever it liked. What would Jane think of her, after all that talk of respectability, and Mr. Blackshear's propriety? What would she think of herself, throwing off this worked-for, planned-for expedition to get a bit of what any man could give her? This man alone had put his trust in her abilities, his fortunes in her hands. She knew better than to misprize that.

"Well, then." He let her cloak fall and took a step

back. His voice wasn't quite steady and his smile, when he raised his eyes to hers, seemed something he must sustain by force of will. "I presume that's the gown a gentleman ought to like?"

"It seemed appropriate for the occasion."

"Exceedingly so. I think I just forgot my own name." His smile came naturally then, an easy admission of his own fallibility, an assurance that their partnership could absorb and transcend a scandalous gown and the animal response it inspired. He half-turned and crooked an elbow to her. "Ready to bring Oldfield's to its knees?" And indeed she'd never been readier for anything in her life.

She did remind him, as the hackney made its way into central London, that they couldn't count on finding a favorable deck the first night. That he must be mindful of the fact that odds needed time and repetition to assert themselves and that even under favorable odds the wrong cards would sometimes come up.

He listened dutifully—or so she must assume, his expressions being lost to her from the opposite seat in the hackney's dark confines—and delivered reminders of his own. Where and how to change her money for counters. The way she was to signal him if she were harassed by any of the establishment's patrons. The location of the side hallway he'd marked out for impromptu conferences, and the place a block away where she'd meet him with the hackney when they'd finished for the night.

"This will be Bury Street," he said when the carriage made a final turn, and shivers of excitement chased down her spine even as the familiar, reliable self-possession descended to cloak her like the scent of her own soap. "I'll be five minutes behind you. I'll settle where I have a view of you. Probably the hazard table. Lydia." Unerringly his hand found hers through the darkness. She felt the stirring of air as he leaned in, caught the bay-rum scent as he lifted her hand and pressed the gloved knuckles to what must be his mouth. "Good luck," he said, and she thought the usual thoughts concerning how a serious gamester knew better than to trust to luck. But she did not, this time, voice them aloud.

*F*IVE HUNDRED pounds in twenty-pound counters. He couldn't hope to pass himself off as an aristocrat in any case, but he might convincingly portray a man newly flush with the proceeds of his commission, and determined to risk it in style.

Will scooped the tokens from the silver bowl and stuffed his pockets. Five minutes ago Lydia must have stood here, trying everyone's patience by purchasing mere ones and fives.

Though perhaps the cashier and the other patrons would be in a mood to indulge her. She would have had her cloak off by the time she'd entered the room.

She was right to dress so, of course. Several other ladies prowled about the room in similar garb, or rather garb of similar intention. No other gown looked quite like hers.

God above, that gown! All over again he felt the electrical frisson, the nerve-sizzling, blood-simmering charge that had raced through him at the sight. Now his brain had had a bit of time to clear and to consider, he could perceive she'd left off some three or four of the usual layers that came between a lady and her gown. At the time he hadn't known how to account for the blunt force of its appeal. Hadn't tried to account, either, nor cared to. That gown had bypassed his brain to address his body directly, and his body had paid it the fervent attention of a treasure-hunter poring over a newly discovered map.

You're here on business. She's depending on you. Time enough for those thoughts later. He clasped his hands behind his back and started a leisurely circuit of the room. Eventually he would come to land at the hazard table, just a bit removed from where Lydia already sat, bidding her scant pound-counters at vingt-et-un. And he would wait for the moment when he could sweep in and use her cleverness to turn his five hundred into more.

$\mathscr{B}$UT AN hour later his nerves were raw from waiting. He was forty pounds down because he couldn't stand apart all night, watching other men play while his own pockets sagged at the seams with counters. People would wonder. So he'd thrown twenty away on the dice, and, after an interval, twenty more. He couldn't afford this. And she, too, must be losing else she would have signaled him in.

Naturally, you couldn't tell the state of her fortunes by looking at her. She was, to all appearances, a good deal more occupied by the would-be Corinthian at her right elbow than by the game. She frequently laughed at things he said, her body twisted toward him like a flower toward an overdressed, fatuous, self-satisfied sun. Twice the cod's-head had to remind her to take her own turn, so caught up was she in marveling over whatever play he'd just made.

Will gritted his teeth and eased a step back, letting another man edge ahead of him in the crowd round the table. He was no idiot. He wouldn't mind her antics if he could have faith that a profit lay waiting on the horizon. But wasn't there some point at which a gambler must say *This is not my night* and walk away before yet more money was lost?

Lydia gave a helpless little laugh—the sound didn't reach him but her attitude was unmistakable—as the banker swept away her wager with his silver rake. She reached out a hand to brush some invisible speck from the Corinthian's coat. The Corinthian puffed himself up like a cockerel on the rut.

Confound it all. Enough. Will stuck his elbow up overhead and stretched that arm with his opposite hand. When she touched her fingers to her lips, to indicate *message received*, he slipped apart from the hazard crowd and made his unhurried way out of the salon.

$\mathcal{S}$HE WAS late. He'd almost made up his mind she'd missed the signal after all when he finally heard slippered footsteps in the main hallway, and put his head round the corner to see her approaching. The underlayer of her purple gown clung in every place imaginable when she moved. The overlayer skimmed and floated, a promise and a shameless tease.

"We have to be patient. I told you." She was speaking before she reached him. Her straight arms ended in fists at her sides. Apparently she'd not had to wonder at the purpose of this conference.

"We're wasting time. I say we ought to quit now and hope for better luck another night." With one hand he caught her elbow and drew her with him, deeper into the darkness of this hallway where perhaps even servants didn't go.

"You know I won't hear any talk of luck." An hour of cards had dissolved the adventurous good nature with which she'd addressed him at her house and in the hackney; she was all rigid determination now.

He sighed, and let go her elbow. "What I know is that I'm out forty pounds, forty pounds wasted at a game I wouldn't ever play but that I cannot just stand about waiting for a signal that might never come. How much have you lost?"

"It's not important. Will." Her hand fumbled at his sleeve, awkward and endearing for the two seconds she took to find a grip. Then less awkward, but still a bit endearing as he felt her concentration, her effort to lend him the confidence she possessed in such abundance. "We knew it might go this way. Remember? This hasn't taken us by surprise."

A broken nose at Gentleman Jackson's wouldn't take a man entirely by surprise either, but that didn't mean he'd be wise to stay in the ring and fight on with blood spouting down his front. "Lydia, you might exhaust your stake without ever seeing a good deck. What will you do then?" She had a hundred pounds in counters, he knew. The idea of her going through that amount in ones and fives, going through so many hands without encountering a situation worth signaling him, had seemed so remote as to warrant no consideration. It didn't seem that way now.

"I'll buy more counters. I brought more money along." She knew no doubt. He ought to be reassured by such unshakeable faith.

But a man could follow unshakeable faith into unequivocal disaster. Ask any soldier of the *Grande Armée* who'd followed Napoleon to Moscow. For that matter ask George Talbot. *I'll get you home to your family. I will not let you die.* God knows his own bold assurances had given him reason enough to mistrust people who didn't doubt.

She moved a step nearer, grip still steady on his arm, the light rose fragrance of her soap infusing his breaths. "Please," she said. "I cannot do this without you."

She knew exactly where his weakness lay, didn't she? He couldn't walk away from a plea for help. Was she using that now, contriving to yank his puppet-strings the same way she was playing that Corinthian at the table? "Lydia." He angled his head to make the shortest path from his mouth to her ear without actually bending, and sent the word out on just enough breath to reach her. "I know I need to trust you, but—"

"You don't need to trust me." Her second hand joined the first, the two of them clasped halfway between his wrist and his elbow. "In fact I don't advise it. But please trust the odds." Her fingers gave a quick squeeze. "If circumstances haven't changed in another hour, we'll consult here again. In the meanwhile, apply yourself to amusements that will keep your counters in your pockets. Have a drink. Find a lady to flirt with. Just be sure you can always see me." Her hands slid down his arm to fold about his hand. His fingers curled in spite of themselves round hers.

The longer they stood here, the more ways she found to seduce him to her will. He drew one more breath. "Very well. I'll drink and flirt. But won't it serve you right if I get into a brawl and go home with someone else."

"That will teach me a lesson indeed." He could hear the shape of her smile. She wiggled her fingers free of his and flattened her two hands with his between for an instant, as though she were patting out a mud pie. Then he heard the shush of her skirts as she spun and left him, striding with adamant purpose back to the gaming salon.

*H*E DIDN'T, however, drink or flirt. Alcohol compromised his quickness; no point in adding *that* impairment to a situation that was likely already to tax his brain. As to the flirting, he'd succeeded in making only one circuit of the room, and ruling out two ladies—both of them already juggling the attentions of several would-be suitors—from the list of contenders before a quick glance at Lydia sent all the rest of his surroundings into a dim haze.

She was talking to the banker, with that same vapid animation he'd witnessed on his every previous glance. But she was leaning forward now, forearms on the table, hands clasped.

The signal. His pulse pelted like hail on a slate rooftop. Finally, the deck had turned and it was time for his part of the scheme.

He made his careless way to the vingt-et-un table, where she glanced up as he pulled out the chair to her left. She smiled. Her glance flicked downward, taking in the ridiculous assemblage of clothing he'd thrown on, and her smile spread like spilled honey, slow and sweet and rich with sensual approbation. When her eyes came to his again they were heavy-lidded, as though she'd been drugged by the mere sight of him.

Yes, he'd known she might play it this way. If her guise was to approach every man as a potential protector, then an indifferent manner with him should have come off as conspicuous. He bowed—not too friendly, not too distant—and took his seat.

Three other men sat to Lydia's right: the Corinthian, to whom she now turned with some remark no doubt calculated to keep him on the string, and beyond him, two older gentlemen who had apparently been proof against her charms. The seating arrangement, of course, would not be accidental. His place at the end, last in every deal, would mean she could incorporate the visible cards of the other players, in addition to her own cards, when she made the mysterious calculations that would drive his wager.

Will took the counters from his pockets and heaped them before him on the table as the first cards came down. Six, eight, three, Lydia's was a four, and he drew an ace. The banker showed nine.

As the first man set out his bet she angled left, facing him with a smile so bewitching it ought to be burned at the stake. "Let me guess." She made a quick survey that took in his person as well as the abundance of counters. One of her hands rose from the table and draped pensively at the ridge of her collarbone. "You've just come out of the Navy and you've got prize money wearing holes in your pockets."

Navy was the pertinent word. Any maritime reference must lead him to *boat*. From boat to *sank*, from sank to *cinq*. Five counters.

She wanted him to bet a hundred pounds on his first card alone. No wading in gradually here.

"Madam, please." The banker's tone of voice suggested he'd had to recall her attention too many times already from the gentlemen about her to the game. "Place your bet."

With her free hand she plucked up one of her pound counters and set it forward, her other hand still at her collarbone performing an idle caress. He could almost hear the drag of her kid-gloved fingertips over her skin.

He could even follow the logic of her strategy in regard to his wager. A ten would bring him twenty-one, and presumably a good quantity of tens remained, to warrant a five-unit bet. "Such a diffident wager from such a forthright lady." He gave her half a smile as he stacked five counters forward of his cards. "I believe in doing a thing boldly if you're to do it at all."

A second card came down before each player. Will lifted the corner. Ten of spades. Good Lord, that was easy.

He flipped his ten faceup and sat back, one elbow atop the back of his chair, his heart going like a runaway wagon down a cobblestoned hill. Of course the banker might still tie him, but at the very least he'd keep his hundred pounds. And he'd made himself popular with the other players at the table. Twenty-one meant the banker must keep drawing in hopes of the tie, and that meant a good chance the fellow would go bust.

The first two gentlemen stuck after their second cards. Lydia and the Corinthian stuck after three. The banker added a six and a queen to his nine, and had to pay every player.

"Do a thing boldly, indeed." What a preposterous figure she made, employing one of the little rakes to sweep in her meager two pounds. "But then I suspect you do all manner of things in that fashion." Neither her face nor her voice betrayed anything beyond the slightly unseemly, slightly desperate attempts to draw him into flirtation. Nevertheless he knew that wrapped up in her tawdry chatter was a private expression of approval and encouragement. She liked the way he played his part.

So, it developed, did he. Well, and why not? What wouldn't he give, after all, to be someone else, someone so complacent in his notions of how the world would dispose itself to oblige him? Perhaps he might have grown into such a fellow, had one or two or fifteen things been different. For tonight, and for as many nights as their scheme persisted, he could at least try on that life, the way he might try on some velvet-trimmed dinner jacket that didn't quite fit and was anyway beyond his means.

Therefore he played the role with gusto, adopting a brooding, fist-to-the-jaw, lower-lip-pushed-out posture between turns and a slight fatalistic flourish of the wrist when he must handle his counters either way.

And with every fresh deal, he caught at Lydia's constant stream of prattle, sifting it through his fingers meticulously as a jewel thief appraising the proceeds of his latest heist.

She addressed herself to the Corinthian: "If I lose five pounds more I vow I shall *quit* this game. You must hold me to that." Quit meant *cease,* and cease meant *six,* and that meant one hundred twenty pounds.

To the banker: "You think to ruin me, don't you? But you see how I hold on, if only by a whisker." Whisker. Cat. *Quatre.* Four counters.

And to him: "You must have my share of luck along with your own." (Luck! A secret jab at him! Numbers overrunning her brain like thistles in a knot garden, and she still had capacity to make a joke that only he and she would apprehend!) "I hope you'll be mindful of that when you see me on the street tomorrow, begging for a crust of bread." Bread. Wheat. *Huit.* God in Heaven, eight counters. One hundred sixty pounds.

But he did as she directed. He handled his cards carelessly, that she might get a look at them and plan how to proceed. He watched for the cues that told him to buy or stick, and measured them against his own understanding. Fifteen against the banker's visible nine; he didn't need to see her touch her right finger to her thumb to know he should buy. Pair of tens against a seven, he'd stick whether or not she fidgeted with her bracelet.

He didn't win every hand. Even with favorable odds he'd sometimes draw an inopportune card or watch the banker get a good one. On those occasions he fancied he could feel her willing him into steadiness, surrounding him with a confidence so solid he almost believed he could lean his weight against it. Not that he needed that, now. Occasional losses notwithstanding, the trend was clearly in his favor. He shrugged at each defeat, and made asinine remarks as to the merits of losing boldly, and waited, always, for her next coded directive.

Devil only knew how much time had passed before she put up both hands to adjust her hair. The quit signal. He'd lost two hands in a row—thankfully on moderate wagers—and she'd apparently decided the composition of the deck was not to her taste.

Half of him wanted to plant himself in that chair and refuse to budge. What rarefied joy it was to work in secret concert with a woman, their shared interest unsuspected by the others at the table, their awareness of each other heightened every moment by the clandestine nature of their bond.

The other half was more than ready to be done. The sooner they both left this table, the sooner they could acknowledge one another, and celebrate together what they'd achieved. He reaped the counters by fistfuls and stashed them in his pockets, and excused himself to go claim a profit of somewhere near a thousand pounds.

ONE THOUSAND, one hundred and sixty-two pounds. Even counting her thirty-eight pounds lost and his forty thrown away at hazard, it was a splendid, splendid beginning.

Lydia slipped from the gaming salon and started down the main hallway. Half an hour more she'd lingered after his exit, flirting with Mr. Keller at her right—a pleasant, innocuous man, Mr. Keller, delighted to flirt and be flattered, but without the means to pursue anything further—and generally making sure no one would have any cause to connect Mr. Blackshear's time at the table with hers.

Oh, but he'd been magnificent, Mr. Blackshear had. She'd feared, after their earlier conference, that he wouldn't have the stomach for it after all. But he'd been a bulwark. He'd been a rock. He'd shrugged off losses of a hundred and two hundred pounds like a stallion twitching its flank to throw off a gnat, and hadn't he looked superb doing it! She would tell him so, in decorous terms. She would praise his resolute poise, and she would joke that he ought to wear that riding coat more often, and perhaps grow his hair to romantic lengths.

Dimmer and dimmer went the light as she moved down the corridor away from the gaming room. By the time she rounded the corner she could scarcely see a thing. She could feel him, though, a warm substantial presence somewhere ahead, and an instant later she felt him beyond any doubt as his hands came out to seize her, and pull her forward into the dark.

He caught her at the waist and lifted her, spinning round with an exuberance that echoed her own. She set her hands on his shoulders, so solid under his coat, and clenched her teeth to forbear laughing aloud. Coins jingled merrily in the reticule that swung from her wrist, and somewhere in his coat-pockets too, a fitting music for this makeshift celebratory dance. Here, unexpectedly, was something new with a man, a chaste congress of body, spirit, and brain, a pleasure she might have dismissed as no worthwhile pleasure at all, had she merely heard it described.

Her skirts twisted round her legs as he spun her, cool and delicious against the few bare inches between stocking-top and chemise, and when he set her on her feet she teetered for a step, hobbled by the skirts that had still to unwind, captive in her own sarcenet snare.

His hands stayed at her waist, steadying. His breaths sounded in the stillness, one breath and two. And of a sudden he crushed her to him: his arm bound her at the waist, his other hand splayed at the back of her neck, and his mouth came down hot and ravenous on hers.

Chapter Twelve

$\mathscr{S}$HOCK UNFURLED from her head to her toes like a sail dropped down from a ship's mast. Her bent arms and the reticule were pinned between their bodies; now she braced her outspread hands on his chest and jerked her head back. "What the devil do you think you're doing?" Had she raised her voice? No. Some dependable corner of her brain stayed mindful of their surroundings, the need for discretion, even as her breaths came shallow from the spinning and the shock.

"One minute." No part of his hold on her slackened. "Sixty seconds." His mouth was so near she could taste the words as he said them. "We'll never refer to it afterward. Nothing will change."

Was that possible? Could a man and a woman give themselves up to passion, even for sixty seconds, and walk away unsinged? Surely things must change.

But maybe she didn't care. His bare hand at the back of her head flexed gently, not like a hand that meant to force her to his will, but like a hand that couldn't get enough of the way she felt.

His breath came warm and ragged against her lips, her

cheeks. A faint flavor of cloves came with it, no doubt from his tooth-powder. He'd cleaned his teeth before setting out tonight. Perhaps with this purpose already in mind.

She might touch her tongue to them, to his clean imperfect clove-scented teeth.

Dear Lord. Of all the factors that could sway a woman into kissing a man. Clearly she was not in her right mind. Drunk on her success at the table, like as not. Their success, rather. She couldn't have done it alone.

Her hands trailed down his chest, over his ribs, to either side of his waist. He shivered once, but didn't otherwise move. He would wait for her word.

"Sixty seconds." She flicked one wrist and her reticule hit the floor. "Make them count."

His mouth closed the distance between them, more patiently this time. His lips brushed over hers and the tiny beard-bristles brushed after, raising gooseflesh all up and down her arms. He was sweet and slow and masterful and he filled up all her perception with the smell of bay rum.

But with only sixty seconds they couldn't afford patience. He had no time to be sweet or slow. She sent a hand up his spine to the very short hairs at the nape of his neck—if only she had time to take off her gloves, and rasp those hairs against her palm!—and when she'd taken a firm hold at the back of his head, she sent her tongue right into his mouth and ran it over his teeth, space between and all.

He made a sound in his throat. Perhaps he wasn't used to bold women. But clearly he didn't mind. He stroked his own fingers down the back of her neck, encouraging her, and a moment later both his hands were at the front of her gown, finding their way under the outer layer to run wild over the purple silk.

Yes. This was exactly what he ought to do. It was right he should read the contours of her corset, and mold her hips, her thighs, with his hands as though she were wet clay. She did feel a bit like wet clay, or warm wax, or some other thing that would take whatever shape he cared to give her. He'd backed her against the wall somehow without her noticing and now she pressed her shoulder blades into that support and swayed and twisted under his touch.

Had it been sixty seconds? Never mind. She found the fastenings that held her overdress together at the bosom and she undid them, deftly, that he might put his hands there too.

Such large hands he had, and so capable. The left one slid over her hip, up her waist, silk bunching before it, and settled, finally, over her breast. His breath roughened in her mouth; he shook that gathered silk free that there might be but one thin layer lying flat over the part of her body he touched; the thinnest possible barrier between his palm and the nipple he'd provoked into ripeness with his kisses and his sculptor's hands.

Thank Heaven—oh, she'd go to Hell for such blasphemy but surely she'd reserved her place there long ago, and at all events thank Heaven she'd cut her chemise down to the top of her corset and left off all her petticoats. Because now she understood the reason for the existence of purple sarcenet. His thumb moved slowly over her nipple, an excruciating tease made doubly excruciating by that cream-smooth knit stuff preventing her from truly knowing his touch; triply excruciating by the way his tongue caressed the curve of her lip, echoing the leisurely strokes of his thumb.

She arched into his touch and he broke off the kiss. She could feel his head angled to watch, though surely he couldn't see anything through the darkness. His right hand came to her left breast and his touch felt . . . wondering, almost worshipful. The touch of a man who'd never put his hands to a woman before, or perhaps the touch of a man who'd come near to dying and meant never to take earthly pleasures for granted again.

That might be true, that last one. That might be his case. She'd think on it later. "Use your mouth," she said now, and her voice was all harshness and need, perfectly fashioned to puncture the illusions of a worshipful man.

But no, he liked that too. He muttered something hot and unintelligible; it ended in low, velvety laughter, and then his mouth was where she wanted it and nothing else mattered in the world.

She pushed herself up on her toes and arched harder, to make this as easy as it could be to him so that he might never, never stop. Because here, in fact, was the reason for sarcenet. She'd been so wrong before. The sweep of his tongue, dragging the fabric to and fro where she was so sensitive. His hands locking her in position, one between her shoulder blades and one at the back of her waist to keep her in thrall to his exquisite torture. His wet mouth dampening the silk, adding sweet complexities to the sensation and meanwhile marking her, staining her, fixing her with a badge visible to any observer, a memento of just what he'd done.

He didn't do *enough*. If he would only grind himself against her, as any decent man could be expected to do, he might finish her off before he had a chance to remember that business of stopping at sixty seconds.

She sent her hands round behind him. Filled her palms and splayed fingers with those particular muscles that would power a man as he drove into a woman, once he was properly persuaded.

He replied with the edges of his teeth, unleashing a riptide of pleasure that nearly buckled her knees. Good.

She knew how to have this conversation. She slipped one hand back round to the front of him, down and down between their bodies, and, oh, good Lord. He'd told the truth.

Well, of course he had. She'd never truly doubted him. But to take his dimensions on faith was one thing. To have the evidence at hand was something else entirely.

She took a grip. Nankeen and man, with his shirttail and a thin layer of linen between. He hissed, a sharp indrawn breath that cost him his hold on her nipple. She could feel his hands and arms go tense. His whole body went tense; she could sense it even in the parts that didn't touch her because the air between them had stilled so.

"Wait." A single hoarse syllable, and her stomach dropped like a partridge shot out of midair. He was remembering all his reasons; the lady in Camden Town and everything else.

She couldn't let him. "Wait for what?" Her hand tightened and stroked up his length. "You're as ready as I've ever felt a man to be."

"I'm not. I don't—" His breath caught and he shuddered as her palm slid back the other way. Say what he would, he wanted this.

Her fingers found the first of his buttons and tipped it through the buttonhole. She would give him what he wanted. She would make him forget. They would be guilty together, throwing off everything either one knew of propriety or obligation to gratify the appetites of a moment, and together they would—

"No." The voice might carry a note of pleading, but the sudden iron grip at her wrist was all command. He put his other hand to the wall and pushed away with a wrenching motion, as though she were some spider who'd snared him in treacherous silk. "No more."

Her hand fell empty at her side. Her skin ached already for the loss of his touch. What had happened to her? A month ago she'd at least had the decency to feel shame during that moment when she'd mistook his sister for a lady he was courting. Tonight she didn't care. She only wanted to possess him, and all the ladies of Camden Town combined would not be enough to stop her.

Only he could do that.

"I'm sorry." His voice shook. He'd leaned against the wall an arm's length away, face to the wallpaper by the sound of his breaths. "I'm sorry, Lydia," he said again. "This isn't what I want."

A candle-flame of sympathy flickered, but she would give it no air. She wasn't that sort. Corruption crawled in her veins, heedless lust fired her every nerve, and countless wadded-up scraps of anger filled the cavity where a woman's warm heart ought to be.

This isn't what I want, he'd said.

As if she hadn't held the evidence in her hand.

I SEE." MISS Slaughter's voice hit the air between them like a sheet of ice, frigid and breakable in equal measures. "My congratulations, then. You counterfeit expertly."

Did she suppose he needed her help to feel wretched? "You know that's not what I mean. I've already admitted I desire you. I just . . ." Confound it, would she even understand? "I want to be better than this. I don't want to be the kind of man who ruts with someone else's woman in the hallway of a gaming hell."

"You'll understand my mistaking you for such a man, I hope." Ice in bitter shards, now. "The part where you had my nipple in your mouth was particularly befuddling."

Befuddling didn't come close. Astounding, staggering, spellbinding, electrifying. As long as he lived he would remember the way she pushed up on her toes to meet him, so sure of what she wanted and so shameless in demanding it.

Bloody hell. Why couldn't he just do this? Why couldn't he take what she wanted to give, and give what she wanted to take, and let pleasure answer for itself?

Because he'd told her he wouldn't. *I'm not another lout looking to make use of you,* he'd said, and she'd begun to trust him. And damn it all, her trust meant something and she needed to know that he knew that. He felt, carefully, for the breeches-button she'd undone and did it back up. "The fault is mine, entirely. I was wrong to begin this, and grievously wrong to let it continue as far as it did. My actions dishonored us both."

"It's not in your power to dishonor me."

Devil take him. Her every lashing-out just made him harder, made him want to take her back in his arms and shape all that fury into searing passion. "You're right, Lydia." Instead he must work to soothe her. "I'm sorry."

"You said that already. In fact you said we wouldn't speak of this at all. I had supposed you a man of your word."

Bitter laughter seized him like a coughing fit: he was helpless to stifle the sound. "That was a resounding error on your part, I'm afraid."

"I'm finished discussing this." Smaller and tighter her voice went, and beneath it, a silken rustle that must be her fastening up the overdress of her gown. "I'm going to go get my cloak."

"Wait." His hand shot out and found her arm, every bit as soft as he remembered. "You can't. You're not . . ." God, could this get any crueler? "I left you unfit to be seen. I'll get the cloak for you."

She twisted from his grasp. "Believe me, Mr. Blackshear, I've survived worse indignities than a damp spot over one nipple." Another rustle and the muffled clink of coins; she'd bent to sweep up her discarded reticule. "Save your pangs of conscience for your graver wrongs."

Her words speared straight through him. She didn't know, of course. There wasn't any way she could. But for a moment, there in the darkness, she sounded like an incarnation of his own tireless self-reproach. Indeed he had such grave wrongs on his conscience as could make her want to scrub raw every place on her body where he'd put his hands.

He didn't say so. She didn't wait for a reply in any case. The purposeful tread of her slippers announced her retreat and he had a glimpse of her silhouette as she reached the faint light of the main corridor and turned left.

He waited the agreed-upon ten minutes, and made his way outside to the agreed-upon meeting place a block away. And it took another ten minutes of waiting, and five more of casting about the neighboring streets in search of her, before he understood she wasn't coming. She'd gone back to Somers Town on her own, and left him behind.

*S*TUPID. *W*EAK. *Gullible. Ineffectual.* Nearly twenty-four hours since the disastrous event, and she hadn't yet found the word harsh enough to describe a woman who tossed away the singular opportunity of her life, and in such craven fashion. *Deficient. Contemptible. Fraudulent.*

"Hell and damnation, Lydia." Edward lay beside her, his bare chest heaving. "I vow you'll be the death of me."

If only it could be the other way round. A woman might destroy her soul by whoring, but for all her most ferocious efforts her body still lingered, with its appetites and its aches and its power to drive her into jaw-dropping folly.

Her knuckles skimmed absently over Edward's near arm. He was damp. She'd worked him to the point of exhaustion, and not once had she permitted herself to close her eyes and imagine other hands. He was her penance and her punishment for having cried, last night, from the minute she got into that hackney to the minute it stopped at her door.

If only he had not kissed her! If he'd set her down from spinning, and stepped away, and asked if she could guess how much money they'd won. Or if she'd stopped him when he'd pressed for sixty seconds: *It's better we don't. Think of how you'd regret it.* She would have gone home warm and fizzing as if she'd downed a glass of champagne on an empty stomach, and she would have recalled the exhilaration of that spinning embrace with pure untainted pleasure. She would have felt full, where now she felt so empty. And their partnership would have remained intact.

"Some men swear by two women in a bed." Edward had more to say. "But I vow you're like two all by yourself."

"You flatter me." Her voice came out lifeless. This inanity was precisely what she deserved.

What had she accomplished in the past two years? Very little, it seemed. Sold herself to a succession of men and learned to despise them. Invited disaster—the pox, prison, an inexorable descent to life on the streets—and met with nothing graver than the unimaginative ill-use any harlot occasionally bore.

She'd sought to eradicate herself and she'd failed to

even wipe out the witless, useless part that wept in a hackney when a man didn't want her.

"I've had to invite that Blackshear fellow to my house party, you know. The one who was at Waterloo." Edward's voice yanked her out of reverie and back into the bed. "Your friend Eliza insisted upon it. Mischief in mind, I suspect." He stretched his arms up overhead and brought his hands back to where he could have a good look at the nails. "It's not a true house party without a bit of that business, eh?"

"That's unseemly. She oughtn't to have asked it of you." Her stomach felt as though it were filling up with lead. "I'm sure Lord Randall wouldn't like it."

"For all we know, Randall's got some intrigue of his own planned. Regardless, she insisted. Only now the gentlemen outnumber the ladies by three or four. I might need to procure a few Cyprians, just to keep it sporting."

Better and better. Maybe she could feign an attack of some illness a week hence and avoid the house party altogether. At the very least she would not bring Jane. The girl could have a week off, and go visit her family. No need to expose her to such sordid things as would surely go on.

She felt for the edge of the sheet, and pulled it up to her collarbone. He wouldn't come, would he? He wasn't sociable with anyone in their set besides that viscount, really. What would he want with a week in Essex among people for whom he didn't care? Disrespectable people, at that. Given to mistresses and scandal. Exactly the sort of people he didn't want to be, if she was to take him at his word.

He wouldn't come. He mustn't. Because for all the trials she'd learned to bear, she might not have it in her to bear seven days under the same roof with Mr. Blackshear.

*   *   *

$\mathcal{W}$ILL LOOKED away from the invitation card, and tossed it back onto his table. It skipped off the stack of mail there and cleared the table's edge to tumble end over end to the floor.

Splendid. He bent to scoop up the bit of malignity, the last mocking punctuation on the mess he'd made of everything, and set it atop a letter from that clerk Grigsby. More mockery. There'd be no need for the man's services if Miss Slaughter never won her two thousand. No need, either, for him to invent some forgotten investment George Talbot had made, because without the capital to entrust to Fuller, there'd be no return with which to benefit Mrs. Talbot.

Abruptly he left the table, reaching the opposite wall in three paces. No escaping one's mistakes in the modest confines of bachelors' lodgings, or probably anywhere else. He turned and leaned against the wall, pushing restless fingers through his hair. A cold wind, yet another cold wind in this dismal pretense at a spring, whistled round the edges of the windows across the room.

She hadn't been at Beecham's last night. He'd gone there, intending to . . . intending to what? Say "I'm sorry" yet again with the expectation that this time she'd be grateful to hear it? Pretend nothing had happened, and ask when she'd be free for another night in the hells? Lure her away from the company, and abandon every dictate of decency to finish what they'd begun?

At all events she hadn't been there. Five days of April gone, and he was near a thousand pounds short of what he needed. He ought to tell Fuller to look for other investors.

But he'd wait. Maybe she'd prove able to put aside her dissatisfaction with him in order to continue in their scheme. He must hope, with all he had, that her heartless determination would come to the fore.

I DID it for you, ninnyhammer." Eliza muttered this behind her fan, leaning in with a dash of jasmine scent. "And perhaps a bit for the gentleman. It's been obvious from the start he's interested, and what other chance is he likely to have?"

"I wish you'd had the goodness to ask me first whether I wanted any such thing." Lydia, too, sank her voice and screened it with a fan. Edward and Lord Randall were guffawing over the play, in particular over that tedious old lady having once again said a word that was not at all the one she meant, and between this, and the usual hubbub of an inattentive audience, the men weren't likely to cast a look over their shoulders to where the ladies sat. Still, she kept an anxious eye on them. "He's never had a *chance*. He can't afford to keep a mistress. And Mr. Roanoke keeps me very well."

"Ha. Keeps you busy in the library, you mean." Eliza's fan fluttered, scarlet plumes dancing in a gleeful taunt. "We barely have your company for an hour together at Beecham's of late." Again, the whiff of jasmine as she leaned close. "Captain Waterloo is despondent. I saw his face, the last time he watched Mr. Roanoke drag you from the ballroom."

"He doesn't *drag* me anywhere." And Captain Waterloo had excellent reasons for despondency. If he hadn't kissed her, if he hadn't laid hands on her and then recovered his conscience, they'd be venturing out to another hell tomorrow night. But he had, and as a result she could scarcely look at him, let alone remain in the same room and risk a conversation. "I'm happy to go with my protector when he wishes."

"Only it strikes me you were happier stealing upstairs to play cards. And in any case, why should you object to the gentleman's presence at Chiswell? It's not as though I've obligated you to an assignation."

That was true. She ought not to mind whether he was there or not. She ought to come up with a reason, credible to Eliza, that would explain why she so clearly *did* mind.

Too late. Eliza's face whipped left as she perceived the hesitation. "Devil take you, Lydia. You *do* have some particular objection. What has he done?"

"Nothing." Another quick look at the gentlemen. "For Heaven's sake try to be discreet. We've ceased to be friendly, that's all."

"Did you quarrel?" A considering tilt of the head. "Where and when would you have had the chance to quarrel? I begin to suspect this has all gone further than any of us knew."

"It doesn't signify. None of it signifies. I doubt he'll even come to the party. It's no concern of mine." Every statement seemed to incriminate her worse than the last, so she clamped her teeth together and gazed down at the stage, where the tedious lady was delighting the easily amused with her substitution of *alligator* for *allegory*.

Eliza could try all the machinations she liked. Even if the gentleman appeared at Chiswell, he wouldn't consent to having his puppet-strings pulled. But that was nothing to the purpose, because he wasn't going to come.

*O*F COURSE you're going to go." Cathcart sawed vigorously at the roast goose. "Who am I to talk to otherwise?"

"May I suggest your wife." Will took a long draught of ale. Not enough ale in the world to make him forget the mistakes that just seemed to compound one upon the last.

"Lady Cathcart? You must be joking. I wouldn't dream of letting her mix with this lot." The viscount speared a slice of the tender meat and transferred it to his plate. "Eat this. You'll turn morose otherwise."

Turn morose? When had he last been anything else?

Eight days now since he'd kissed Miss Slaughter. This was his fourth visit to Beecham's in that span, and he had yet to exchange so much as a glance with her. His hopes of resuscitating their scheme had dwindled like a millpond in an August drought.

Worse than that—he missed her. Missed her teasing and her temper and oh, Lord, though he'd only had it on one occasion he missed the taste of her mouth. And the way her body fit his hands, the way she swerved and twisted to accommodate whatever he did.

But no, that wasn't really worse, was it? The loss of their scheme was far worse. Ale was trifling with his brain.

"What are you to do in London, anyway, with everyone else gone?" Cathcart had served himself with goose, potatoes, and peas, and was now tucking in. "Sit in your rooms, drinking your meals?"

That sounded as reasonable as anything else, at the moment. Nevertheless he put down his ale and took up the knife and fork.

"There'll be chances to win money up in Essex. All the regular cardplayers will be there, and I hear the house has a billiard room with two tables."

"I haven't played billiards in years."

"I'll stake you a six-point lead, then." The viscount reached over to stab a few potatoes and load them onto Will's plate. "I don't believe you've been in my newest carriage yet, have you? Excellently sprung. Just the thing for a journey of forty miles."

He made a noncommittal sound, and forked a bite of goose into his mouth. Were any of Cathcart's arguments compelling? Difficult to determine, through the fog of too much ale.

He chewed and swallowed. He would consider it. He'd leave off drinking for the night, and fill his stomach with victuals, and in two or three hours he'd have the necessary faculties to give the question some thought.

Chapter Thirteen

ℋOW DIFFERENT Chiswell had looked on her first visit! There'd been a harvest in progress then, and weather suitable for walking from the manor to the village to the remotest of the tenant farms. So she'd done each morning, half dazed with the novelty of a gentleman who strove to please his mistress in bed.

Lydia caught the windborne edges of her cloak and tugged them together in front. Two nights she'd been here now, and the guests had come in yesterday. She hadn't wanted him to touch her either night. The rash mauling hunger that had possessed her, that last week in London, had apparently not made the journey to Essex. And so she'd gone to bed ahead of him both nights and feigned deep sleep when he'd crawled in alongside her. Little chance of pulling off that ploy a third night. A man didn't keep a mistress to watch her sleep.

Her stockings were damp above her half-boots. She'd walked the opposite direction from last September's rambles, out across the lawn that fronted the house and into tall grass wet with last night's rain. The hem of her gown, too, hung heavy and waterlogged already. Never mind. When Edward had got up and gone to church she would go back to their room, take off all the wet things, and sleep.

The ground rose up into hills at some distance from the house. Gentle hills and then more rigorous. She went over one and the next, pushing on as though she had some destination, filling her lungs with air that carried a hint of salt from the coast. Farther and farther from the house she forged, into bold terrain with unfamiliar foliage, until she crested one last hill to find the figure of a man on a ridge some fifty feet distant.

She stopped. She would have sworn no one but herself would be up and out at this hour, let alone so far afield.

He stood with his back to her, hatless, one side of his unbuttoned greatcoat furled out on the wind. He faced east. Toward the sea. Toward Belgium and Waterloo, if you kept going. It could have been any tall, dark-haired man at this distance, but it wasn't. She knew.

How impossibly far away he looked. Lonesome and unreachable, not even bothering to shelter from the wind as he gazed out into something she couldn't see. He'd arrived late yesterday afternoon with the viscount and her heart had somersaulted to earth like a fledgling bird pushed from the nest too soon.

Not her heart. Something else. A few of those balled-up remnants of anger that lived in that space now, no doubt.

A stronger wind kicked up. Her cloak slipped her grasp and flew out sideways in imitation of his coat. He turned.

If he felt any surprise at the sight of her, it didn't show from this distance. He only considered her, as though she were but one more feature of the landscape he'd been studying. Then he lifted one hand and mimed tipping a hat.

She'd gone out hatless too, in spite of the clouds that threatened more rain. They made quaint mirror images, both of them underequipped for the weather, their coats whipping out to the south.

They hadn't spoken in eleven days. She gathered her cloak round her again, and went to him.

"You can smell the ocean here," he said when she reached him. No greeting. He pivoted again so they stood side by side, both looking eastward to where the sloping green met a curtain of mist.

"It's not far. In pleasant weather it makes a fine excursion." Did that sound frivolous, to a man who'd crossed the Channel to fight in a war?

He didn't say so. After a moment he angled his head. "Are you not going to church with the others?"

A rush of laughter threatened. "No, Mr. Blackshear." She folded her arms tight across the lapped edges of her cloak. "A harlot is still a harlot on Sundays."

"Other ladies are going, I'm sure. And the gentlemen who keep them." He kept his eyes on what could be seen of the horizon.

"That's their affair. I take it you won't be among them."

He shook his head. "I'm less fit for it than you."

"How do you say so? You're the most upright man of this whole company."

"Forgive me for hearing that as faint praise." A smile caught at his mouth. He didn't turn to share it with her, and in another second the wind chased it away. "A murderer is still a murderer on Sundays." With careful precision he formed the words. "I believe my sin would trump yours if we came to reckoning up our hands."

"Murder! Do you refer to what you did in the war?" One heard of it sometimes, soldiers who never came to terms with taking lives. The reasoning wasn't entirely without logic. Young Frenchmen left grieving mothers and sisters too.

"I do." His jaws moved just enough to let those syllables out. He continued to stare into the distance, but she could feel him waiting for her response.

They were speaking again. By some miracle of the Essex air, they were finding a way to leave every difficult thing behind and just converse.

And she knew what response to make. "You did your duty. You preserved your life and the liberty of England, and I doubt you took any pleasure in killing."

"No pleasure at all." One shoulder flicked, as though he were shaking off a memory.

"There is the difference between us." She set her feet to face him. "Repentance. I contend you'd be more welcome than I in any church."

His head turned and he looked at her with an expression she couldn't read. And all at once there was something she needed to say.

"Will, I'm sorry. For that night at Oldfield's," she added when his look went quizzical.

"Don't." He shook his head, a tight, minimal motion, and his eyes stayed fast to hers. "I'm the one who began it."

"I'm sorry for how I responded, I mean. For my lack of understanding. I fear wounded vanity got the best of me." That wasn't the whole truth. He'd pierced other things besides her pride. But it was truth enough for this moment.

He dropped his glance to the ground between them, and his voice dropped likewise. "You have ample reason to be vain, where I am concerned. But surely you remarked that for yourself."

A fresh gust of wind drove her cloak against the back of her legs and carried her wet hem into contact with his boots. His coat billowed out behind him.

"You know I'd like to be your lover." He spoke just loudly enough to be heard over the flapping of their garments. "I have been, in my dreams, more than once."

"But you can't. I know." Her voice sank to match his.

"But I *won't*." He raised his eyes again. The wind was blowing full into his face but he didn't turn aside. "I want to be something different to you. I want to be someone . . ." His eyes cut past her to some horizon where the rest of his thought must lie. "Someone you can trust. Not only at cards."

Now she was the one to look away, down to where the edge of her windblown skirt still lingered about his boots like an emissary for the rest of her, a scout demonstrating how easily the gap between them might be bridged. "Don't hope for that." She dug her fingers into the folds of her cloak. "It's not something I can give."

He nodded once, still gazing past her. His shoulders rose and fell with a great breath, and she knew beyond any doubt that he was letting go of a hope that had meant much to him. The middle of her chest burned, painfully, as her limbs would if she'd come in from freezing weather to sit too near a fire.

A lock of her hair escaped its pin and rode out on the wind, one more insubordinate part of her reaching for him. She put up a hand to tuck it back, but his hand got there first.

Carefully, he set the lock behind her ear, smoothing it in a futile attempt to resist the wind. His solemn eyes traveled from her hair to her face. "You ought to go back to the house. Your hem is soaked and you haven't any hat."

He hadn't asked why she couldn't trust him. He'd accepted her edict so readily, with such resignation, as though there were really nothing extraordinary in her saying so.

And suddenly she needed him to know. "Will you walk with me?" Her hand closed over his and the lock of hair whipped free again. "I have a story I'd like to tell."

Swift comprehension kindled in his eyes. He bowed, and slipped his hand free to offer her his elbow.

She shook her head. Proximity would make some parts of this too difficult to voice. She caught up her skirts and started down the hill, and he fell in beside her.

"This isn't a story I've told before. It's sordid, I'll warn you now. But it will help explain why I don't have it in me to trust you."

"You needn't explain. I'm not expecting—"

"Mr. Blackshear." Her pulse was pounding in her ears. "I've resolved to tell you this. Do not give me the smallest opportunity to turn coward and run from that resolve."

He inclined his head. She saw it sidelong. His hands went deep in his greatcoat pockets and he walked on, waiting for her to speak.

One big breath. "In short, I trusted a gentleman once and paid a steep price. My subsequent experiences with gentlemen have been . . ." But he could guess what those experiences had been. "I suppose trust is like a muscle that wastes away for lack of use."

No answer for a minute besides the woolen rustle of his clothing and the squeak of his boot heels on the wet grass. "Did he seduce you, the man you trusted?" he then said.

"No more than I seduced him." To put all the blame on Arthur's side would put all the mastery there as well. It hadn't been like that. "We were in love, I suppose. He was a neighbor, of family somewhat better than mine, though somewhat less well off."

"He hadn't the liberty to marry for love."

"He said he would make his own liberty. I think he believed he would. At all events we entered into a secret engagement, but his promises—but his love, I suppose— proved insufficiently stalwart in the face of his parents' disapproval."

One sideways glance at his dark undissembling eyes told her exactly what impression he'd formed of Arthur. He was all but biting his tongue to keep from voicing it.

The ground sloped upward again and she pushed her stride longer. She would go over the next part quickly, lightly, like one of those insects who skated across water without ever breaking the surface to drown. "When I discovered myself to be in a difficult condition I wrote to him and received my letter back, its seal unbroken. I've heard reports he married a lady with thirty thousand pounds."

"Wait." He sounded half strangled. He'd halted ten feet back and he stood there now, downhill from her, face tilted to stare as he might at some grisly apparition. "I thought you couldn't . . ." He was blushing. She would concentrate on that novelty, that she might not linger on other thoughts.

Her hands let go her cloak edges and her arms fell straight at her sides. Facts, plain and unadorned, one after the next. That was the way to get through this. "I was with child for several months. Then I bled, and I had a fever, and I nearly died. And since then I've never conceived again, nor even . . ." Of a sudden she needed to take a breath. She twisted so as not to face him, and sucked in chilly air. "It's made me convenient, you know. At the brothel I could entertain men every day of every month, and there was no risk I would ever . . ." But that was obvious. She didn't need to say it. "I don't delude myself Mr. Roanoke would ever have engaged me without that advantage. I wonder if we might start walking again."

Two or three forceful strides brought him up the slope and he fell in at her side. "Did he know? Your young man?" He sounded ready to slap a glove in Arthur's face. "Did he hear of your illness?"

"I assume so. I think most of the neighborhood did."

She'd begun this story too soon, she could now see. They had a long walk ahead of them and he might wish to fill it with such questions. "He didn't come beg my forgiveness on bended knee, if that's where your questions tend. By then I didn't hope for it. I ceased to love him with remarkable speed."

He didn't answer at first. In the lull she heard the steady march of his Hessians, felt the way he weighed what she'd told him. "Were your parents still living then?"

"Indeed." Abruptly she stooped to pluck a sodden wildflower from out of the grass. Maybe she wouldn't say any more than that. Or no, she might say just a bit. "No one would have blamed them if they'd turned me out of the house. But they never did, though I know I shamed them terribly." She tore a petal from the flower and threw it away.

"That must have made the loss of them doubly difficult." He spoke like a doctor, tranquil and reassuring as he prodded at her broken places. Her broken places hurt like fire all the same.

"It should have been difficult in any case. No other family would take me in, and the cousin who inherited claimed that my portion had all been spent on doctor's bills. I was penniless and disconsolate. You can see, I trust, how such a woman ends in an establishment like Mrs. Parrish's." She let the flower fall. "I believe that concludes my tale. I'd be obliged if you didn't repeat any of it to others."

"Of course. You honor me with your confidence."

He must know without her saying so that she'd left herself raw from unburdening, because he didn't ask any more questions. What a singular man he was, too principled for careless pleasure in a gaming-hell hallway, but drawing her into such delicate intimacy as no lady in Camden Town could possibly approve, if she knew of it.

Maybe it's not what you think. His understanding with that lady. Maybe it was some bargain of convenience that left both free to love elsewhere. Maybe it was . . . some poor but respectable aunt for whom he'd taken responsibility.

Nothing to the purpose. He would not be her lover. How many times did he have to say so, for her to grasp the fact?

They parted ways at some distance from the house, for discretion's sake. And when she crawled into bed a short time later, finally free of her damp gown and stockings, her thoughts did not dwell on the things she'd told him or other maudlin details of her past. Neither did she indulge in recollections of his graceful, tactful attention. Instead she fell asleep on a memory of the picture he'd made when she'd come upon him, poised on that ridge with his coat carried by the wind, a desolate figure looking out toward the vast indiscernible sea.

$\mathcal{B}$Y THE time he took up a place along the wall in the billiard room that night, he thought he might really run mad. Not one word had he exchanged with Lydia since they'd come to the end of their walk. She'd spent the day in Roanoke's room, or in retirement with the other ladies, or too far away from him at the dinner and supper tables. While he'd spent the day seething with the wrath he'd swallowed when she'd told him her story, not one bit of it given voice because he'd known she wouldn't welcome that.

Lord above, what the world did to people. What people did to each other. He should like to hunt down that spineless cad who'd abandoned her and thrash him within an inch of his life. And then he'd find every swiving bastard who'd despoiled her, who'd reduced her to a convenient barren womb, and he'd darken their day-lights, one by one.

Will flexed his fingers, fitting his hands together and stretching his arms before him, palms out. One swiving bastard, at least, was within reach. Roanoke held court at one of the room's two tables, hitting hazard after can-non after hazard with an irksome unnecessary flourish, and also an irksome degree of skill. He wouldn't look near so smug with half his teeth knocked out.

But what good would that do her? Prince Square-jaw was but a minor pestilence in a life of relentless calamity. Even if he should be brought to repent, and apologize for how he'd misprized her, and perhaps even settle some amount of money on her as would guarantee her independence, so many wrongs would remain unrighted. Every man who'd ever touched her could make recom-pense and it would not bring back her parents, or her brother, or the possibility of motherhood, or the hope and faith with which she must once have approached her life.

"Back for more punishment, are you?" Lord Cathcart slouched into place at his left. "I should have thought you'd be consoling yourself with a woman tonight. Our host laid in a few spares, you know."

It was true. Alongside the by-now-familiar faces of the assorted mistresses he'd remarked several new ones, la-dies hired for the purpose of amusing the un-mistressed male guests. He'd exchanged pleasantries with one for a full minute in the library last night before grasping that something was on offer.

"If I gave up that easily I shouldn't have come back alive from the Continent. Last night's games were prac-tice, merely. Tonight you shall see what I can do." Of women he said nothing. He was near to climbing the walls of this room on account of a woman; near to boil-ing over with outrage at what she'd borne and fury at his utter powerlessness to remedy any of it. What he wanted was distraction, and not in any feminine form.

"I'll see, to be sure." The viscount rubbed his hands before him. "Five pounds says my first ball lands nearer the cushion than yours."

Ten minutes later they had a table, and Will had something immediate on which to fix his thoughts. Billiards rewarded practice: he could see at once he'd improved since those few rusty games last night. Cathcart won the five-pound bet, but Will went on to win the game.

There was an art to it, or perhaps a science, or perhaps both. Yes, art, without question, in the gleam of the ivory balls, the neat thrust of the cue arm, the clack of one ball against another or the muffled carom off a cushion. And science, to be sure, in the invisible lines a player sketched from cue ball to red ball, cue ball to cushion, red ball to pocket, cue ball to opponent's ball until an imaginary spiderweb of lines and angles overlaid all six by twelve feet of baize.

She would enjoy that aspect. Did she ever play billiards? Yes, here was a better, calmer way to think of her. Doubtless she'd be one of those players who studied a table and saw possibilities, not just for the immediate lie of the balls but even four or five shots into the future.

Now they were speaking again, he might try whether he could talk her into a game some quiet afternoon when the tables were free. If she'd never played before he could show her how to hold the cue, his arms carefully circling her from behind, his body held a conscientious inch away from hers.

"Fine shot, there." He glanced up to see Roanoke watching from the wall, his coat put off and a glass of rum in one hand. He and Cathcart were into their third game—rather he'd just won their third game by sinking the red ball in the middle right pocket, the viscount's cue ball in the top-side right, and his own off the cushion into the middle left, ten points with one stroke of the cue. A fine shot indeed, by any measure.

"Lucky shot, you mean to say." Cathcart had lit his pipe and now spoke round its stem. "Any bacon-brain can have a game or two where the balls line up in his favor. You ought to have seen him last night."

"Last night was practice, I told you." He moved round to the left side to fish the ball out of that pocket. "I hadn't played in a while. I needed to get back my touch."

"It's all in the touch, to be sure." Roanoke stood directly in his field of view now. His eyes narrowed slightly, as though taking Will's measure at the table. A well-launched cue ball would crack him in the nose. Get the carom right and it would land in the glass of rum. Three points for that. "Had some experience playing, have you?"

"A bit." The man's voice stirred up every rash, heedless impulse in him. *Had some experience playing with your woman just the other week. You can ask her about my touch.* He bit his tongue and rolled the ball down the table to the baulk cushion. The viscount's ball came rolling alongside. "I'd left it off the past few years."

"And for my part, more than a bit." Cathcart came round to the baulk end of the table, rotating his right wrist and flexing all the fingers in unhurried fashion. "We used to play at school and I, at least, kept it up."

"We ought to have a round, then." Arrogant coxcomb wouldn't know his company was unwelcome if the fact was spelled out before him in letters of fire. He gave a nod as though it had all been decided. "I'll play the winner of this match."

"Are you prepared to wager?" The rash impulses were coalescing into one whirlpool of reckless intent. "His Lordship's been lining my pockets handsomely. I should need some inducement to play anyone else."

"You need to win this match before you go setting

conditions for the next." The viscount frowned at his cue ball as he leaned forward and drew back his right elbow. In fact they hadn't wagered at all since that five pounds on the first shot, but he made no comment on the fact. He was game for whatever contrivance Will had in mind.

"Glad to hear it. The more you win from him, the more you can lose to me." Roanoke lifted his glass again.

That's right, souse yourself stupid. Get your hands and your eyes speaking two different languages. That will suit me just fine.

Cathcart prodded his cue ball down the table to two inches shy of the cushion. He'd got it within an inch on all three of their previous games. He didn't speak or look up but the message was clear: this game, and the pleasure of playing Prince Square-jaw, were Will's for the taking.

They kept it close. By aiming for flashy shots they assured frequent misses and frequent swapping of turns, which gave a man ample opportunity to sort out the question of just what he thought he was doing.

What he *was* doing, rather. Thought played little part. Anger had hold of the reins, and goading it onward was an overwhelming ache, a yearning to just seize her with both hands and pull her out of her grim circumstances, if only for a night.

His nerve-endings all sizzled like drops of water flicked on a hot grate. How much could he persuade the man to risk? What would he have to risk on his own side? Ought he to start with a modest wager and a loss, and work his way from there?

The final shot was a gift. Cathcart took out his pipe and swore when his ball rebounded off the top-side cushion to lie an inch apart from the red ball, for all the world as though he hadn't used every bit of his skill to effect the arrangement.

Will sank the pair, red to the top-side right pocket and white to the left, with one clean shot down the middle. Three points for the winning hazard on red, two for the winning hazard on white, and two more for the cannon. "That's fifty more you owe me," he said, just in case Roanoke had supposed they'd be playing for half-crowns.

"I'll take it out of what you'll lose to me tomorrow at piquet." The viscount tossed his cue to Square-jaw, who grabbed it one-handed—perfectly adequate reflexes—and set to wiping it with the opposite shirtsleeve while simultaneously balancing his drink in that hand.

Will laid his own cue on the table and turned away to take off his coat. One button, two buttons, three buttons. It wasn't decided yet, what he would do. Nothing wrong with a fair cash wager. Lord knows he could use fifty pounds.

The soft thunk of ivory on baize. Someone was setting up the cue balls. "What stakes do you like?" said Roanoke, and the mere sound of the man's voice decided him after all. No starting modest. No fifty pounds.

He slid out of his coat and let it fall on the nearest chair, turning to fix the other man with a considering look. "Let's make it interesting." He hefted his cue and balanced it between both hands. "What do you say to putting up your mistress?"

Three or four colors of surprise chased across the man's countenance before he muscled his features into aplomb. He tipped his head back a bit, giving him a shrewd, superior aspect. "Fancy Lydia, do you?" He'd paused in wiping his cue, but now he resumed that action. "None of the pullets I hired in are to your taste?"

Cathcart, who'd come round to put the cue balls in place, maintained an eloquent silence.

"They're entirely agreeable." He ran an idle finger over the tip of his cue. "Only I expect I should enjoy a lady more if I won her than if I plucked her up like a cake off a footman's tray."

"And a choice bit of cake she is, I assure you. Don't expect me to put her up cheap." Fool couldn't resist the sensation of being envied. Even if he meant to ultimately refuse, he was going to play this out as long as he could. Already he was raising his voice a bit, that the half-dozen men round the other table might be privy to this drama.

Well, that was to Will's benefit too. Square-jaw would find it difficult to back down from the bargain in front of witnesses. "Undoubtedly a permanent arrangement would be beyond my means. I had a single night in mind. What would be a reasonable wager on my side?"

"You tell me." He had the whole room's attention now, and he knew it. "She's got tits the size of plum puddings, she'll rake your back like a wildcat, and she can suck a man into next week. What's a night of that worth to you?" He drained the rest of his rum and set the glass down hard on the table's cushion.

"Plum pudding. Who wouldn't be tempted by that?" The viscount sent this mild remark into the silence that vibrated between the two men. He'd taken one step this way as well. He didn't look at Will, or raise a hand, but he'd clearly positioned himself to stop his friend doing anything idiotic.

Will's hands clutched tight on his cue. Cathcart could block some things. Not all. One elbow brought up, one fist jerked down, a lunge on one leg and Roanoke would have the butt end of his cue across the face. Teeth flying like wheat-kernels out of a mill chute. Blood spouting down and spreading like contagion on the crisp white of his cravat. *Let that remind you of what's due to a lady.*

He wasn't going to do that. He was going to win her away. His hand relaxed its grip and he tapped the cue against his palm. "Two hundred. It happens I'm fond of pudding."

It was a ridiculous amount of money. If he hadn't already been aware of the fact, he certainly should have learned it from the reactions of the men listening.

"Three hundred." Square-jaw's eyes had gone glittery with greed.

"Two-fifty." More astonishment from the audience, and a jocose remark or two questioning his sanity.

"Two-fifty it is." Roanoke caught up his cue, grinning, and came to the bottom of the table to take his first shot.

"Good God, man, there's girls can be had for a guinea will do all those same things." A dandy in a purple velvet waistcoat made this appeal to reason.

"Doesn't matter." Will rolled one shoulder to loosen it. "I'm not going to lose."

And he didn't. He needed to win, so he won. Now and again life really was that simple. Every violent impulse channeled itself into the next smooth stroke of his cue. Cue ball off the red ball. Red ball in the pocket. Cue ball off the cushion and all the way into baulk, out of Roanoke's reach. No flourish and no gloating, just quiet, lethal accuracy.

When he stroked his final shot he turned and handed off his stick without even waiting to see the balls drop in. "You may send her as soon as you like. Do you remember which room you put me in, or shall I provide directions?" He reached for his coat.

_D_o you know the one called Barbara?" Eliza leaned forward in her armchair, elbows on the arms and fingers laced between. "I spoke to her this afternoon. She said they had a conversation in the library last night, but when it came to the point, he excused himself and went away."

"Is that so very wonderful? Perhaps he's courting someone and doesn't want to do anything unseemly." Lydia smoothed her skirts, carefully avoiding Eliza's eyes.

"Then I question his decision to come to this house party at all. What young lady would like to hear that her suitor was . . ." Maria's voice trailed off. Lydia glanced up to find her twisted to face the door, a single line of disapproval wrought into her brow.

She turned. There stood Edward, his coat over one arm and his eyes roving round the ladies' sitting room. His gaze connected with hers, and held. He cleared his throat. "Lydia." He shifted his coat to the other arm. "Might I have a word with you?"

Chapter Fourteen

WILL STOOD at the fireplace, facing the open door, perfectly still but for the restless toes tapping in one boot. From the moment he'd left the billiard room, a notion had been creeping over him—like a great double handful of snow plunked atop his head and left to melt and trickle down his skin—that he might after all have made a mistake.

At least it's not the worst mistake of your life. His mouth twitched, grim laughter surging up from some mutinous place inside him and nearly making its way out. Devil take honorable intentions. Would he never learn his lesson? He tried to do good, and he only made an infamous farce of everything.

Footsteps sounded in the hallway—too many footsteps—and a memory flared through his muscles before his brain could lock it down. That first night at Beecham's, his refuge in the library disturbed by approaching footsteps, one set heavy and one set light. She hadn't come on her own, then. That might not augur well.

Indeed it did not. When she arrived in the doorway it was with Roanoke at her side, gripping on to her elbow as though to prevent her dashing away. She wore only nightclothes and a dressing gown, with her half boots clutched in one hand and a pile of what must be tomorrow's clothing pinned against her chest by the opposite arm. Her hair hung down her back in plaits.

Hell. He hadn't known she'd be paraded through the corridors half-undressed. She stood rigid as a bedpost and stared straight ahead, her eyes blank as he'd ever seen them.

"Well, I've delivered her." Square-jaw's face, too, was impossible to read. "More than that I cannot guarantee." Indeed his mistress's reluctance rolled off her like mist off a moor. Even a man as thick as Roanoke couldn't fail to perceive it.

"Very good." Will gave a slight nod but stayed where he was. "I shall manage the rest."

"Manage as best you can." He propelled Miss Slaughter a few steps farther over the threshold. "Only don't send her back to me if she doesn't please you. I've made other arrangements for that place in my bed tonight."

Will's heart sank like a boot heel in muck. The lout must have engaged one of the hired ladies. Curse his lack of foresight: the possibility had not occurred to him, and certainly the idea that the man might wish to announce it in Miss Slaughter's presence never had.

She stood precisely where he'd pushed her, and made no response at all. She looked the way she would surely look if she should ever be pilloried in a public square: neither shamed nor defiant, but willfully absent, rolling all her sensibilities smaller and smaller until she need feel nothing at all. Any crowd pelting her with rotten fruit would be pelting a mere empty shell.

"Close the door on your way out, if you please." He didn't spare Roanoke another glance.

The door clicked shut and Miss Slaughter stirred to life, crossing briskly to the window seat where she dropped her half boots and clothing. "Had a change of heart, have we?" Her voice could curdle milk.

"I'm so sorry, Lydia." He advanced only a step or two; to go to her felt presumptuous. "Believe me, I had no idea of spurring him to such a coarse betrayal."

"I'm not naïve enough to suppose it's the first." She kept her straight back to him. "I don't know what he promised you, but I do not consider myself bound by that promise. He had no right to offer me up."

"He didn't. It was I who proposed the wager."

She half-turned, showing her face in profile. A muscle seized in her cheek. "Then what the devil was all that nonsense this morning? Is this your way of courting a lady's trust? Or did you abandon that plan and decide to settle for a quick tumble after all?"

"Can you really think me capable of that?" He went a few steps nearer the window, to be in her field of vision. "Do you believe *that* is the response I would make to the things you told me this morning?"

"I don't know *what* I'm to think!" She turned her face to the window again. "I'm in your bedroom for the night because of a wager of your own making. Tell me how I ought to construe that."

He rested a hand on the nearby armchair's high back, and raked the other hand through his hair. "I lost my head at the table. I confess it." Lord, but he was an idiot. "I wanted to goad your protector and I wanted . . . I wanted to free you from your obligation to him, just for a night. Now that I know the things you've borne, I couldn't help—"

"I'm not some bedraggled kitten for you to rescue from a ditch." Her anger came cleanly as arrows from a bow, no energy wasted. "I chose to be obligated to Mr. Roanoke. I *enjoy* my transactions with him. And I don't go about staggering under the weight of those things I told you today. I've learned to keep them out of my thoughts."

Her words resonated as though he were all made up of harpstrings inside. Didn't he know exactly what it was, to gain that particular mastery over one's thoughts.

He could tell her. *I understand. I have things that don't bear thinking of, too.* But he hadn't brought her here to be his confessor. She had burdens enough.

He pushed away from the chair and crossed to a pier glass in the room's corner. "Be that as it may, you have the night off from your duties. You needn't entertain me in any way." He started on his coat buttons. "Needn't even converse with me, if you'd rather not."

"That's very noble of you, to give me a choice in the matter." Caustic. If he touched her she would probably burn his skin, like lye. "Ought I to offer myself in gratitude?"

He sighed, slipping out of his coat. Clearly he oughtn't to have wagered for her. She'd developed certain views of men who treated her as a commodity, and she wasn't able to make an exception for him. "I don't think there's anything to be gained by our speaking further. The bed is yours." He flicked his coat up over one shoulder and pivoted. "I shall sleep on the floor. I'll go to the dressing room now, unless you'd like to put your clothes away first."

She didn't. When some ten minutes later he returned in nightshirt and dressing gown she stood in the same place he'd left her, still facing the window. Perhaps she meant to defy him by standing there all night—but no, as soon as he was far enough clear of the door that she needn't sidle by him, she picked up her clothing and retired to the dressing room. And when he came near to the bed he saw a pillow and the heaviest of the blankets had been put down on the carpet alongside.

A peace offering, maybe. Or maybe a proud partial

rejection of his charity. Things would never, never, never be simple with her.

He left one candle burning that she might find her way back, and he rolled onto his side, scrupulously facing away, when the floor creaked with her footsteps. The candlelight went out with a puff of her breath. The mattress sighed. The sheets and blankets rustled.

And there they were. The woman he wanted above all others in his bed, and he a million miles away on the floor. Confound the perversity of things.

He rolled onto his other side, and pulled the one blanket up to his ears. Nothing to do now but wait for morning.

_H_E'D LEARNED, in the army, to recognize the sounds of a nightmare. Her first one came just after he'd slipped into sleep.

Will sat up, then rose to his knees. Damnably tall bed. She hadn't pulled the bedcurtains, and her terrible closed-mouth cries told him exactly where to find her. His hand was on her shoulder before he'd stopped to think of whether there might be some more proper way to do this with a lady. "Lydia." He shook her gently. "Lydia." He found her other shoulder and shook with both hands.

She came awake with an awful gasp, sitting straight up and nearly knocking him in the face. Her hands scrabbled at his as though she believed she were being overrun by great spiders.

"Lydia." He took a tighter grip. "Nothing's the matter. It was only a nightmare."

"I don't know where I am." The panic in her voice was like a bayonet plunged straight into his conscience.

"You're at Chiswell. Mr. Roanoke's house. But in Mr. Blackshear's room." He needed a second to gather the next words, and her rapid breathing filled the silence. "There was a wager. Do you remember?"

She breathed. "I . . ." He could feel the force of effort with which she mastered herself. "Yes. I remember." Somehow her hands had ended up on his wrists, clamped tight as if he were all that stood between her and drowning. She loosened her grip now, and let her hands fall away. "I woke you. I'm sorry."

"I'm the one sorry." He found her forehead with the knuckles of one hand. Damp. "It's disconcerting to wake in a strange place. I oughtn't to have brought you here."

"Yes. Well." She pulled away from him and lay back down. "You're paying now, aren't you?" Thank God for her pertness: it was just the salve his bayoneted conscience required.

"I suppose I am at that." He sank to the floor again and waited for her breathing to lengthen.

But scarcely had he dropped back into slumber, or so it seemed, when the same desperate sounds started up again. Lord above, he'd thought he'd left nights like this behind him when he'd sold out. He hauled himself to his knees and got his arm across her to stop her springing up.

"It's Mr. Blackshear," he said this time as soon as she woke. "You're in my room. I gave you my bed. You're safe. I woke you because you're having a nightmare."

Her chest heaved under his arm, but she didn't scrabble at him this time. "I'm sorry," she said again as soon as she'd come to herself.

"Don't be." He could feel the way she grew calmer. The reassurance he gave, and she took. "Is this common for you?"

"Sometimes." Embarrassment muted the word. "I often sleep in daylight."

"I see." He let his hand go to her forehead again, and pushed back a few damp strands of hair. "Would you like me to light the candles? I could sit up with you. I might find some cards."

"No. Thank you. I'll be fine. Thank you."

He might have argued with a single *thank you*, but two added up to a dismissal. He withdrew and rolled himself up in his blanket.

A pack mule on a three-day march could not be so bone-weary as he was. Still, he didn't go to sleep. And when the third nightmare started he climbed right into the bed and folded her in one arm. "It's Will," he said, near her ear. "You're in my room. Nothing can hurt you here. Go back to sleep."

She woke, just barely. The twitching and the thwarted cries stopped. Her breaths sounded, shallow at first and then deeper, slower, as her body went limp in his arm. Against his chest. Lord only knew where she thought she was, or with whom. It didn't matter. He wanted nothing in the world but this: to be someone's balm, to have the power of comforting, to know he kept her safe from whatever terrors haunted her sleep.

Such peculiar creatures, human beings. He had thought it was only men who managed their torments so, cramming them into some closet at the back of the brain from which they poured forth to run rampant at night. He would think more on it in the morning. Perhaps they'd discuss it then. He was so tired.

He didn't go back to the floor. He slept when she did, and he woke when she needed him to wake, and again and again he reminded her of the same few facts. Chiswell. Will Blackshear. It was a nightmare. You're safe. By the time the sun was rising some bit of her mind had retained enough that he need only tighten his arm at the first stirrings and murmur the single word *safe*. Then she'd sigh, and slacken, and be at peace. And so would he.

* * *

*S*HE WOKE in a bed that was not her own. That was the first odd thing. The linens felt different and sunlight came in at the wrong angle. If she were to open her eyes she would see strange wallpaper. She held still, and kept her eyes shut.

The second odd thing was the weight of an arm laid across her. She lay on her side. The arm indicated someone was lying behind her, and for all the times she'd had a man in her bed, she did not sleep or wake up with one there. Though this wasn't, as had already been established, her bed. Things must have gone awry in consequence.

The third odd thing . . . Oh, the third odd thing. She pressed her lips together and drew in as deep a breath as she could, to fill all her perception with the third odd thing. Her brain clamored to name it and to declare, like a gossip, what it meant, to whom it belonged, but she would not make room in her perception for that. There would be only the scent, during these seconds she'd come up out of the ocean of sleep. She would fill her lungs—one more deep breath—and submerge herself again, beyond the reach of whatever all this meant.

"You're awake." His voice was soft but clear. Its tone suggested he himself had been awake for some time. The words vibrated in his chest, which touched her back.

"I'm so tired." She let her eyes open part of the way. There was a hand. He had his right arm about her middle, his left laid over the pillow above her head. That couldn't be comfortable. "Do you know the time?"

"Past noon, I think. My watch is in the dressing room." His ribcage pressed and receded with a breath. "You slept poorly."

"So did you, I fear." She sounded shy. Like a bride who'd gone to her wedding bed a virgin, fumbling for things to say to her husband on the morning after. Not like herself.

"You're wrong." He might have been waking up after a wedding night himself, to judge by the warm satisfaction in his voice. "I didn't sleep as long as I might like, nor as deeply. But I can't remember when I slept so well."

There was an erection. Ordinarily she would have noticed that first out of everything. Her whole body had been gathered in against his, with only the cotton of her nightgown and his nightshirt, two modest layers, between them. With his arousal between them as well. It pressed hard and redoubtable against her. She wouldn't speak of it. "How long have you been awake?"

"A while. I don't know. I've been thinking."

Thinking. Why on earth would he want to do something like that? When he might have just lain here, balanced at some thin height from where he could tip either into sleep or to passion?

"There will be talk when we rejoin the company, I expect." One of his feet stirred and the coarse hairs on his shin tickled over her calf. "There will be questions."

Questions? But surely no one in the company would have any doubt as to what—Ah. "Impertinent questions, you mean, concerning particulars."

"Perhaps not among the ladies. But I assure you the gentlemen will have questions for me."

"Ladies ask those questions too. Some ladies. Not precisely the same questions, I suppose." She held her body still, to avoid disturbing the erection. "I'll tell them whatever you like."

"That's exactly the offer I'd thought to make you." His words came out on the ghost of a laugh. "Left to my own devices I'd refuse to speak of it at all. But it occurs to me it may benefit you with Mr. Roanoke to have it known nothing happened."

"I expect it would have benefited me more with Mr. Roanoke to spend the night in his room instead of yours. Did that not occur to you?"

"Of course." Somewhere under the covers his right hand moved, lifting from the mattress as he stretched that arm. "But to let you go with him last night was beyond my power. To tell the company I slept on the floor is not." The arm settled over her again.

Beyond his power, indeed. How was a lady to make sense of so many conflicting messages? The gentle patience with which he'd tended to her in the night. The lover-like clasp to which she'd awakened. His arousal, and his obstinate refusal to put it to use. "How do you propose to explain sleeping on the floor? It will sound a very odd thing to do with a woman for whom you gambled."

"Easily enough. You made it clear you didn't desire me, and I don't force. Any man who objects to that explanation deserves a black eye."

She closed her eyes. She'd been very rude to him last night. *Ought I to offer myself in gratitude?* And he'd only wished, as always, to be decent.

"Lydia." This near, his breath and his body told her of his every small change in mood. He'd gone grave. "You'd tell me, wouldn't you, if you believed yourself to be in any real danger from him?"

There he went, trying to rescue her again. "He doesn't beat me. I told you that already. And he agreed to the wager. He can blame no one but himself for its outcome." But of course that wasn't true. If he preferred to blame her he would do so, unhindered by the claims of logic. Her stomach contracted, faintly. "I wonder if we oughtn't to get up. The later we appear, the more time we give the others for scandalous conjecture."

"Of course." His arm tightened on her, infinitesimally. "I'll go first, and send for a maid to help you." He lay behind her a moment longer, arm over her middle, breath at the back of her head, erection still in force. Then he rolled away, taking all that and the bay-rum scent with him, and forsook her company to go wash and dress.

WILL PAUSED in the breakfast-room doorway to gird himself. He would do this if it killed him. And if Square-jaw made any trouble for his mistress, he'd kill *him*. He crossed to the sideboard where Roanoke stood.

The man glanced up, perceived him, and, through an impulse he no doubt would have preferred to rein in, sent a quick, intent look about the room.

"She's not here." He took a plate. "When I left she hadn't risen yet."

"Quite worn out, is she?" There was something grotesque in the attempt at jocular indifference. For all his effort, he couldn't hide the fact that he truly didn't want his mistress enjoying herself with another man.

Will knew an instant of ferocious temptation. *Indeed I could only persuade her to let me leave the bed by promising to return with my stamina renewed.* But he'd been resisting temptation since the moment of waking, and he could resist this one too. For her sake. "Worn out?—not by me, more's the pity. She wasn't inclined to oblige me, and I wasn't inclined to press the matter." Plum cake. That was probably decent. He took a slice. "I prefer my women willing. I left her alone."

"Really." Lord, didn't that pluck the blackguard right up. "Unfortunate it didn't come out the way you imagined, but I did warn you there were no guarantees. I hope you don't seek some sort of restitution from me."

"Nothing of the kind. I did wish to ask you, though, whether she's frequently troubled by nightmares."

"Not at all, in my experience." Roanoke applied himself to pouring a cup of chocolate. "Was she so troubled last night?"

Interesting. He'd never seen one of her nightmares. *I often sleep in daylight,* she'd said. Perhaps she left the bed after her protector had gone to sleep, and him none the wiser.

She hadn't left *his* bed. She'd stayed even after he rose.

"Indeed she slept but little. I suppose she was distraught at being parted from you, or something of that nature." Like casting up a stomachful of rocks, to say those words.

"Very likely." Roanoke helped himself to rolls and butter with the cool satisfaction of a man who'd just thoroughly trounced a rival. If he had any curiosity on the subject of his mistress's nightmares and her general well-being, he did not show it.

He doesn't beat me. Was she telling the truth? Was the unease he'd felt in her, when he broached the subject, only to do with the prospect of losing her position? Will forked a slice of ham onto his plate while studying her protector sidelong. *I enjoy my transactions with him.* No use dwelling on that. He pivoted away to find a place at the table.

"What in blazes was that all about?" said Lord Cathcart when he'd taken the empty seat beside him.

"Diplomacy. I didn't tumble his woman last night and I wanted him to know, for her sake." He cut a strip of the ham and speared it with his fork.

The viscount took a long swallow of coffee. "You confound me." He set the cup firmly in its saucer. "You put yourself out some last night to get her into your bedroom. Why would you go so far only to pull up shy of the finish line?"

"It was she who pulled me up." Might as well get used to telling the tale. "She didn't like the arrangement, or perhaps she didn't like me. At all events she wasn't willing, and I don't go in for force." The words came more easily already than they'd done with Roanoke. "That being the case, I took it upon myself to let her protector know she hadn't been unfaithful."

"Honor makes a fool of you, Blackshear." He jerked his chin at where Square-jaw sat, feasting on his rolls and butter. "He's been telling everyone who'll listen about the piece he enjoyed last night. Do you really think he deserves to rest easy in the knowledge of his mistress's constancy?"

"I did what I thought would serve her interest. What he deserves is beside the point." He shrugged and took another bite of ham, the very picture of a man who heeded his own conscience with no regard to the individuals involved. Not at all the picture of a man who'd spent the morning battling his body's demands because he dreaded to lose what he'd gained of a lady's trust.

She hadn't pulled away from him on waking, though she could not have failed to notice his arousal. She knew he desired her, and she trusted, yes, *trusted*, that he would not act upon that desire. How could he, when her nightmares, and the story of her fall, were so fresh with him? Bedraggled kitten or no, she deserved to know what it was to be delicately handled. She deserved a night, and a morning too, of respite from the demands of men.

He'd given her that. Square-jaw never could. And in return she'd given him the soul-deep satisfaction of calming her, soothing her terrors, putting himself between her and the harrowing dreams.

"Are you going to eat your cake, or have you resolved on wasting romantically away? I daresay the effort will be lost on her." Cathcart's voice brought back the immediate environs, the table, the plate, the fork arrested halfway down. Will shook off his reverie and ate his plum cake.

Chapter Fifteen

$\mathscr{I}$ BEGIN TO believe he has unnatural proclivities." Halfway through this pronouncement Eliza swung her racket at the shuttlecock, freighting her words with an accidental emphasis quite apart from the louder tone she'd already adopted in order to be heard halfway down the gallery. "Who ever heard of a man installing a lady in his bed only so that he could sleep on the floor?"

"Lydia explained that already. She refused him, so he didn't touch her." Maria declined to swing, the trajectory passing too near a portrait of some Roanoke ancestor in a magnificent powdered wig. She stepped back, ceding her place in the game as the shuttlecock hit the floor. "Do we really think so little of our due as to be astonished that a man wouldn't overpower and ravish her in that circumstance?"

"There's a great swath of ground between ravishment, and giving up the hunt at the first refusal." With her free hand Eliza clutched up a fistful of skirts, that she could run and lunge if need be without tripping on a hem. "If he truly hoped to have her, surely he would have made some attempt at persuasion. At seduction." She shifted her address to Lydia. "Are you absolutely sure he didn't? Were there no efforts to change your mind, or at least to make himself more agreeable to you?"

"He was kind, I suppose." Lydia scooped up the shuttlecock and served it with an underhand swing. "He was respectful. But he said nothing of changing my mind."

"And surely *that* made him agreeable beyond anything else a man can do." Maria stood with her back to one of the tall gallery windows, racket on her shoulder like an elegant parasol, watching the other ladies sustain their volley. "She said no, and he didn't assume she only needed the right sort of persuasion. He credited her with knowing her own mind. I vow it's a pity he hasn't any money. A lady would be lucky to be kept by such a man."

Luckier than you know. Lydia lunged right to bat back a wide shot. She'd said nothing, naturally, of her nightmares and how he'd responded to them. Nothing of his presence in the bed. Not one word of the erection or the feel of his strong arm draped over her middle. But it was all nearly enough to make even a rational-minded lady believe in luck.

"I still suspect something irregular. We have his refusal of that Barbara the night before to consider as well, recall." Finally Eliza missed a return and stopped, racket hanging idle, to finish her thought. "If he has deviant inclinations, then surely he'd hope to conceal the fact. What better way than by publicly making a bid for another man's woman?" For the fourth or fifth time that afternoon she threw Lydia that glance that said *I won't expose you, but I know you haven't told us all.* Lydia looked away, busying herself with re-pinning a lock of hair that had come loose.

"Nonsense." Maria came away from the window to take Eliza's place in the game. "If he wanted to deceive the company, why would he admit to sleeping on the floor? He told Mr. Roanoke directly he came to break-fast. So says Mr. Moss." She caught up the bird and sent it sailing down the gallery. "The most reasonable expla-nation is that he's developed a *tendre* for Lydia—that explains why he'd have nothing to do with that Barbara—and when he found she didn't return the sentiment, he went out of his way to repair whatever damage he might have done to her standing with her protector. It's a fine, courtly kind of devotion. Quite romantic. Some other gentlemen could take a lesson."

Romantic. That word had meant something to her once. If the past three years had not happened, and if a man like Mr. Blackshear had come to love her, she might have loved him back. She might even have loved him first, and known the breathless hope that her feelings would be returned.

If, if, if. A waste of a thinking brain. She missed a re-turn and withdrew to the window.

"Have you spoken to Mr. Roanoke today?" Even Eliza possessed sufficient tact to save this question for a moment in which her face was averted as she bent to retrieve the shuttlecock. All day the ladies had tiptoed round the fact of Edward's indiscretion, blessed as they both were with gentlemen who would presumably never do such a thing.

"I haven't." Lydia bounced the netting of her racket rhythmically off the heel of her hand, as a lady might do if her protector's slights were a matter of no great con-cern or even notice to her. "He's been quite occupied all day with boasting to the other gentlemen of last night's conquest. Perhaps we'll speak when he's had his fill of that."

Or perhaps not. What was there to say? No explana-tion could undo the insult he'd served her, and yet what could she do but carry on with him? As she'd told

Mr. Blackshear, she cherished no illusions of Edward's fidelity.

"He's lucky to have you." Eliza lobbed up the shuttlecock and swung. "If I'd been subjected to that affront, I promise you I would have entertained Mr. Blackshear whether I desired him or not, and seen to it we could be heard as far away as Mr. Roanoke's room."

"Yes, but you would have done that in any case." This remark proved to the others that her spirits were not suffering, and also shifted the conversation away from Mr. Blackshear and herself in favor of some general good-natured teasing.

Lord knows she'd need all the good nature she could hoard up before going to Edward's room tonight. As the day went on it became increasingly apparent he was angry. For all that Mr. Blackshear's admissions—which must surely have come at some cost to Mr. Blackshear's pride—ought to have assured him, he was still stung by the ignominy of having lost his mistress in a game of skill. She could see it in his exaggerated unconcern, in the gusto with which he congratulated himself on last night's exploits with his hired partner. In her own presence he carried on this way, which meant a share of his anger was directed at her.

Well, she'd foreseen this possibility, after all. And she'd gain little by pointing out the illogic of his pique. Men's anger sprang from odd sources, from perceived injuries to their dignity, and a prudent woman just stood back and let the mood run its course.

So she did to the best of her ability all day, idling in the gallery with the other ladies, taking a walk to the stables and back, avoiding her protector in hopes his ire would burn itself out by evening. But when the company assembled for supper it was immediately evident that Edward had spent those same hours feeding his ill humor, and that his food of choice was drink.

He was no five-bottle man. He drank his fill at parties or card games, as did any gentleman, but he wasn't one of those who began the day with a bottle and learned to go about with no signs of impairment. When he drank in earnest the effects were visible to all.

To begin, he put his new favorite lady at his right hand and set to lavishing her with compliments at a volume either distorted by the drink, or expertly calibrated to reach the place where Lydia sat. At great length she heard of the merits of the lady's golden hair, and of her snow-white skin, and of her eyes that put sapphires to shame.

Objectively considered—and the only wise way to receive any of this was in strict objectivity—what he said was quite true. Caroline, as her name proved to be, was pretty after Maria's fashion, if less dazzlingly so. Caroline was also embarrassed at having the fact proclaimed to such a degree, though Edward, of course, was beyond taking note of this detail.

If you cared for him, this would hurt like swallowing broken glass. Another instructive reminder, as though any were wanted, of the disadvantages of love. Absent that emotion, she could even feel a bit of sympathy for the lady, who had only done what she'd been hired to do and never bargained with playing a role in some tawdry melodrama between a man and his mistress.

Still, by the time they came to the fish course this was beginning to feel like the most interminable supper in human history. And clearly she wasn't alone in that opinion. Maria, who sat near to Edward, had bodily angled herself away from him. An auburn-haired lady who sometimes joined them for whist was wincing at every upsurge in the vigor of his speech. Even Eliza's Lord Randall, with whom she'd never exchanged two words, sent her one eloquent look of tight-lipped commiseration.

And when she happened to glance at Mr. Blackshear, across the table and four seats down, he looked up from his turbot in Dutch sauce with an expression just as eloquent as Lord Randall's, though its message was something different. Something like *Say the word and I will eviscerate him with this knife and fork.*

She dropped her gaze to her own plate, her insides buzzing like a hive of bees. He was a man who'd killed, of course—so he'd told her—but she'd never before glimpsed murder in his eyes.

"I vow that wager with Blackshear proved to be excellent sport." The name yanked at her attention as none of the rest of Edward's tirade had done, and she twisted to face his end of the table. "I've half a notion to try it again." He delivered these words to the company at large but his eyes were on her. "Who's come without a mistress and might like to take his chances at winning one? Lord Cathcart?"

The viscount lifted his napkin and dabbed calmly at his mouth. "I find myself unable to perpetrate such injury upon the lady who has joined her life to mine, else I should already have a mistress of my own." He sent a slight bow her way. "Perhaps even one as charming as Miss Slaughter."

Heat was creeping up her cheeks in spite of every effort at aplomb. She set down her fork. A person couldn't eat under so many covert glances and open stares.

"Someone else, then?" He'd either missed or was willfully disregarding the reprimand in Lord Cathcart's answer. "Some man of more sporting tastes?"

"I don't consent to this." Even on so short a statement, her voice wavered. She pressed her lips together before it could have a chance to waver anymore.

"Neither did you consent last night, and yet I've heard remarkably little complaint from you all this day." He'd been only waiting for her to provoke him to this lashing-out. "A night in Blackshear's bed seems to have been everything agreeable to you."

How could a lady even make any reply? She'd only done what he himself had arranged. He'd have been equally angry if she'd defied him. "I don't know what I've done to incur your displeasure, but I wish you would have the goodness to resolve it with me in private, rather than attempting to punish me with these uncivil words and coarse machinations in view of the entire company."

"Resolve it with you in private?—don't you wish I would." His eyes and his laugh made lewd allegations, apparently heedless of the accusation he'd just issued regarding her partiality for another man. He was utterly beyond reason now.

She took the napkin from her lap and put it on the table. "I cannot speak to you when you are in this state. Nor can I remain here and be the target of your abuse." Her pulse hammered like an overzealous blacksmith. She'd never addressed him so—doubtless he'd be angrier than ever—but to stay had become insupportable. "If everyone will excuse me, I shall take my distracting presence elsewhere that you may enjoy the rest of your meal."

"My room, Lydia. I trust you remember the way?"

She'd avoided, these last few moments, any glance toward the place where Mr. Blackshear sat, but this utterance brought her round to face him before she could think whether she ought. Indeed everyone at the table swiveled likewise, more than one piece of cutlery clanking or screeching against a plate as a diner was brought up short by this unexpected development.

He, in contrast, was the picture of unruffled poise. He'd lifted his goblet and now brought it to his lips, eyelids lowered, without the smallest sign of awareness that he'd just hurled a firebomb into the proceedings. His use of her given name alone must throw into doubt their previous accounts of what had transpired last night.

Someone touched her chair. The footman, come to draw it out. One deep breath, and she would rise.

Will lowered his glass and leaned a bit forward. "That will be agreeable to you, I hope?" He laid the slightest emphasis on *agreeable,* the word around which Edward had built his accusation. He was smiling with everything but his eyes.

Without waiting for an answer he shot a brief glance to the end of the table where her protector sat. "I trust you won't mind. I had the impression, from your recommending her to others, that you weren't wanting her company tonight." Like a single scarlet thread in white-work, the strain of menace in his voice. Perhaps no one else in the room knew him well enough to discern it.

"Please yourself." Edward laid hold of his own glass and brought it halfway up before a witticism occurred. "I daresay that's what you did last night, all primed for a woman only to find her not inclined to open shop to you."

Anger surged up in her then: all those wadded-up portions of anger she'd hoarded away sprang out to full size and drove her finally to her feet. "Would it be any wonder if I did prefer his bed to yours?" This was imprudent. This was precisely the kind of outburst she couldn't afford. But so help her, she'd been prudent long enough. "He behaved with honor. He treated me with respect. A lady recognizes a debt to a gentleman who conducts himself so." Was she really going to say this next bit? She oughtn't. She courted disaster. But the words sat hot on her tongue; they'd burn her if she didn't let them out.

She revolved just enough to face Mr. Blackshear, who watched her with calm interest, only his eyes betraying any trace of turbulence to match her own. "Your room, to be sure." Her own blood roared in her ears. She curtseyed, eyes never leaving his. "Give me half an hour, then you may come after."

No one could miss her meaning. Half an hour was the time it took a lady to undress.

And here was that gaze she'd seen before, the one that made her naked without ever roving away from her face. One hand dropped to his waistcoat and came back with a pocket watch. "Half an hour." His eyelids lowered to consult the watch as he flicked it open. "You'll have at least that long before I come." He set the watch by his plate and didn't look up again when she turned and left the room.

*S*HE HADN'T meant it, had she? He'd assumed she was only saying what she thought would spite Roanoke, and he'd been more than happy to abet her in that.

Will looked about him, and saw two or three glances hastily withdrawn. One of Miss Slaughter's friends, the porcelain blonde, broke the short silence by forcefully proposing a round of charades after supper. Her gentleman protector seconded the scheme, and a number of well-intentioned souls who'd had their fill of unpleasantness chimed in with such zealous, dogged gaiety as charades had probably never before inspired in all the years of its existence. When the half hour ended they were still on the topic.

He set down his fork with his cutlet half-finished, and rose. No remark seemed quite suitable for the occasion, but he bowed. Several of the gentlemen nodded in return. Everyone pretended ignorance of the circumstances surrounding his departure save for another of

Lydia's friends—the dark-haired one—who caught his eye and winked, unabashed approval written all across her face. He picked up his watch and walked out.

What would he do if she'd meant it? *Oblige her, you nodcock.* But oblige her in what? If she intended to do this only for the purpose of avenging herself on her protector, then it really had little to do with him. And if he were ever to bed her, he wanted it to have *everything* to do with him.

More than likely she hadn't meant it. Or if she had, her wrath would have subsided in the half hour. They'd have a good laugh at their outrageous counterfeit, and then retire to the bed and the floor as they'd done last night.

The walk upstairs and down the hall to his room gave him time enough to convince himself of this, and almost time enough to convince himself it was what he desired. He swung the door open, and every conviction fled before the sight of Miss Slaughter, in nightclothes, with her hair taken down.

She perched on the window seat, legs bent to one side in mermaid fashion, bare ankles visible past the hem of her dressing gown. Or rather, *his* dressing gown. A low humming started in his blood as that detail came clear.

She didn't look at him. In her hand she held a glass of claret and she raised it to drink. Matter-of-factly she did this—no angling her neck to show him the delicate ripples of her swallow, no licking the wetness from her lips—but when she lowered the glass, one side of his too-large gown fell away from her shoulder, exposing the gleam of dark, dark purple silk beneath.

It was no nightgown she wore. His palms and fingers remembered, with a charge like static electricity, every quality of that fabric. So did his mouth. The humming in his blood kicked up to a low-level clamor.

He pulled the door shut behind him, his hand lingering at the knob. Eighteen or so inches higher was a bolt. *Lock it,* came the prompting from his hand and his blood and every other hasty part of him.

But to throw that bolt home would be to commit to the deed. In the slide and click of metal would be acquiescence to a drama with no worthy role for him. *Yes,* that action would say. *I'm willing to serve as a mere convenient erection in your scheme.* And was he?

He took his hand from the door and folded his arms across his chest. He wouldn't decide just yet.

Miss Slaughter stirred: her shoulders rose with a breath. "I pride myself, you know, on acting rationally and deliberately." Though the words must be for his benefit, she delivered them into her glass of claret. Now he'd absorbed the spectacle of her dress, he could perceive the half-empty bottle beside her on the seat.

Splendid. She'd be foxed. Another good reason not to succumb to the temptations of purple silk and his too-large dressing gown. He shifted to his left and leaned against the wall. "Indeed you're one of the most rational and deliberate people I know."

"I was not so at supper." She lifted the glass and took another healthy swallow. Probably he ought to be calculating how best to get that bottle away from her.

"You were provoked." He'd listen, he'd humor her, he'd coax the glass out of her hand, and he'd put her to bed before they could do anything ill-advised.

"He was so unreasonable." Still she addressed the claret, her body perfectly still and her voice afire with vehemence. "I don't only mean that he was rude and unkind. He had no consistent argument behind his attacks."

Of course. Never mind that the man had crudely bullied her; she saved her outrage for his disregard of logic.

"His reasoning did leave something to be desired." He pushed off the wall and made his leisurely way to the armchair, unbuttoning his coat as he went. "He ought first to have made up his mind whether I debauched you, or spent a frustrated solitary evening on the floor. Insults lose a good deal of their sting when they contradict each other."

"His remarks to you were despicable." She set down the claret and fixed her gaze out the window. Near a full minute he'd been in this room, and she hadn't looked at him once. "His worst conjectures of what we're doing now are no more than he deserves."

"Perhaps." Here was precarious ground; he would cross it with care. He shrugged out of his coat and tossed it over the chair's arm. "Though I must say I cannot occupy my mind overmuch with the matter of Mr. Roanoke and his deserts."

"Nor should you." In the line of her back he could see another deep breath. She turned, then, and rose from the window seat. She hadn't fastened the dressing gown and it slipped right off as she stood, cascading down to pool about her ankles like water round the feet of some just-emerged ocean goddess.

But where a new-made goddess would wear only innocence, her bare skin in harmony with nature itself, Lydia Slaughter was dressed for sin. She hadn't even bothered with the diaphanous overdress. Purple-black silk flowed from shoulder to ankle, inviting the eye to roam everywhere and to loiter most especially on the lascivious places: the ripe full breasts with nipples standing up in sharp relief; the curve of her belly down to the Y-shape at the juncture of her thighs.

Devil take him; how could he have been so utterly unprepared for this? He'd seen her before in this dress. He had ample acquaintance with her shape. He'd known, from the instant he entered the room and glimpsed her, what might be her intent.

And still his throat went dry. His brain stuttered and slowed. The clamor in his blood mounted to importunate heights.

You can't. Not like this. She's not in her right mind. If her eyes would only meet his, his body would recognize her for a lady deserving of respect—for another man's mistress—for something other than a luscious assemblage of parts—and he would find the words to make them both understand why they ought not to do this.

Maybe she knew that. At all events she kept her eyes from his. The silk rearranged itself in enthralling ways as she bent and twisted to pick up her claret. She drained the glass's contents and set it decisively down. "Blackshear." Finally she looked at him. "Don't make me beg."

And he'd be hanged if he could remember how to form any words at all. He could only watch, heart pounding like the charge of oncoming cavalry, as she turned and went to the bed.

Confound him a thousand times. He fooled precisely no one with his principles. When it came to the point he was entirely willing to be reduced to a convenient erection.

The claret, though. He wrenched himself from where he stood and went to the window seat. "How much of this have you drunk?" He hefted the bottle. Drink was suddenly sounding like a very good idea. "You scarcely ate any supper."

"Don't try to take care of me. That's not what I need from you now." They were a pair, she and her protector. Belligerent drunks, the two of them. And once again she'd found his weak spot; she'd gone to the word—*need*—that could make him crawl a mile on his belly over jagged rocks.

She *needed* something he could give. He set one steadying hand on the wall. "It's not that I don't want it, Lydia."

"Then take it." If he looked at her now he would be lost.

He drew in a ragged breath. "It's not right this way." Here was some small return of reason. "You're in no condition to know what you want. I'd be taking advantage." He tipped the bottle and splashed claret into the glass.

"I've known what I wanted since I left that dinner table." A brief silence. "And I only had one drink."

"Liar." But he'd always admired the ruthless resolve with which she went after a thing she wanted. And when he himself was that thing . . .

He set down the bottle and picked up the glass. This was six different kinds of wrong. Cuckolding his host. Bedding a woman too drunk to know better. Risking this relationship all over again, this time with delicate confidences at stake. But somewhere between the first sight of her with her hair down and the unsporting use of the word *need*, choice had slipped through his fingers. "Shall I lock the door, or not?" He tossed off the drink in one grim string of swallows.

"As you please." Oh, wasn't she wallowing in her triumph now. Her syllables poured over him like honey from a spoon. Would she say his name in that voice when the time came, or would she cry it out, harsh as a hawk sighting prey?

He pivoted to face her and nearly had to sit down. She'd discarded her purple sheath while his back was turned and lay naked atop the covers, elbows propped behind her, knees bent up, feet flat on the counterpane. Her contours swerved here and subsided there, pale and lush and precise as if she'd been sculpted out of butter.

There was not one part of her he didn't want to sink into, not one inch of her he didn't want to taste.

Devil take honor, and conscience, and all those tyrannical principles that harassed him sunup to sundown with their incessant promptings. He was a man who'd shredded his own soul, and tonight he was going to act like one. He went to bolt the door.

Chapter Sixteen

$\mathscr{S}$HE WAS watching him, expectant and wholly without shame, when he turned to face the room. Her eyes glittered, hard and intent.

Now. Four steps brought him to the bed. He set one knee on the mattress and her legs edged apart. Greedy impatient thing. Just for that, she could wait a bit. He bent and pressed a luxuriant kiss on her kneecap.

"Stop that." Her knee twitched away. "Take off your clothes."

A dictatorial drunk as well as belligerent. But to obey this command was no hardship.

He pulled off his boots and his hose. Waistcoat, cravat, braces, shirt, all over his head and dropped helter-skelter on the floor. He stood.

She shifted, propping herself higher on the pillows, angling unabashedly for a better view.

His blood thundered like a river's rapids as he obliged her, turning himself so she could see. One button after another slipped free and the front-fall of his breeches dropped away. He undid his drawers. He looked at her.

She swallowed. The tip of her tongue flicked out to wet her lips.

"Is this what you want?" All velvet and shadow, his voice, and pitched just loud enough to reach her. With his fingertips he stroked up his length. She'd been waiting for this. And Lord, so had he.

"I think perhaps . . ." She bit her lip, still staring. "Um." Her eyes came to his, soft and uncertain. "Can you go in very slowly?"

It was beautifully done. But he knew her too well. He stepped out of his breeches. "Flattering minx." He crawled back onto the bed, parting her knees with his hands to find his place between them. "You say that to every man."

Her concerned expression dissolved into a deliciously wicked grin. "Every man loves to hear it. Even a man who knows it for flattery."

He couldn't argue. He couldn't say anything at all. Was he really here at last? The insides of her thighs touching his hips where her knees bent up? His hands flat to the mattress on either side of her, his chest brushing over the unholy abundance of her bosom, her shoulders elevated from the elbows still propped behind her and her mirthful face mere inches from his? This was so wrong in so many ways. How could it feel so magnificently right?

"Lie back." He nudged her forehead with his.

"No." She stayed where she was.

So it would be that way, would it? Well enough. They had all night to negotiate who was in charge. He lowered his hips and the head of his cock met her soft flesh, honey-slick from desire.

He closed his eyes and shuddered. "I want you so much," he whispered. Damnation. He wasn't going to last long, this first time. But he'd make it up to her. Repeatedly.

"Don't *tell* me." He opened his eyes to meet bold unblinking defiance very like what he'd seen that first night in the library when she'd caught him watching. "Show me. Now."

"In truth, Lydia." He sounded as though he were being stretched on the rack. "Do you need me to start slowly?"

"No, Mr. Blackshear." Her eyes glinted like agates, a mere handsbreadth away. "I need you to fuck me as hard as you can."

The breath burned inside him and the edges of his vision went hazy. Bloody hell. This was going to be a battle every step of the way, wasn't it? He shook his head, and braced himself on one hand as he sent the other to caress her thigh. "I've waited a long time for this." With his voice, too, he could caress her. "I mean to savor it."

"No." She swatted at his hand. "No lingering."

"I'll only linger over the parts you enjoy." Hanged if he'd let her turn this into something quick and brutish and utterly devoid of meaning.

"I've told you what I enjoy. You may believe I know my own tastes." Her voice was growing thin with agitation. She twitched like a cornered animal. "Don't dare fancy you'll be the man to teach me the pleasures of tenderness." *Tenderness* was a rat whose neck she wrung with her own hands before hurling it over the hedge to rot with *feelings*.

And of course he'd fancied he'd be exactly that man. Or at the very least, that they'd do this with some acknowledgment of what had been between them. He'd already had intimacy of her in her confidences on their walk outside, in the way she'd trusted him to comfort her last night in this same bed. What on earth did she expect to gain by treating him like a paying customer now?

He drew back a few inches and saw panic flare up in her eyes. She might want only an impersonal fuck, but she wanted it very much. "I won't try to teach you anything. I wouldn't presume." He bent to kiss one nipple, just to reassure her of his lustful intent. "But surely there's some ground for compromise between what you want and what I want."

"*Compromise* is but an over-nice way of saying neither person gets what they want. Do that again. This time use your tongue."

Leverage, finally. "I'll do it as much as you want." He retreated to knees and straight arms, too far away to do anything but talk. "After we settle how we're both to come out of this satisfied."

Her eyes narrowed. They shifted back and forth, reading his face. "You'll be satisfied. Have no fear on that count." Half promise and half threat, the way she said it. "And if you find any hungers unappeased, we'll do it again, to your taste this time."

It sounded . . . so much like a transaction. A trade. She would use him, and then he could use her. Any man might have taken his place, provided the cock was to her liking, and apparently she thought any woman would do just as well for him.

He could refuse. He could clamber over her and right off the bed to where his clothes lay discarded. *I'm sorry but this isn't what I want,* he could say while buttoning his breeches over his rampant erection. She would probably throw something at him.

Stop thinking. The woman you want is underneath you with her legs apart. Why in the name of all that is holy do you hesitate? Very well, this round went to her. His eyes still on hers, he lowered his mouth to her other nipple and made a circle round it with his tongue.

She arched to meet his mouth and then sank slowly down, as he followed, until her shoulders lay flat on the mattress. "Yes," she muttered, eyes fluttering closed. "Good. Now put your cock in me. Anywhere you like."

Debauched past all redemption. He stroked a hand

down her belly, through her maiden hair, to the place where he could make her melt like butter. "Right here is where I like." His voice descended to a growl. "Where you're wet for me, and hot. Spread your legs wider."

She liked that, if he could judge by the shiver that ran through her. And, because she was constitutionally incapable of acceding to any of his commands, she did not spread her legs but rather brought them about, by some miracle of flexibility, until her ankles sat at his shoulders. His cock found the place where she opened to him and he slipped in, all the way in, with no effort at all.

He stayed for a moment, just so. His throat had gone tight and his breath unsteady.

Nearly a year, it had been. Some camp follower in Belgium would have been the last, an anonymous and forgettable encounter that left him vaguely ashamed and not at all satisfied. Then had come that feeling of unfitness; the fear that his darkness, his corrupted soul, might somehow leach out of him to contaminate any woman he touched.

And maybe this was what he'd needed all along. Not a pure-hearted woman who could lift him out of darkness, but one who dwelt there herself. Already corrupted to such a degree that nothing remained to ruin. Incorruptible, now, more incorruptible than the most virtuous maiden.

A furrow traced itself in her brow, above her still-closed eyes. "Hurry," she said.

He could do that. He half withdrew, and pushed in hard. Her lashes trembled as her hands came up and took hold of his biceps. Again. She tipped her head back, exposing her throat. Once more. Her lips parted and he heard her harsh breaths as he worked to find the right rhythm.

"Lydia, open your eyes," he whispered on what breath he could spare. "Look at me."

"No. Harder." Her lip drew up at one side to show her teeth, again the cornered animal. Her fingers dug into the bunched-up muscles of his arms.

He thrust on, but desolation began to trickle through him in chilly drops, one by one from that icicle of desolation he kept somewhere inside. She didn't care to look at him, to *be* with him. He'd thrown away whatever remaining claim to honor he had in order to bed this woman, and he might as well have been with a camp follower again. An imperious, ill-tempered camp follower who meant to leave no doubt of her contempt for him.

"Faster. Don't slow down." Her eyes half-opened and glared at him, from between her ankles, without the slightest glimmer of warmth.

Confound her drunken hostility. He would stop this. He would haul himself out of her and flop down beside her and tell her: *I'm not your enemy. I'm not your punishment. I won't play that part for you.*

Any minute, he would do that. For now he clenched his teeth to hold back the tide of pleasure and made his strokes swift and shallow.

"Harder. Hurt me." Her voice was a feral snarl and her face half contorted with loathing.

"I can't. I don't want to." There was a way to ask for such things, and it wasn't the way she'd just done. He'd tell her so afterward, if she was still inclined to speak to him then. At the moment he couldn't spare the breath.

She writhed under him and took a new grip on his arms. "You said you'd do what I wanted. My way first, your way after. We agreed."

His patience snapped, then, and with one monumental effort he halted, half inside her. Her narrowed eyes flew wide with outrage.

"Listen to me." His chest was heaving and one wrong move would make him spill, but he kept his voice steady.

"Against my better judgment and all my principles I am fucking you under your protector's roof." One great swallow of air. "I'm plowing you harder than I've ever plowed a woman in my life. I'll probably end with bruises and I won't be surprised if I make myself ill." One more lungful. "I'm sorry it's not enough for you, but this is all you're getting. I suggest you find a way to like it."

Her eyes flicked back and forth on his face, as though he were some new adversary whose measure she must take. And devil take her, she got hotter for him. She took her legs from his shoulders to wrap them round his back and tilted her hips to take him deeper. Her whole body roiled under him like molten metal in a blacksmith's cauldron.

Hell. She'd wanted rude handling and she'd goaded him into it. She had what she wanted and he had . . . his cock in her hot wet quim. And he was too near his crisis now to complain, particularly as she'd set some muscles in there to doing things he hadn't even known a woman's body could do.

Sweet holy mother of . . . He wasn't going to last. He would disgrace himself, and leave her wanting. He squeezed his eyes shut, and slitted them open again to see how she arched and gritted her teeth on his every thrust, to see the face that went with those rapturous sounds she was making in her throat. "Come, Lydia. Hurry." The words rasped out like a death rattle. But at least he was speaking her peremptory tongue.

And this command, thank the fates, she obeyed. She whipsawed under him, head thrown back, and snatched her hand up to her mouth, sinking in her teeth to stifle her cries.

Not a second too soon. Two more thrusts he gave her before climax seized him in its unforgiving talons, bearing him up and away with no regard for his sensibilities, his better nature. This coupling had been so far from what he'd wanted, and pleasure swamped him all the same. He pushed up on straight arms, his head thrown back, and spent himself to the sound of Miss Slaughter's muffled cries.

He'd never spilled in a woman before. A gentleman always withdrew. This ought to have been . . . uncharted bliss. Unlooked-for privilege. Something, anything, more than it was.

Pleasure left just enough room for that thought to sidle through. Then pleasure rolled out like a spent ocean wave, and nothing rolled in to take its place. He lifted his body clear of hers and settled to the mattress beside her, limp and unspeaking and utterly barren inside. The whole thing had been just an exercise in her pushing him away. She hadn't said his name in the end, or if she had, she'd withheld that gratification from him by smothering the syllable with her fist.

He lay on his stomach, head turned away from her, breathing slowly in and out. He had nothing to say.

Her own breaths sounded behind him, more rapid than they ought to be. She wasn't relaxed. Perhaps regrets had begun to crash in on her, now she wasn't addled by lust.

"Have we betrayed someone?" Her words spilled forth with a vehemence that suggested she'd had to launch them before losing her nerve.

"Mr. Roanoke? I think that's for you to judge." He turned his head on the pillow. She was staring straight up, tense and unmoving but for the rise and fall of her naked bosom.

She shook her head, lips pressed tight. "I don't mean him."

"Someone on my side?" Now he lifted his head, that she might meet his eyes. "There's no one." *And really, oughtn't you to have considered this* before *luring me into bed?*

Her eyes cut sideways to him. "There's a lady who depends on you, I think. For whose sake you want to earn money. I've thought she might be the one on whom you called, that day. In Camden Town."

"No, Lydia. Can you really think I'm the sort of man who—" He stopped. He was the sort of man who took someone else's woman to bed and used her brutishly. And in regard to Mrs. Talbot, perhaps he was even worse. "The lady you're thinking of is the widow of one of my men. I promised him I would do what I could for her and their small son. I'd like to see her independent of the relations with whom she now lives. But that's the whole of it. I don't think of courting her."

She'd let down some guard, or maybe the claret had let it down for her. And for a moment he could read her: he saw the shift from trepidation to relief to curiosity in her eyes. "That's an extraordinary promise for you to make."

"He was dying." How much more was he prepared to tell? He knew so many of her secrets—her brother, the loss of her parents, the cad who'd ruined her—and she knew almost nothing of him. "It had been a long day, and a longer night, and I wanted—I wanted to give him what comfort I could."

"What an honorable man you are." Her eyes tracked about his face, assessing him all over again. "Not many would make such a promise, let alone strive to fulfill it."

He couldn't say more, after that. *Honorable man* crawled over his skin like a centipede. And what if she was still feeling the effects of the claret? She might receive his story one way now; another way altogether when she woke clearheaded.

She watched him, calm and patient, willing to hear whatever he said and equally willing to bear his silence.

Where the devil had this woman been ten minutes ago? Where did she go when that hissing, spitting succubus usurped her body?

For an instant he thought of gathering her in and demanding his turn, his way, as she'd agreed to. But now he'd been sated there was no clamorous appetite to shout his conscience down, and his conscience had a litany to deliver.

He permitted himself one touch: a hand sent out to smooth her hair. "Go to sleep now, Lydia. You've had a long day." He pushed himself from the bed, and went to put out the candles.

𝒯HE DREAMS came again, more fiercely than ever. Gunshots. The terrible scream of a horse. Shouting in the darkness outside, and the bang of the coach door yanked open.

Every bit as fierce, though, was the watchful presence beside her, who hauled her out of each dream before the images could progress any further. He pulled her against him, and mopped her forehead with a corner of the sheet, and said things. *Lydia,* he said. *Sweetheart,* he called her at least once. *You're safe here. I won't let anything hurt you.* Because he believed the dreams were about herself.

He might have run from her after the coupling, but he hadn't. He knew of her coarse impatient self-obliterating hungers now. He'd glimpsed the appalling depths of her need. And he'd gone with her into those depths, absorbing every bit of her fury because he was a man of limitless strength, limitless patience, limitless understanding for the frailties of others.

His forehead touched her hair in back. His breath warmed the nape of her neck. He kept an arm over her, as he'd done the night before, though now no nightclothes came between them. Every time she woke, the feel of his naked skin astonished her anew.

Lydia blinked her eyes open. Was it morning? Her head hurt. She oughtn't to have drunk so much claret.

They hadn't pulled the curtains last night and now a whisper of light permeated the room. Morning, in strictest terms. But they needn't rise for hours.

The alertness of his muscles told her he was awake, even as his stillness told her what care he took to keep from waking her. His erection told her how they might pass the time before breakfast, if they so chose.

His arm stirred. His hand found hers, under the covers, and he threaded their fingers together. He knew she was awake.

Some time this morning she would have to confront the consequences of what she'd done. But not yet. She had a distraction in her bed, a magnificent willing distraction who was not promised to any lady anywhere, and she would forget herself entirely with him. She drew his hand up and set it on her breast, her nipple meeting the center of his palm.

He sighed, the sigh of a man who'd lain for long minutes just waiting for a lady to wake up and put her breast in his hand. "How is your head this morning?" He made his voice soft, to spare her. His palm bestowed a slight, sweet friction that made her nipple draw tight.

"It's rather poor." He wouldn't decide he must leave her alone, would he? "Other parts of me fare better."

She felt a thrumming in his chest, laughter so deep and private it didn't need to come out into air. "Other parts of you can fare better still if you wish it." His palm skated over her nipple, striking sparks as it went.

Yes. It was prayer and exultation. *Yes yes yes yes yes.* "What parts did you have in mind?"

"I shall have to review them and consider." A soft, unexpected touch: his lips just behind and below her ear.

"Turn this way." His voice dropped to a whisper. "Let me see you."

She rolled onto her back and he pushed up on one elbow. His face in the pale bare light of morning took her breath away. Those dark thick brows that gave him such a serious aspect; the eyes colored like strong coffee; his cheeks rough with the stubble of a beard, and all of it limned with unmistakable purpose. His hand left her breast to tug the covers down, baring her to somewhere near mid-thigh. Baring him as well: she could see the distribution of dark hairs over his chest, the ridges of his collarbone, the place where his ribcage gave way to the first course of flat muscle that continued down his stomach. These subtler details had escaped her notice last night.

His hand came back to her breast, this time to take the nipple between thumb and middle finger. His eyes rose to hers. He wanted to watch her pleasure.

His mouth tautened into a straight line of concentration as he stroked the pad of his thumb slowly back and forth. When she swallowed, his eyes flicked to her throat. "Do you like this?" he murmured.

A shiver went through her. He'd used that same voice last night to ask a similar question. *Is this what you want?* he'd said, standing before her in all his unbuttoned splendor. A Catholic nun could not have said no.

"Do you?" He whispered the words as his fingers gave a slight squeeze.

"Yes. Harder." Her breath was beginning to shorten.

He shook his head, the corner of his mouth ticking up. "My way this time, remember? No ordering me about. I place an embargo on the word *harder.*" His thumb resumed stroking, more slowly than before and with barely any pressure at all.

This would kill her. "What if I beg? Instead of ordering."

His brows twitched together; his eyes told her he was imagining the idea thoroughly. "It will have no effect," he said nevertheless. "I have a program in mind and I mean to follow it."

Panic drove pinpricks all up and down her spine. She knew how to lie back and take whatever a man cared to give her. There were ways to retreat deep inside one's body, beyond the reach of what went on; there were ways to stand one's ground and wrest pleasure from the jaws of degradation. Even last night she'd managed him like any other man, taking what she wanted while holding him an arm's length away.

But she'd woken in his embrace, tired and warm and wide open to him. She'd misplaced her armor in the night and it might be too late to retrieve it now.

"Don't worry." He could feel her agitation. "It's an excellent program. You'll enjoy it."

"Sure of yourself, aren't you?" She would not flinch. She would not writhe, though he'd moved his hand to the other nipple and commenced his same slow torture there. "I should think I'd be the one to say whether or not I enjoy it." She swallowed again.

"You're so sensitive." An awestruck address to her bosom, heedless of the words she'd just spoken. "I'm barely even touching you and you're on fire. Why do you insist that everything be so hard and fast and brutal when the slightest pressure sends you to the stars?"

"Because I like it that way." Maybe she could writhe a bit. It wasn't as though her stillness would fool him into thinking her unmoved.

"You like it this way too." He flicked at her with a fingernail.

"Yes." An undulation wove through her, from her toes all the way to the top of her head. "Slide that hand lower and see just how much I like it."

"Not a bashful bone in your body, is there?" His

mouth curved, its lopsidedness dizzyingly sensual somehow. "Patience, Lydia." He reached across her, balanced his palm on the mattress, and lowered his mouth to her breast.

A short keening cry drove itself out from her lungs. His tongue on her nipple was fire itself.

He lifted his head just enough to look in her eyes. His own were dark and fierce with the primal triumph of a man who had made a woman make that sound. "You could convince the greenest schoolboy to think himself a virtuoso lover," he said. "No wonder your man wanted me to put up three hundred pounds for you."

Three hundred. That was ridiculous. He'd better not have agreed. She could tell him so later. "Don't stop." That was the important thing to say now. "Please." So he couldn't accuse her of commanding him.

He chuckled low in his throat, as if he were following her thoughts exactly, and sank his mouth to her once more.

Men liked her bosom. Better than they liked her face, most times. And so she'd had ample experience of hands and mouths, strokes and pinches and bites and sucking and the astounding things tongues could do. Will Blackshear did them all, with a thorough, intricate care that lit up nerve endings one by one. She gasped and twisted, desperate as an eel on dry land. If this kept up it would all be over before he even got inside her.

"Enough." It didn't sound like command, did it? "That's enough." No, it sounded like abject pleading for mercy.

He raised his head and fixed her with a look that made the room spin around them. "It's not enough for me. Spread your legs." He swung his knee up and over, pushing her thighs apart even as she obeyed.

The sheet slid all the way off him. He was naked above her, impressively erect, his eyes glinting with sinful intent. He planted his second knee in between hers, and she spread her legs even wider to make room.

But instead of bringing his body forward he drew back, and back again, still kneeling, and she knew what was coming and she dug her heels in the mattress to lift up her hips, greedy wanton that she was, without even waiting for his hands to slide under her.

He caught her hips in a firm grasp and bent his head, and he dragged her into a whole bright world made of just his mouth and hands. No, his mouth and hands and the stubbly nascent beard on his chin, prickling all her most sensitive places into a frenzy as he rubbed his mouth over her.

No doubt he could be thorough. No doubt he could pleasure her nerve by intricate nerve here, too. But he'd primed her too well. His tongue stroked once, plunged once, and circled once, and she was done for. She shook all over, hips pushing to answer him of their own volition, hands clapped over her mouth to stop up cries that could have woken people in the next parish.

She was his. The taking would be but a formality. Every nerve, every cell in her body sang for him and him alone. Her hips sank slowly back to the mattress, his hands bearing her weight, cupping her arse in a fit so perfect that they stayed there, between her flesh and the linens, even after she'd come all the way back down.

He knelt at a forward pitch, his hands under her and his head bowed like some heathen worshipper. He didn't speak. He didn't look up. He remained in his prayerful posture for one long moment, and when his chin finally came up and his eyes met hers he was smiling with such serene satisfaction she might really believe he'd found a revelation between her thighs.

"Come here." She reached out with both arms. "If you please."

His hands slid out from under her and he stretched out to his full height on the horizontal. Instead of settling atop her, though, he eased himself to her side and lay facing her, his fingers venturing out to trace her hairline, his eyes roving over every inch of her face.

"That was a fine program." She turned her body to face him as well. "I liked it very much."

"There's more to it, actually." He trailed a finger down her cheek.

"I should hope so. You didn't take your pleasure."

"Nor do I intend to."

Oh. Well, not much was novel to a lady who'd worked at Mrs. Parrish's, and she'd encountered more than one man who liked to have his crisis denied. If he wanted her to—

"I shan't take, this time." Along her jaw his finger went, from under her ear on out to her chin. His eyes narrowed ever so slightly. "You shall give."

Chapter Seventeen

He was challenging her, as surely as if he'd bid her name her friends. The back of her neck prickled. "Do you think I cannot?"

"I don't know." Brows straight and serious, he let his hand fall from her face to the pillow. "I expect I'll find out."

Oh, he'd find out, to be sure. "I can give you anything you want." Likely he thought he'd seen her at the height of her powers in the gaming hell. He hadn't seen the half of what she could do. "I can give you things you didn't even know you wanted." Her voice was sloping into its duskiest timbre, thick with promise and potency. In one smooth motion she rose above him and pushed his shoulder down to make him lie flat. "I can leave you begging for mercy *and* begging for more."

"No." With a granite grip he halted her as she was halfway to straddling him. "No arts. Save your showing-off for the card table. That's not what I want."

Not what I want. For Heaven's sake, not again. Did he prefer a *mediocre* fuck, perhaps? She fixed him with exactly the blank look such sentiments deserved.

"I want *you*." The more gently he spoke, the more

resolute the pitch of his brows. "The Miss Slaughter with whom I've grown acquainted." He eased her down so she sat across his thighs, just back of his erection. "I don't want to spend myself in a stranger again. I want to do this with the woman for whom I've come to care."

"Don't." He'd turned into a bright sun of a sudden, or a blazing fire threatening to leap the hearth. "Don't say that." She had to angle her face away.

"Don't worry." His hands stroked up her arms. "It needn't be tender. It can be a good rollicking fuck. We can say as many filthy things as you like. Only it needs to be you here with me."

"It was, last night." Her eyes stung and she was blinking. "That was me too." She ought to have known he wouldn't truly accept that part of her.

For a moment he was silent, and finally she had to risk a glance. His eyes had gone slightly unfocused. He was busy with his own thoughts. "Of course," he then said. "Forgive my mistake. I just . . . want *all* of you this time."

"I can't." He had no idea what he was asking of her.

"Most of you, then. More of you. Lydia." He would have an answer for her every objection. He would prevail no matter what she did. "It needn't be so difficult. Trust me. Trust yourself. We'll find our way."

His soft exhortations kindled a memory: that night at the gaming hell, when he'd called her out to the hallway because he wanted to retreat, and she'd willed the necessary confidence into him. Now she was the one wrestling an urge to flee, and his were the steady hands holding her in place.

She could do this. She'd writhed and wailed and come for him already this morning without anger. She could meet him on what ground he liked, and she could do it without betraying herself.

She grasped his cock, rose up on her knees, and slid down hard until she had him to the hilt. That meant *yes*.

He closed his eyes and exhaled forcefully. "Yes," he said in his turn. "Good. Just like that." One of his hands left her arm to claw up a fistful of the rumpled sheet.

He didn't need her to be careful, then, or warm. "Open your eyes." She could command him without shoving him away. "Watch me fuck you."

A spasm shot through him, feet to scalp. His eyes half-opened and his hand trailed from her arm to her waist, settling there to ride her movement. "You are wanton beyond my wildest dreams, Lydia Slaughter. You are the lewdest, filthiest, most irredeemable . . ." His paean ended in a curse as he succumbed to another bolt of pleasure.

"You make me that way. I've wanted to see you naked since the first time we spoke in the dark upstairs at Beecham's." That was a confidence, not altogether easy to say. But it was what he wanted, so it was what he would have, in a caressing whisper, with her fingertips wandering through the hairs on his chest.

"Only since then? I think I wanted you on sight." He was addressing her bosom, watching, unabashedly, the bounce with which it echoed her every movement on him. He nudged her arm aside where it blocked his view. "Damnation, but your tits are exquisite," he growled.

"Would you like to watch me touch them?"

"Hell. What do you think?" His voice was hoarse and his eyes burned with appetite.

She lifted her hands, slowing her movement to a delicate writhing, and crossed her arms in front to cover her breasts with her palms. This might be more interesting if she played the shy virgin lured into lechery.

He stared, and swallowed. "Touch them."

"I am." Her eyelids fluttered modestly down.

"You ruthless, pitiless tease. Stroke them."

She couldn't help smiling. This was art, and it was showing off, and despite what he'd said he wanted it.

She let her smile tell him so, and he understood precisely. He smiled in answer, making it a sweet shared joke that sent currents of warmth through every part of her.

She dragged her fingers, one after the next, hesitant as a maiden in her bath. His throat rippled with a harder swallow. His smile evaporated and his gaze sharpened until it was fit to cut diamonds.

"What else would you like me to do?" She half-whispered the question, eyes averted to his chest.

"Put your fingers in your mouth. Make them wet."

Not bad, Blackshear. But she could do better. She met his gaze. Then she sent her hand down and slipped her fingers in between her body and his, between her legs, and brought them back wet.

His chest gave a quick heave as he sucked a breath in through his mouth.

She fetched her wet fingers back to one nipple, and the slick contact was almost as good as his tongue. Better, when you factored in the heat of his stare. She let her head fall back—why not?—and moaned aloud.

"Lydia." He near-strangled on her name. His solid hands landed on her hips, where they shaped her movement. Harder. Tipped back ten degrees or so. She'd remember. She was a quick study. Then his thumb was roaming down through her curling hairs, and then it was upon her, stroking nefarious circles. "Lydia," he said again. "Let me see you come."

She quivered. But no. Her eyes came to his and she shook her head. "Your pleasure first." She put his hand away from her.

Give, he'd said. She could do that. She kept hold of the one hand and reached for the other, lacing her fingers through his, palm to palm. She leaned forward, pushing his hands back down to the pillow, bringing her face nearer to his, thrusting on him all the while.

"Talk to me," he murmured, in such a voice as the serpent must have used with Eve.

So she told him a few things. Regarding the broadness of his shoulders, and the superiority of his cock, and the way his eyes alone could make her feel naked. And when his hips began to rock roughly under her and his face went grim with concentration, she told him more. How she'd worn the plum-colored sarcenet only for him. How the scent of bay rum would forever bring him to mind. How she'd never slept beside a man until two nights since.

Fraught confidences these were, requiring all her nerve. But how could she regret them, seeing their effect? His hands slipped free of hers and groped for a hold on her waist. His breath came in harsh pants. He was on the doorstep of delirium, and she would push him over the threshold.

She touched herself. He was close enough now that she might risk it. She wouldn't go ahead of him but she wouldn't be far behind.

He watched her fingers slip in between her thighs and he swore, thrusting up with furious strength. His teeth showed in all their imperfect glory as his lips pulled back in a grimace. His brows, like inky scrawls on his taut face, drove down and his eyes shut hard. His grip convulsed at her waist.

Climax took him like a lightning strike, all in one bright instant. He arched up from the bed and went rigid, gasping for breath, holding her hard to him that he could stay deep inside. His fingers would leave bruises. She didn't care. She stroked herself harder, faster, riding the wave of his pleasure, welcoming the bruises, claiming the fierce grasp of his hands right alongside the shudder of his release inside her. *I did this. I gave him what he thought I couldn't. His seed and his cock and his climax are mine.*

Then she was shuddering too, the back of her free hand pressed to her mouth against a squall of desperate sounds. Everything shuddered: the bedposts faltered in her vision, the wallpaper swam, the walls themselves lurched out and away. Nothing remained but pleasure, and rightness, and then nothing at all. A perfect void cradled her, or cradled what would have been her but that she'd shed her self to fuse with this perfection and now she need never come back.

She did come back, though. She always did. And this time she was lying naked atop one man when within hours she must make account to another. Claret and drowsy waking lust had obscured the outlines of her predicament—of her brash and profitless transgression—during all the hours before. Nothing remained to obscure those outlines now.

*H*IS BREATHS demanded a certain effort still, partly because he'd got out of practice with such exertions and partly on account of a singularly agreeable cause, namely the weight of the woman collapsed over his chest.

Will inhaled, and settled his outspread hands carefully on her back. She'd worn herself out with him. Let her take as long to recover as she liked.

If only there were some way . . . but he wouldn't spend these few glorious minutes thinking of that. There wasn't any way. Beyond this bed lay cold realities woven out of his small means and prior obligations, and her wish to be independent of a gentleman's protection.

Never mind. Nearly a year he'd waited for such a night and morning, and this moment alone was worth every minute of the wait.

Her ribs expanded against him with a sudden sharp breath. Oh, hell. She was crying.

"Lydia." One stab of disappointment would not be

denied, but quickly enough solicitude slipped into its place. "What is it, sweetheart? What's wrong?" He wrapped his arm across her and put his other palm to the back of her head.

For a few awful seconds she couldn't shape her breath into words, and he must wonder at what thoughts possessed her, in this moment when he'd believed her to be as contented as he. "I don't want to stay here," she finally said. "I want to go home to London." The admission apparently taxed her to the limit: she fell into soft hopeless sobbing, her muscles against him all wracked with misery.

"I'll take care of it, then." He could make no other answer in the world. "Don't worry. I'll get you home. Today, I will." A deep, deep breath was needed for the next words. "I promise."

MR. BLACKSHEAR proposed to speak to Edward, that she would not have to. "I'll tell him you fell ill, and that the viscount had already meant to return home today and offered to convey you. I can say your illness prevented anything improper from transpiring here."

But Edward was not so gullible as to credit such a tale. And even if he could be convinced that she and Mr. Blackshear had failed to consummate matters, he would still hold her guilty of the intent. She had defied him before the company. He would not soon forgive her for that.

Indeed the machinery of her punishment seemed already to be set in motion: when she rang for a maid, and sent her to Mr. Roanoke's room to fetch her burgundy muslin and a clean chemise, the girl came back empty-handed. Her clothing had all been banished from Mr. Roanoke's room. She was to dress in yesterday's gown and wait upon Mr. Roanoke in his study.

Her stomach wrung itself as she made her way to that room. Mr. Blackshear had dressed and gone ahead of her to effect the necessary persuasion on the viscount and then, presumably, to notify Edward of their departure. He might himself be in the study at this moment, ready to brace her up with his own unswerving resolve.

But no. She passed through the open study door to find Edward in consultation with some gentleman who had the appearance of a steward. He glanced up as she crossed the threshold and, without any interruption in his conference, gestured toward a chair where she was presumably to sit and wait her turn.

She moved near the chair, but stayed standing. To sit at his command felt like the action of a penitent woman. And she might be apprehensive, and a bit aghast at her recklessness of the past fifteen hours, and utterly unable to imagine how she and Edward could ever mend matters between them after the betrayals of these few days—but one thing she was not, was penitent.

Some five more minutes he and the steward conferred, and when the man had gone on his way Edward got up from the desk where he'd sat and strode to a window, not sparing her so much as a look. He settled there, hands clasped behind him, feet planted apart. "I trust you had a pleasant evening?" he said in an acid-laced voice.

"Just as pleasant as yours, I hope." If he expected her to act like the only guilty party in this drama, then he was in for a disappointment.

"My congratulations. Now listen." His chin lifted slightly. He didn't turn. "Your things have all been put into your trunk. You have twenty minutes to eat breakfast and make what good-byes you wish. You and your trunk will go in a cart to Witham, where you may catch the mail coach. At the end of this week, when I return to

London, you will have removed yourself from the house in Clarendon Square. Is all that quite clear?"

Half her innards dove downward; the other half twisted themselves in knots. Of course she'd known this might be the price of her indulgence. More than that: she must have known, if she paused to consider, that she could not go to bed with him again regardless his sentiments on the matter. And still, to hear it as an edict both chilled her and sent a warm flush of anger to her face.

"I see." She clasped her hands behind, like his, and advanced several steps toward him. "I'm a commodity to be wagered and passed about to other men when it suits you, then? But I'm to be chaste otherwise, and silent when you fling your own transgressions in my face?" She would gain nothing from this mutiny—even if he could be made to acknowledge his injustice, she would not go back to him—but the words poured forth nevertheless. "You're free to amuse yourself with other women as they catch your eye, even on a night you were to take me to the theater, and I must sit and wait and never ask you to account for yourself when I see you next?"

He turned then, and his hazel eyes glowed with the anger he was working to suppress. He'd never hit her, not once. But she'd never been quite sure he wouldn't. "I am the gentleman. You are the mistress." A pause of two seconds, the muscle in his cheek twitching as he composed his next words. "I've paid all your expenses these seven months. You've paid none of mine. You have no more right to dictate my behavior than does a footman or a maid."

Curse him, he served up his hostility with a dollop of undeniable logic. And he reminded her of a concern she'd neglected to weigh, in her heedless chasing after revenge and gratification. Behind her back her fingers laced themselves tighter. "What will become of Miss

Collier?" Footsteps sounded at a distance: it occurred to her she had still to face the unpleasantness of announcing she was to leave with Mr. Blackshear and his friend, rather than in the decreed cart and mail coach.

"To whom?" His regal brow quirked and his head canted several degrees to the side.

"My maid. Miss Collier." Her pulse was pounding of a sudden. How could she have been so careless? Who would look after Jane, if she did not? "I should like to take her with me." Her mind raced. She had nearly four hundred pounds. She might take a modest house, and persuade Will to go back to the hells with her. "You may keep all the jewels, and everything you ever bought for me. I only want to keep my maid."

Foolish, foolish, foolish of her to say so. A seasoned card player ought to know better. She'd just put a weapon in his hands and shown him where to strike.

"I'm afraid that won't be possible." He sent a glance over her shoulder while speaking, and raised his voice. Someone had arrived in the room, someone he was only too pleased to have as a witness to her humbling. "She's a pretty thing, that maid. She can divert me until I engage a new mistress."

He'd said it on purpose to wound her, of course; to insult her and to drive home just how little power she had with him. He might really have no such intentions.

It didn't matter. His words unleashed twin furies in her: rage at her failure to protect the girl, and wrath at every man who'd ever thought a woman existed only for his own diversion. Without thought she lunged forward and slapped him, hard as she could.

His arm moved so quickly. For an instant the whole world was hot pain; only in the next instant did she grasp the cause. Her face. The back of his hand. She stumbled back and sideways into sudden, steadying, unfamiliar arms. There were sounds, and a blur of motion,

and when the swimming stars receded from her vision
Edward was down on the Aubusson rug.

Mr. Blackshear, standing over him, swung about and
looked past her to the person supporting her, a grim,
urgent query in his eyes. He must have had the answer
he sought because he swung back to the man he'd
knocked down. "You may send your friends to call on
Lord Cathcart when you return to London. We'll meet
at your convenience."

Edward nodded, rubbing his jaw. Her jaw hurt too.
Her cheek still stung. He'd hit her.

Her whole body felt like eggshells cracking. He'd hit
her, and Mr. Blackshear had hit him, and now they
would meet with pistols drawn. "Don't," she said. "I
don't want this."

But nobody answered her. What was done was done,
and no words, no acts, no bone-deep, soul-wringing
penitence from her could undo any of it now.

*W*HAT NOW, Blackshear?" Lord Cathcart sprawled across
the opposite seat, one arm laid along its top, swaying
with the coach's movement. For the first half hour of the
journey they'd conversed on innocuous subjects, by tacit
agreement keeping up the pretense that nothing extraordinary had led to this early departure from the house
party. But gradually Miss Slaughter had dropped into
sleep, listing and listing until her head came to rest on
Will's shoulder, and now they might speak on topics
they would not broach in her hearing.

"Target practice, I suppose." Confound Fate and the
way it toyed with him. He could have just goaded Roanoke into calling him out that first night at Beecham's.
Save them both a deal of time and all the intervening
trouble.

The viscount shook his head. "I'm in no doubt of the

duel. I count that as already won." Proper thing for a man's second to say. "I'm asking, rather, what you intend in regard to the lady."

"I don't know." Self-reproach, his most faithful companion, lapped him in its python coils. "I wish I could do something for her, but I haven't the means to keep a mistress. I oughtn't to have trifled with her, knowing I could be the cause of her losing her place when I could offer no remedy."

"Don't take all the blame upon yourself. She's no green girl. She knew what were the stakes and she chose to play."

This was true, of course. True, and no consolation whatsoever. Not when every rose-petal-infused breath tugged his attention back to the slumbering presence at his side. "She was foxed, you know." He dropped his voice lower. "When I got to the room last night she was half the way through a bottle of claret. I ought to have slept on the floor."

"Did she reproach you this morning? Was her manner cold?" Cathcart angled his head quizzically and drummed his fingers on the leather squabs.

Vivid memories of this morning flooded in. *Would you like to watch me touch them? I've wanted to see you naked since the first time we spoke in the dark.* "No." He shifted in his seat, gently, to keep from disturbing her. "She was neither reproachful nor cold."

"Then trust her to look out for her own interest. A woman doesn't last long in her trade without that ability."

No doubt this was true as well. Yet how was she to manage? Banished from her house. No family with whom to take refuge. Cut off from all the security she'd known.

She sighed, audibly, and sank farther into him, the sweet solidity of her body accompanied by a staggering weight. Trust. Trust it was that let her drop into sleep beside him, here as well as in bed.

He ought never to have asked for her trust. How could he have been so presumptuous, when all he could offer was the demolition of her carefully pieced-together existence? How could he have been so foolish, knowing what he knew of this burden and how ill he bore it?

He closed his eyes. Let Cathcart think he'd gone to sleep. With any luck, he would. Then he could have a few minutes' respite, at least, from the prospect of the duel, the apprehensions for Miss Slaughter's welfare, and the incessant hammering of regret for all he'd done wrong.

*H*AD THINGS just gone smoothly at the posting inns, they would have reached London well before dusk. A carriage with three passengers, and the trailing equipage that bore the viscount's valet and baggage, oughtn't to have taxed the resources of any competent establishment. But here they met with a shortage of horses, there with three postilions taken ill, and the result was they were still on the road, the second carriage a full change of horses behind, when the shadows descended and their luck took one more turn for the worse.

The hoofbeats came all at once, out of nowhere. Christ. *Highwaymen*. Will was on his feet, lunging for the pistol box strapped back of Cathcart's seat, even before the footman's shout of alarm sounded, or the gunshots from their pursuers.

Two pistols, both loaded—he'd assured himself of that on the drive out to Essex. Two footmen riding up top, each with a blunderbuss, and two hired postilions to whom he would never have committed any share of their safety but that the sun had been sinking, and he simply couldn't wait for better horsemen to come along. He wouldn't rely on them, either to outrun the brigands—four sets of hoofbeats, did he count? Five?—or to risk themselves in a firefight.

The carriage swayed hard; he dug his feet into the floor, clamped the box against his body, and flung out his free arm to stop Miss Slaughter from pitching out of her seat. Her eyes, wide with terror, met his, and for an instant his stomach felt like the hull of a boat scraping bottom.

He'd promised to get her home. She'd trusted his word.

The discharge of a weapon directly overhead yanked him back into action. No time for self-indulgent despair. He was the only one here with a soldier's training, and two civilians were depending on him to keep his head in the midst of chaos.

He steadied Miss Slaughter, put the box on his knees, pulled out one ivory-handled pistol. Grip first he held it out to the viscount. "Tuck this in the back of your breeches, where it won't be seen straightaway."

"The footmen . . ." Cathcart said even as he closed his hand around the gun.

Will shook his head. "One's fired his shot already. I expect the other will be disarmed. The postilions as well. Numbers are against us." *We shouldn't have let the second carriage fall behind.* Futile regret, not worth voicing. They'd chosen to chase the daylight, and nothing could be done about that choice now.

The viscount busied himself with the pistol, his tight-pressed mouth outlined in white. Frightened, as any reasonable man would be, but ready to do what was asked of him.

"Lydia." He swung about to face her. An officer learned ways of dealing with a terror-stricken man. He might manage a terror-stricken woman by the same methods.

"Do you know how to fire a pistol?" He sent up a silent, fervent prayer.

She nodded. "My brother taught me to shoot."

Thank God, and thank Henry Slaughter, might he rest in peace. "I need you to be as heartless as you've ever been, Lydia." The carriage was slowing. They didn't have much time. "I'm going to ask you to shoot a man. Can you do that?"

And bless her cold soul, *that* was the way to blot out the terror. Every angle in her face hardened and she held out her hand for the gun.

Already he was sliding to the floor as he released the pistol into her grasp. "You shall counterfeit to faint. Hide the pistol in your skirts." Still speaking, he held the gun box out to Cathcart, who took it and put it back in place. "The viscount and I will contrive to be taken from the carriage, and to get the men facing away. You must shoot one in the back."

She nodded again, her eyes like shadowed ice as she laid herself down and hid her gun. If she had any qualms over shooting a man in the back, she did not show it.

"Presumably there will be a moment of confusion, and then you, Cathcart, must bring out your pistol and shoot another." From outside came the thump of boots hitting the ground, dropping from horse height. "We'll do what we can with what numbers remain." One last look to the viscount, one last look to Lydia. His heart beat hard but steady. Strong. "Don't shrink from killing. We can't afford that. I'm counting on you both." He just had time to take hold of her wrists, to feel her runaway pulse, before the carriage door was wrenched open.

Chapter Eighteen

$\mathcal{D}$ON'T SHOOT." Will half-turned, one hand chafing Lydia's wrists, the other raised in a show of surrender. "We haven't any weapons. We'll give you no trouble. We only want to go on our way." His fingers itched madly for the grip of a gun, and every sinew in his body protested this decision to play the lame deer before a pack of wolves. But he would do whatever he must to draw all attention away from his armed companions.

"Set your money and your jewels down here by the door. No quick movements, now." The voice bit through the twilight dim like the jaws of a man-trap. A pistol barrel poked in through the open door. Enough daylight remained to show a second man just back of the one speaking, and one more at a distance, keeping hold of the horses. Five, at least. The three in sight had left their faces uncovered, which did not bode well.

Beneath his thumb Lydia's pulse beat a scattershot rhythm. The sensation was horribly familiar. Never mind. At this moment, his old private anguish was the least important thing in the world.

"My wife's jewels are all in her trunk." He locked his gaze on a spot in midair where it would meet with none of the men's. "Money as well." Thank goodness his trunk and Lydia's had gone on this carriage instead of the other; they might make a useful distraction now. He cleared his throat. "What money we have is in the trunks. Will you take them, please, and let us go on our way? You see my wife's fainted from the fright."

"From disgust at her cringing dog of a husband, more like." This came from one of the other men, and inspired a spurt of laughter from the one with the horses. Good. Further distraction. The more they occupied themselves in bullying, the less watchful they'd be for any threat.

"Take down the trunks," the first man snapped in the footmen's direction. He leaned in through the doorway and used the pistol to lift Will's chin until their eyes met. "Now, my fair fellow, I'll give you one last chance." He was an ugly sod, with two visible rotten teeth and the breath to match. "Hand out your purse, and the other gentleman's purse too. If we must search your pockets and find you've been lying, it won't go well for you or your fainted wife."

A hot tide of rage swept through all his poised muscles; he shaped it into the more manageable form of grim intent. They would not touch her. If he had to take fire from every pistol these blackguards had among them, if he had to stagger after them and flatten them one by one as his own life gushed out—But he wouldn't have to. He was luring them into a neater trap.

That's right, whoreson. Take us out of the carriage to search us. I expect you'll be the one at whom she points her pistol, now. He blinked and fidgeted as though his underclothes were all made of scratchy wool. "We haven't any—that is—" A quick glance at Cathcart who was watching, ready, in perfect dependence on the efficacy of his plan. More *trust*, devil take it. And what could he do—what could he, or any man on this earth, ever do when trust came, but strive to be worthy? "I don't think . . . I'm almost certain all we have is in the trunks." He said this last in a thin watery voice, eyes now averted to the floorboards. The pistol under his jaw was an irritant, merely. A man serious about shooting him would have done it by now.

"Very well. Crawl on out and we'll see, won't we?" The pistol receded and a ripple of anticipatory mirth went through the brigands—here were the other two, now, hands full of what had been the footmen's and drivers' weapons—as they all shuffled back to make room. Clearly they thought great sport was in store.

To let go of Lydia's hand then felt, for an interminable second, like stepping off a cliff. But he did it. With one slight press for courage, to remind her he'd put his faith in her, he released his grip and scuttled, ungraceful and unthreatening as he could make himself, through the carriage door and to the ground below. The viscount jumped down after, and Will managed to collide with him, to pivot, to stumble several steps before regaining his footing, hands atop his head, at some little distance from the carriage.

The highwaymen hooted, making plain their contempt for such a shabby specimen of masculinity. But they had to turn their backs to the carriage to face him now.

Cathcart slipped silently to his side, hands likewise held overhead. This near, Will could sense his coiled-spring tension. He'd been a crack shot in university days—please God he'd kept that up as well as he'd kept up his billiards.

A quick, habitual inventory: on the ground, four robbers of varying size; the coach beyond, footmen weaponless but still possibly of use; postilions dismounted; a woman with a pistol somewhere within. Off to the right, the outlaws' five horses with one mounted man holding on to all the bridles. He, too, had fixed his attention on the two prisoners, though half a turn would give him a view into the carriage.

Nothing to be gained by imagining that. Will clenched his teeth. The purse in his breast pocket felt like a great hot coal, heavy, smoldering, and surely glowing right through the wool of his coat as the burliest of the villains stepped forward, ham hands rising to make a search. *Now, Lydia. Now.* "Ought I—ought I to hold my hands up, like so, or out to the side?" He must divert them as thoroughly as he could, lest they think of swiveling about and catch a glimpse of—*There.* Movement in the carriage doorway; fabric, a face, an arm—his heart whirlpooled round his ribcage and bloodlust woke in his bones.

"For the love of God, will you shut your mewling mouth and—" The air split with a crack and Will seized the man before he had time to turn; seized him by the ears and slammed his face down against one upraised knee. His knee would hurt like the devil, later. No time to feel it now.

A second shot rang out beside him and an answering shot came from ahead. His heart clambered halfway up his throat. If she'd been hit—but there was no time for *ifs.* He shoved aside the dead weight of the man who'd meant to search him, and launched himself in the direction from which the last shot had come.

How many of them were still standing? Had Lydia and Cathcart both hit their marks? He'd sort it out later. Just now the brigand before him was pulling another pistol from his belt—confound these bastards to Hell; how many did they carry?—and Will swung his arm in a hard arc to send the weapon flying. Dimly he was aware of hoofbeats and commotion somewhere on the right; then the disarmed man kicked out and connected with his kneecap and Christ, it did hurt now. Stupid swiving shin-kicking son of a goat; after all the trouble he'd been at to take away the advantage of pistols *and* the advantage of numbers—he shifted the weight to his good leg and threw a fist at the blackguard's face, dead center.

The man went staggering backward, arms windmilling for balance, blood already running from his nose. He'd nearly regained his footing when one more shot sounded, and he jerked, and crumpled like a scarecrow cut down.

For a disorienting instant it was like being back in the little room upstairs at Beecham's, struggling to bend his brain to some principle of odds that made no intuitive sense. Two ivory-handled pistols; two shots. Then how to account for the third?

He swung his gaze leftward and saw her, kneeling by the body of a fallen bandit, the man's own smoking pistol clutched in both her hands. Her wide eyes met his with no recognition whatsoever. She let the gun fall, and twisted to look at the lifeless form beside her. Her shoulders rose with a mighty inhalation, and her fists rose too, and of a sudden she was flailing at the man as though he stood between her and her next breath.

One quick glance around the clearing: they'd felled four. The fifth was gone, and the horses with him. "Cathcart." The viscount stood arrested, staring at Lydia the way he might stare at some banshee dropped into their midst. "See if any of them are still alive, and bind any that are. Your men can cut the rope from the trunks."

He went to her. She didn't look up, or slacken in her grim exertions, so he crouched. "Lydia." This near, he could hear that she was panting. She gave no sign of having heard him.

"Lydia," he said, more forcefully. He might as well have been whispering into a whirlwind. He shifted behind her and wrapped his arms round, pinning her elbows to her waist, then stood, lifting her right off her feet.

"Smash him." Her voice shook with passion. She twisted, struggling to get free, but his grip was too solid. "Smash his face like you did those others."

"There's no need." No inclination, either. His appetite for violence never did outlive a threat. But he'd seen re-actions like hers before, among his fellows in battle, and he'd heard of worse. Several of the more senior in his regiment had been at Badajoz, and come away with tales that could curdle a man's blood. He bent his head to bring his voice closer to her ear. "He can't hurt you, this man. You're safe from him."

"You don't *know*." It sounded like a sweeping and final pronouncement on his character, and to be sure there were many, many things he didn't know.

Nevertheless he held her. Ignorant as he was, he stood with his arms locked fast, absorbing all her residual fury. His kneecap ached and his knuckles stung and his whole body felt the effects of two largely sleepless nights. But he was alive, and so was she, and so was the vis-count. Easily it might have been otherwise.

She didn't speak again. Her body, too, went quiet at last, and he set her on her feet—she would want some time alone to collect herself—and went to see how Cath-cart got on.

"The one whose face met with your knee is the only one still breathing." The viscount jerked a thumb toward where his footmen were just knotting a length of rope round the ankles of the form in question. "Well, that one and the bloody coward who ran away with the horses." He laughed, a bit manically, passing the back of a glove across his forehead. "Thank God Miss Slaughter proved aptly named."

"One of the shots was yours, I think. I owe my life to you both."

Cathcart shrugged, and gestured imprecisely at one of the fallen figures without turning his eyes that way. His complexion wore a grayish tinge that Will had seen on other men more than once.

"They would only have gone to the gallows, you know, if we'd left them alive." Sometimes you put a hand on a man's shoulder, in this moment. But the viscount was his elder, halfway in years between him and Nick, and possessed of a rather delicate dignity. Will flexed his fingers but kept his hand where it was.

"Oh, I know. They deserved what they got. If one of them rose up alive I'd shoot him again. And still it's . . ." He hesitated, jaw working as though to find the proper word. ". . . odd . . . to know you've ended someone's life."

That it was. No getting round it. In this one matter, he had a great deal more experience than his older friend. "That you say so is testament to your humanity." His hand lifted after all, just to glance lightly off Cathcart's shoulder. "And I won't do you the disservice of trying to persuade you into callousness. I'll only suggest you turn your thoughts to Lady Cathcart and everyone else who would have been grieved if it were you instead of these villains lying facedown in the dirt." He dusted his hands together. "Now let's move this last fellow nearer the road. If he's lucky his friend with the horses will come back and find him. If he's less lucky it will be the law."

He couldn't help glancing back at Lydia on the word *lucky*, just to see what might be her response.

She didn't respond. She stood just where he'd set her, arms wrapped round her midsection as though to steady herself in the absence of his grasp. For all her bravery, she'd surely been harrowed by the past quarter hour. They'd best finish up here and get her home.

* * *

*H*E'D RELOADED the pistols, shaken powder from the horn into both pans, wrapped them in their flannels and put the whole box neatly away by the time they pulled into the outskirts of London. He had not found the proper words to say to Lydia in that time.

I'm so sorry to have brought you into danger. I'm grateful beyond measure for your courage. Will I ever see you again after tonight? That their acquaintance might close this way—a near encounter with death followed by a polite farewell not twenty-four hours after he'd finally found release in her arms—made him want to put a fist through the nearest window. For pity's sake, might he really fight a duel at the end of this week over a woman who'd be nothing but a vivid memory by then?

The carriage swayed going round a turn, and her body leaned briefly into his before she was able to pull herself away and back upright. She'd brushed aside his and Cathcart's every attempt at solicitude, insisting she had no need of brandy or a seat to herself. She was fine, she'd assured them, and then she'd pressed herself into the seat's farthest corner and stared out into the dark.

Clearly she was not fine.

Well, why should she be? With everything she'd undergone in this one day it was a wonder she wasn't curled up and raving on the carriage floor. So why the devil wouldn't she let him help her?

"Is there a friend with whom we can leave you?" Did she have any, besides the two ladies they'd left behind in Essex? "I fear your maid will be caught unprepared by your early return. She won't have had a chance to light all the fires, or see to supper."

"She's not there. I sent her to visit her family for the week." She turned from the window. The carriage-lamps shed scarcely enough light to show her face, and of course her face showed him nothing. "And you're not leaving me anywhere. I'm going to your rooms with you." She sent her attention back to the dark outside, not waiting for his response.

Her words gutted him, or rather the combination of her words with that flat, brook-no-dissent timbre he remembered so well. Devil take it all, were they really here again? After what they'd just borne together, after the honest intimacy they'd attained this morning, after he'd engaged himself to a duel with her damned protector on her behalf, could she really think to drag him through another antagonistic coupling?

Cathcart watched him, one eyebrow raised. The viscount's eyes cut to Lydia and back. *She's not well,* said his face with mute eloquence.

Yes, I know. And that's exactly why I can't just set her down at her empty house and drive off. He turned his hands palm-up, a gesture of quiet resignation. "Did you catch that, your lordship? My lodgings. One less stop for you." He angled away to look out his own window. Lord only knew what would happen when they reached his rooms and she found out he wasn't going to give her what she wanted. Doubtless they were in for a long night.

Somewhere in the bustle of unloading the trunks and directing the porter, Cathcart pulled him aside. "Are you sure this is a good idea?" he muttered, throwing another significant glance to where Lydia stood, arms folded, surveying the facade of Lewes Buildings.

"I'm almost sure it's not." A thoroughly inappropriate spasm of laughter threatened; clearly the events of the day were taking their toll on him too. "Only I don't know what else is to be done. I'd have gone mad with worry if I'd left her off in Clarendon Square in this state."

He mightn't have said so much, had he been in fuller possession of his faculties. Going mad with worry suggested a stronger attachment to Miss Slaughter than he'd so far owned, and the viscount's expression made it clear he hadn't missed that nuance.

So be it. He was too weary to dissemble with a friend, particularly a friend who'd proved his worth more than once today. "Write to me when you've arranged matters with Roanoke." He put out his hand, and the viscount shook it, and in another minute he was gone. Three or four minutes more, and Will was slipping a shilling to the porter in gratitude for his discretion as well as the work of hauling trunks and lighting the lamps and fires.

Quiet descended as he shut the door and turned to put his back against it. Lydia stood facing away from him in the middle of the . . . parlor, one might call it. Sitting room. The room that was not the bedroom. He could imagine the sweep of her gaze across the plain curtains, plain unpapered walls, plain cabinet, and single stout armchair.

He'd never been ashamed of his lodgings. Lewes Buildings was a bit on the Spartan side, perhaps, when compared to the Albany or any other first-rank bachelor-quarters, but there was nothing shabby in these rooms. Still, the rooms numbered only two. No pantry; no place to house a personal servant. If she'd harbored delusions of his keeping her, those fancies must be crumbling like slipshod plasterwork.

"It's nothing very grand." He crossed to the table and set to clearing away the ink and paper, the few letters that sat there. Somewhere in the cabinet he had a table-cloth. Didn't he?

"It's as I imagined." He could see her face now, taking in his living quarters with keen attention. "Modest and well maintained."

It was exactly that. And of course she hadn't harbored

delusions. No hint of disappointment intruded on her quiet approval of his rooms. He put his papers and ink in the cabinet and came back for his jar of sand. "Are you hungry? There's a public house round the corner that makes a fair pigeon-and-mushroom pie. I could fetch us a pair, and some ale."

"I'm not hungry." Her expectancy rippled outward to fill the small room. "I presume that door leads to your bedroom?"

Damnation. He'd hoped for a few peaceful minutes more. "It does. But Lydia." Now for it. He put away his sand and faced her. "I'm not going to bed you tonight."

"Yes, you are." Not even the slightest pause to absorb his refusal, nor any trace of uncertainty in her features.

"I'm not. It's been a long and trying day, and you, in particular, are in no condition for such—"

"Neither was I in any condition last night, as I recall." She shrugged. Her eyes hardened and left him altogether as she began to tug down her right glove. "Maybe you ought to have a drink. Claret seems to overcome your scruples quick enough."

One flash of temper, one quick knife-twist of guilt; then he recovered his resolve. "No." He folded his arms and put his back to the wall. "I'll stand here all night if you like, listening to every angry thing you can think of to say. I will bear as much acrimony as you care to deliver, if that does you good. Out here, though. Standing up. Fully clothed. I will not couple with you."

"You ought to have left me at my house, then." She was starting to crumble. He'd taken away her plan of action and she clearly had no idea how else to proceed. Her glove slipped off her right hand and hung limp in her left. She stood still, blinking and pressing her lips tight together.

It was all coming down on her now, he knew. The fear she'd held at bay in order to play her part with the pistols. The shock and humiliation of having been struck across the face by the man who kept her. The question of where she was to live, in a few days' time, and how she was to provide for herself. Probably the old familiar losses were joining in as well, adding their practiced voices to the general dirge.

He pushed off the wall and went to where she stood. "I think you ought to get into your nightgown and go to bed." He took the glove, put it in his pocket, and started easing the second one off. Soothingly as he could, he spoke. "There's nothing more to be done tonight. You'll feel better when you've had some rest, and in the morning we can consult about what to do."

Her hand closed convulsively on his. "I *won't* feel better. I won't ever feel better again." She stared past his shoulder, her words barely clearing a whisper.

He waited for her to say more, and when she didn't, he pried her fingers gently loose and drew off the glove. "It's natural to think so, after such a day as you've had. Fear, in particular, has a kind of residue. But it does lose strength over time. Soldiers couldn't very well come back to marry and raise families if that weren't so." Glove in his pocket, he moved round behind her. "With your permission I'll unbutton your gown and unlace your corset. Only so that you may dress for bed. My intentions regarding your person haven't changed."

Her head dipped forward, the back of her neck impossibly stark and vulnerable. The sight made him light-headed, his breath suddenly shallow. So easily he might have lost her tonight. If her pistol had misfired, if her aim had been less true, if just one highwayman had been a bit quicker in his reaction . . .

No. That way lay madness. He bent his attention to her buttons, small flat bone-colored things with carved edges that pressed unevenly into the pads of his thumbs.

Layer by layer, careful and chaste, he got her out of her clothing and down to her chemise. She could manage the rest without his help. He ought to withdraw to the bedroom and pour water into the basin so she could wash.

She was so tired, though. Her shoulders sagged. She hadn't made the least attempt to play on what she must know of his susceptibility as he'd undressed her. She hadn't even spoken since confiding her fear that she'd never feel better again.

Devil take it. He bent and lifted her into his arms. Her hand took a hold on his coat and her muscles all subsided against him, an acquiescence as gratifying as if it had been the first salvo of intimacy between them, rather than an overlooked piece of ordnance pitched in after the skirmish was well under way.

He stood for a moment, eyes closed, breathing in her scent. If only . . . Truly, it didn't bear thinking of. But they'd been near in station once, youngest son and youngest daughter in respectable families, both with unstained, marriageable souls. If he could have met her then . . . he might have one day lifted and carried her in just this fashion, over a threshold and—

Madness, again. No use indulging those thoughts. The bedroom door stood partly open; he used his foot to swing it the rest of the way in. She lifted her head to view this room's furnishings, shadowy shapes in the firelight. Chair, table, washstand, clothespress, and the bed, in all its austerity of black posts and white linen. He bore her there, and sat. If she asked what he thought he was doing, he would have no answer.

Her hand tightened on his coat. Her head ducked against his shoulder. Where his arms met her, round her shoulders, at the back of her knees, he could feel the muscles tensing as though to shrink herself small. "I want to tell you something," she said, and his heart began to race like a coursing hound.

"You can tell me whatever you wish." He tightened his hold.

Twice she drew in breaths as though to begin speaking, only to let them out again. On the third breath, she managed it: "I spoke of my parents having died in an accident."

Hell. Suddenly he knew the rest.

"In fact they were killed in a highway robbery. Murdered by men just like the ones we—" Her voice faltered and she pressed her face into his coat.

He let out a long breath, and touched his chin to her bound-up hair. "Were you with them?"

She shook her head, forehead brushing out a rhythm against the wool at his shoulder. "I was still recovering from the illness of which I've told you. They'd gone to look at a house, in another part of Lancashire. They intended . . ." She started trembling then, giving in to tears. "They planned to sell our house and move to a new neighborhood, where we could live among people who wouldn't know . . ." Her hand let go his coat to swipe at her face. "Because of what I did, they would have had to give up everything familiar and start over among strangers. And because of what I did, they were on the road that night."

He gathered her in closer, close as he could. She shuddered like some hapless small prey seized in the very jaws of grief. "It was bad luck." With his flesh he would absorb her every shudder, just as he'd absorbed her rage when he held her back from the body of the man she'd shot. "Bad luck, and an evil act by villainous men. You're not to blame."

"I've told myself that." She let the reference to luck pass unchallenged. "But I don't find any comfort in it." She pressed her head against his coat as though she meant to burrow in there. "I try so hard not to think of what their last moments must have been."

"I know, sweetheart." Everything he had went into those words. *I know exactly how hard you have to work to keep that out of your thoughts.* He knew how banished memories, banished images hovered, only waiting to spot some breach in your defenses by which they might slip in. "Your nightmares . . ."

She nodded against his shoulder. "I think I've seen their end a hundred times or more." She was breathing in gulps now, not well able to talk.

"I've lost my own parents, as I told you." His left arm braced her shoulders and his left hand stroked her upper arm, a painfully paltry gesture of reassurance. "My mother in childbed when I was ten; my father after a long illness some few years ago. It's difficult enough when it comes of a natural cause. No one should have to bear what you've borne."

Should. That was the flimsiest of notions, wasn't it? Like pebbles from a slingshot against a raging tidal wave. Things happened to people, and they bore them, or failed to bear them, and *should* really played no part in the matter.

She pressed the heels of both hands to her eyes. "I didn't bear it, truly. I wasn't strong enough." A hesitation. Her voice sank near a whisper. "I wanted to . . . quit life altogether."

"Did you . . ." He swallowed. "Did you make any attempt to . . ." And then he saw. "Of course you did. You went to work in a brothel."

Again she nodded. "I thought I would catch the pox, at least. I thought the suffering might . . . cleanse me even as it consumed me. Like fire." For a moment she was silent, studying her own hands. "I was ignorant." She wiped her palms together and let her hands fall.

"You were stronger than you thought." He could see the rest of her story without her telling. She'd set out to destroy herself layer by layer, but at her core she'd found an unexpected will to survive, and with it, the ruthlessness that had powered her through life ever since. Out of the ashes of catastrophic misfortune she'd reinvented herself as something formidable, honed and tempered by each disaster she weathered.

She hadn't, thank God, succeeded in destroying herself. She'd lived. And he'd found her. And here she was, in his lap, in his arms, confiding all her most difficult secrets, and he could not for the life of him see how he was ever to let her go.

"Stronger in some things, perhaps." Her words tugged him back to the conversation. "But in others, wrecked beyond any hope of repair." She shifted in his lap. He knew the language of her body now; she was preparing to say something important. "I will never love anyone again, Will. I cannot. You understand, I hope?" She didn't look at him. She waited, still and taut, for his reply.

"Because . . . you don't want to risk that kind of loss again?" Everything in his field of vision wobbled a bit, the way it might if he'd run at full speed into a brick wall.

"I *cannot.*" She articulated the syllables with painstaking precision. "Forgive my presumption. I don't mean to imply that I believe you had any hopes of . . . I only want you to understand."

"Of course." Dry husks, those words, rattling all the way up his throat and out into the air. He did have hopes. And he didn't understand. How could she give him this gift, spilling out her dark history, leaning on him for comfort, trusting him as he knew in his marrow she'd never trusted another man, and then slam a door and bolt it against what ought logically to follow?

He filled his lungs on one slow breath. She was waiting, hushed and motionless in his arms. She knew *Of course* could not be the whole of his answer. "I won't lie to you, Lydia. If I'm not in love with you already I'm within striking distance of the state. There's nothing presumptuous in your wanting to warn me, given what you must have observed these past few days."

"We couldn't ever have—"

"Shh. I know." He set his hand at the back of her head, smoothing her hair to tell her she needn't comfort him with all the reasons his love could never have come to fruition. "I can't afford to keep you, and I know you don't want to be kept. Our stations put marriage out of the question. And there are other reasons, besides, that prevent my offering myself to a lady. Nevertheless I wish you would love me. For all that I know better, I can't help what my heart wants." He eased his right arm out from under her knees until she sat upright on his lap, supported only by his left arm at her back. "There, I suppose, is another difference between us."

"I'm sorry." Her face was near his. Her eyes were red and swollen. "I like you very much, and I—I think my body spoke for itself this morning. But that's all I can give. I wish I could grant you what you want, but it's too late for me."

"Never mind about it." He pressed a kiss on her forehead. "It's been a frightfully long day. Let me pour you some water and you can wash and go to bed."

He lay awake for well over an hour after she'd dropped into sleep, partly on the watch for nightmares, partly reviewing all the scenes of their acquaintance as though he could somehow rearrange them to arrive at a different ending.

There *ought* to be a different ending. They belonged with one another. Her broken edges fit with his.

But Fate had no use for neat arrangements. Here they were, just as they'd been that first morning at Chiswell when he'd looked over his shoulder and seen her, hatless, in her insufficient cloak. Here after all was their condition, perched on their separate wind-whipped summits, in view of each other, but too distant to reach.

Chapter Nineteen

WOULD SHE never wake in the right bed again? That thought barely had time to take a toehold in her brain before a bolder, more reckless thought shoved it aside: *This* is *the right bed*.

Nonsense. She was sleep-addled, and not thinking clearly. The last few days had taken too much of a toll. Her brain had more important matters to weigh.

She lay still and let her senses wake one at a time. Linen against her skin, her hair loose on the pillow, no body touching hers. Several scents threaded together and apart. Bay rum and the man who wore it. Coffee, making her mouth water. Chocolate? Toast. Breakfast had somehow appeared.

A rustle of paper interrupted the silence: the page of a newspaper turned. She opened her eyes. Will Blackshear sat fully dressed in an armchair near the bed, the *Times* in one hand and the other hand feeling for his coffee on the bedside table. He landed upon it and lifted it just that way, palm curved over the top, fingertips spaced all round the cup's perimeter, with no regard for the handle. He drank from it that way too, the arch between his thumb and forefinger providing sufficient space for the purpose. When he set it down again he found the saucer on the first try, never looking away from his paper. She might just lie here, and watch that, and never get up from this wrong bed again.

His fearlessness took her breath away. Facing highwaymen unarmed. Telling a lady he was near to loving her after she'd already warned him the sentiment could meet with no return. She would never regret anything she'd shared with this man; not her body, not her numberish skills, not the grueling confidences of last night.

On her side of the table sat two cups. Coffee and chocolate, they must be. He hadn't known which she preferred so he'd brought both. He'd set the saucers atop the cups, too, to keep them warm.

She closed her eyes. Something about the sight of those two covered cups struck at the rawest place inside her, the part that never gave up wishing for things she could not have.

If she were able to love him . . . if she could somehow undo the corrosion that had overspread her heart . . . if they could forge an arrangement as independent men and women sometimes did . . . she would only lose him in the end. No matter how he might love her now, he must finally leave her for a respectable lady who could give him children.

And it was right that he should. He ought to have children. He deserved a blooming, sunlit, *honest* kind of love, not a connection built on heedless grappling in dark hallways and other people's beds. He deserved a wife who could know his family and take her place among them.

He deserved, first of all, to be released from any obligation that might jeopardize such a future. "Will." Her eyes opened. "I don't think you ought to meet with Mr. Roanoke. I think you must call off the duel."

He frowned, slightly, letting his paper fall as he studied her. Indeed they were odd words with which to make a morning greeting. He reached for his coffee. "Why?"

"Because it could end in your death." Her fists clenched under the covers, where he wouldn't see. "And it would be a very poor reason to die."

"Don't think much of my chances, do you?" He raised his cup, this time by its handle and this time holding the saucer beneath with his other hand. There was a formality in his manners this morning, a distance that had not been there last night. She could see him seeking the proper tone to take with her, now he knew he could not hope for her love.

"Your chances might be excellent. I don't know enough about your marksmanship and Mr. Roanoke's marksmanship to render a judgment. But the consequences of losing are too great to justify even a marginal risk."

A smile flickered over his lips, as though there were something comical in evaluating risk. Then he shook his head and went grave. "He hit you, Lydia. I don't have it in me to let that pass."

"You didn't let it pass. You knocked him down." She had reason on her side, and if reason wouldn't sway him, she had a few unscrupulous tricks up her sleeve as well. "What will become of that soldier's widow, if you're killed? What will become of Mr. Fuller, and the ship you meant to help him buy?"

He frowned again, at his coffee this time. He'd asked himself these same questions, obviously. And obviously come up with no good answer. He set his cup aside and rubbed an absent palm on the knee he'd hurt in fighting the highwaymen. "I don't know what will become of them. But the only way out of the duel is to apologize. And I simply cannot do that." His gaze, gentle but resolute, came to her. "You know the difference, I think, between *won't* and *cannot*. You know it's not a matter of persuading me."

She knew no such thing. His weak spot, clearly, was his sense of duty to the people depending on him. She would go after that weak spot without mercy.

He reached across to her side of the table and took first one, then the other of the saucers off the cups, replacing them underneath. "You ought to drink one of these before it gets cold. Did you know you slept the whole night without any nightmares? At least, none that announced themselves to me."

Her hand stopped halfway to the coffee. Her whole body remembered the way he'd held her last night as she'd delivered up her sorrow. As though he'd known she might fly apart into irretrievable pieces if he were to let go. She felt for the cup, and finally had to turn her eyes away from him. "You must be a very light sleeper."

"When I have cause to be." So clearly could she picture him lying beside her, attuned to her slightest sound and movement because he had . . . feelings . . . tender feelings . . . for her. She'd spat as hard as she could on *feelings* and *tenderness*, and she hadn't dissuaded him one whit.

This, too, is his weakness. Use it against him. She pushed herself to a sitting position, took up the cup and saucer, and forced her gaze to his. "You said last night we might speak of my prospects this morning, and what is to be done."

"Indeed." He crossed one leg over the other, angling his whole body to face her. "What day do you expect Mr. Roanoke back in London?"

"Sunday." This was Wednesday. In the space of four days she must find new lodgings, secure Jane's safety, and persuade Mr. Blackshear to abandon the duel. "Will." There could be no question as to where she must start. "I'm sixteen hundred and twenty-eight pounds short of what I require for my annuity. How much more money do you need to buy your ship?"

"Eight hundred and some." His eyes quickened with alertness. He knew where her thoughts were tending.

"I need to go back to the hells. I need you to come with me." *Need, need, need.* The chisel at which she would tap, relentlessly, until his resistance lay in pieces at her feet. "Allowing me an extra hundred for expenses until the annuity begins to make its return, and let us say two hundred to keep you until you see a profit from that ship, we'll want two thousand, five hundred, and twenty-eight, altogether."

"We can't possibly win that much in four nights." But everything in his face said he was waiting, hoping, to hear his assertion refuted.

"We'll have five nights, at least." She bolted a quick swallow of coffee. "If Mr. Roanoke returns on Sunday, then Monday at dawn would be the soonest you'd meet. Tuesday is more likely. I scarcely imagine he'd rush straight out upon coming home to enlist a second and send him off to arrange things with the viscount. Let's presume six nights." She sat straighter. "We need only win an average of four hundred twenty-one pounds, six shillings, eight pence per night. You'll recall we won eleven hundred sixty-two in a single evening, our first time out."

"You presume we'll win every night." A sound, sensible objection, but hope was blazing through him now like a wildfire over parched cropland. He wanted, so badly, to make his word good with Mr. Fuller, to keep his promise to that dying soldier, and to be of service to her, even though she would not love him.

"Not at all. I spoke of an average. Some nights we may lose, and some nights we'll surely win more." Another bracing swallow of coffee, and one last well-aimed thrust. "In any event, there's no question I must go. All my hope of a decent life, for my maid as well as myself, depends upon my winning more money."

"We'll play, then. Beginning tonight. You know perfectly well I cannot stand by and let you go into those places alone."

She drank more coffee and said nothing. The silence would give him time to reflect, to note that if he lost his life in the duel she certainly *would* be going into the hells without his protection. And once they were at the table tonight, and winning, he would be reminded of all the good he could do with those winnings. By the time he'd amassed what he needed to be a partner in Mr. Fuller's business, and to see to the security of that widow, he would surely feel such an attachment to life, to his own bright prospects, as would render the very idea of the duel preposterous.

That night they lost twelve hundred. He, of course, lost most of it. She called him in at a presumably advantageous moment, and he played every hand and wagered just as she cued him to do, and still the cards fell out wrong and he watched his pile of counters shrink to almost nothing.

"Do you think the banker may be cheating?" Will said when she'd finally signaled for a conference. The establishment, which used no name beyond its address, was grimmer altogether than Oldfield's. It offered no convenient corridors or anterooms for a private meeting: the door to the gaming parlor led straight to the stairs and the further doors that shut out the world beyond. They had to speak in a corner of the very room, in full view, pantomiming a drunken flirtation in contrast to their hushed, sober words.

"I don't think so. If he is, they're better tricks than any I know." She let a hand fall on his sleeve and curved her lips into a smile that promised such tricks as no gaming-hell banker ever dreamed of. "The wrong cards come up sometimes, in spite of the odds. Just like when I showed you three cards and you found the ace of spades on your first try. Over time the odds will prevail."

But they didn't *have* time. After tonight they had five, maybe four nights remaining, and an even greater mountain to climb than when they'd walked in here, some hours since. He grazed a knuckle along her jaw, but he could not come close to matching her show of *sangfroid*. "Do you want to play on? I'll trust your judgment." He sounded every bit as ill as he felt.

"I confess I'm distracted by our losses, and consequently duller than I'd like to be." She caught his hand and brought the knuckle to her lips. Her lashes fluttered down. "Let's leave."

His body couldn't even muster a proper animal response to the tickle of her breath on his skin. That she would admit to being concerned by their losses only confirmed him in his kindling alarm. With effort he contorted his mouth into what might pass for a leer, and coasted his hand from her lips to her shoulder and on down her arm. "Very well." He took hold of her fingers. "We'll go."

Her flirtatious warmth vanished the instant they passed through the last door to the street. She went silent, remote, worry hanging over her like a small private cloud, and he didn't have the least idea of how to drive it away.

Ought he perhaps to take her to bed? He might at least distract them both from their worries for an hour or two. She'd be in his bed in any case. With the hells all in nearby St. James's, and no maid to help her dress at home, they'd agreed she'd stay with him until—well, they hadn't exactly filled in the *until*. *Until she has her two thousand pounds and can take a house* was the most hopeful way to end that sentence, but other possible endings loomed as well. *Until Cathcart sends her word of my loss in the duel,* for example.

A streetlamp up ahead shed its halfhearted illumination into the fog and shadows of the quiet street. He couldn't help a fleeting vision of her walking these same streets alone, going unprotected into the gaming hells or even soliciting gentlemen because he was no longer here to look out for her. The prospect would spur white-hot panic through all his veins if he dwelt on it.

He touched her elbow. "Are you hungry? Shall I order something to be sent up when we reach my rooms?" Laughable, really, this compulsion to see to her bodily needs when he found himself powerless in regard to the larger questions of her future.

"No, thank you." Her opposite hand touched his, almost absently, where he still clasped her elbow. "I think I'll just go straight to bed, if you don't mind. But feel free to order something and dine without me."

Well, that certainly didn't sound like a carnal invitation. "Is there nothing at all I can do for you?" In the heavy night air his words hung and twisted, gathering weight. If all his utterances could be tossed in a pot and boiled down to their purest essence, these ten words would surely be what remained.

"I wish I could be sure of your being here in a week's time." She made her answer without turning to look at him. "I wish you would give up the duel."

He sighed. "I told you this morning why that's not possible. Nothing has changed since then."

She only nodded, and they finished the walk to Lewes Buildings in silence. He helped her out of her gown and corset when they reached his rooms, and they sidled round one another in the small space, carving out what privacy they could for washing and teeth-cleaning and the last layers of undressing.

In bed, she lay on her back and felt for his hand. He closed his fingers over hers.

"I don't know what to do about my maid," she said.

"In regard to what Mr. Roanoke threatened, you mean?" He'd walked into the study just in time to hear the man's coarse taunt. "Surely she wouldn't agree to such an arrangement."

"I would hope not. But sometimes, for want of other options . . . if he refused to give her a character, for example, she'd have a difficult time finding another situation. She'll face that same predicament if he doesn't survive the duel. And a young lady in want of money can fall prey to so many different . . ." She trailed off, slipping into thoughts where perhaps no gentleman could follow. "I hoped to have enough money to employ her myself."

"You must be good friends, I think. You and your maid."

"Not really. Not at all, in fact." Her hair brushed over the pillow as she turned. In the dim light, her face was all vague contours; no glimmer from her eyes. "We haven't much in common and I suspect I bore her with talking of cards and calculations. It's foolish, I suppose, that I should feel so responsible for her as I do."

"I shouldn't say foolish. I'd call it admirable." He stroked his thumb in circles on her palm.

"You would, wouldn't you?" He could hear her smile even if he couldn't see it. And he could feel, through the air between them, the sudden shift in her thoughts. "Will you take me to call on that widow?"

"I beg your pardon?" Foreboding slipped uninvited into the room. "Why would you want me to do that?"

"She's your obligation, as my maid is mine. I suppose . . . I'd like a clear picture of her. It will help me know you. I think you said she has a child?"

The back of his neck prickled, as any soldier's did

when some unspecified thing was not as it ought to be. Given that she could not love him, and given that she seemed to think it likely he'd be breathing his last on some greensward early next week while Prince Square-jaw put up his pistol and walked away, why should she hope to know him any more than she already did?

Might she suspect there was more to the story of his obligation than he'd so far divulged? A stronger current of unease came, washing over him in the silence. He'd said more than one thing at which any half-clever woman must wonder. That the war had changed him, that he wasn't fit for church, that he had reasons against offering himself to a lady. Perhaps she'd begun to piece those clues together. Perhaps he'd wanted her to, all along.

"Do you wish to know me, truly, Lydia?" His thumb went still against her palm. "There are things I can tell you that you might rather not have heard."

"I know." Her fingers curled round his thumb to trap it. "I've known for a while that you have secrets." She faced him, still, though surely she couldn't make out his features any more than he could make out hers. "I know I might not be the most suitable confidante. But I'm not afraid of anything you can tell."

"You're a more suitable confidante than you can imagine." Indeed who in the wide world was likelier to understand than a woman with deaths on her own conscience? And yet . . . if she *didn't* understand, then he must surely give up hope that anyone ever would.

He lay silent. How would he even begin?

"You needn't tell me anything if you don't wish it." She was steadiness itself, a dark beacon in the shadowed room. "I haven't any claim on your secrets."

"May I have a day to consider? Only it's a new thought with me, to speak to you—to speak to anyone—on this subject. I'm not sure it would be for the best."

"Of course." Her fingers uncurled from his thumb. "Perhaps we could call on that widow, though, and I could come to know more of you that way. Without prying into things you might rather not tell."

The proposal still didn't make sense. How exactly would a visit to Mrs. Talbot help her know him? Never mind. A call on the widow suddenly felt like the most innocuous of diversions, beside the prospect of confessing himself. "If you like," he said, and then there was nothing to do but lie awake, wondering at her motives and at whether he had the fortitude to risk losing her good opinion.

*H*E WAS responsible, in some way, for the loss of this woman's husband. That was the obvious explanation, and one did not seek an explanation beyond the obvious without good cause. *Entia non sunt multiplicanda praeter necessitatem,* as Henry had been fond of quoting. No unnecessary multiplying of things.

Lydia sat on a tired sofa in a small parlor in Camden Town, fighting the urge to knead her hands in her lap. Will sat at her left. Unease furled off him like a vapor, troublesome and distracting to her, undetectable to the other two women in the room. She'd been foolish, perhaps, to hope a visit here might help strengthen his attachment to life.

"Are they an older branch of the family, the Slaughters? I'm almost sure I've heard of a Lord Slaughter." Mrs. John Talbot, wife of the soldier's brother and mistress of this house, seemed determined to take all the consequence of this call to herself and now must discover exactly how much consequence was involved.

"I'm not familiar with him. I doubt he can be any relation." The less said of Slaughters here, the better. "Most of our family distinction resides in the Blackshear line, truth be told."

"My cousin flatters us." Will cast his eyes to the carpet, looking suitably modest and all the nobler for it. "The Blackshears are common country gentry; not so much as a Sir among us." He made a small, unconscious adjustment to one of his cuffs.

"That can change, though, can't it?" The woman would not be deterred. "One hears of knighthoods, and new-created baronetcies. Even new peerages, sometimes."

"Indeed." He acknowledged her contention with a bow. "But my eldest brother already has a reputation for conduct and dignity quite the equal of any lord, and a stubborn pride that prevents him ever wishing to change his state. My next-eldest, I believe, would rather have influence with a peer than be one himself. And both my sisters have already married, neither into the aristocracy. So I don't anticipate any titled Blackshears, at least in this generation."

Two brothers, one dignified and one political. A sister besides the one who'd driven Jane home that day. People she would never meet, even if he forsook the duel or survived it. He couldn't very well pass her off as a cousin with *them*.

"I think perhaps the modern way is for a gentleman to forge his own distinction, by his actions." Mrs. Talbot the widow broached this radical sentiment with a certain hesitancy—it seemed entirely possible Mrs. Talbot the wife might lean over and cuff her for her effrontery—underlaid by the strength of quiet conviction. "Only think of Wellington, a younger son and Irish into the bargain, but more highly regarded in the land now than even the Regent, I daresay."

"My point exactly." Mrs. John Talbot was quick to seize back command of the discussion. "Even younger sons can hope for titles, if they only bring themselves to the notice of the right people. A man like yourself, Mr. Blackshear, might rise above your elder brothers one day."

Mrs. George Talbot sank into a mortified silence. Clearly she'd meant nothing so impertinent as to suggest Will ought to concern himself with a title.

I don't think of courting her, he'd said. If indeed he bore some responsibility for her widowhood, this was certainly understandable. But a lady *like* Mrs. Talbot, if not Mrs. Talbot herself, would do him some good. She set an admirable example of how to bear disaster with grace. To lose her husband and fall on the charity of these relations must have been a terrible blow, but she found the strength to forge on. She did not go seeking her own extinction in a brothel, as some weaker, more impetuous women did.

Of course she couldn't afford to be impetuous, having the child to think of, but then wasn't that the very point of bringing Will here? To remind him of the people *he* must think of; the people who depended on him and for whose sake he must not risk himself in a duel.

"Well, Miss Slaughter." The other Mrs. Talbot sat forward with abrupt vivacity. "I'm sure I'd like your opinion of the garden I've just put in. Will you walk out with me?"

Beside her, Will started. Across from them, the widow Talbot blushed. Mrs. John Talbot's intent could not have been clearer.

Lydia groped for the sofa's arm and missed it entirely. Her limbs were icing over. To sit upright, to draw breath, suddenly required conscious effort.

"Let's all walk out." Beside her, Will had come to his feet. "I've taken a recent interest in agriculture and I'm particularly intrigued by what can be done on a small scale." He spoke with such enthusiasm as surely convinced the other Mrs. Talbot that he was not angling to escape the private interview, but rather had not grasped what was intended.

This would only make a temporary reprieve, though. There could be little doubt of what must follow, if he survived the duel. He would hold himself guilty of leading the Talbots into expectations. Being the man he was, he would want to honor his obligations, even if they were founded on misunderstanding. There was a promise involved, after all, and a solemn burden. He'd forsake his own happiness before he'd abandon Mr. Talbot's widow.

There mightn't be any forsaking of happiness. Weren't you just thinking that this woman is precisely what he needs? She rose, sluggish and ungainly as if she were hauling herself out of a bog, and she walked out with the others.

A thought bloomed, feebly, as she staggered through the ordeal of the Talbot garden: maybe now he would give up the duel. What respectable woman, after all, would want her husband to have fought for such a cause?

I don't think of courting her. If I'm not already in love with you, I'm within striking distance of the state. It could never have come to anything. She'd never hoped for it in the least. So why did she feel like she'd been turned outdoors coatless in the dead of winter?

The garden tour came finally to a merciful end, and after a round of good-byes and well-wishes and other excruciating politeness she found herself once more on the street with Mr. Blackshear. She started walking. Discussion would change nothing, so she did not speak.

"Lydia." He fell in beside her, his voice low with urgency. "I assure you, I had no idea of—"

"It doesn't matter." She pulled her cloak more snugly about her, and walked faster.

"Only I want you to know I didn't lie, when I told you there was no understanding. I would never have bedded you if there were. I don't even know how to account for—"

"I've said it doesn't matter." The words emerged more brusquely than she intended. She evened out her voice. "I don't doubt you. I can see the family's assumption came as a surprise to you."

"I haven't called there above a few times. And she's in mourning." He was reasoning with himself as well as with her. "Her husband hasn't even been dead a year. It simply never occurred to me that—"

"You've made that plain. And you don't have to make account to me. None of this is my concern." She couldn't seem to be civil. And of a sudden the two-mile walk to St. James's, with her no doubt cutting off his attempts at conversation all that way, was more than she could bear.

She stopped where she was, and pivoted to address him. "I think I'll go home, since I'm so near Somers Town. I need to get the rest of my money for tonight, and I need to sort through some belongings."

His already-stricken eyes showed new dismay. "I thought—" He took a step back from her, and dropped his gaze to her boots. "That is, I had supposed we would go back to my rooms and . . . talk, for a bit."

Oh, God. He'd made up his mind to tell his dark secret. He was ready, finally, to unburden himself, to honor her with his deepest trust, and she was not equal to it, not now. "I think it will be more convenient if we just meet at Oldfield's tonight."

His eyes came back to hers. He didn't understand. Well, how should he? She only half understood herself.

"Very well." He accepted this latest setback with soft words and a nod, when he had every right to demand an explanation. "I'll see you home." He put out his elbow.

"You're kind, but no. Thank you." Already her legs were moving, backing her away and down the street. "I shall be at Oldfield's from ten-thirty. I'll expect to see you around eleven."

He didn't argue, as he'd done in a similar situation some weeks since. He didn't make any reply at all. He pushed his hand into his greatcoat pocket and stood there, watching her recede.

Her heart—her stupid poisoned heart that had lurked for years beneath the rubbish-heap of anger, just waiting for the worst possible moment to reemerge—her heart would surely break if she had to see the look in his eyes for a single second more. With a whirl of skirts and cloak she turned, and went on her way.

$\mathcal{T}$HAT NIGHT she wore her plain white muslin to Old-field's, since her more elegant gowns were all in the trunk in Mr. Blackshear's rooms. Anyone recognizing her from her last visit here must suppose her fortunes had undergone some change—if not by the evidence of her subdued dress, then by her manner.

She counterfeited drunkenness this evening. She hadn't the heart to flirt, with Will or with anyone else, so she alternated between morose silence and bouts of bad-tempered loquacity in which she embedded his cues. Bet five. Bet four. Bet seven. Now stick.

Behind her, the roulette wheel clattered. At her left, the dice clacked together in someone's hands before tumbling down the baize. And from all about came the buzz of conversations that did not concern her. The sounds knit themselves together and retreated a discreet distance, and then the world was nothing but cards and reckoning and cool resolve, a world where the only hearts that mattered were those that could be numbered in pips.

She had no place in any decent man's life. Not as a wife, not as a lover, not even as a sympathetic ear. But by

all she held sacred, she had a place here. Graceless disrespectable wanton that she was, she would take what she
wanted from Oldfield's in handfuls, with mercy for
none.

And the cards, as though to welcome her back from
having wandered astray, fell out again and again in her
favor. Mr. Blackshear's favor, rather. He was the one
making the large wagers. *Eight units. Nine. Eleven,* with
a reference to pawning all her worldly possessions, because *possess* led to *own,* and *own* to *onze.* Truly, she
hadn't expected to ever need that one when they'd de-
vised the code.

Without clocks, one measured the night in money
rather than hours, and somewhere near the dizzying
mark of eighteen hundred pounds he stretched his arm
to signal for a conference. She looked the other way. If
he was fatigued, he could excuse himself for a few minutes without making any account to her. If he thought
they'd won enough and ought to quit for the night, he
sadly underestimated her firmness of purpose. And if he
meant to address her on some other subject, he needn't.
They'd said all there was to say.

When twenty minutes elapsed with no response, he
made the signal again. Carelessly, languorously, he
raised his right elbow behind him and took hold with
his left hand.

A cog slipped somewhere in the workings of her brain.
The teeth of one wheel failed to meet the teeth of another, or perhaps a spring leaped free of its mooring,
and suddenly she was all too conscious of the unseen
muscles that would be stretching up and down his near
side, from his waist to his skyward-pointing elbow.

*Leave him alone. The only good you can do him is by
staying here in this seat and playing on.* But her next
breath brought with it the scent of bay rum, and then

cards and numbers receded the way the room's sounds had already done.

Very well. She tapped her lips and set to scooping up her counters with outward calm even as one unsteady impulse after another chased through the tangled pathways of her nerves. She'd abandon a favorable deck to go await him in that corridor, if he insisted. But if he thought to corner her into a painful and profitless discussion, he had better think again.

WHAT THE devil had gone wrong between them? Obviously it had coincided with that visit to the Talbots, but what, precisely, had made his company so unbearable to her?

Will clenched and unclenched his hands as he drew nearer to that side hallway, site of the last time their partnership had foundered. He'd told her he hadn't lied regarding his connection with the widow, and she'd said she believed him. What, then, could account for the stone-like impassivity into which she'd sunk since this afternoon's call?

She's guessed. A cold whisper down his backbone, frosting each vertebra in turn. The details, she wouldn't know. But she might very well have divined the general nature of his wrong, and his ill-disguised unease during the visit would only have confirmed whatever dark suspicions she entertained.

He rounded the corner. No sign of her. He went a few steps deeper into the hallway and paused. Might she have tired of waiting for him and gone back to the table? No, he would surely have passed her. A sudden uneasy memory flashed through his muscles: the late-night chill as he'd waited for her, looked for her in the streets outside before grasping that she'd left in the hackney without him. Had she quitted the table only to fetch her cloak and forsake him altogether?

"Here." The syllable just reached him from the dark far end of the hall. The nape of his neck prickled. What was she doing all the way back there, and why hadn't she announced herself at once?

He made a straight path to where he'd heard her voice, only to put his hands against empty wall. Now his scalp prickled as well.

"Here." She'd moved. She was to his left and behind him. His eyes hadn't adjusted enough to make out her shape, though he was surely visible to her.

A faint rustle of muslin told him she was moving again, circling him. The air between them was thick enough to stir with a spoon. "Lydia, will you tell me what's the matter?" He flung those words out into the thick air, before he could forget the purpose with which he'd come here.

"Nothing, just now." Her silken murmur sank straight through his skin, and a hand crossed the darkness to land on his arm.

"I think you're angry." His words nearly caught in his throat on the way out. He knew exactly what she was doing: she meant to avoid this conversation and she would use every weapon in her arsenal to divert his attention. Certain susceptible parts of him were diverted already.

"Am I?" She spoke from directly before him. Her hands took hold of his coat and she went up on her toes, giving him a noseful of rose-petal soap before her lips found his in the darkness.

She tasted of unalloyed temptation. He knew this because his tongue was in her mouth. Likewise his arms had gone round her and he'd crushed her body to his, entirely without conscious thought. To give in to her manipulation, to forget himself and to bury once more the secrets he'd meant to tell, would be the easiest thing in the world.

But she wasn't . . . his brain groped blindly for a hand-hold on reason . . . she wasn't doing this out of honest desire. She strove only to use his own lusts against him, and that wasn't the way he wanted to . . . "Lydia, wait." He caught his breath, his mouth just far enough from hers to allow speech. "This isn't . . . I called you away from the table that we might speak." He grasped her at the waist and eased her from him, opening up space between her body and his.

Obstinate anger poured off her to fill up that space. She loosed her grip on his coat and laid her palms flat on his chest. For a moment she stood just so, defiance pulsing in her touch. Then her palms dragged down his front as she sank right out of his grasp in a whisper of skirts. "Speak all you like," she said from where she knelt. "I shall be unable."

Bloody hell. "This isn't what I intended." But his treacherous hand had already found its way to the first button of his breeches. "This isn't what I want from you." *Liar.* He was fumbling from one button to the next as he spoke, and his hand was nearly shaking with how badly he wanted it.

He hadn't had her since that last morning at Chiswell. Nearly three days, now. And he'd never yet known the secrets of her mouth. *She can suck a man into next week.*

Confound him, was he no better than that coarse bastard who'd kept her? No. He *was* better. He could still stop this. "For God's sake, this is madness. Someone could pass this way." His fingers met hers: she'd been unbuttoning from the other side of his frontfall, which now dropped away. She wore no gloves. She'd shed them, no doubt, in expectancy of his capitulation.

"Don't worry." Her voice carried that easy assurance that came with the upper hand. "We won't be seen. It's dark, and I can work quickly."

He still held her fingers, adept and devious and naked in his grasp. He let two breaths pass in silence. "No." His hand loosed her fingers. "Go slowly. Make it last."

Linen tormented him with its delicate friction as she freed him from his drawers. She tugged down his breeches and he braced his outspread hands against the wall at his back. He could discern her shape in the darkness now, and he watched with unholy greed as she leaned close and took him inch by inch into the merciful heaven of her mouth.

And now nothing in the world mattered—not his sins, not his promises, not the things he'd meant to tell her or the duel he must fight in a few days; not anything but her lips and her tongue and the expert way they coaxed him into madness. Or perhaps her hand mattered too, as it came up to cradle his balls and send jagged bolts of pleasure to the middle of his brain.

"Not too fast. Not too much." *You'll make me lose my mind.* His body clamored to thrust but he was not quite so lost, so bereft of decency as to use her that hard. He fought the urge and moved his hips instead in slow circles, grateful for the darkness that prevented his being seen like this, given up to sinuous gyrations like some Amazon queen's slave-dancer. She stayed with him as he moved. Her free hand settled behind him, fitting itself to his bunched muscles while one careful finger teased just at the edges of where he was cleft.

Could a person die of pleasure? His heart felt as though it might batter itself to extinction on his own ribs. What an ignominious end that would be, and what an embarrassment for his family. Home safe from Waterloo only to be discovered on an out-of-the-way gaming-hell floor, his breeches down to his knees and a grimace of agony etched into his face. She'd better have the good sense to leave him where he lay if it happened.

He brought one hand off the wall to set it at the back of her head, to caress her in meager recompense for the tempest of sensation she'd set going. Devil take it. He *was* her slave. And better than any Amazon queen, she was mistress of all his flesh. Her hands steadied him, and her tongue drove him, and her finger no longer teased but tortured, boldly stroking where it had no business to be.

She would turn him inside out. She would annihilate him and he didn't care. "Harder," he muttered as her tongue slowed and he felt the soft pull of her mouth. "Suck me harder."

Her favorite word. And she took the command as readily as she gave it. He clawed at the wallpaper, his head tipped back, his teeth bared in a feral grimace. He'd spill in another minute. He ought to warn her. She wouldn't want—

Oh, but ruthless torrents of pleasure rocked him and he couldn't find the words. It was her own fault, with her hand tightening on his balls and her mouth taking him in so deep and her finger doing unspeakable things. Her other fingers splayed themselves on his arse and she pushed, gently. Then again. Inviting him to thrust.

He didn't need telling a third time. He set his hands by either ear to hold her steady, to keep her just where she was, and he gave it to her in small pulses. Not too hard. Not rough. Just enough to bring the relief of that primal motion she'd known his body so desperately craved, and all the while the words he ought to say, the warning that would spare her, slipped further and further beyond his grasp.

No words. Hands. He fumbled to push her away as climax came thundering toward him. She didn't move.

"Lydia!" he gasped, and she only held her ground and pleasured him harder, harder, until he shuddered and staggered and finally sank down into the sweet, sweet shame of flooding a woman's mouth with his seed.

She sank with him: when he came to his senses he was sitting on the floor, his back to the wall, and she crouched beside him, just lifting her head.

"I'm sorry." Shame washed over him, not an ounce of sweetness to it now. He'd meant to speak to her; to discover what had gone wrong and to repair their understanding, and he'd pitched all good intentions aside at the chance to get his cock in her mouth. Then he'd befouled her into the bargain. "I tried to spare you—"

"I know. You tried to be a gentleman to the last." She wiped the heel of her hand across her lips. "You forget I haven't any use for a gentleman." Her hand fell on his thigh, still bared above his tugged-down breeches. "Take me to your rooms. Let's cash in our counters and go."

She was a stranger again, all appetite and command, no interest in addressing the rift that had opened up between them. And Lord help him, he didn't care, so long as she wanted to fuck him.

"Yes," he said, and covered her hand with his. "Let's go."

$\mathscr{S}$HE COULD not repent. Days from now she might look back on this night as a dreadful mistake, as one more source of pain when *that* river had quite enough tributaries as it was. Never mind. This was *what should be,* a whore and the man she'd collared walking wordless through the midnight streets of St. James's.

Once, he stopped to press her up against a lamppost and kiss her, with a hunger he made no effort to conceal. A multitude of convenient shadows and he chose the place where they would be most visible to anyone who happened to look. If he'd bid her lift her skirts then and there she would have done it. That was her mood.

They gained his rooms and he undressed her, deft and silent, pausing only to transfer his roll of banknotes from his pocket to a drawer. Not one stitch of his own clothing did he remove, not even his boots. He put her on her knees before the pier-glass in his bedroom and he knelt behind her, his dark infernal eyes watching over her shoulder as his gloved hands wandered with utter liberty over her naked form. Shoulders. Elbows. The curve of her hips. One hand cupping her breast; one fingertip stroking across her belly and catching in her navel. Again he made her think of a sculptor, studying all her dimensions and committing them to memory for future use.

"Mine." It was the first word he'd said since they'd left Oldfield's. He dipped his head and whispered it with a breath that tickled her ear. His hands slipped down to her thighs. "All of this is mine."

"For tonight, yes." That much was true. If she could be nothing else to him, she could certainly be all the wanton he desired for one night.

"That's not enough." His eyes found hers in the mirror. His fingertips trailed through the curls at the juncture of her thighs. "Tell me you're mine entirely."

Yearning scalded the back of her throat, but the answer he wanted wouldn't come. She hadn't enough imagination to push aside a future that might see him perish, or see him prevail in the duel and bind himself to Mrs. Talbot. Whether he loved her, whether her heart answered him, was nothing to the purpose. They could not belong to one another.

"I can make you tell me." Undaunted by her silence, he took hold of his right glove and tugged it loose.

Not one spark of protest rose within her. "Do your worst," she said, and it was not defiance but invitation.

His glove hit the floor and his hand went straight to work. Both his hands. The left one, still gloved, slid up to tend to her nipples while the right, bared and deliciously warm, slipped between her thighs.

She closed her eyes and forced them open again. She would store up this sight. She would watch the way his hands pinned her, possessed her; she would watch the perspiration on her body catch the candlelight when pleasure made her flinch, and she would watch the look in his eyes as he watched her.

"Show me you like it, Lydia." He could persuade her to throw herself into a blazing hearth when he used that voice. "Show me how good it feels."

A half-formed joke shimmered in the remoteness of her rational mind, something about him finally having his erotic spectacle, but to complete the thought, let alone voice it aloud, was more than she could manage. She writhed, all abandoned, and that was the answer he wanted anyway. In the mirror they looked like a tableau from some ancient myth, a nymph escaping a demigod's rude grasp by turning into smoke, or a dancing fountain, or moonlight on uncalm waters.

But the demigod in this myth possessed her all the same. He was tireless, and staunch, and he would follow her through every metamorphosis with his unswerving will and his divinely clever hands. "Have I enslaved you, Lydia?" he said by her ear, and his fingers quickened to coax out the response he desired.

"Yes." That was the beginning of surrender.

"So have you done to me. Do you want me?"

"Yes." A great shudder seized her.

"And so do I want you. Are you mine, now?" Urgency burned bright in his eyes.

One word: *yes*. One scant syllable, but it might as well have been an operatic aria with multiple occurrences of high C, so absolutely was it beyond her power to voice.

Instead she gave him inarticulate cries, eager and savage, and she thrashed in his hands so he could know how he pleased her. Crisis was within sight, then within reach, then it was upon her, blinding her to the picture she made with him, shutting out whatever thing he was murmuring, robbing her of every sense and setting her ablaze like a pagan pyre.

When the flames died down she was limp, his arms across her chest and waist to keep her from collapsing. She opened her eyes and he'd been just waiting for that: he shifted his hold on her, arms behind her knees and shoulders, and lifted her up and carried her to the bed. Then he shucked his clothes, finally, and climbed in beside her.

"You're a wicked man, Will Blackshear." She could almost blush, remembering the look in his eyes as he'd watched himself drive her all out of her mind. "You try to act the gentleman, but you've got sin in your blood and your bones."

He ought to reach for her now, roll onto her or pull her on top of him. She'd seen when he'd stripped that he was ready.

But he only smiled, a thin smile that went away as quickly as it came. His eyes grew grave and looked past her.

She'd said the wrong thing. *Wicked.* He had reason to believe he was worse than that, and she'd reminded him. And suddenly she felt able, as she had not that afternoon, to hear what he had to say.

She turned on her side. Her right hand reached out to take hold of his arm. "You can tell me now." She waited until his eyes went dark with comprehension. "Tell me, Will. I want to know."

* * *

$\mathcal{F}$OR AN instant his every muscle tensed with the urge to flee. At least he ought to put out the candles. If her face paled in horror as he spoke, that might be more than he could bear to watch.

But of course her face wouldn't do that. She never did wear her sentiments there. She lay on her side watching him with that unreadable falcon stare. Was that better than horror, or worse?

He filled his lungs. "It has to do with Talbot, the widow's husband. I expect you've guessed that."

She nodded. Her fingers flexed delicately on his arm.

He was going to tell her. God help him, though his love for her could meet with no answer, though they could not look forward to a future of relying upon one another, bearing one another's burdens, being one another's shelter from the world's cold winds, he was going to tell her everything.

"He might have died in any case, Mr. Talbot." So had the doctor said. There was no reason to doubt it. He fixed his gaze on the ceiling, where a crack in the plaster had worked itself from one corner of the room to the center.

"You blame yourself, though." No warmth, no condemnation. She was simply stating a fact.

"I oughtn't to have moved him." He could feel some great sagging surrender at his core as every memory flooded in. Sights and sounds and scents and crushing desperation. "He'd been caught in a charge of cavalry and had damage to his spine, and . . ." He sucked in another breath, forcefully this time, as though he'd come up from three minutes underwater. "And he hadn't died. He lay in the mud among corpses, in horrific pain, for hours before I found him, and more hours after."

He threw her a look. Still the blank stare. One could believe she heard such stories every time she took a man to bed.

"And it was night. I was exhausted, and I couldn't persuade any of the medical staff to carry him to the hospital. I ran out of hope that anyone would stop to help him, so finally I carried him myself, and . . . I made things worse with his spine. By the time the surgeon saw him he couldn't move his limbs."

Here was where she might have attempted absolution: *Surely anyone in your situation would have done the same. Surely all hope for him was already lost.* But no sound came from the presence at his right side but her steady breathing.

And God help him again, only now could he see just how badly he'd hoped she would bathe him in sympathy and tell him, with the full force of her deliberating mind, that for him to blame himself was irrational.

But it wasn't. That truth thudded deep inside him like an underwater bell. She couldn't pardon him any more than he could pardon himself.

"Go on," she said, because her sharp falcon eyes read him and she knew there was more.

He took one more breath, to dive down again. "I carried him to three different field hospitals because I thought . . . I was so tired, I wasn't thinking clearly. I hoped another surgeon might give me a different answer. I didn't want to give up."

"Because you knew he had a wife and child."

"Yes."

"And because you hoped to undo the wrong you'd done in moving him."

"Yes." His voice came out raw and ragged, exactly as it had been that night. Memory had its claws in him and was dragging him back there; he could taste the sour torment of too many hours without water. "Most of all, though, because I'd promised him he'd be all right, and he trusted my word."

"How did it end?" Calm and direct as a corporal interrogating a prisoner.

"I couldn't do him any good." That awful, awful sense of uselessness, helplessness, dropped back in to wrap him like a shroud. "I couldn't even get him opium. I only dragged him about, prolonging his agony for hours. He ended by begging for a bullet to the head."

A short silence as she absorbed this. "Did you oblige him?"

"We didn't carry rifles, in our regiment. I should have had to use a musket, and I . . ." *I was fastidious in how I murdered the man.* "I used my hands."

Another silence, this one long enough that he must finally turn his head to look at her. The only mark in her countenance was a thoughtful crease in her brow. "Will you show me how?"

Good God. The darkest deed of his life and her first concern was with the mechanics. She needed to fill in the outline his story made, or perhaps she meant to make use of the knowledge someday.

No matter. He'd chosen to confess himself to her, when he might have waited until he'd met a lady with a warm, sentimental nature. Patience and a hopeful disposition. All those qualities he couldn't seem to want anymore.

He found her hands and brought them to his throat, feeling for the right place to set her thumb. "There's a vein." She frowned, faintly, watching the placement of her hands. "If you press on it you can stop the flow of blood. Then everything ends."

Her eyes, empty and glittering, came again to his face. Her hands stayed where they were. For an instant it seemed possible she might—and would he resist her, if she did? Might he make that final surrender, and let her relieve him of all his burdens for the rest of time?

But she didn't. She took her hands back, and this time

neither one settled on his arm. Both lay curled on the pillow under her chin. She didn't speak.

He oughtn't to have told her. Or he ought to have told her long ago. Before he'd touched her, pleasured her, fitted his body to hers.

"I wish you would speak, Lydia." If there was a way to say that without sounding pathetic, he didn't know it. He felt hollow, unmoored, lying beside her without the least idea of her thoughts. "I never could read you. I don't know . . . I've no idea what you want, now. Whether you want me to . . ." *Help you dress and hire a hackney to take you home. Apologize for having lain with you. Shut my mouth and just go to sleep.*

Two silent seconds passed. Then she rose up and threw one knee over him. Her palms sank into the mattress at either side of his shoulders and her eyes stayed fast on his. "Fuck me," she said. "I want you to fuck me."

He recoiled to his core. To do this now, to follow so grim and solemn a confession with carnal enjoyment, would profane his last remnants of honor. "I can't." Could she really not grasp that? "Not after what I've just told you."

"*Now* you mean to be delicate?" Her eyes shone cold and accusing in the dim light. "None of what you've told me is new. All of this was true the first time you kissed me." She brought her hips down until she sat astride him, her wet warmth a taunt to all his pretensions of decency. "It was true when you bedded me at Chiswell. When you put your mouth on me. When you demanded I bring my whole self to bed with you. When I knelt for you in the hallway at Oldfield's, and when I knelt for you in front of that mirror right there." She was moving, barely, against him, and damn him to Hell, he was getting hard again. "Whatever you think must prevent you now, surely ought to have prevented you then."

"I ought to have told you, I know, and given you the choice." His whole body was declaring mutiny: his hands drifted up to settle on her arms. "But I couldn't resist you. I can't resist you. Even now." There was his frailty, laid out before her.

"You're not so honorable as you'd like to be." Her hand left the mattress to feel for his cock—shamefully, indecently hard—and she slid it inside.

Of all the occasions when he'd tried to stop her—how many times had she had to hear *Lydia, this isn't what I want?*—surely this was the occasion when he ought to insist, before he could drown in self-disgust. Instead he arched up into her and groaned aloud. Sensation aside, there was a bone-deep comfort in knowing she still wanted him. Knowing that, despite the worst he could tell her, she still had this use for him. A woman of kindness and patience and virtue never would have done.

Her hands braced herself on the mattress again and her icy gaze sank nearer. "You're not a good man, Blackshear," she whispered.

"I know." It felt like a pound of flesh given up. He closed his eyes.

"You break your promises and you fuck other men's women and you haven't even a soul to your name."

A shaft of hot, grief-tainted pleasure stabbed through him. "I know." He jerked his chin in a nod.

"You went to bed with me in the guise of an honorable man, but you never were."

He shook his head, jaw clenched tight. He'd betrayed her. He'd betrayed himself. He could make no earthly defense.

"You threw away your soul when you stopped that man's blood and you can never, never have it back again."

"I know." One more pound of flesh torn away. He'd never wanted to own that truth aloud. He caught his breath on another spasm of sensation, in spite of the despair, and shook his head side to side. *Stop. I can't bear any more of this.* Those were the words he ought to say but he'd forgot how to form them. He opened his eyes.

And he knew there'd have been no point in asking for mercy. It was a word with no meaning to the creature whose gaze met his.

She stared down at him, his judge and his ravisher, appalling as the eagle who'd feasted every day on Prometheus's liver, and he as powerless as that Titan, chained to the rock, rent open, his darkest, most unspeakable secrets laid bare to her view.

Her eyes hardened. Her lips pressed tight. She leaned an inch nearer. "I love you," she breathed, just loud enough for him to hear.

He gasped, one great rush of sustaining air. And he seized her with unyielding hands, and rolled her beneath him and drove himself into her, into her truth and her terrible strength and the pitiless love that was his only redemption in this world.

And came, claiming her, giving himself up to her, a woman so beautifully broken she could love a soulless man.

Chapter Twenty-one

He FELL almost immediately to sleep—he was thoroughly wrung out—and when the slumberous breaths started, she slipped from the bed and left the bedroom, pulling the door soundlessly to. In the corner where her trunk still sat was just space enough for her to wedge herself in by the wall. She slid down to sit on the floor, knees up, and she put her face in her hands and wept until she shook with grief.

He would never know what it had cost her to hear his story. Never. If she'd shown the smallest sign of being affected he would have bottled up his own anguish and turned his energies to comforting her, when for God's sake he'd borne his burden long enough and it was damn well time someone was strong enough to listen, to bear witness to the enormity of what he'd undergone, beginning to heart-lacerating end.

Had she done wrong, though, in speaking to him so? She curled her hands into fists and pressed them against her eyes. She might have been kind, and told him the truth. *You are a good man, the finest I know. You drew a dismal hand, and played it as well as anybody could.*

The state of your soul is not for you or me or any church to pronounce upon.

But surely these were the things he'd expect a listener to say. And he would not believe them. He'd think she said them because she shrank from beholding the awful corruption that crawled beneath his skin.

Now he knew she shrank from nothing. The worst thing he could tell of himself would not be enough to drive her away. She'd listened unflinching to his darkest confessions and she'd answered with the darkest confession she could make in her turn.

I love you. She wiped, with open palms, where tears ran down both cheeks. He'd been so grateful to hear it. So relieved. She wouldn't be sorry she'd told him, even if only pain could follow.

A few minutes more she cried, and when she'd poured out sorrow enough to make her steady again she crept back to the bedroom. A lone candle still burned; she snuffed it and crawled under the covers. He muttered in his sleep and turned, his hand brushing hers. She lay motionless, measuring his breaths and the intervals between, marveling at the place—his first and second knuckles, the back of her hand—where their bodies met.

"Will." One word only. If he woke, they'd speak. If not, she'd let him sleep on.

"Hmm?" Her need was like a fishhook, drawing him unerringly out of the deep.

Long breath in. Long breath out. "I can't let you fight that duel."

She could feel him groping, sleepily, for the best way to reassure her. "Don't fret yourself." His hand moved in soothing strokes up and down her arm. "Go to sleep. Let me worry about the duel."

"I can't let you die. And I can't let you . . ." *I can't let you have another man's death on your hands.* Couldn't he see how important that was?

"There isn't always a death." He was coming all the way awake, now. "Sometimes only wounds result. One or both parties might miss the target altogether." His hand stopped at her wrist and he made a bracelet of his thumb and first two fingers. "Regardless, for me to walk away from the defense of your honor is more than ever unthinkable. Surely you see that."

"I *don't* see." Her voice was raw with desperation. She'd played all her best cards: his duty to the living, her need of him in the gaming hells, even the heart that would break with the loss of him. What else was left to try? "I should think a woman's honor would be her own concern and no one else's."

"A wife's honor would be her husband's concern." His words pooled out to fill every corner of the room in the two or three seconds it took her to gain command of her tongue.

"I'm not your wife." That was all the reply she could manage.

"Not yet." His fingers let go her wrist; that hand skimmed across her belly to take a grip at her waist and pull her whole body close to his. "Will you marry me, Lydia?"

Her heart twisted like laundry fresh out of the tub. He didn't mean to be unkind, of course. But to know he loved her, to know he would bind himself to her, honorably, if he could, only made the remaining insurmountable obstacles that much crueler. "You know that's impossible." She would remind him of the reasons one by one if she must.

"Circumstances are very much against it. That's not the same as impossible." She could feel the strong beat of his heart where her upper arm touched the middle of his chest. "I love you. You've said you love me. I trust you won't doubt me if I say that, after tonight, I cannot think of making a life with any woman but you."

The choice of words sent a sharp stab of laughter half-way up her throat and pricked her eyes with tears. "*Making a life* is the very thing I cannot do. Have you forgotten?"

For several seconds he was silent, leaving her to imagine what transpired on his face. "I'm a youngest son," he then said. "The world does not clamor for a copy of me."

"You know I refer to more than that." He'd hesitated for a reason. He was not so sanguine on this topic as he'd like her to believe. "Think what it would be, to know your line would die out with you. No descendants to have a care for you in your old age. No infants to cherish. No little faces growing to resemble yours." Oh, Lord. Already she was maudlin.

"I don't say I won't think of that sometimes, and grieve the loss. But we'll grieve it together. And I'll have you for consolation. That's no small thing." He rolled from his side to his back, his sizable palm guiding her head to a place on his shoulder. "I've told you my mother died in childbed." In the darkness, this near, his every syllable sounded like an exquisite confidence. "It was her tenth confinement and she'd been worn down to nothing. I don't think my father ever recovered from losing her, and I don't think he ever ceased to blame himself." He'd caught a lock of her hair between his fingers and was twisting it, slowly, round one finger and then another. "I've seen my eldest brother nearly crawl out of his skin when his wife was brought to bed. I'll never know that fear, if I marry you. We can enjoy one another with no such cloud hanging overhead. Not many men are so lucky."

She allowed herself four seconds to just drift, his words and aching-sweet sentiments buoying her up like warm sulfured water. "It's not that simple," she finally said.

"Of course it isn't. It's not simple at all." He let go the lock of hair and brought his palm against her scalp again. "My family will probably throw me off, I've got to find a way to put things to rights with Mrs. Talbot, I need a home and income suitable to share with you, and I have to get through that damned duel. It's the farthest thing from simple." His voice slowed, shifted, like a violin changing keys as it moved toward the resolution of an intricate concerto. "But we both have some experience with difficulty, haven't we? We've been tried, and tempered. Beyond doubt we'll meet with obstacles and adversity. Haven't we ample reason, though, to hope we'll be equal to whatever challenges come?"

It was the prettiest, grandest, best-argued marriage proposal a lady could ever hope to hear. Her heart bobbed in its wake like an empty cask tossed into choppy seas.

The hour was late, though. He'd been glutted with pleasure, and likely was still light-headed, tender-hearted, from the relief of finally bringing his secrets into the light. He might feel differently in the morning. At the least he might recognize the folly of plotting out his future when the meeting with Edward loomed so large in his way.

She found his hand and wound her fingers between his. "If you love me—if you want a life with me—then I should think you'd want to give up the duel."

He sighed, his chest swelling and subsiding under her head. She'd answered poorly. *Yes,* she ought to have said. *I love you. I want to face adversity with you at my side.* Instead she'd circled back round to where they'd begun, receiving his declarations and promptly converting them into ammunition for her single-minded campaign. "Let's go to sleep now, Lydia." He shifted out from under her, consigning her to the inferior comforts of her pillow. "We're at a stalemate for the night, I think.

We can speak again in the morning. I'll convince you to marry me then."

*B*UT WHEN morning came he found he only wanted to let her sleep. Devil of a long night it had been, in hours alone. And hours were the least of it.

He lay on his side, facing her. She lay on her back. She knew now, and here she still was. Once or twice he closed and opened his eyes, just to make sure.

This was the woman he would marry. Life had shaped them for each other. He would wake every morning to this view: the stark lines of her nose, her brow, her chin, and the soft, slightly parted lips that undercut her fearsome mien. He had only to convince her that there could be no other course.

Well, no. He had a great deal more to do than that. He rolled onto his back, very slowly, so as not to disturb her. This interlude in a room with a cracked ceiling was just that, a brief connective chapter, a respite from the world in which they must find their way. He had arrangements to make, failures to confess, people to disappoint, and Lord, that damnable duel with which to contend. Might as well get a start on all of it.

He rose. An hour's worth of dressing and letter-writing later she still hadn't woken, so he went back to his table and penned one more note, this time to her. The paper whispered as he laid it on the pillow where he'd been, a hushed promise, a token of all he would bear and sacrifice in exchange for a life with her.

*E*ARLY THAT afternoon he stood on the threshold of the first sacrifice, in his eldest brother's drawing room, and looked a bit too long at each of the assembled faces, the way he might if he were getting set to board a ship to

India. Andrew and his wife. Kitty and her husband. Martha and Mr. Mirkwood. Nick, by himself in an armchair with the same keen expression he must wear in court.

"Out with it, Will." His eldest sister, bossy as she'd always been. "We know well enough it can be nothing good."

He clasped his hands behind him and stood straight, back to the fire. His toes curled and uncurled in his boots, all his nervous energy pushed down out of sight. "You're quite right. I'll get straight to it. I'm engaged to a duel in several days' time, for a cause that can bring no credit to the family. I've involved myself in the fortunes of another man's mistress."

He'd imagined, beforehand, what might be each sibling's reaction to the news. More or less they stayed true to pattern: Andrew, a muscle in his jaw flinching as his hands tightened on the arms of his chair. Nick, his brows ascending to give his eyes all the room they needed for spelling out *Have you taken leave of your senses?* Kitty, her disapproving countenance suddenly swamped with sisterly concern. And Martha, straight and serious, her mouth pinched small.

"Is it Miss Slaughter?" His younger sister addressed him quietly, as though he and she were the only ones in the room.

He nearly bit his tongue, the question came so unexpected. "How the deuce did you know?"

"Her maid is an inexpert dissembler. We spoke a bit, when I drove her to Somers Town, and she said things that led me to suspect her mistress might be living in such an arrangement as you now say she is. I didn't realize—" Her mouth shaped and reshaped itself as she sought for the proper phrase. "I had supposed her but a slight acquaintance of yours."

"Who issued the challenge?" Andrew had no use for such details as the lady's name, or the terms of her acquaintance with his brother, but must go directly to the meat of the matter; the part he could get his hands on and repair. "Can it be withdrawn?"

"There's no chance of that." Behind his back he flexed his fingers, the one slight expression of impatience he'd allow. He was six and twenty, he'd been to war and back, and still his brother seemed to think he could not manage these things for himself. "I knocked him down after seeing him strike the lady. For me to apologize is out of the question."

"For you to *die in a duel* is out of the question. Have you any idea how your sisters worried while you were on the Continent?" Andrew's face was flushing red and he looked to be some few seconds away from snapping the arms of his chair with his bare hands. "We've had you back for less than a year. I've no intention of— of . . ." Abruptly he jerked one hand from the chair and passed it over his brow. And for the first time Will understood, in his sinews, how much his loss could grieve his family.

Would grieve his family. If they didn't lose him through the duel, they would lose him by what would come after. He shoved himself a step forward. "I'm sorry. I wish there might have been some way to spare you. But I mean to fight this duel, and provided I'm neither killed nor arrested, my intention is then to marry Miss Slaughter."

Oh, Lord. He ought to have worked up to it gradually. Kitty was staring as though he'd suddenly sprouted boils all over his face, Nick was leaning farther and farther forward in his chair, and Andrew looked ready to combust.

"I'm not insensible of what this will mean to your families. Please believe I don't make this choice lightly." He could feel six and twenty years of fondness, of needling, of shared jokes slipping through his fingers. But he'd known this must be the cost. It didn't, at least, take him by surprise. "I can only say that the war wrought certain changes in my views. Among other things, I'm unwilling to condemn a lady—a lady every bit our equal by birth—for choices that were forced upon her by the most unenviable circumstances."

Martha's already straight posture went straight enough to lay bricks by, and she sent her hand abruptly to cover her husband's. "You'll honor Mrs. Mirkwood and myself with the first introduction, I hope," the man said as if nothing untoward had passed.

Will nearly sagged to the floor under the sudden warm weight of gratitude. He clenched his jaw and nodded, his sentiments too raw and unwieldy to shape into words.

Nick snorted and lurched up from his chair. "Yes, you would welcome this, wouldn't you? The two of you would look positively respectable by compare." He wheeled to the window, eloquently turning his back on his shambles of a family.

"I liked her." Calm resolve colored Martha's voice. "She showed a very becoming concern for her maid. And people in desperate circumstances do what they must."

Kitty was not so magnanimous. Her daughters were older than Martha's, of course, and the damage this connection would do to their prospects therefore loomed larger with her. "I'll allow she might have been a worthy lady who would sooner not have entered into such a life. I'll believe she treats her maid, and anyone else of humbler station, with such graciousness as sets the example for us all." She angled forward, hands earnestly clasped. "Can you not see that none of that makes the least difference?"

"A gentleman of good family isn't always free to love

where he likes." Her husband, beside her, offered this gentle underscore to her argument.

"I beg your pardon, he is perfectly free to *love* as he chooses." Nick pivoted and set his hands on the back of the armchair. "Gentlemen fall in love with unsuitable women all the time. What they don't do is marry them. If you would only keep her, discreetly, there need be no scandal at all."

"I'm sorry for the scandal. Truly, I am. I'm sorry for any injury to your name, and your practice, and I'm sorrier than I can say if my nieces' fortunes should be affected. But the fact is I cannot seem to find my place any longer in a society where to keep a woman in sin is a more respectable path than to give her my hand and my name."

"Don't dare try to cloak this act in morality." Andrew had finally found his voice, and a fearsome voice it was, low and taut and suggestive of temper just barely contained. "And don't insult us with *if*s. You *will* do harm to your brother's name and practice, either through the duel or through this . . . connection . . . you would impose upon the family. You *will* hurt my daughters, Kitty's daughters, Martha's daughter, by crippling their chances to make an advantageous marriage. If you insist on going forward with this astounding show of selfishness, you must count yourself a stranger to this house, at least."

He'd expected it. He'd borne reversals ten times as brutal. And still, it pierced his middle like an icy blade. He dropped his gaze to the carpet for a moment. "I don't dispute anything you've said. Indeed, to cut my acquaintance would probably be the reasonable course for all of you." He raised his eyes again for another look round at the familiar faces. "If I'm so fortunate as to . . . Well, I shall strive to keep my name out of gossip, and be as little known in your circles as I can."

No one spoke—really, what more was there to say?—so he bowed, and made to leave the drawing room. Martha jumped up and was at the door before him, hand extended. "Any day next week will do for a call. I look forward to knowing her." With fierce determination she gripped his hand and said this, as though by making plans for the future she could will him safely to the other side of the duel.

"I look forward to her knowing you, too." Irrepressible hope fizzed through him at the thought that he might after all have more to offer Lydia than just himself. She would gain a sister, a brother, and a niece, if only—no, he would follow Martha's example, and pass over the *if only.* "Thank you." He kept his voice low. "And thank your husband. I've scarcely been acquainted with him. I shall strive to correct that."

His sister nodded, flushing with pleasure. She knew a bit, didn't she, about the cost of marrying a black sheep. No wonder she'd spoken up for him. Please God he'd live to repay her loyalty.

With a last squeeze of her hand he made his exit. He was in the entry hall, waiting for his hat and coat, when brisk, purposeful footsteps sounded on the stairs behind him. Nick. Save for when he was being dragged into a gaming hell, his brother always walked as if he had somewhere important to be and something important to do once he got there.

Will straightened but didn't turn. For all that he knew better, he couldn't wholly suppress a hope that his siblings had relented *en masse,* and sent Nick to fetch him back among them where he belonged.

He checked the hope. "Don't try to argue me out of the duel or the marriage. For more reasons than I can share, this is the only possible course for me."

Nick's step slowed, and halted. "I didn't intend . . ." His voice trailed off, uncharacteristically hesitant. "That is, I do wish you'd change your mind. And I'm sorry you can't tell me your reasons. But I only came after you to ask whether you're in need of a second for your duel."

He turned, then. His brother stood on the lowest step but one, hand on the railing, jaw set with dutiful resolve. Will inclined his head. "Thank you for thinking of it. But Cathcart's already agreed."

"Ah. Well, then." Nick glanced away, almost as though he were stung by not having been asked.

Will felt all over again the distance that had opened up between him and his brother—hell, between him and every other Blackshear—since he'd gone away to war. This last, decisive estrangement had perhaps been inevitable, and still, if he should be mortally wounded in a few days' time, among his regrets would be that he hadn't tried harder, in the months since returning, to reforge those familial bonds.

Nothing for it now. "I *am* sorry, Nick." Here was the footman with his coat; his parting remarks must be brief. "I know what your work and your good name mean to you. I would gladly have sacrificed my own happiness, if it were only my happiness at stake." He settled his hat. "But she loves me. She trusts me. I'll give my life before I'll abandon her."

He might give his life indeed, not many days from now, and he couldn't help wondering, as he left his brother's town house and descended to the street, whether some in his family might not prefer that less scandalous outcome.

An hour later he sat before Fuller's desk, elbows on the arms of his chair, frowning out the window at the sunstarved greenery of Russell Square. "I don't know why you're not angry." He twisted to face the man again.

"Because you're angry enough at yourself." Fuller

shrugged, hands clasped atop some piece of correspondence. "And you've lost the better part of your family already today. And you might be dead by next week." A grin cracked his face. "Altogether I'm more inclined to offer you a drink." He set his palms flat on the desk and pushed to his feet.

"What will you do, though? Is there any chance of finding another investor in time?"

"Possibly. I have prospects. None I like as well as you; I'll be frank about that." At the other side of the room he fetched a bottle and two glasses from a cabinet. "None so likely to impress my trading partners with fine English manners. None with your gift for inspiring confidence."

"I think it may be more curse than blessing on balance, that gift." He pressed the thin edge of one cuff-stud hard into the pad of his thumb, a tiny act of self-mortification. "People like yourself put their trust in me when perhaps they oughtn't."

"Really, Blackshear, you lay it on a bit thick." Brandy gurgled musically as he tipped the bottle over one glass, then the other. "What would a trustworthy man have done, that you didn't? Turn your back when you saw Miss Slaughter's gentleman hit her? *Sorry, sweetheart, but Jack Fuller is expecting me to help him buy a ship and I can't go risking myself.*" He corked the bottle and put it away. "You dealt with me in good faith. You never planned to fall in love, to wind up in a duel, to have to provide for Miss Slaughter in the event of your death." Carefully he took up the glasses and crossed the room again with his uneven step. "If you'd plotted it all from the beginning that would be different. I'd be more than happy to heap abuse on your head."

"I admire your equanimity." Will took his brandy and tossed back a good swallow. "You ought to have seen my brothers."

"It's an advantage of my class, I think." Fuller resumed his seat. "We merchants get a good deal of practice, early, in contending with things that don't go the way we'd like. We learn to take a philosophical view." He tipped a mouthful from his own glass. "I recommend trade to any man, if only as a forge of character. Tell your brothers I said so."

Ha. Maybe he would, by letter at least. Another swallow of brandy, and already he was beginning to feel its warming effect. Or perhaps the warmth had other sources.

It was all true, what Andrew had said—he was making a selfish choice, besmirching the family name—and yet here, in Russell Square, there were other truths. Other expectations. Not once had his friend suggested he ought to abandon Miss Slaughter, or keep her as a mistress and avoid all scandal. In this world, such a marriage might not be so very remarkable.

He set down his glass and leaned forward. "Fuller." The brandy had surely gone straight to his head. "I'll want an income, if I survive that duel. Not a great one—the money we've won at cards can establish us, at least—but if I'm to marry, I'll want a steady source of funds."

He paused for a quick breath. To ask this of the man was impudent in the extreme. But devil take it. He might be dead in a few more days. "Whatever qualities you found appealing in me as a prospective investor . . . might I be able to bring those qualities to your business in some other capacity? It's not just the income, you know. I had looked forward to being part of this. I've studied to learn about ships and shipping." Now the brandy had hold of his tongue. He stilled it. He'd made his case and he could wait for an answer.

Fuller rubbed a considering hand over his jaw. "To be sure I could use you when the Americans come. I might have other uses as well." He was silent for a moment, gone somewhere else, picking his way through the intricacies of his business to find the places where Will might fit. "Come call on me after the duel, if you're able." He grinned again. "If you'll promise to bring your wife sometimes to have a look at my ledgers, I think perhaps something can be arranged."

His wife. That sounded excellent. If he could live to see his own wedding, he had every reason to be hopeful. They'd work hard, the two of them, and scrape their way from subsistence to comfort. And with an income to look forward to, he could think again of carving out part of his winnings to provide for Mrs. Talbot.

A muscle somewhere deep inside him twitched. Guilt. How was he to forgive himself, if he'd led the widow to expect an offer and now must disappoint her? What if he died some several days hence? The nearly twenty-eight hundred pounds he'd amassed could buy independence for one woman, but not two.

He pressed the cuff-stud to his thumb once more, but the guilt-muscle only twitched harder. Sometime in the next few days he must call in Camden Town. He would swallow the medicine of correcting any mistake as to his intentions. But how to honor his promise to Talbot, while still securing a future for the woman who now had every claim on his heart, was a calculation requiring more dumb genius and depth of understanding than he knew how to summon.

Chapter Twenty-two

$\mathscr{A}$ wife's honor, he'd said, was her husband's concern. Then surely a husband's honor was his wife's concern, and his debts and obligations likewise her own. And so here she stood on the steps of the little house in Camden Town, waiting for the widow Talbot to fetch her cloak and come out for a walk.

Lydia unwound and rewound her reticule strings until the purse sat snug in her palm. He'd gone to brave the wrath of his family for her, according to the note on the pillow, and then to withdraw from his partnership with Mr. Fuller. She'd woken too late to prevent him in that. Not for the world, though, would she give him any chance to default on this most solemn of debts. Not in her name.

"You're very good to call again." Mrs. Talbot descended the steps, a polite wariness in her manners. Pity *would* well up, despite all Lydia's firm intentions. The woman had lost her husband through circumstances too horrible for her to ever know. Nor could she ever have the consolation of being Mrs. Blackshear. For Will to marry her, bearing the secret he bore, would only be a cruelty to both. She understood that now.

"It's very forward of me. I beg your pardon for that. Shall we walk?" They started south, the widow's skirts swishing in rhythm with her own. Time to set her shoulders and plunge ahead. "In fact I've come on a particular errand. My cousin left yesterday's visit in a state of some confusion."

"I should be surprised if he hadn't." Mrs. Talbot dimpled suddenly, blushed, and shook her head, averting her gaze to the pavement. "Please tell him I'm sorry for the awkwardness. Assure him he was no more astonished than I was to hear of Mrs. John Talbot's assumptions."

"You did look . . . startled."

"Perhaps I oughtn't to have been." She lifted her chin and frowned into the distance. "My sister-in-law would like very much to have the house to herself and her husband and her own children again. Little wonder, I suppose, that she'd jump at any chance of another establishment for me and my son."

This was near enough, wasn't it, to a denial of any expectation? It wasn't as though he could marry the widow in any case. And yet to know for a certainty—to be able to go back to him and say *you have not disappointed her hopes in the least*—would be a prize worth some risk. Lydia tightened her fingers where they gripped her cloak together. "I should think you must wish for that too. It must be very hard, living with relations who make you feel you're a burden. Marriage, to say nothing of marriage to a man with Mr. Blackshear's merit, must be an attractive option by compare."

"Not for me." She studied the pavement again, then brought her chin round to address Lydia straight on. "I'll be frank, Miss Slaughter. Your cousin appears to be an excellent man. Mr. Talbot spoke well of him in his letters, and his kind attentions speak for themselves. He deserves a wife who will love him, not one whose heart was buried with another man." Her eyes shone blue and pristine as a reflecting pool under a cloudless sky. "I'd never remarry at all, if I could avoid it. I certainly won't inflict such unhappiness on Mr. Blackshear."

And now she had the prize, a balm to his conscience, to take back to him. Better yet, she had a prize for Mrs. Talbot too. With the hand that wasn't clutching her purse she caught the widow's elbow and ushered her to one side of the walk. "Mr. Talbot must have known what would be your wish." Was this a convincing story? Through the mounting haze of happiness she couldn't be quite sure. "You'll forgive Mr. Blackshear, I hope, for not telling you of this before now, but he wanted to wait until there was a result worth telling. The fact is your husband made an investment and left it in my cousin's charge, and now that investment has made its return, and . . ." She was doing the right thing. Without doubt she was doing the right thing. ". . . and it's my privilege, Mrs. Talbot, to ask whether you can spare an hour to journey with me to the bank."

M̃rs. Talbot wept in the hackney. Her sweet dainty features concealed nothing, and Lydia could see the exact second when she understood that she was to have her independence. Her eyes widened, and her lips parted for an instant before she pressed them together in a futile attempt at command. But by then her whole lower face was trembling. She brought her hands halfway up and let them fall again, helplessly, and turned to the window. Then she gave up altogether and just let the tears come.

It was wonderful, one of the most wonderful things Lydia had ever seen. Her foolish heart felt like a teacup into which someone had forgot to stop pouring. But that was all right. Such untidy brimming-over warmth kept the widow company in her untidy weeping.

"I recommend you set aside two hundred in ready money, to see you through the year and to discharge whatever obligation you choose to recognize toward your husband's kin." One helpless peal of laughter spilled out from between the helpless tears, prompting another slosh of sentiment in her heart. "That will leave you with twenty-five hundred to invest, which will bring you one hundred and twenty-five pounds per year."

Mrs. Talbot found a handkerchief and pressed it to her eyes. "I scarcely know what to think. It's Providential, isn't it? That this money should come when I had no earthly hope of it?" She turned the handkerchief over to find a dry place, and dabbed at her eyes again. "My Jamey has two thousand pounds of his own from another such arrangement; did you know?"

She hadn't known. But she remembered, of a sudden, the night she'd asked after the proceeds of Will's commission. Part of it was tied up elsewhere, he'd said. She touched a gloved knuckle to each eye. "I'm so happy for you. I'm sure you've deserved it."

Let her believe it was the work of Providence. Well, and it was. Good people provided for one another. The best people made a solemn duty of it. People like herself could at least make sure they didn't stand in the way of such noble intent.

At the bank she waited in that same line again, drawing inexorably nearer to the clerk whose insolent manners had thwarted her in a similar mission six weeks since.

Six weeks had wrought changes, though. She'd struck a man in that time, and shot two. She'd recovered her heart, with all its frailties and its strengths as well.

Besides, Mrs. Talbot was depending on her, as Jane

never truly had. So was Mr. Blackshear, though he didn't know it. And the dependence of other people proved a remarkably fortifying tonic—by the time they reached the front of the line she could have faced a dozen leering clerks, naked, if she had to, without so much as a blush.

She only had to face one. And he never even worked up a proper leer. "Good afternoon, sir," she said the instant she and the widow sat down. "May I present Mrs. Talbot, a widow of one of our brave fighting men. She'd like to invest in the Navy fund. She hasn't a man of business, but she does have twenty-five hundred pounds." She paused for an unhurried breath. "And she has me. And I will not leave this bank until she has her certificate, not if I have to sit down with a dozen of your worthy colleagues until I find one willing to help." *Colleagues who might be interested to hear a few things I can tell of you.*

She didn't have to say that aloud. His face told her, plainly, that his imagination had supplied it. He dipped his pen and began to take down the widow's information, avoiding her own eyes all the while.

Thirty minutes later they passed through the doors onto the street, Mrs. Talbot clutching tight to her certificate and fumbling for her handkerchief again. "You've been so kind, Miss Slaughter. If I can ever be of service to you in any way—"

And *that* was all that had been wanting; the final value that would make the whole equation come out right. "In fact you can do me a very great favor. You'll have means enough to employ a maid-of-all-work, and I happen to know one who's in want of just such a respectable situation."

*H*E COULDN'T say how long he'd been sitting in that same place on the bed when she finally walked through his door. He'd spent some time on his feet, to be sure. He'd gone inch by inch through the rooms to see whether anything else had been disturbed, then searched every surface for a note of explanation. But the bulk of his time had been spent right here, staring at the drawer he'd ransacked and ransacked again. He'd left it out after his last rifling and it jutted from the dresser with a certain truculence, as though conscious of having failed him and determined not to care.

The latch hardware clicked and he turned his head slowly. He did not rise.

She was wearing the plain dark blue gown she'd worn that day he and Martha had encountered her on the street. A reticule swung limply from her wrist. She glanced about the room, and crossed with careful steps to the bedroom door.

He waited for her eyes to register him, to register the pulled-out drawer. He brought his own gaze back to the dresser. He couldn't seem to form the question, but then he didn't have to. A woman with only a tenth of her cleverness would know he wasn't despairing over a lost pair of stockings.

"I took the money." Damn her, she didn't even sound sheepish. "I called on Mrs. Talbot. I told her Mr. Talbot had put you in charge of an investment, and it had come out well."

"How much did you give her?" The air was feeling too thin, too insubstantial to breathe.

"Two thousand, seven hundred pounds."

He surged to his feet, the desperate misgivings of these past hours galvanized into a panic that seized his whole form. "Lydia, that was *everything*." In two strides he made the dresser and shoved the drawer back in. "That was all the money I had to my name."

"Not altogether." *Now* she sounded self-conscious,

because she knew this wasn't the appropriate reply, but she could no more avoid making it than a clock could keep silent at the top of the hour. "You had sixty-two pounds three shillings sixpence besides. Have." She corrected herself, holding up the reticule as though for proof. "You still have that." A faint jingle of coins testified to the fact.

He rested his palms on the dresser-top and let his head sag until all he saw was faded mahogany. "I might have secured your future with that money." His mouth filled with the familiar bitter taste of good intentions thwarted by circumstance. "I might at least have gone to that duel with the peace of mind brought by knowing I wouldn't leave you destitute and alone in the world."

"I know. That's what I was afraid of." Without the smallest sign of repentance she slipped into the place beside him and laid her right hand over his left. "You made a vow to provide for Mrs. Talbot before you ever laid eyes on me. She has the prior claim."

"She has a roof over her head. She has relations, however far from ideal. If I can only provide for one of you . . ." He stopped. He hated himself for even thinking of renouncing his promise to Talbot.

"Do you see?" Her fingers fitted themselves between each of his, knitting their two hands together. "You don't even like to speak the idea aloud. You know the act would be unworthy of you."

"I've been too much concerned with what would be worthy of me." He turned his head aside. He might hate himself, yes. But self-hatred was a price he would have willingly paid in exchange for her security. "I begin to think honor is just another kind of vanity, and honor satisfied will be the poorest of consolations if—"

"No." The brief utterance carried all the authority of a rolling thunder-peal. "Honor is the best part of you,

Will Blackshear. And I don't make that pronouncement lightly. No woman could, who's ever seen you naked."

He let his head fall back. He wanted to laugh. He wanted to break the nearest breakable object, he wanted to run from the room, he wanted to pick up this woman and throw her over his shoulder and haul her straight off to the bed. Instead he drew his hand out from under hers and sent that arm, carefully, round her waist. Her head tipped to rest on his shoulder. "You called on Mrs. Talbot," he said.

"She never had any thought of marrying you. She would refuse you if you offered, even if it meant remaining with those relations." She craned back to look up into his eyes. "She was so happy to have the prospect of living independently. So grateful. I wish you could have been there to see."

The intelligence did bring some solace, as did her nearness and the weight of her head on his shoulder and the knowledge that she was telling him this—that in fact she'd gone to find this out—because she knew the state of his conscience and wanted to deliver him from self-blame where she could.

He touched his cheek to the top of her head. "My sister will still know me, if I marry you." Now he would tell her how he'd spent *his* day. "The one you met, Mrs. Mirkwood. Her husband as well. We're to call on them next week provided I . . . provided we're able. And I may take a position in Mr. Fuller's business. I'm to speak to him next week too."

An ache crept into the back of his throat. Even a day ago he hadn't minded the prospect of dying so very much. But now that he had such a worthwhile future almost in reach, things took on a different complexion.

No point in dwelling on that. "You still have your own few hundred, I hope." They would just have to fatten that stake as best they could, tonight and for as many nights as remained. He couldn't guarantee her security. He must let that ambition go. All he could do was shoot straight, when the moment came, and privately pray for luck.

𝓑ʏ Monday, when a note came from Lord Cathcart with the time and location of the duel, she had six hundred eight pounds, two shillings, and a farthing. They'd won at a decent pace these last three nights, but Mr. Blackshear had insisted on keeping their wagers conservative and, well, she cared too much for his feelings to argue. Hence, six hundred eight pounds and some coins. Not enough to keep a woman safe from want.

"I've written my sister's direction on a paper and left it in that top drawer," he said that night in bed. "I think she won't refuse you help, if you go to her." They lay chastely side by side. Gravity had shouldered its way into the bed and left no room for passion. "Or you might see how far you can prevail upon Mrs. Talbot's gratitude. If she's to have a home of her own . . ."

"Yes. Thank you." A corpse would sound like this, if it could talk. But if she had been a corpse, she would at least know the peace of inertia. Instead she felt the way she did in her nightmares, screaming with all her might and never producing a sound.

The way she *had* felt in her nightmares, rather. She'd slept six nights in this bed without one.

Life needn't be entirely devoid of purpose if you lose him, nor of joy. Remember how it felt to rescue Mrs. Talbot. Remember how it felt to make provision for Jane.

No. Tomorrow she would begin meditating on those consolations, if she must. Tonight it was her prerogative to dwell unreservedly on the horror of watching him slip through her desperate clutching fingers.

"I do intend to survive the duel, Lydia." He'd turned his head. Sidelong she could see his solemn dark eyes, glimmering in the moonlight. "But to prepare you for the other eventuality is only sensible." His hand drifted across several inches of mattress to find hers. "I'll have Cathcart send a message to you straightaway, whatever the outcome. You won't have to wait and wonder."

"That won't be necessary." Ah. She hadn't known she intended this. "I'm coming with you tomorrow to Primrose Hill."

"Lydia . . ." Her name came out on a sigh. He was too weary, too preoccupied, to make a forceful argument. He was depending on her recognizing the absurdity of what she proposed.

"Don't try to dissuade me. You must have known this might be the outcome, when you didn't trouble to hide the viscount's note. If you don't let me come with you, I'll go by myself in a hackney."

"It's a duel. It's no fit place for—"

"No fit place for the woman who's at the center of the dispute? No fit place for my delicate feminine sensibilities? Don't even try to say so. Surely you haven't forgot the highwaymen." She would win this argument, because nothing else was left to her. The sooner he saw that, the better.

"I don't want to quarrel with you. Not tonight." His hair made a scrubbing sound on the pillow as he turned to face the ceiling again. His hand clasped steadfastly about her own.

And every proof of his affection—every reminder of all that might be taken from her before she'd properly learned to enjoy it—touched her heart like the cut of a lash.

"I'm going with you," she repeated, in place of half a dozen things she couldn't bring herself to say.

* * *

$\mathcal{S}$TARS HAD just begun to dwindle against the the waning black of night when Cathcart's carriage pulled up. Will helped Lydia in and then took his own seat beside the surgeon procured for the occasion, a dour-faced man who scowled over his spectacles at this unexpected distaff addition to the party.

Cathcart opened his mouth and closed it again. He raised his eyebrows, hard, at Will.

"It's her concern." He turned to stare out the window. On what might be the last morning of his life, he was in no mood to make explanations.

If he'd been able to slip from the rooms without waking her, the seat across from him would be empty now. But of course she'd chosen this day to finally rise ahead of him, and he found himself unwilling, still, to part with her on a quarrel. Well enough. If it was his lot to die today, he would at least have her at hand to be the last thing he saw.

The drive to Primrose Hill passed mostly in silence, or rather, passed in that absence of conversation that lent prominence to every incidental noise. The springs creaked, the wheels rumbled over cobblestones in counterpoint to the horses' clopping hooves, and something in the surgeon's bag gave an occasional metallic rattle.

He remembered this from the hours before combat, this bodily need to perceive every last insignificant sight and sound and sensation. The grim morning taste in his mouth, because he'd got up too early to have hope of even coffee in the breakfast room downstairs. The texture on the inside of his gloves, usually as unnoticeable as his own skin. The way light from a streetlamp would crawl from one side of the carriage to the other as they passed, bathing Lydia's somber face and glinting off her eyes before leaving her to darkness once more. Today, of all days, he could read her. But then again he'd authored what was there.

He reached for her hand and held it, devil take the two men watching, until the wheels and hoofbeats finally slowed and came to a stop. "I won't interfere," she said, though he'd been in no need of that promise. He stood, leaned over to press his lips to her forehead, and stepped down from the carriage, winding his muffler an extra turn about his neck. Devil of a year for someone to die, with this endless winter.

Night had given way to a meager dawn: he could see the layout of the place. Bare ground, clumps of straggling trees, a downhill slope that might afford a prospect of distant London rooftops, if the fog should ever lift.

"They're here before us." The viscount, at his elbow, nodded toward a landau some thirty feet off. "That's his second, standing by the carriage. Kin of some sort."

Indeed he might have guessed that himself, once he'd drawn near enough to make out the man's features. He proved fairer-colored than Roanoke, but the eyes were similar and he had that same blockish quality about the chin. He inclined his square-jawed head, when Cathcart made the introduction, and said nothing. The expression on his face was very like the expression Lydia had worn all this morning.

Some small thing splintered somewhere in Will's chest. Here was where a duel differed from battle, or from defending yourself against a band of highwaymen: there, you knew in an abstract way that your adversary likely had a mother or sister who would mourn his loss, but you needn't *face* that person. You needn't see their pallor, or the grim set of the mouth. Needn't sense the effort they took to project an air of nonchalance while privately rehearsing for grief.

A vision shimmered, unbidden and unwelcome, of a summer day in his boyhood spent with his brothers out of doors. Nothing of moment had occurred—they'd passed an afternoon in setting up targets and hitting them with rocks—but he prized the memory, as he prized a hundred other such memories of hours spent with Nick and Andrew. No doubt this fellow had golden-hued recollections of his own from a childhood in which Prince Square-jaw might have loomed as an admired elder.

Well, Square-jaw ought to have valued that admiration, then, and worked to stay worthy of it. Will excused himself; Cathcart and Roanoke's second had details to sort out concerning pistols and the surgeon, and he'd caught sight of the opponent himself, leaning one shoulder against a tree a little way off with his back to the others. He'd put off his hat and greatcoat already, perhaps to make a show of his indifference to the cold. Not wise. His reflexes would pay a price.

He glanced up at Will's approach and then put his hands behind his back, not quickly enough to hide the fact that they were shaking. Possibly due to the cold. But then his cheeks ought to be ruddy, not dull and wan as spent tallow.

Hell. Will dusted his own hands together. He had every right to fire a pistol at this coxcomb, and to enjoy whatever advantages nature and his experience had seen fit to give him. "You ought to put your coat on," he said nevertheless. "Warm muscles will serve you better when the time comes."

Roanoke jerked his head in a nod, eyes averted, but he didn't move from the spot.

Confound him. Confound this whole cursed undertaking. Will shoved his hands deep in his greatcoat pockets. The pair of seconds had gone to consult with the surgeon now, and the carriage door stood open. Dimly he could see Lydia's shape within. "Is it your brother who's come with you?" The fellow really did look like a more refined edition of the Roanoke template, as sometimes happened with the succeeding issue in a family.

Square-jaw nodded again, not turning that way. He brought a hand from behind his back just long enough to pass it across his mouth. One couldn't help wondering whether he'd recently cast up his accounts. Then his eyes met Will's. "He doesn't know all the circumstances. If he should ask you—if this is the end of me, for instance, and he wants to know more of how it came about—you'd oblige me by omitting any mention of my striking Lydia."

"Please to call her Miss Slaughter now." Those words rang and rattled swift as a sword unsheathed, and if he'd *had* a sword, he couldn't answer for what it might have done in that moment. "You'd descend in his opinion, you mean, if he knew you'd struck a woman."

"He has notions of what's proper." Roanoke frowned at his feet, and rolled his shoulders one at a time against the cold. "I never hit her, you know, besides that one time." He half-mumbled, though he must know his brother was well out of earshot. "And I don't think I would have, if she hadn't hit me first. Only it took me by surprise, and I didn't stop to think and I forgot myself." His weight shifted from one leg to the other and he adjusted his position against the tree.

"Are you making an apology?" He could see his own breath before him, small puffs of mist in the chilly air.

The man hesitated, and shook his head. Stupid stubborn bastard. Shaking and puking and pale as a ghost at the prospect of being fired upon, but ready to take a bullet rather than risk being thought a coward. "I never hit her before. I only wanted to say that."

A number of responses rose up and subsided. *Do you think that signifies at all? Am I to forget that you were vile to her the entire time we were at Chiswell? Are you angling for a more lenient judgment in the afterlife, perhaps?—because I assure you your testimony makes no impression on me.*

He let his gaze drift back to the carriage, where he could see the gray of a cloak and a face in shadow. "You might speak to her, if you like. If you've anything to say to her." Probably he oughtn't to make this offer without her permission. Too late now. "She insisted on being present, since the duel was entered into for her sake."

Roanoke straightened with surprise, and threw a furtive look toward the carriage before facing forward again. "I don't see what I'd have to say to her. She knows I never hit her before."

Will shrugged, and took a half step back. His muscles needed that outlet, and that distance, in order to sidestep the temptation to knock this obstinate lack-wit down all over again. "It's none of my business what you have to say." He tipped his head back and frowned at the sparse branches above. "Only I speak from experience. It's a useful kind of tidying-up, an emptying of your pockets. You don't like to go into battle with things hanging unreconciled, when they might have been reconciled." One more half step back, one more lift of the shoulders. "Perhaps you haven't got anything to say to her. I wouldn't know. But if you have, then now's the time to say it."

Roanoke shot another look round the tree. He folded his arms, shoulders hunching against the cold, hands gripping tight to the opposite elbows. He inhaled, and for the length of the inhalation it seemed possible he would scrounge up what honor he possessed, turn on his heel, and go make some sort of account to Lydia.

Then he let the breath out, shaking his head. "I've nothing to tell her." He fixed his gaze on a patch of ground several feet past Will's boot.

Pathetic. Pitiful. Pitiable. Good God, was he really pitying this man? When had his clean, bracing contempt lost its shape and sagged into pity?

But he couldn't help it. To see a man grope so feebly toward honor—and without doubt he did have some concept of the virtue, else he shouldn't care whether or not he were tarnished in his brother's eyes—but to see the fellow recognize, if only dimly, the standard of which he fell so far short, must necessarily pluck at the sympathies of any fair-minded man. He knew what it was, after all, to lose a brother's good opinion. He knew about smothering a clamorous conscience. Didn't he owe the keenest joy of his life, in fact, to the lapses and deceptions and willful transgressions that had brought this man's own mistress into his bed and his arms?

Movement by the carriage snagged his attention: she'd stepped outside. Doubtless she'd noted the multiple glances cast her way by both men, and now she stood, just clear of the wheels, clutching her cloak against the wind, poised to approach if summoned. Her eyes held him as fast as they'd done that first night in the darkened library, but this time there was nothing of indifference in her gaze. For all her strength and steadiness he could see the ardent hope burning there. Even now she let herself believe he and Roanoke could be coming to some terms that would avert the duel.

The splintering sensation started up in his chest once more. This on its own might not have swayed him; even in tandem with that odd sunlight-shaft of pity, it might not have done. But his right thumb chose that instant to recall the hushed cadence of Talbot's pulse, and that impression acted upon the other two like the final drop in an alchemist's potion, or the prism that splintered a shaft of sunlight into something brilliant and new.

And now all was clarity, and decision, and action. "Listen, Roanoke." He didn't have much time. Cathcart and the Roanoke brother had finished with the surgeon and pistols and were turning this way. "I'm going to delope."

Square-jaw's head jerked up, eyes wide, nostrils flared, disbelief writ large across his brow. To be sure it was a disgraceful act, deliberately missing one's target. Apology was the honorable way out of a duel.

Well, hang that. After all he'd gone through, he'd surely wrested from life the right to decide for himself what was honorable. "The truth is I find myself uninclined to kill, this morning. If I could be certain of my aim I'd probably shoot you in the leg. But I don't know these pistols." Quickly. Here they came. "They might kick just enough to put a bullet in your vitals. Altogether I think it's safer to aim away. Ah—is it time, then?" He swung away to address the seconds before Roanoke had a chance to reply. He wanted no reply. He'd made up his mind.

Prince Square-jaw was no more deserving of mercy than he'd been ten minutes since. *That* part hadn't changed. Rather the shift had come in his perspective, as though he'd climbed some peak to look down on the terrain of his life and seen the duel from a different angle. He had the privilege and power of granting mercy, regardless of whether it was earned. And if he did this—if he waived his right to dispatch a worthless bounder—then his history would have an act of irrational grace to balance, in some small way, the memories of his helpless complicity in the death of a man who'd never deserved such an end.

Besides, he'd be doing a kindness to this fair-haired younger Roanoke who stood before him now, proffering the pistols and reminding everyone of the agreed-upon terms. One shot apiece, simultaneous fire, and a misfire counted as a shot. Cathcart said something too, as to the surgeon and his qualifications and the steps they would take to avoid notice by the law in the event there was need for medical treatment. He'd proven himself a surprisingly generous and dependable friend, the viscount had. He'd see his goodness repaid, if he didn't mind friendship with the husband of a demimondaine—and if, of course, Roanoke didn't choose to fire on a man who'd already told him his own shot would go wide.

His heart pounded, robust and regular, as he took a pistol and followed to the patch of ground the seconds had picked out. If he was mortally wounded he would have a devil of a time explaining, with his dying breaths, why he'd declined to inflict a wound in his turn.

Never mind. To condition his deloping on an assurance of his opponent's doing the same would have been but a timid gesture. And a dueling-ground was no place for timidity.

Twenty paces. He took the left-hand direction, because that was the one that would leave him facing Lydia, and when he set his feet he had a good long look at her.

She'd let go her cloak, to bring her arms straight down at her sides. Her hands were balled into fists. Her chin jutted at a deliberate angle, as though to emphasize to any viewer how she did not shrink from the scene. Her eyes glittered like a mishap in a chemist's workshop, quicksilver mingled with broken glass.

I love you for your quickness and your brokenness and your sharp edges too. Let her read that in his eyes, on his face, in every part of his body even as his right arm rose and extended straight out to the side, pistol in hand. He turned his head to the right, sighted down his arm, and bent his elbow in close. Forty paces away Roanoke was doing the same, and somewhere out of his view one of the seconds was counting down.

Let happen what would. He angled his face for a sight

of Lydia again, for one more draught of that fierce, irregular beauty. She saw him look away from his target, saw the sudden slant of his wrist, and as the powder flashed and the pistol kicked he was conscious of nothing but her smile, spilling out across her face with such warm incandescence as put the sunrise to shame.

Epilogue

I'M FAIRLY certain your parents will think better of this someday. Such a connection does no credit to any young lady." Lydia kept her voice down, as the parents in question were walking several paces behind. Miss Mirkwood, to whom the words had been addressed, received them with an expression of as much sagacity as an infant could manage, while occupied with cramming her own bonnet strings into her mouth.

Of course she'd heard this admonition before, more than once. Lydia took care to repeat some version of it every time she saw the child. If the Mirkwoods eventually came to their senses and cut the connection, she would at least have been prepared.

"However, provided they continue so careless in these matters long enough for you to reach a reasoning age, I shall teach you a great deal about playing cards. A little skill at vingt-et-un can make a lady's fortune in more ways than one." Miss Mirkwood must wonder, if she understood the words, what kind of fortune brought a woman down into this neighborhood, all narrow streets and ramshackle buildings and every offensive smell of close city living mixed with every foul odor that came off the river. "Are you quite sure you want to go on?" Lydia said over her shoulder. "If you'd rather, you could wait back a block or two with the baby and I could go the rest of the way on my own."

"Not at all. Mrs. Mirkwood is fond of squalor." That lady's husband flashed his perfect teeth—some women did prefer that kind—in a smile of such mischief as ought by rights to try a serious-minded wife's patience.

But other people's marriages were things of mystery, and to have her patience tried seemed to suit Mrs. Mirkwood very well. "I take an interest in the *alleviation* of squalor, as must any country landowner." She had her brother's disarming direct gaze as well as his dark-chocolate eyes. "Poverty doesn't belong only to the city. I expect I've seen enough, in Sussex, to prepare me for whatever we encounter on this walk. That is what Mr. Mirkwood meant to say."

"Precisely what I meant to say," agreed her husband, just as satisfied to be corrected by her as she was to be teased by him. "We fear nothing. Lead on."

So on she led them, past dockworkers staggering out of public houses, harlots soliciting sailors flush from the last voyage, children chasing after drays in hopes some merchandise might tumble off into the street. She would never have been easy in this neighborhood, if she'd remained respectable. She would have missed so much.

A thrumming started up in her chest as the stones underfoot gave way to the timber of the massive dock, with its warehouses and offices and ongoing bustle of industry. A small crowd of emigrants thronged ahead of her, waiting for the boats that would ferry them to one of the ships moored out in the river proper. She wove through their ranks, one Mirkwood on her hip and two more in tow, and cut right to arrive at the office that had been their destination. The door stood open and she paused, on the threshold, just to look.

Her husband stood at a table directly in line with the door, coatless, cuff-buttons undone and sleeves pushed up to the elbows. His palms lay flat on the tabletop, at either side of a document in which he was absorbed, and as he leaned forward, head bent, hair falling over his brow, the beauty of his forearms alone was enough to make her dizzy.

At his right was a man she recognized as the ship's first mate, explaining something at which he nodded with that easy authority that must come from his time leading soldiers on the Continent. He glanced up to ask the crewman a question, caught sight of her, and smiled.

His smile—and with all due respect to Mr. Mirkwood, *here* was what a man's smile ought to be, crooked and imperfect and crammed with character—made all her innards bloom like flowers under a tropical sun.

So had she bloomed under his smile that morning on Primrose Hill, in the instant when she understood he'd chosen to leave Edward standing. Granted she would have killed Edward herself if he'd been so craven as to answer that clemency by inflicting even a flesh wound— but she hadn't had to. Something had bloomed in Edward, too, at least for the span of time it took him to fire at the ground and mutter a few imprecations on shoddy pistols and how they kicked. Such was the influence of a nature like her husband's.

"Bringing the gentry in to gawk at those of us who labor for our bread, are you?" *Just one moment,* said the gesture he made to the crewman as he came from behind his table. "I don't know but we ought to charge admission. Sixpence, or a firstborn child." Miss Mirkwood had by now spied him and was reaching out her arms; he hoisted her neatly from Lydia's hip to a perch on his shoulder. "What say you, Fuller?"

Mr. Fuller, at his own desk by the east wall with its windows, had come to his feet. "All order in my account books is owing to Mrs. Blackshear. She may bring in whatever visitors she likes." He directed a bow toward the Mirkwoods. He'd met them, of course, at the wedding breakfast. And he was exaggerating about the account books, but she could let that pass.

Happiness still felt, at odd moments, like something with which she oughtn't to be trusted. A delicate and costly music box put into the hands of a maladroit child. Yet happiness felt, too, like a prize she and Will had fought for and seized. An edifice they'd built with their own bare hands out of the scrap heap of mistake and misadventure.

There would never be any but borrowed children to sit atop her husband's shoulder. They must live modestly, with tradesmen for neighbors and only a slight income from what remained of their winnings to supplement his wages. Their friends would probably always be few. And still, knowing what she knew—what they both knew—of fortune and misfortune, the bounty of their life together seemed sometimes almost too much to bear.

"Don't let us interrupt." She advanced a step or two farther into the office, yet another improbable place where she'd begun to feel at home. "Mr. and Mrs. Mirkwood have come to town on business, and called to invite us to dine with them. I said I'd carry the invitation to you and they proposed to come along."

"Excellent." He sent her insides spinning with one more smile as he shifted himself toward the crewman again. "Give me a minute to finish here and then I'll show you all about the place." And on he went with his business, one hand steadying the child on his shoulder just as though that were the ordinary way to conduct these things.

Hours later he still glowed with the pride and pleasure of having his work thus acknowledged by what family remained to him. Stretched out in her bed, sated by the six courses they'd enjoyed in Brook Street that evening and at least temporarily sated in other appetites as well, he looked as though sparks might jump from his skin to set the sheets ablaze.

"Lydia," he said. "Mrs. Blackshear." He gave the words a moment to shimmer in the air between them as his eyes roved over her face. "You know I have reason to disbelieve in the benevolence of Fate."

"I know. So do I have reason." It was the most sober of their intimate bonds. She lifted a hand to rasp her fingertips on his unshaven cheek.

"Then how do we account for this? How do *you* account for it?" He caressed without touching her, through his voice and his bay-rum scent and his reliance on her reason. "That we should have found each other. That of all the epochs in which to be born, our souls should both have chosen this one, and that we both should have been in England, when it might have been me in France and you in China."

"That we both survived to adulthood."

"Exactly. That's no small accomplishment." He was caressing with his hand now as well, following the curve from her lowest rib to her waist to her hip. "That one outrageous circumstance after the next should have led to our both being in the same gaming club on the same night."

"And that you didn't wash your hands of me after I fleeced you that first night."

"That too, yes." A grin tugged at the corner of his mouth. "The odds against our being in this bed together, happy in the life we have, must be nearly beyond human reckoning. And yet here we are. How are we to understand it?"

"Some of the odds can be reckoned. If we begin, for example, with the numbers of people presently living in each country of the world, and if we could arrive at an approximate count of all people who have *ever* lived . . ." But that was the wrong answer. She knew, not from any change in his expression—he only watched her with a fondness that made her vision go hazy—but because the right answer was suddenly there, square in the middle of her thoughts.

"Luck," she said, and meant it. "I think we must ascribe it all to luck."

If you loved *A Gentleman Undone*,
you won't be able to resist

A Woman Entangled

The next breathtaking novel from Cecilia Grant
Coming Spring 2013

Read on for a sneak peek
at this unforgettable story . . .

FEBRUARY 1817, LONDON

*D*ISCOMFITURE, FOR all that it felt like a constant companion, never failed to find new and inventive guises in which to appear.

"I'd like to take out *A Vindication of the Rights of Woman*, the first volume." Her sister's voice soared into every corner of the lending library, all but rattling the bay window in whose alcove Kate had taken refuge. "I'm engaged at present in a work of my own that will build on Miss Wollstonecraft's foundation. Where she restricted herself to theory, however, and broad societal prescription, I address myself directly to the individual woman of today, arming her with practical methods by which she may begin even now to assert her rights."

She wouldn't speak of *bodily emancipation* in such a setting, would she? Kate held her breath. Surely even Viola had better sense than to—

"In particular I introduce the idea that women will never achieve true emancipation until we have absolute governance of our own persons, within marriage as well as without."

A stout young man, sitting at the long table nearest Kate's alcove, looked up sharply from his book. An elderly woman seated on the opposite side of the room did the same. So, no doubt, did every peacefully reading patron in this establishment. Vi's was a voice that commanded attention, all crisp consonants and breath support, exactly the voice you'd expect from the granddaughter of an earl.

Or the daughter of an actress.

The young man's table was scattered with volumes, all perused and discarded by patrons who hadn't bothered to return them to the desk. Kate swiped one up and bent her head over a random page, to avoid meeting anyone's eyes. *To Elizabeth it appeared that had her family made an agreement to expose themselves as much as they could during the evening, it would have been impossible for them to play their parts with more spirit or finer success . . .*

Pride and Prejudice. That single line was enough to set her bones vibrating like a struck tuning fork. Surely it had been written for her, this tale of a young woman struggling under the incessant mortifications thrust upon her by a family that did not know the meaning of discretion.

She turned a page. No more sound from the library's other end; the clerk must have gone to fetch the requested volume, and to escape any more discussion of practical methods for asserting a woman's rights. In the book, meanwhile, the party at Netherfield dragged dismally on, plaguing Elizabeth with the disagreeable attentions of Mr. Collins and the cold silence of the Bingley sisters and Mr. Darcy.

Of course, Mr. Darcy had already begun to take note of Elizabeth's fine eyes by this point in the story, and Mr. Bingley was so smitten with Jane that he never noticed half the graceless things the Bennet family did. Could there really be such men in the world? And if so, where did they reside?

"There you are." Viola stood at the other side of the book-scattered table, *Vindication* volume in hand, peering at her through those plain glass spectacles she always insisted on wearing in public. "Are you ready to go?"

The stout man glanced up again, no doubt recognizing Vi's voice. He sent a quick look from one lady to the other, piecing together their relation.

And then he saw her, properly. Though he'd been sitting no great distance away all this time, a mere half turn of his head necessary to bring her into view, his eyes apparently had not landed on her until now.

A dozen or more variations she'd seen of this response, on too many occasions to count. Some men managed it without looking witless. Most, unfortunately, did not.

The portly man's features stalled, then veered away from the jolly smirk they'd been forming in favor of a glazed-eyed reverence. He blushed and bowed his head once more over his book.

Not terribly useful, the admiration of such a man. Still, it gave a girl hope. If she could one day drive a marquess, for example, into a like slack-jawed stupor— and why should she not? Title notwithstanding, a marquess was a man with the same susceptibilities as any other—then she might make something of the triumph.

"Novels and more novels." Her sister, indifferent to such small drama, had begun turning over the discarded volumes on the table. "I suppose nobody wants to read what might actually improve his mind." The man abruptly closed up his book—doubtless a novel—and shoved it away as though he'd only just noticed its offending presence in his hands. His gaze averted, his cheeks pink as fresh-butchered pork, he pushed to his feet and fled to some other sector of the room.

"Yes, I'm ready." Her own voice, of course, had all the patrician clarity of Viola's, though she aimed it for shorter distances and always took care to stir in a bit of sugar. "Help me gather up these books. They oughtn't to be left lying about."

How long could a marquess, once stunned, be counted on to remain in that state? Could he procure a special license and marry her that same day, before his first rabid infatuation receded to the point where he might think of meeting her family? Or maybe she'd do better to get him out of London altogether, that he might not encounter any friends who would feel it their duty to knock him back to his senses. She'd have to count on sustaining his state of stupefaction, in that case, for the length of the journey from Mayfair to Gretna Green.

Difficult and unlikely. But not, perhaps, beyond her. Stupefaction was her stock in trade, and she would not stoop to the tedious false modesty of pretending not to know it.

The library clerk, when she stopped at his desk, accepted her armload of stray books with an effusion of gratitude such as no plain lady would ever have received for the same task, and fetched her the other two volumes of *Pride and Prejudice*. She signed her name, paid her pennies, and emerged with her sister into the chill February afternoon.

"You've read that already," was Viola's pronouncement on ascertaining what book she held.

"Indeed I have. But you *own* that volume of the *Vindication of Women*, and every other volume, too. I cannot see on what grounds you think you can find fault with my borrowing habits."

"*A Vindication of the Rights of Woman*, it's called. The meaning is entirely different. And my purpose wasn't to borrow a book but to begin making myself known." She drummed her gloved fingers on the volume's binding, a rhythmic accompaniment to the ring of their heels on the paving. "The more library clerks and booksellers I make aware of my project, the more likely it is that they'll mention me in discussions with one another—perhaps even in discussions with publishers. In fact I think it very likely that publishers spend time in just such establishments. One day I may well be overheard and approached by some enterprising man who sees that the time is ripe for a book like mine."

Oh, she'd be approached, certainly enough. Behind those false spectacles and taut-pinned hair and the sensible Quakerish garments she favored, Vi had her share of the Westbrook beauty. One day some man would see past her brusque manners to notice the fact, and if he was enterprising, it would surely occur to him to feign an interest in her book, perhaps even to present himself in the guise of a publisher.

That was why Kate could not allow her to undertake these errands alone. For a young lady of intellect, Viola was shockingly ignorant in some matters.

"I wonder, though, if a more gradual kind of persuasion might be to your benefit." At the corner she turned east, steering her sister along. "If perhaps you concentrated your efforts at first on pleasantries—on asking the clerk to recommend an interesting book, for example, or even speaking on commonplace topics such as the weather or an amusing print you recently saw—then by the time you introduced the subject of your own book, you might have a reservoir of goodwill already in place. Even a clerk who doesn't necessarily subscribe to your book's ideas might be disposed to advance your cause with his publisher friends, simply as a favor to a charming customer."

"But I don't want to be a charming customer." Viola's voice sank into the low passionate chords of the instrument with which she shared a name. "I want to be taken seriously. I want to know my book is appreciated on its own merits—not because the reader finds me sufficiently *charming.* I'm sure Thomas Paine never concerned himself with whether or not he was *charming.*" The word apparently furnished endless fuel for disgust. She jabbed at *Pride and Prejudice.* "Your Mr. Darcy isn't the least bit charming, and yet everyone tiptoes about him in awe."

It's different for women. She needn't say it aloud. Vi knew well enough.

Kate shifted the volumes to the crook of her other arm and fished in her reticule for a penny as they approached the street crossing. She wasn't without sympathy for her sister. The constraints of a lady's life could be exceedingly trying. Demoralizing, if one allowed them to be.

The trick was not to allow them to be.

"Lord help us all if you mean to pattern yourself after Thomas Paine. Perhaps he wouldn't have got into such trouble if he'd spent a little effort on charm." She paid the crossing sweep, a ragged dark boy, with the penny and her sweetest smile. "And Mr. Darcy had ten thousand a year and a grand house to his name. Much will be forgiven in the manners of such a man." She caught up her skirts and stepped into the street, sister alongside.

"What of his Elizabeth, then?" The unavoidable legacy of a barrister father: progeny always on the lookout for an argument. "*She* never takes pains to charm anyone, least of all Mr. Darcy, and yet—Where are we going?" She halted, abrupt as a fickle cart horse. "We ought to have turned north by now."

"The girls won't be through with lessons for a good half hour yet." Kate took her sister's elbow to usher her the rest of the way across. "That gives us time to go by way of Berkeley Square."

"Berkeley Square?" The way Vi pronounced it, you'd think she was naming the alley where the meanest residents of St. Giles's went to empty their chamber pots.

"Berkeley Square, indeed. I have a letter for Lady

Harringdon." Might as well serve up the objectionable news all at once, rather than by spoonfuls.

"Lady Harringdon? The dowager, or the present one?" What difference this detail could make was beyond fathoming, as Viola's lip curled and nostrils flared equally for both ladies.

"The countess. The present Lord Harringdon's wife." *What can you possibly have to communicate to her* would be the next question; no need to put her sister to the trouble of asking it. "She's just married off the last of her daughters this week. I'm offering my congratulations, as civil people do on such occasions to their kin."

"Kin, do you call her?" An audible snort, now, in case the sneer and the tone of voice had been too subtle.

"She's married to our father's elder brother. That makes her our aunt."

"Well, somebody ought to tell that to her. Her and Lord Harringdon and whatever mean-spirited offspring they spawned." Viola walked faster, swinging *Vindication*, volume one, in a pendulum motion as though she were winding up to brain one of that family with it. "Really, Kate, I would have thought you had more pride than to toady to such people."

"A brief note of congratulations is hardly toadying." She made her voice light, unruffled. "Indeed I should think it will provide an instructive example of proper manners to Lady Harringdon, while proving that her own lapses in civility do not guide the behavior of Charles Westbrook's children. You see I'm partly motivated by pride after all."

Partly. But in truth she had grander ambitions than to simply make a show of unbowed civility to her aunt.

They weren't really so unlike, she and her sister. She, too, intended to be known. One day the door to that glittering world of champagne and consequence—the world that ought to have been her birthright—would crack open just long enough to admit a girl who'd spent every day since the age of thirteen watching for that chance, readying herself to slip through. Even at two and twenty, she hadn't given up hope. Enough attentions to people like Lady Harringdon, and *something* must finally happen. *Someone* must recognize the aristocratic blood that ran through her veins, and the manners and accomplishments worthy of a nobleman's bride. Then she'd dart through that open door, take her place among her own kind, and free herself forever from this trial of daily mortification.

"Do what you must." Viola's shoulders flexed, as though the insult of a trip to Berkeley Square had an actual physical weight that wanted preparation to bear. "*My* pride shall take the form of waiting across the street while you go about your errand. Anyone looking out the window may see that *I* am not ashamed of our mother."

That was petty; the argumental equivalent of jabbing her with a sewing pin. And it smarted every bit as much.

Papa had made what must be termed an imprudent marriage. Never mind Mamma's quick wit and generous heart; never mind that she came of a proud theatrical family whose women studied Sophocles and spat on indecent offers from gentleman admirers. Never mind the affection undimmed by twenty-three years of wedlock. All that mattered in the eyes of Society was that the late Earl of Harringdon's second son had married an actress, thereby forsaking every privilege to which he was born.

She wasn't ashamed, precisely. But she recognized, as no one else in the family seemed to do, that Society's judgment mattered. And that privileges were worth having.

A *Pride and Prejudice* volume was pressing a sharp edge into her forearm, so she switched to a one-handed grip, like Viola with her *Vindication*. No, she couldn't accuse herself of being ashamed. But if Mr. Darcy had come to *her* with that first grudging proposal, openly acknowledging his abhorrence at so lowering himself, she would have swallowed her pride long enough to choke out a yes. Affection and understanding could come afterward—or if they never came at all, she would have a good name and the grounds at Pemberley for consolation.

She tipped back her head for a view of Mayfair's rooftops, stretching off in the distance. Surely somewhere in London was a gentleman who would suit her needs. Surely some aristocrat—some marquess ripe for stupefaction—must appreciate a beautiful bride with such pragmatic expectations of the wedded state. Surely someone, someday, could be brought to lower himself as Mr. Darcy had, and spirit her out of that middling class in which she had never truly belonged.

Surely that man did walk and breathe. The trick was only to find him.